THE BEST MAN
& THE WEDDING
PLANNER

BY
TERESA CARPENTER

Published in Great Britain 2015
by Mills & Boon, an imprint of Harlequin (UK) Limited,
Eton House, 18-24 Paradise Road, Richmond, Surrey, TW9 1SR

© 2015 Harlequin Books S.A.

Special thanks and acknowledgement are given to Teresa Carpenter for her contribution to The Vineyards of Calanetti series.

ISBN: 978-0-263-25189-0

23-1215

Harlequin (UK) Limited's policy is to use papers that are natural, renewable and recyclable products and made from wood grown in sustainable forests. The logging and manufacturing processes conform to the legal environmental regulations of the country of origin.

Printed and bound in Spain
by CPI, Barcelona

Teresa Carpenter believes that with love and family anything is possible. She writes in a Southern California coastal city surrounded by her large family. Teresa loves writing about babies and grandmas. Her books have rated as Top Picks by *RT Book Reviews*, and have been nominated Best Romance of the Year on some review sites. If she's not at a family event, she's reading, or writing her next grand romance.

This book is dedicated to my editor Carly Byrne
for her patience, understanding, speed and good cheer.
I never see her sweat. Even when I do.
Thank you for everything.

CHAPTER ONE

"NOW BOARDING, FIRST-CLASS passengers for Flight 510 to Florence."

Lindsay Reeves's ears perked up. She glanced at her watch; time had gotten away from her. She closed her tablet folio, tucked it into her satchel and then reached for the precious cargo she was personally escorting across the ocean. She hooked the garment bag holding the couture wedding dress for the future Queen of Halencia over her shoulder and began to move as the attendant made a second announcement. "First-class passengers now boarding."

"Welcome aboard." The attendant looked from the second ticket to Lindsay. "I'm sorry, both passengers will need to be present to board."

"We're both here. I bought a seat for this." She held up the garment bag.

The woman smiled but her eyes questioned Lindsay's sanity. "You bought a first-class ticket for your luggage?"

"Yes." She kept it at that, not wanting to draw any further attention. With the wedding only a month away, the world was alive with wedding dress fever.

"We have a storage closet in first class that can hold it if you want to refund the ticket before takeoff," the attendant offered.

"No, thank you." Lindsay pressed the second ticket into the woman's hand. "I'm not letting this bag out of my sight."

On the plane she passed a nice-looking older couple already seated in the first row and moved on to the last row where she spied her seats. She draped the garment bag over the aisle seat and frowned when it immediately slumped into a scrunched heap on the seat.

That wouldn't do. She pulled it back into place and tried to anchor it but when she let go, it drooped again. The weight of the dress, easily thirty pounds, made it too heavy to lie nicely. She needed something to hold it in place. After using her satchel to counter the weight temporarily, she slid past a young couple and their two children to speak to the flight attendant.

"We have a closet we can hang the dress in," the male attendant stated upon hearing her request.

"I've been paid not to let it out of my sight," she responded. True enough. Her reputation as a wedding planner to the rich and famous depended on her getting this dress to the wedding in pristine condition without anyone seeing it but her, the bride and her attendants.

"Hmm," the man—his name tag read Dan—tapped his lips while he thought.

"Welcome aboard, sir." Behind Lindsay another attendant, a blonde woman, greeted a fellow passenger.

Out of the corner of her eye Lindsay got the impression of a very tall, very broad, dark-haired man. She stepped into the galley to give them more room.

"You're the last of our first-class passengers," the attendant advised the man. "Once you're seated, please let me know if you need anything."

"Check," the man said in a deep, bass voice and moved down the aisle.

Goodness. Just the one word sent a tingle down Lindsay's spine. She sure hoped he intended to sleep during the long, red-eye flight. She wanted to get some work done and his voice might prove quite distracting.

"I've got it." Dan waved a triumphant hand. "We'll just put the seat in sleep mode and lay the bag across it."

Ma'am? Seriously? "I'd like a pillow. And a blanket, please."

"We'll do a full turndown service after the flight gets started." She gave Sullivan a smile and disappeared behind the curtain to the coach area.

Lindsay stared after her. Did that mean she didn't get a pillow or a blanket? This was her first time flying first-class. So far she had mixed feelings. She liked the extra room and the thought of stretching out for the long flight. But Blondie wasn't earning any points.

Lindsay draped the garment bag over the window seat as best she could until the seat could be reclined. Unfortunately that put her in the aisle seat directly across from Mr. Tall, Dark and Inconsiderate.

Nothing for it. She'd just have to ignore him and focus on her work. It would take the entire flight to configure the seating arrangement for the reception. She had the list of guests from the bride and the list of guests from the groom. And a three-page list of political notes from the palace of who couldn't be seated next to whom and who should be seated closer to the royal couple. What had started as a private country wedding had grown to include more than a hundred guests as political factors came into play.

It was a wedding planner's nightmare. But she took it as an opportunity to excel.

Before she knew it she was being pushed back in her chair as the plane lifted into the air. Soon after, Dan appeared to fold down the window seat. He carefully laid the heavy garment bag in place and secured it with the seat belt and a bungee cord. She thanked him as she resumed her seat.

She glanced out of the corner of her eye to see Sullivan had his pillow—a nice, big, fluffy one. Ignore him.

Easier thought than done. He smelled great; a spicy musk with a touch of soap.

Eyes back on her tablet, she shuffled some names into table seats and then started to run them against her lists to see if they were all compatible. Of course, they weren't. Two people needed to be moved forward and two people couldn't be seated together. That left four people at the table. She moved people to new tables and highlighted them as a reminder to check out the politics on them. And repeated the process.

A soft snore came from across the way—much less annoying than the shrill cry of one of the toddlers demanding a bandage for his boo-boo. Blondie rushed to the rescue and the boy settled down. Except for loud outbursts like that, the two boys were actually well behaved. There'd been no need for Sullivan to move seats.

"Would you care for a meal, Ms. Reeves?" Dan appeared beside her.

She glanced at the time on her tablet. Eight o'clock. They'd been in the air an hour. "Yes, please."

"You have a choice of chicken Cordon bleu or beef Stroganoff."

"I'll have the beef. With a cola."

He nodded and turned to the other side of the aisle. Before he could ask, Sullivan said he'd have the beef and water.

Her gaze collided with his. Brown eyes with specks of gold surveyed her, interest and appreciation sparkled in the whiskey-brown depths, warm and potent.

Heat flooded her, followed by a shiver.

"What's in the bag?" he asked, his voice even deeper and raspier from sleep. Way too sexy for her peace of mind.

"None of your business." She turned back to her table plan.

"Must be pretty important for you to get so upset. Let

me guess, a special dress for a special occasion?" He didn't give up.

"Yes. If you must know. And it's my job to protect it."

"Protect it? Interesting. So it's not your dress."

She rolled her eyes and sent him a droll stare. "I liked you better when you were snoring."

He grinned, making his dimples pop. "I deserve that. Listen, I'm sorry for my attitude earlier and for sitting on the dress. I had wine with dinner and wine always gives me a headache."

Lindsay glared at Sullivan. "So you did sit on the dress." She knew it. That had definitely been a butt print on the bag.

He blinked, all innocence. "I meant I'm sorry for dumping it over there."

"Uh-huh."

His grin never wavered.

"Why did you have wine with dinner if it gives you a headache?"

The smile faded. "Because dinner with my folks always goes better with a little wine. And I'm going to have a headache at the end either way."

"Okay, I get that." Lindsay adored her flighty, dependent mother but, yeah, dinners were easier with a little wine. Sometimes, like between husbands, a lot of wine was required.

A corner of his rather nice mouth kicked up. "You surprise me, Ms. Reeves. I'd have thought you'd be appalled."

"Parents aren't always easy." She closed her tablet to get ready for her meal. "It doesn't mean we don't love them."

"Amen. Respect is another matter."

That brought her attention around. He wore a grim expression and turmoil churned in his distracted gaze. The situation with his parents must be complicated. It was a sad day when you lost respect for the person you loved most in the world. She understood his pain only too well.

Thankfully, Dan arrived with a small cart, disrupting old memories. He activated a tray on the side of her seat and placed a covered plate in front of her along with a glass of soda. Real china, real crystal, real silverware. Nice. And then he lifted the cover and the luscious scent of braised meat and rich sauce reached her.

"Mmm." She hummed her approval. "This looks fantastic."

"I can promise you it is," Dan assured her. "Chef LaSalle is the pride of the skies."

She took her first bite as he served Sullivan and moaned again. She couldn't help it, the flavors burst in her mouth, seducing her taste buds.

"Careful, Ms. Reeves," Sullivan cautioned. "You sound like you're having a good time over there."

"Eat. You'll understand." She took a sip of her drink, watching him take a bite. "Or maybe not. After all, you've already eaten."

"I wasn't hungry earlier. Damn, this is good." He pointed to the video screen. "Shall we watch a movie with our meal?"

She was tempted. Surprising. After the disaster of last year, work had been her major consolation. She rarely took the time to relax with a movie. She was too busy handling events for the stars of those movies. A girl had to work hard to make the stars happy in Hollywood. And she had to work harder than the rest after allowing an old flame to distract her to the point of putting her career at risk. But she'd learned her lesson.

Luckily she'd already signed the contract for this gig. And she planned to make the royal wedding of the Crown Prince of Halencia, Antonio de l'Accardi, to the commoner, Christina Rose, the wedding of the century.

Thirty days from now no one would be able to question her dedication—which meant returning to the puzzle of the table seating.

"You go on," she told Sullivan. "I have to get back to my work."

"What are you doing over there? Those earlier moans weren't as pleasant as your dinner noises."

"It's a creative new form of torture called a seating arrangement."

"Ah. It sounds excruciating."

"Oh, believe me. It's for a political dinner and there are all these levels of protocols of who can sit with whom. And then there's the added element of personal likes and dislikes. It's two steps back for every one step forward. And it's a lot of manual double-checking…talk about a headache."

"Politics usually are." The grimness in his tone told her there was something more there. Before she had time to wonder about it, he went on. "The information isn't on spreadsheets?"

"It is, but there are more than a hundred names here. I have to seat a table and then check each name to see if they're compatible."

"You know you can set up a program that can look at the information and tell you whether the table mates are compatible at the time you put the name in."

She blinked at him. "That would be wonderful. How do I do that exactly?"

He laughed, a deep, friendly sound, then rattled off a string of commands that had her eyes glazing over. "The setup will take a few minutes but will likely save you hours overall."

"Yeah, but you lost me at the word 'algorithm.'" She wiped her mouth with the cloth napkin. "You really had my hopes up for a minute there."

"Sorry, tech talk. I own a company that provides software for cyber security. A program like this really isn't that difficult. Let me see your computer after dinner and I'll do it for you. It'll take me less than an hour."

This man was tempting her left and right. She weighed the hours she'd save against the confidentiality agreement she'd signed and sadly shook her head.

"Thank you for offering but I can't. This is a special event. I'm not allowed to share information with anyone except my staff, designated officials and pre-approved vendors."

"This is for the royal wedding of Prince Antonio of Halencia, right?"

Her eyes popped wide. How could he know that?

"Come on, it's not hard to guess. The wedding dress, the seating chart. We're on a flight to Florence. And I know they have an American event planner. Hang on, I'll take care of this."

He pulled out his cell phone and hit a couple of buttons.

"What?" she challenged. "You're calling the palace in Halencia? Uh, huh. I don't think so. You can hang up now."

"Hey, Tony." He raised a dark eyebrow as he spoke into the phone.

Tony? As in Antonio? Yeah, right.

"I got your text. Don't worry about it. I'm here for a month. I'll see you next week." He listened for a moment. "Yes, I had dinner with them. They were thrilled with the invitation. Hey, listen, the wedding planner is on my flight and she needs some programming to help her with the seating chart. She's bound by the confidentiality agreement from letting me help her. Can you give her authorization? Great, I'm going to put her on."

He held the phone out to Lindsay. "It's Prince Antonio."

CHAPTER TWO

LINDSAY ROLLED HER eyes at the man across the way, wondering how far he meant to take this joke and what he hoped to achieve.

"Hello?"

"*Buona sera*, Ms. Reeves. I hope you are having a nice flight."

"Uh, yes, I am." The voice was male, pleasant and slightly accented. And could be anyone. Except how had he known her name? Sullivan hadn't mentioned it.

"Christina is thrilled to have your services for the wedding. You have my full support to make this *il matrimonio dei suoi sogni*—the wedding of her dreams."

"I'll do my best." Could this actually be the prince?

"Duty demands my presence at the palace but I look forward to meeting you at the rehearsal. Zach is my best man. He will be my advocate in Monte Calanetti for the next month. He is available to assist you in any way necessary."

She turned to look at the man across the aisle and quirked a brow at his evil smirk. "Zach…Sullivan?"

"Yes. We went to college together. He's like a brother to me. If he can assist with the meal plan—"

"The seating chart." She squeezed her eyes closed. *OMG, I just interrupted the royal prince.*

"Of course. The seating chart. If Zach can help, you must allow him to be of service. He is quite handy with a computer."

"Yes. I will. Thank you."

"It is I who thanks you. You do us an honor by coming to Halencia. If I can be of further assistance, you have access to me through Zach. *Buona notte*, Ms. Reeves."

"Good night." Instead of giving the phone back to Sullivan she checked the call history and saw she'd spoken to Tony de l'Accardi. She slowly turned her head to meet chocolate-brown eyes. "You know the Prince of Halencia."

"I wouldn't take on the best man gig for anyone else."

The flight attendant appeared with the cart to collect his meal and sweetly inquire if he'd like dessert.

Lindsay rolled her eyes, barely completing the action before the blonde turned to her.

"Are you done, ma'am?"

Ma'am again? Lindsay's eyes narrowed in a bland stare. Her displeasure must have registered because the woman rushed on. "For dessert we have crème brûlée, strawberry cheesecake or a chocolate mousse."

Lindsay handed off her empty plate and, looking the woman straight in the eye, declared, "I'll have one of each."

"Of course, ma... Ms. Reeves." She hurriedly stashed the plate and rolled the cart away.

Lindsay slowly turned her head until Sullivan's intent regard came into view. Okay, first things first. "I'm only twenty-nine. Way too young to be ma'am."

He cocked his head.

She handed him his phone. "Why didn't you tell me you were the best man?"

He lifted one dark eyebrow. "Would you have believed me?"

She contemplated him. "Probably. I have a file on you."

His slanted eyebrow seemed to dip even further. "Then I'm surprised you didn't recognize me. You probably have profiles on the entire wedding party in that tablet of yours."

She lifted one shoulder in a half shrug of acknowledgment. "I've learned it's wise to know who I'll be working with. I didn't recognize you because it's out of context.

Plus, you don't have an eight-o'clock shadow in your company photo in which you're wearing glasses."

"Huh." He ran the backs of his fingers over his jaw. "I'll have to get that picture updated. I had Lasik eye surgery over a year ago. Regardless, I didn't know you were involved in the wedding until you started talking about the meal arrangements."

"Seating arrangements," she corrected automatically.

"Right."

The flight attendant arrived with dessert. She handed Zach a crystal dish of chocolate mousse and set a small tray with all three desserts artfully displayed in front of Lindsay.

"Enjoy," she said and retreated down the aisle.

"Mmm." Lindsay picked up a spoon and broke into the hard shell of crystalized sugar topping the crème brûlée. "Mmm." This time it was a moan. "Oh, that's good."

"Careful, Ms. Reeves, you're going to get me worked up if you continue." Zach gestured at her loaded tray with his spoon. "I see you like your sweets."

"It's a long night." She defended her stash.

"I guess you don't plan on sleeping."

"I have a lot of work." She gave her usual excuse then, for some unknown reason, confessed, "I don't sleep well on planes."

"It may help if you relaxed and watched the movie instead of working."

No doubt he was right. But work soothed her, usually. Over the past year she'd found it increasingly more difficult to believe in the magic of her process. She blamed her breakup with Kevin last year. But she hoped to change that soon. If a royal wedding couldn't bring back the magic in what she did, she needed to rethink her career path.

"Thank you for that insightful bit of advice. What don't you like about being best man? The role or the exposure?"

"Either. Both. Seems like I've been dodging the limelight since I was two."

"Well, you did grow up in a political family." That brought his earlier comment and reaction into context. Her research revealed he was related to the political powerhouse Sullivans from Connecticut. "Never had any aspiration in that direction?"

The curse he uttered made her glance worriedly toward the toddlers. Luckily the lack of sound or movement in that direction indicated they were probably asleep.

"I'll take that as a no."

"I wished my father understood me so well."

She empathized with his pain. She felt the same way about her mother. Perhaps empathy was why she found him so easy to talk to. "I've found parents often see what they want to see. That addresses the exposure…what do you have against the role of best man?"

"I hate weddings. The fancier the event, the more I detest them. There's something about the pomp and circumstance that just screams fake to me." He licked his spoon and set the crystal dish aside. "No offense."

No offense? He'd just slammed everything she stood for. Why should she be offended?

And he wasn't done. "It's like the couple needs to distract the crowd from the fact they're marrying for something other than love."

"You don't believe in love?" It was one thing for her to question her belief in what she was doing and another for someone else to take shots at it.

"I believe in lust and companionship. Love is a myth best left to romance novels."

"Wow. That's harsh." And came way too close to how she felt these days.

The way his features hardened when he voiced his feelings told her strong emotion backed his comment. Kind of at odds with his family dynamic. The Sullivans were touted as one of the All-American families going back for generations. Long marriages and one or two kids who were all upstanding citizens. They ranked right up there with the Kennedys and Rockefellers.

The attendants came through the cabin collecting trash and dirty dishes. They offered turndown service, which Lindsay turned down. She still had work to do.

"Just let us know when you're ready."

Across the way Zach also delayed his bed service and got the same response. Once the attendants moved on, he leaned her way.

"Now you know you can trust me, are you ready for me to work on your spreadsheet? I'd like to do it before I start my movie."

"Oh. Sure." Could she trust him? Lindsay wondered as she pulled out her tablet. Just because she knew who he was didn't mean he was trustworthy. Too charming for her peace of mind. And a total flirt. "Do you want to do it on mine or should I send it to you?"

"Little Pixie, I'd like to do yours." His gaze ran over her, growing hotter as it rolled up her body. Her blood was steaming by the time his gaze met hers. "But since I have to work, you should send it to me."

"It'll do you no good to flirt with me." She tapped in her password and opened her spreadsheet. "What's your email?" She keyed in the address and sent it. "This wedding is too important to my career for me to risk getting involved with the best man."

"Oh, come on. The best man is harmless." Zach had his laptop open. "Got it. He's shackled for the whole event."

"The best man is a beast. His mind is all wrapped up in the bachelor party and strippers. He feels it's his duty to show the groom what he'll be giving up. And more than half the time he's on the prowl for some action just to re-mind himself he's still free, whether he is or not."

Zach flinched. "Wow. That's harsh."

Oh, clever man. "With good cause. I have a strict 'no fraternizing with the wedding party—including guests'—policy for my company and the vendors I work with. But, yeah, I've had to bolster a few bridesmaids who took it too far and expected too much and went home alone. Or refer them back to the bride or groom for contact info that wasn't shared."

"That's a lot of blame heaped on the best man."

"Of course, it's not just the best man, but in my expe-rience he can be a bad, bad boy."

"It's been a long time since I was bad."

"Define long."

He laughed.

"Seriously, I just want you to rewind the conversation a few sentences and then say that again with a straight face."

His gaze shifted from his laptop to make another slow stroll over her. Jacking up her pulse yet again.

He needed to stop doing that!

Unremorseful, he cocked an eyebrow. "I'm not saying I don't go after what I want. But I'm always up front about my intentions. No illusions, no damages."

Sounded like a bad boy to her.

"Well, you have fun, now. I'm here to work."

He shook his head as he went back to keying com-mands into his computer. "All work and no play makes Ms. Reeves a dull girl."

"I'm not being paid to have fun." And that was the problem right there—the one she'd been struggling with for nearly a year.

Her work wasn't fun anymore.

And the cause wasn't just the disillusionment she suf-fered in her love life. Though that ranked high on the motive list. She'd started feeling this way before Kevin had come back into her life. Instead of being excited by the creative endeavor, she'd gotten bogged down in the details.

Maybe it was Hollywood. Believing in the magic of happily-ever-after got a little harder to do with each repeat customer. Not to mention the three-peats. And the fact her mother was her best customer. Hopefully, husband number six would be the charm for her.

Seriously, Lindsay crossed her fingers in the folds of her skirt. She truly wished this marriage lasted. She liked Matt and he seemed to get her mom, who had the attention span and sense of responsibility of a fourteen-year-old. There was nothing mentally wrong with Darlene Reeves. She could do for herself. She just didn't want to. Darlene's dad had treated her like a princess, giving her most everything she wanted and taking care of all the little details in life. He'd died when she was seventeen and she'd been chasing his replacement all her life.

She'd had Lindsay when she was eighteen and then she learned to get the wedding ring on her finger before they lost interest. In between love interests, Lindsay was expected to pick up the slack.

She loved her mother dearly. But she loved her a little easier when she was in a committed relationship.

"Did you fall asleep on me over there?"

His question called her attention to his profile. Such strong features—square jaw dusted with stubble-defined cheekbones, straight nose. He really was beautiful in a totally masculine way. Too much temptation. Good thing her policy put him off limits.

"No. Just going over what I need to do."

"Perfect timing then." He swirled his finger and hit a single key. "Because I just sent your file back to you."

"So soon?" She reached for her tablet, excited to try the

new program. The file opened onto a picture of circles in the form of a rectangle. Each circle was numbered. She'd refine the shape once she viewed the venue. She ran her finger across the page and as it moved over a circle names popped up showing who was seated at the table.

"Cool. How do I see everybody?"

"You hit this icon here." He hung over his chair, reaching across the aisle to show her. He tried showing her the other features, but his actions were awkward. Being left-handed, he had to use his right hand to aid her because of the distance between the seats.

"This is ridiculous." Unsnapping her seat belt, she stood. "Do you mind if I come over there for a few minutes while we go over this?"

"Sure." He stood, as well, and stepped aside.

Standing next to him she came face to loosened tie with him. She bent her head back to see him and then bent it back again to meet his gaze. "My goodness. How tall are you?"

"Six-four."

"And the prince?"

"Six-one." Long fingers tugged on a short dark tendril. "Does this brain never stop working?"

"Not when I get a visual of a tall drink of water standing next to a shot glass."

"I'm not quite sure what that means, but I think there was a compliment in there somewhere."

"Don't start imagining things at fifty thousand feet, Sullivan. We're a long way from help." She tugged on his blue-pinstriped tie. "You can ditch this now. Was dinner a formal affair?"

The light went out of his eyes. He yanked the tie off and stuffed it in his pants' pocket. "It's always formal with my parents."

She patted his chest. "You did your duty, now move on."

"Good advice." He gestured for her to take the window seat.

She hesitated for a beat. Being trapped in the inside seat, surrounded by his potent masculinity, might be pushing her self-control a little thin. But his computer program blew her mind. From the tiny bit she'd seen, it had the potential to save her hours, if not days, of work.

"Ms. Reeves?" His breath wafted over her ear, sending a shiver racing down her spine. "Are you okay?"

"Of course." She realized he'd been talking while she fought off her panic attack. "Ah…hmm." She cleared her throat to give herself a moment to calm down. "Why do you keep calling me by my last name?"

"Because I don't know your first name," he stated simply.

Oh, right. The flight attendants had used their last names. The prince had given her Zach's name and then she'd read it on her spreadsheet.

"It's Lindsay."

A slow grin formed, crinkling the corners of his eyes. "Pretty. A pretty name for a pretty girl."

So obvious, yet the words still gave her a bit of a thrill. She pressed her lips together to hide her reaction. "You can't help yourself, can you?"

"What?" All innocence.

"Please. That line is so old I think I heard it in kindergarten."

She expected to see his dimple flash but got an intent stare instead. "It's not a line when it's true."

A little thrill chased goose bumps across her skin. Oh, my, he was good.

She almost believed him.

Shaking her head at him, at herself, she slid past him and dropped into the window seat.

He slid into his seat, his big body filling up the small

space. Thankfully they were in first class and a ten-inch console separated their seats, giving her some breathing space. Until he flicked some buttons and the console dropped down.

"That's better."

For who? She leaned away as he leaned closer. Just as she feared, she felt pinned in, crowded. When he dropped the tray down in front of her, the sense of being squeezed from all sides grew stronger. Not by claustrophobia but by awareness. His scent—man and chocolate—made her mouth water.

"So is it easy for you?" He half laughed, going back to their previous conversation. "To move on?"

"It's not, actually. My mom problems are probably just as bad as or worse than your parent problems. Yet, here I am, jetting off to Italy."

Mom's words, not hers. Darlene couldn't understand how Lindsay could leave and be gone for a month when Darlene's next wedding was fast approaching. It didn't matter that Lindsay had booked this event well before Darlene got engaged or that it was the wedding of the year—perhaps the decade—and a huge honor for Lindsay to be asked to handle it.

"I doubt it."

"Really? My mother is my best customer."

"Oh-hh." He dragged the word out.

"Exactly. Soon I'll be walking her down the aisle to husband number six."

"Ouch. Is she a glutton for punishment?"

"Quite the opposite. My mother loves to be in love. The minute a marriage becomes work, it's the beginning of the end. What I can't get her to understand is that you have to work on your marriage from day one. Love needs to be fostered and nourished through respect and compromise."

"Honesty, communication and loyalty are key."

"Yes!" She nudged him in the arm. "You get it. Maybe you won't be such a bad best man, after all."

He lifted one dark eyebrow. "Thanks."

"Anyway. I can waste a lot of time worrying about Mom or I can accept that it's her life to live. Just as my life is mine to live." She didn't know why she was sharing this with him. Her mother's love life wasn't a secret. Far from it. But Lindsay rarely talked about her mother. "Until the next time she comes crying on my shoulder, I choose the latter."

"At least she lets her suckers off the line."

"What does that mean?"

"Nothing." He ran a hand around the back of his neck, loosening tight muscles. "It's hard to let my parents just be when they keep harping on me to join the campaign trail."

"They want you to run for office?"

"Oh, yeah. I'm to stop messing around with my little hobby and turn my mind to upholding the family name by running for the next open seat in congress."

"Hobby? Didn't I read an article that your company just landed a hundred-million-dollar government contract to upgrade electronic security for the military?"

"You did." While he talked he opened the seating arrangement program. "And between that contract and Antonio selling me his share of the business, I've met a goal I set the day I opened my business."

Clearly, resignation overshadowed pride, so she ventured, "You exceeded your father's net worth?"

He shifted to study her. "So you're psychic as well as a wedding planner?"

"When you work with people as closely as I do, you get to know how they think."

"Hmm."

"It's an impressive accomplishment."

The Sullivans came from old money made from banking and transportation. Their political dynasty went back several generations. "Your parents must be proud of you."

"They didn't even mention it. Too focused on when I'd leave it all behind and fall in line with my family obligations." He tapped a few keys and her seating arrangement popped up on the screen. "Feels kind of hollow now."

"I'm sorry."

He didn't look up. "It doesn't matter."

"You mean it didn't matter to them."

He gave a negligent shrug. "I'm a big boy. I can handle it."

"Well, I officially call the parent battle a draw. I know it's not the same but…congratulations."

That earned her a half smile and a nod. Then he started to run her through the features of the computer program.

"This is fabulous." All she had to do was type a name into a seat slot and all the notes associated with that name appeared sorted by category and importance. "You have saved me hours of work."

His eyes gleamed as he went on to show her a few additional options. "And if you do this—" he punched a couple of keys "—it will auto-fill based on a selected category." He clicked social standing and then pressed Enter. Names popped into assigned seats.

She blinked. "Wow. What do the colors mean?" Many of the names were in red and blue.

"Blue means there's a conflict with someone else at the table. Red means there are two or more conflicts."

While he showed her how to access the conflicts, she impulsively pressed the button to call the attendant. The blonde appeared with impressive speed, her smile dimming slightly when she saw Lindsay seated with Zach.

"How can I help you?"

"We'd like two glasses of champagne, please. And some strawberries if you have them."

"I think I can find some. Be right back."

"Champagne?" He cocked his head. "You turned it down earlier."

"That was before. Now we have things to celebrate. I have this to help me finish my seating plan and you met a career-long goal."

The attendant arrived with a tray, setting it down between them. "*Buon appetito!* Ms. Reeves, would you like us to do your turndown service now?"

"Sure." Maybe the champagne would help her sleep. The woman turned away and Lindsay lifted a flute of bubbling gold wine. "To you. Congratulations and thank you."

Zach lifted his flute and tapped it against Lindsay's. "To you." A crystal chime rang out as pretty as the sound of her laughter. Her simple gesture almost undid the butcher job his parent's self-absorption had done to his pride. He didn't get them, probably never would. They couldn't spare the smallest show of affection. But this prickly little pixie put her animosity aside to toast his success.

She didn't know him except as a helpful jerk and a few dry facts on paper. Heck, she hugged the window in an attempt to maintain her distance yet she still celebrated his accomplishment.

It almost made him feel bad about sabotaging the wedding.

CHAPTER THREE

It was a drastic plan. One Zach took no pleasure in. But he'd do whatever necessary to ensure his friend didn't suffer the frigid existence his parents called marriage. Antonio was already sacrificing his life for his country; selling off his business interests in America to Zach. He shouldn't have to give up all chance of happiness, too.

Zach reluctantly agreed to be best man. He didn't believe in big, lavish weddings. And he didn't approve of Tony's insane sacrifice. So why would he agree? Because Tony was the closest thing he had to a brother. Of course, he had to support him.

And of course he felt compelled to talk him out of throwing his future away.

Zach knew the circumstances of Antonio's marriage and it made him sick to think of his honorable, big-hearted friend locked into a miserable existence like his parents had shared.

He wasn't thinking of doing anything overt. Certainly nothing that would embarrass the royal family, especially his best friend. But he could cause a few delays. And earn enough time to talk his friend out of making the biggest mistake of his life.

Tony had a lot on his plate taking on the leadership of his country. Halencia had reached a state of crisis. Antonio's parents were gregarious, bigger-than-life characters madly in love with each other one moment and viciously in hate the next. There'd been public affairs and passionate reconciliations.

The country languished under their inattention. The

king and queen lived big and spent big, costing the country much-needed funds.

The citizens of Halencia loved the drama, hated the politics. Demands for a change had started years ago but had become more persistent in the past five years. Until a year ago when the king was threatened with a paternity suit. It turned out Antonio wasn't getting a new sibling. It was just a scare tactic gone wrong.

But it was the last straw for the citizens of Halencia.

The chancellor of the high counsel had gone to Antonio and demanded action be taken.

Antonio had flown home to advise his father the time had come. The king must abdicate and let Antonio rule or risk the monarchy being overthrown completely.

The citizens of Halencia cheered in the streets. Antonio was well loved in his home country. He lived and worked in California, but he took his duty as prince seriously. He returned home two or three times a year, maintaining a residence in Halencia and supporting many businesses and charities.

Everyone was happy. Except Tony, who had to leave everything he'd worked to achieve and go home to marry a woman he barely knew.

Zach knew the truth behind Tony's impromptu engagement four years ago. He was one of a handful of people who did. And though it was motivated by love, it wasn't for the woman he'd planned to marry.

Tony was a smart man. Zach just needed a little time to convince him that marriage was drastic and unnecessary.

Lindsay seemed like a nice person. She'd understand when this all played out. Surely she wouldn't want to bring together two people who were not meant to be a couple. Plus, she'd get paid either way. And have a nice trip to Italy for her troubles.

Once he was in Halencia and had access to Tony and

Christina, he'd subtly hound them until one or the other caved to the pressure. And maybe cause a snag or two along the way so the whole thing just seemed like a bad idea.

Of course he'd have to distract the pretty wedding planner with a faux flirtation to keep her from noticing his shenanigans. No hardship there. He was attracted enough to the feisty pixie to make it fun, but she was way too picketfence for him so there was no danger of taking it too far.

He saw it as win, win, win. Especially for those not stuck in a loveless marriage.

She lifted her glass again. "And thanks again for this program."

"I hope you like puzzles, because there's still a lot of work there."

"Not near what there was." She picked up a strawberry, dipped it in her flute and sank dainty white teeth into the fruit. The ripe juice stained her lips red and he had the keenest urge to taste the sweetness left behind. "In fact, I may actually watch the movie."

"Excellent." He all but had her eating out of his hand with that act of kindness. And he'd needed something after stumbling onto the plane half blind with a migraine and sitting on the blasted dress. He'd popped some over-the-counter meds just before boarding. Thank the flight gods the headache had finally eased off.

He needed to stick close to her if this sabotage was going to work. He'd do his best to protect her as he went forward, but if it came down to a choice between her job and the happiness of the man who meant more to him than family, he'd choose Tony every time. No matter how pretty the wedding planner.

He'd revealed more about himself than he meant to, than he ever did really. But her attitude toward parental problems appealed to him: do what you can and move on. How refreshing to find someone who understood and accepted that not all parents were perfect. Many people didn't get along with their parents but most loved and respected them.

He tolerated his parents, but he wasn't willing to make a total break, which probably meant he harvested hope for a better relationship at some point. He couldn't imagine what might bring it about so he pretty much ignored them except when he was on the east coast or at a family function requiring his presence.

Next to him Lindsay sipped champagne and flipped through the movie choices. The dim lights caught the gold in her light brown hair. She had the thick mass rolled up and pinned in place but soft wisps had broken free to frame her face. He wondered how long the confined tresses would flow down her back. Her creamy complexion reminded him of the porcelain dolls his mother collected, complete with a touch of red in the cheeks though Lindsay's was compliments of the champagne.

She shot him a sideways glance, a question in her pretty baby blue eyes.

He realized she'd asked a question. "Sorry. I got lost in looking at you."

A flush added to the red in her cheeks and a hand pushed at the pins in her hair. "I asked if you preferred the comedy or the World War One drama." She turned back to the screen, fidgeted with the buttons. "But maybe I should just go back to my seat."

"No. Stay. This is my celebration, after all."

She glanced at him through lush lashes. "Okay, but you'll have to behave."

"I'll have you know my mother raised me to be a gentleman."

"Uh-huh." She made the decision for them with the push of a button. "That might be reassuring, except I doubt you've been under your mother's influence for quite some time."

He grinned and reached up to turn off the overhead light. "Very astute, Ms. Reeves."

Lindsay came awake to the rare sense of being wrapped in warm, male arms. She shot straight up in her seat, startling the man she cuddled against. His whiskey-brown eyes opened and blinked at her, the heat in his slumberous gaze rolling through her like liquid fire.

Escape. Now. The words were like a beeping alarm going off in her head.

"Can you let me out?" She pushed away from him, gaining a few inches and hopefully reinforcing the message to move. Now.

"Is the movie over?" He reined her in with an easy strength. His broad chest lifted under her as he inhaled a huge breath and then let it go in a yawn.

"Yes. This was fun." Too much fun. Time to get back to the real world. "But I need to get past you." He tucked a piece of her hair behind her ear instead of moving. The heat of his touch called for desperate measures. "I've got to pee."

He blinked. Then the corner of his mouth tipped up and he stood. "Me, too." He helped her up and gestured for her to go first.

"You go ahead," she urged him. "I want to grab a few things to freshen up with."

"Good idea." He opened the overhead compartment and grabbed a small bag. "Can I help you get anything?"

"Thank you, no." She waited until he wandered off to gather what she needed from her tote.

The attendants had performed her turndown service so both beds were down for the night. She automatically checked the garment bag holding the royal wedding dress.

It lay nicely in place, undisturbed since the last time she checked. She bent to retrieve her tote from under the seat in front of hers and decided to take the bag with her. Strap looped over her shoulder, she hurried down the aisle.

It was after one and the people she passed appeared to be out for the count. Even the attendants were strapped in and resting. Good. Lindsay intended to take her time. She wanted Zach to be back in his seat and sound asleep when she returned.

He was too charming, too hot, too available for her peace of mind. She hadn't needed to hear his views on marriage to know he was single. From her research she'd already gathered he had commitment issues. The only hint of an engagement had been back in his college days.

She'd found that snippet of information because she'd been researching his history with the prince. They'd both been going to Harvard's school of business but they'd met on the swim team. They both broke records for the school, Zach edging out Antonio with a few more wins. Antonio explained those extra wins came from Zach's longer reach. In the picture accompanying the article it was clear that Zach had at least three inches on all his teammates.

Tall, dark and handsome. Tick, tick, tick. The stereotype fit him to a tee, but did little to actually describe him. He was brilliant yet a terrible flirt. Could apologize when he was wrong and laugh at himself. But it was the touch of vulnerability surrounding his desire for his parents' approval that really got to her. She understood all too well the struggle between respect and love when it came to parents.

Bottom line: the man was dangerous. Way out of her league. And a distraction she couldn't afford. She may be headed for one of the most beautiful places on earth, but this was so not a vacation. She needed to stay sharp and focused to pull off the wedding of the century.

Face washed, teeth brushed, changed into yoga pants and a long-sleeved T-shirt, she glanced at her watch. Twenty minutes had passed. That should be enough time. She gathered her clothes and toiletries and tucked them neatly into her tote before making her way quietly back to her seat.

Zach lay sprawled on his bed. He was so tall he barely fit; in fact, one leg was off the bed braced against the floor. No doubt he had a restless night ahead of him. For once she'd sleep. Or pretend to. Because engaging in middle-of-the-night intimacies with Zach Sullivan could only result in trouble. Trouble she couldn't afford.

Climbing into her bed, she pulled the covers around her shoulders and determinedly closed her eyes.

She had this under control. She'd just ignore the man. If she needed something from the groom, she'd get it from the palace representative or Christina. There was no need for her to deal with Zach Sullivan at all. That suited her fine. She'd learned her lesson.

No more falling into the trap of self-delusion because a man paid a little attention to her. But more important—work and play did not go together.

"There must be some mistake." Lindsay advised the car-rental clerk. "I made my reservation over two months ago."

"*Scusa*. No mistake. My records show the reservation was canceled."

"That's impossible," Lindsay protested. Exhaustion tugged at her frayed nerves. This couldn't be happening. With everything she needed to do for the wedding, she absolutely required a vehicle to get around. "I had my assistant confirm all my reservations a week ago."

The clerk, a harried young man, glanced at the line behind her before asking with exaggerated patience, "Perhaps it is under a different name?"

"No, it is under my name." She gritted her teeth. "Please look again."

"Of course." He hit a few keys. "It says here the reservation was canceled last night."

"Last night? That doesn't make any sense at all. I was in the middle of a transatlantic flight." Enough. Arguing did her no good. She just wanted a car and to get on the road. "You know it doesn't matter. Let's just start over."

"*Scusa*, Ms. Reeves. We have no other vehicles available. Usually we would, but many have started to arrive for the royal wedding. The press especially. And they are keeping the vehicles. We have requested more autos from other sites but they won't be here for several days."

"There you are." A deep male voice sounded from behind her.

She glanced over her shoulder to find Zach towering over her. Dang, so much for losing him at the luggage carousel. Assuming her professional demeanor, she sent him a polite smile. "Have a good trip to Monte Calanetti. I'll keep you posted with updates on the arrangements. I'm going to be here for a bit." She smiled even brighter. "They've lost my car reservation."

"They didn't lose it. I canceled it."

"What?" All pretense of politeness dropped away. "Why would you do that?"

He held up a set of keys. "Because we're going to drive to Monte Calanetti together. Don't you remember? We talked about this during the movie last night."

She shook her head. She remembered him asking her what car-rental company she'd used and comparing their accommodation plans; he'd rented a villa while she had a room at a boutique hotel. Nowhere in her memory lurked a discussion about driving to Monte Calanetti together. There was no way she would have agreed to that. Not only did it go against her new decree to avoid him whenever possible, but she needed a vehicle to properly do her job.

"No," she declared, "I don't remember."

"Hmm. Must be champagne brain. No problem. I've got a Land Rover. Plenty of room for you, me and the dress." He grabbed up the garment bag, caught the handle of her larger suitcase and headed off. "Let's roll."

"Wait. No." Feeling panicked as the dress got further out of her reach, she glared at the clerk. "I want my reservation reinstated and as soon as a car is available, I want it delivered." She snatched up a card. "I'll call you with the address."

Dragging her smaller suitcase, Lindsay weaved her way through the crowd, following in Zach's wake. Luckily his height made him easy to spot. She was right on his heels when he exited the airport.

Humidity smacked her in the face as soon as she stepped outside; making her happy she'd paired her beige linen pants with a navy-and-beige asymmetrical short-sleeved tunic.

Champagne brain, her tush. What possible motive could he have for canceling her reservation if she hadn't agreed?

This just proved his potent appeal spelled danger.

Okay, no harm done. She handed him her smaller case and watched as he carefully placed the garment bag across the backseat. It should only take a couple of hours to reach Monte Calanetti. Then she could cut ties with the guy and concentrate on doing her job.

"How long to Monte Calanetti from here?" she asked as he held the door while she slid into the passenger seat.

"I've never driven it, but I can't imagine it's more than a few hours." He closed her in, rounded the front of the Land Rover and climbed into the driver's seat. A few minutes later they were in the thick of Florence traffic.

The old world elegance of the city charmed her, but the stop and go of the early evening traffic proclaimed work-force congestion was the same worldwide. She could admit, if only to herself, that she was glad not to be driving in it.

"Have you've been to Tuscany before?" she asked Zach.

"I've been several times. A couple of times with Antonio and once with my parents when I was twelve."

"So you know your way around?" She smothered a yawn.

"I do." He shot her an amused glance. "Enough to get us where we're going."

"I was just going to offer to navigate if you needed me to."

He stopped at a traffic light, taking the time to study her. "Thanks." He reached out and swept a thumb under her left eye in a soft caress. "You're tired. I guess relaxing didn't help you sleep."

She turned her head away from his touch. "I slept a little, off and on."

"Disrupted sleep can be less restful than staying awake." He sympathized. "Are you better at sleeping in a car?"

"Who can't sleep in a car? But I'm fine. I don't want to miss the sights. The city is so beautiful."

He drove with confidence and skill and a patience she lacked. He'd shaved on the plane; his sexy scruff gone when she woke this morning. The hard, square lines of his clean-cut jaw were just as compelling as the wicked shadow. The man couldn't look bad in a bag, not with a body like that.

Unlike her, he hadn't changed clothes, he still wore his black suit pants and white long-sleeved shirt, but the top two buttons were open and the sleeves were rolled up to his elbows. The suit jacket had been tossed onto the backseat.

"Florence is beautiful. The depth of history just draws me in. Halencia is the same. Since I'll be here for a month, I'm really hoping to get a chance to play tourist."

"Oh, absolutely. They have some really fantastic tours. I plan to stay after the wedding and take one. I'm torn between a chef and wine-tasting tour or a hiking tour."

"Wow, there's quite a difference there."

"I'm not going to lie to you. I'm leaning toward the pasta and wine tour. It goes to Venice. I've always wanted to go to Venice."

"Oh, yeah," he mocked, "it's all about Venice and nothing about the walking."

"Hey, I'm a walker. I love to hike. I'll share some of my brochures with you. There are some really great tours. If you like history, there's a Tuscan Renaissance tour that sounds wonderful."

"Sounds interesting. I'd like to see the brochures."

"Since technology is your thing, I'm surprised you're so into history."

"I minored in history. What can I say? I'm from New England. You can't throw a rock without hitting a historical marker. In my studies I was always amazed at how progressive our founding fathers were. Benjamin Franklin truly inspired me."

"You're kidding."

"I'm not." He sent her a chiding sidelong look. "I did my thesis on the sustainability of Franklin's inventions and observations in today's world. He was a brilliant man."

"And a great politician," she pointed out.

"I can't deny that, but he didn't let his political views define or confine him. I respect him for that. For him it wasn't about power but about proper representation."

"I feel that way about most of our founding fathers. So tell me something I probably don't know about big Ben."

"He was an avid swimmer."

"Like you and Antonio. Aha. No wonder you like him—" A huge yawn distorted the last word. "Oh." She smothered it behind a hand. "Sorry."

"No need to apologize." He squeezed her hand. "Don't feel you have to keep me company. Rest if you can. Jet lag can be a killer."

"Thanks." He'd just given her the perfect out from having to make conversation for the next hour. She'd snap the offer up if she weren't wide-eyed over the sights. Nothing in California rivaled the history and grandeur of the buildings still standing tall on virtually every street.

Zach turned a corner and the breath caught in the back of Lindsay's throat. Brunelleschi's Dome filled the skyline in all its Gothic glory. She truly was in Italy. Oh, she wanted to play tourist. But it would have to wait. Work first.

Riding across a beautiful, sculpted old bridge, she imagined the people who once crossed on foot. Soon rural views replaced urban views and in the distance clouds darkened the sky, creating a false twilight.

Lindsay shivered. She hoped they reached Monte Calanetti before the storm hit. She didn't care for storms, certainly didn't want to get caught out in one. The turbulence reminded her of anger, the thunder of shouting. As a kid, she'd hated them.

She didn't bury her head under the covers anymore. But there were times she wanted to.

Lightning flickered in the distance. Rather than watch the storm escalate, she closed her eyes as sleep claimed her. Her last thoughts were of Zach.

Lack of motion woke Lindsay. She opened her eyes to a dark car and an eerie silence. Zach was nowhere in view. Stretching, she turned around, looking for him. No sign. She squinted out the front windshield.

Good gracious, was the hood open?

She pushed her door open and stepped out, her feet crunching on gravel as a cool wind whipped around her. Hugging herself she walked to the front of the Land Rover. Zach was bent over the engine using a flashlight to ineffectually examine the vehicle innards. "What's going on?"

"A broken belt is my best guess." He straightened and directed the light toward the ground between them. "I've already called the rental company. They're sending a service truck."

She glanced around at the unrelenting darkness. Not a single light sparkled to show a sign of civilization. "Sending a truck where? We're in the middle of nowhere."

"They'll find us. The vehicle has a GPS."

Relief rushed through her. "Oh. That's good." She'd had visions of spending the night on the side of the road in a storm-tossed tin can. "Did they say how long before they got here? *Eee!*" She started and yelped when thunder boomed overhead. The accompanying flash of lightening had her biting back a whimper to the metallic taste of blood.

"As soon as they can." He took her elbow and escorted her to the passenger's-side door. "Let's stay in the car. The storm looks like it's about to break."

His big body blocked the wind, his closeness bringing warmth and rock-solid strength. For a moment she wanted to throw herself into his arms. Before she could give in to the urge, he helped her into her seat and slammed the door. A moment later he slid in next to her. He immediately turned the light off. She swallowed hard in a mouth suddenly dry.

"Can we keep the light on?" The question came out in a harsh rasp.

"I think we should conserve it, just in case."

"Just in case what?" It took a huge effort to keep any squeak out of her voice. "The truck doesn't come?"

"Just in case. Here—" He reached across the center console and took her hand, warming it in his. "You're shaking. Are you cold?" He dropped her hand to reach behind him. "Take my jacket."

She leaned forward and the heavy weight of his suit jacket wrapped around her shoulders. The satin lining slid coolly over her skin but quickly heated up. The scent of Zach clung to the material and she found it oddly comforting.

"Thank you. You won't be cold?"

She heard the rustle of movement and pictured him shrugging. "I'm okay right now. Hopefully the tow truck will get here before the cold seeps in. Worst case, we can move into the backseat and cuddle together under the jacket."

Okay, that option was way too tempting.

"Or you could get another one out of your luggage."

His chuckle preceded another crash of thunder. "Pixie girl, I don't know if my ego can survive you."

Maybe the dark wasn't so bad since he hadn't seen her flinch. Then his words struck her. "Pixie girl? That's the second time you called me that."

"Yes. Short and feisty. You remind me of a pixie."

"I am average," she stated with great dignity. "You're a giant."

"You barely reach my shoulder."

"Again, I refer you to the term 'giant.'" She checked her phone, welcoming the flare of light, but they were in the Italian version of Timbuktu so of course there was no service.

"Uh-huh. Feisty, pretty and short. Pixie it is."

Pretty? He'd called her that before, too. Pleasure bolstered her drooping spirits. She almost didn't care when the light faded again. Not that his admission changed her feelings toward him. He was a dangerous, charming man but she didn't have to like him just because he thought she was pretty. He was still off limits.

Hopefully he took her silence as disdain.

Right. On the positive side, the bit of vanity served to distract her for a few minutes. Long enough for headlights to appear on the horizon. No other vehicles had passed them in the twenty minutes she'd been awake so she said a little prayer that the approaching headlights belonged to their repair truck.

"Is the repair service coming from Monte Calanetti? How far away do you think we are?" She feared the thought of walking, but she didn't want to stay in the car all night, either.

"We're nowhere near Monte Calanetti," Zach announced. "By my guess we're about ten miles outside Caprese."

"Caprese?" Lindsay yelped in outrage. Caprese was the small village where the artist Michelangelo was born. "That's the other direction from Monte Calanetti from Florence. What are we doing here?"

"I told you last night. I have an errand to run for Antonio before I go to Monte Calanetti. It's just a quick stop to check on his groomsmen gifts and do a fitting."

"You so did not tell me."

"I'm pretty sure I did. You really can't hold your champagne, can you?"

"Stop saying 'champagne brain.' When did we have this conversation? Did I actually participate or was I sleeping?"

"You were talking, but I suppose you might have dozed off. You got quiet toward the end. I thought you were just involved in the movie. And then I fell asleep."

"Well, I don't remember half of what you've told me.

You should have reminded me of the plans we supposedly made this morning. I need to get to Monte Calanetti and I need my own car. I know you're trying to be helpful but…"

"But I got you stuck out in the middle of nowhere. And you're already tired from the flight. I'm sorry."

Lindsay clenched her teeth in frustration watching as the headlights slowly moved closer. Sorry didn't fix the situation. She appreciated the apology—many men wouldn't have bothered—but it didn't get her closer to Monte Calanetti. She had planned to hit the road running tomorrow with a visit to the wedding venue, the Palazzo di Comparino and restored chapel, before meeting with Christina in the afternoon.

Now she'd have to reschedule, move the interview back.

"Lindsay?" Zach prompted. "Are you okay?"

"I'm trying to rearrange my schedule in my head." She glanced at her watch, which she'd already adjusted to local time. Seven-fifteen. It felt much later. "What do you think our chances are of getting to Monte Calanetti tonight?"

"Slim. I doubt we'll find a mechanic willing to work on the Land Rover tonight. We'll probably have to stay over and head out tomorrow after it's fixed."

"If they have the necessary part."

"That will be a factor, yes. Here's our help." A small pickup honked as it drove past them then made a big U-turn and pulled up in front of them.

Zach hopped out to meet the driver.

Lindsay slid her arms into Zach's jacket and went to join them.

"Think it's the timing belt." Zach aimed his flashlight at the engine as he explained the problem to the man next to him. Their savior had gray-streaked black hair and wore blue coveralls. The name on his pocket read Luigi.

"Ciao, signora," the man greeted her.

She didn't bother to correct him, more eager to have

him locate the problem than worried about his assumption that she and Zach were married.

The driver carried a much bigger flashlight. The power of it allowed the men a much better view of the internal workings of the Land Rover. The man spoke pretty good English and he and Zach discussed the timing belt and a few other engine parts, none of which Lindsay followed but she understood clearly when he said he'd have to tow them into Caprese.

Wonderful.

Luigi invited her to sit in his truck while he got the Land Rover hooked up to be towed. She nodded and retrieved her purse. Zach walked her to the truck and held the door for her. The interior smelled like grease and cleanser, but it was neat and tidy.

"From what I remember from my research of Italy, small is a generous adjective when describing Caprese. At just over a thousand residents, 'tiny' would be more accurate. I'm not sure it has a hotel if we need to stay over."

"I'm sure there'll be someplace. I'll ask Luigi. It's starting to rain. I'm going to see if I can help him to make things go faster." He closed the door and darkness enveloped her.

The splat of rain on the windshield made her realize her ire at the situation had served to distract her from the looming storm. With its arrival, she forgot her schedule and just longed for sturdy shelter and a warm place to spend the night.

A few minutes later the men joined her. Squeezed between them on the small bench seat, she leaned toward Zach to give Luigi room to drive. The first right curve almost put her in Zach's lap.

"There's a bed-and-breakfast in town. Luigi's going to see about a room for us there." Zach spoke directly into her ear, his warm breath blowing over her skin.

She shivered. That moment couldn't come soon enough. The closer they got to town, the harder it rained. Obviously they were headed into the storm rather than away from it.

Fifteen minutes later they arrived at a small garage. Lindsay dashed through the rain to the door and then followed the men inside to an office that smelled like the truck and was just as tidy. Luigi immediately picked up the phone and dialed. He had a brief conversation in Italian before hanging up.

He beamed at Lindsay and Zach. "*Bene, bene*, my friends. The bed-and-breakfast is full with visitors. *Si*, the bad weather—they do not like to drive. But I have procured for you the last room. Is good, *si*?"

"*Si. Grazie,* Luigi." Zach expressed his appreciation then asked about the repairs.

For Lindsay only two words echoed through her head: one room.

CHAPTER FOUR

THE B AND B WAS a converted farmhouse with stone walls, long, narrow rooms and high ceilings. The furniture was sparse, solid and well worn.

Lindsay carried the heavy garment bag to the wardrobe and arranged it as best she could and then turned to face the room she'd share with Zach. Besides the oak wardrobe there was a queen bed with four posters, one nightstand, a dresser with a mirror above it and a hardback chair. Kindling rested in a fireplace with a simple wooden mantel, ready to be lit.

The bathroom was down the hall.

No sofa or chair to sleep on and below her feet was an unadorned hardwood floor. There was no recourse except to share the bed.

And the bedspread was a wedding ring quilt. Just perfect.

Her mother would say it was a sign. She'd actually have a lot more to say, as well, but Lindsay ruthlessly put a lock on those thoughts.

Lightening flashed outside the long, narrow window. Lindsay pulled the heavy drapes closed, grateful for the accommodation. She may have to share with a near stranger and the room may not be luxurious, but it was clean and authentic, and a strong, warm barrier against the elements.

Now why did that make her think of Zach?

The rain absorbed the humidity and dropped the temperature a good twenty degrees. The stone room was cool. Goose bumps chased across her skin.

She lit the kindling and once it caught added some wood. Warmth spread into the room. Unable to wait any longer, she made a quick trip down the hall. Zach was still gone when she got back. He'd dropped off her luggage and had gone back for his. She rolled the bigger case over next to the wardrobe. She didn't think she'd need anything out of it for one night.

The smaller one she set on the bed. She'd just unzipped it when a thud came at the door.

Zach surged into the room with three bags in tow.

"Oh, my goodness. You are soaked." She closed the door and rushed to the dresser. The towels were in the top drawer just as the innkeeper said.

Zach took it and scrubbed his face and head.

She tugged at his sopping jacket, glad now she'd thought to give it back to him. "Let's get this off you."

He allowed her to work it off. Under the jacket his shirt was so damp it clung to his skin in several places. He shivered and she led him over to the fireplace.

"Oh, yeah." He draped the towel around his neck and held his hands out to the heat.

"Take the shirt off, too," she urged him. She reached out with her free hand to help with the task, but when her fingers came skin to skin with his shoulder she decided it might be best if he handled the job himself.

To avoid looking at all the tanned, toned flesh revealed by the stripping off of his shirt, Lindsay held the dripping jacket aloft. What were they going to do with it? He handed her the shirt. With them?

A knock sounded at the door. Leaving Zach by the fire, Lindsay answered the knock. A plump woman in a purple jogging suit with more gray than black in her hair gave Lindsay a bright smile.

"Si, signora." She pointed to the dripping clothes, "I take?"

"Oh. *Grazie.*" Lindsay handed the wet clothes through the door.

"And these, too." From behind the door Zach thrust his pants forward.

Okay, then. She just hoped he'd kept his underwear on.

"Si, si." The woman's smile grew broader. She took the pants while craning her head to try to see behind Lindsay. She rolled off something in Italian. Lindsay just blinked at her.

"She said the owner was sending up some food for us."

As if on cue, Lindsay's stomach gurgled. The mention of food made her realize how hungry she was. It had been hours since they'd eaten on the plane. *"Si."* She nodded. *"Grazie."*

The woman nodded and, with one last glance into the room, turned and walked down the hall.

"You have a fan." Lindsay told Zach when she closed the door. "Oh, my good dog." The man had his back to her as he leaned over the bed rummaging through his luggage. All he wore was a pair of black knit boxer briefs that clung to his butt like a lover. The soft cloth left little to the imagination and there was a lot to admire.

No wonder the maid had been so enthralled.

And Lindsay had to sleep next to that tonight.

"What about a dog?" He turned those whiskey-brown eyes on her over one broad, bare shoulder.

Her knees went weak, nearly giving out on her. She sank into the hard chair by the fire.

"Dog? Huh? Nothing." Her mother had taught her to turn the word around so she didn't take the Lord's name in vain. After all these years, the habit stuck.

He tugged on a gray T-shirt.

Thank the merciful angels in heaven.

"I'm going to take a quick shower. Don't eat all the food."

"No promises."

He grinned. "Then I'll just have to hurry."

He disappeared out the door with his shaving kit under one arm and the towel tossed over his shoulder.

Finally Lindsay felt as though she could breathe again.

He took up so much space. A room that seemed spacious one moment shrank by three sizes when he crossed the threshold. Even with him gone the room smelled of him.

She patted her pocket. Where was her phone? She needed it now, needed to call the rental agency that very moment and demand a car be delivered to her. They should never have allowed a party outside the reservation to cancel. They owed her.

The hunt proved futile. Her phone wasn't in her purse, her tote or either suitcase. She thought back to the last time she'd used it. In the Land Rover, where it had been pitch-black. It must still be in the vehicle.

That was at the garage.

There'd be no getting her phone tonight. Dang it.

Stymied from making the call she wanted to, she took advantage of Zach's absence to gather her own toiletries and yoga pants and long-sleeved tee she'd worn on the plane. And a pair of socks. Yep, she'd wear gloves to bed if she had any with her. And if she had any luck at all, he'd wear a three-piece suit.

There'd be no skin-to-skin contact if she could help it.

Loosen up, Lindsay. Her mom's voice broke through her blockade. *You're young and single and about to share a bed with one prime specimen. You should be thinking of ways to rock the bed not bulletproof yourself against an accidental touch.*

How sad was it that her mother was more sexually aggressive than she was?

Her mom was forever pushing Lindsay to date more, to take chances on meeting people. She'd been thrilled when Lindsay had started seeing Kevin again. She'd welcomed him; more, she'd invited him to family events and made a point of showing her pride in Lindsay and her success.

Right, and look how that turned out.

To be fair, Mom had been almost as devastated as Lindsay when Kevin showed his true colors. She may be self-absorbed but Lindsay never doubted her mom's love. She wanted Lindsay to be happy and in her mind that equated to love and marriage. Because for her it was—at least during the first flush of love.

Lindsay wanted to believe in love and happily ever after, but it was getting harder to do as she planned her mother's sixth wedding. And, okay, yeah, Mom was right; Lindsay really didn't make an effort to meet men. But that wasn't the problem. She actually met lots of interesting men. While she was working, when it was totally inappropriate to pursue the connection.

The problem was she was too closed off when she did meet a nice guy. After stepfather number two, she'd started putting up shields to keep from being hurt when they left. She and Kevin had been friends before they were a couple and when they'd split up, her shields just grew higher.

She hadn't given up on love. She just didn't know if she was brave enough to reach for it.

You're in Italy for a month with a millionaire hunk at your beck and call. It's the perfect recipe for a spicy summer fling. Every relationship doesn't have to end with a commitment.

Mom didn't always practice what she preached.

The food hadn't arrived when Zach returned smelling of freshly washed male. He wore the same T-shirt but now his knit boxers were gray. She could only thank the good Lord—full-on prayer, here—that the T-shirt hung to his thighs, hiding temptation from view.

"Bathroom is free," he advised her.

Her stomach gurgled, but he looked so relaxed after his

shower and the storm had her so on edge she decided to get comfortable. Grabbing up the cache she'd collected, she headed for the door.

"Don't eat all the food," she told him.

"Hey, you get the same promise I did."

She stared at him a moment trying to determine if he was joking as she'd been. His features were impassive and he cocked a dark brow at her. Hmm. She better hurry just in case.

The bathroom was still steamy from his visit. As she pulled the shower curtain closed on the tiny tub she envisioned his hard body occupying this same space. His hard, wet, naked body. Covered in soap bubbles.

Oh. My. Dog.

She forced her mind to the nearly completed seating chart to remove him from her head. But that, too, reminded her of him so she switched to the flowers. Christina had yet to decide between roses and calla lilies or a mix of the two. Both were beautiful and traditional for weddings.

It may well depend on the availability. Christina wanted to use local vendors and merchants. She'd said it was for the people so should be of the people. Lindsay still puzzled over the comment. *It* was obviously the wedding, but what did she mean "it was for the people"?

Was the royal wedding not a love match?

Lindsay could ask Zach. He'd know.

No. She didn't want to know. It was none of her business and may change how she approached the wedding. Every bride deserved a fantasy wedding, one that celebrated the bond between her and the groom and the promise of a better future together. It was Lindsay's job to bring the fantasy to life. The reality of the relationship was not in her hands.

Her musings took her through the shower, a quick attempt at drying her hair, brushing her teeth and dressing. Fifteen minutes after she left the room, she returned to find

Zach seated on the bed, his back against the headboard, a tray of food sitting beside him.

The savory aroma almost brought her to her knees.

"Oh, that smells good." She dropped her things into her open case, flipped the top closed and set it on the floor before climbing onto the bed to bend over the tray and the two big bowls it held. She inhaled deeply, moaned softly. "Soup?"

"Stew."

"Even better. And bread." She looked at him. "You waited."

He lifted one shoulder and let it drop. "Not for long. It just got here. Besides, we're partners."

Her eyebrows shot up then lowered as she scowled at him. "We are so not partners." She handed him a bowl and a spoon. Tossed a napkin in his lap. Then settled cross-legged on her pillow and picked up her own bowl. "In fact, I think I should arrange for my own car tomorrow. I need to get to Monte Calanetti and you have to wait for the Land Rover to be repaired, which could take a couple of days."

"Getting a car here could take longer yet. You heard the rental clerk. All the vehicles are being taken up by the media presence here for the wedding."

"Oh, this is good." No point in arguing with him. She was an adult and a professional. She didn't require his permission to do anything.

"Mmm." He hummed his approval. "Are you okay with sharing?"

"The room?" She shrugged. "We don't really have a choice, do we?"

"The bed," he clarified and licked his spoon. She watched, fascinated. "I can sleep on the floor if you're uncomfortable sharing the bed."

"It's hardwood." She pulled her gaze away from him. "And there isn't any extra bedding."

"I can sleep near the fireplace. It won't be comfortable, but I'll survive. We're still getting to know each other, so I'll understand."

Crack!

Thunder boomed, making Lindsay jump and spill the bite of stew aimed for her mouth.

"Dang it." She grabbed her napkin and scrubbed at the stain on her breast. "Are you uncomfortable?"

"No." He took her bowl so she could use both hands. "But I'm a man."

Oh, yeah, she'd noticed.

"If something happened between us, I'd be a happy man in the morning. You, on the other hand, would be satisfied but regretful."

She glared at him. "Nothing is going to happen."

He held up his hands, the sign of surrender blemished by the bowls he held. "Of course not."

"So there's no reason not to share."

"None at all."

"It's settled then."

"Yep." He handed her bowl back. "Now you want to tell me what your deal is with storms?"

Zach watched the color leech from Lindsay's cheeks, confirmation that his suspicions were right that her reaction to the thunderstorm exceeded the norm.

She was nervous and jumpy, which was totally unlike her.

Sure she'd gone ballistic when he'd sat on the wedding dress, but considering the cost of the gown she could be forgiven for hyperventilating.

Generally he found her to be calm and collected, giving as good as she got but not overreacting or jumping to conclusions. Efficient but friendly. The storm had her shaken and he wanted to know why.

"Nothing." She carefully placed her bowl on the tray. "I'm fine."

"You're jumpy as hell. And it started before we got to the room so it isn't the sleeping arrangements. It has to be the storm."

"Maybe it's you." She tossed the words at him as she slid from the bed. "Did you consider that?"

"Nope." His gaze followed her actions as she put the suitcase back on the bed and began to organize the things she'd dumped in. "We're practically lovers."

Ice burned cold in the blue glare she sent him. "You are insane."

"Oh, come on." He taunted her. "You know it's going to happen. Not tonight, but definitely before the month is up."

"In your dreams. But I live in reality."

"Tell me about the storms."

"There's nothing to tell." The jerkiness of her movements told a different story.

"Okay. Have it your way." He relaxed back against the wall and laced his arms behind his head. "I like storms myself."

"You like storms?" The astonishment in her voice belied her indifference. "As I said, insane. I'm going to take the tray downstairs."

Zach grabbed the bread and wine from the tray and let her escape. Pressing her would only antagonize her.

He'd had nothing to do with the engine failure, but he approved of the results. If he were a man who believed in signs, he'd take it as karma's righteous nod.

He'd been playing with her when he'd alluded to them being lovers. Or so he thought. As soon as the words had left his mouth, he'd known the truth in them. He generally preferred leggy blondes. But something about the pixie appealed to him.

Her feistiness certainly. At the very least it was refreshing. With his position, family connections and money, people rarely questioned his authority and never dismissed him. She'd done both. And still was.

He had no doubt she'd try to make a break for it tomorrow.

He sipped at the last of his wine, enjoyed the warmth as it rolled down his throat. The fire had burned down to embers and he stirred himself to get up and feed it. The thick stone walls and bare wood floors kept the room cool so the fire gave nice warmth to the room. Plus, he imagined Lindsay would find it a comforting offset to the storm.

She was more pretty than beautiful, her delicate features overshadowed by that lush mouth. His gut tightened as heat ignited his blood just as flame flared over the fresh fuel.

Oh, yeah, he wanted a bite of that plump lower lip.

He'd have to wait. He'd put her off limits when he concocted the sabotage plan. He couldn't use her and seduce her, too. That would be too much. But she didn't need to know of his restraint. Just the thought of him making a move on her would keep her on edge, making it easier for him to cause a little chaos.

A glance at his watch showed the time at just after nine. Early for him to go to bed most nights but tonight, fatigue from travel, the time change and the concentration needed to drive an unfamiliar vehicle on unfamiliar roads weighed on him.

The room held no TV so it was sleep or talk.

He wouldn't mind getting to know his companion better but somehow he knew she'd choose the escape that came with sleep. Whether she actually slept or not. His feisty little pixie had a bit of the ostrich in her.

The door opened and she slipped inside.

"You're still up?" She avoided his gaze as she crossed to the bed and zipped the case that still sat on her side.

"Just feeding the fire."

She lifted the case and he stepped forward to take it from her.

"I can do it," she protested, independent as always.

"So can I." He notched his chin toward the bed. "You're falling asleep on your feet. Go to bed."

"What about you?" Caution filled her voice and expression.

"I'm going to tend the fire for a bit. I'll come to bed soon."

Relief filled her blue eyes and he knew she thought she'd gotten a reprieve; that she hoped to be asleep before he joined her in the far too small bed.

Truthfully, he hoped she fell asleep, too. No point in both of them lying awake thinking about the other.

Lindsay pretended to be asleep when Zach came to bed. His presence kept her senses on edge. Between him and the storm that still raged outside her nerves were balanced on a fine-edged sword.

She tried to relax, to keep her breathing even so as not to disturb Zach. The last thing she wanted was another discussion on why storms bothered her. It was a weakness she preferred to ignore. She usually plugged in her earphones and let her playlist tune out the noise.

Tonight there was nothing in the still house to disguise the violence of the weather outside the window. Everything in her longed to press back into the strong male body occupying the other half of the bed. Instead she clung to the edge of the mattress determined to stay on her side.

Thunder boomed and lightening strobed at the edges of the closed drapes. Lindsay flinched then held herself very still.

"Oh, for the love of dog, come here." Long, muscular arms wrapped around her and tugged her against the hard planes of a male chest.

Shocked by both action and words, Lindsay chose to focus on the latter. She glanced over her shoulder into dark eyes. "What did you say?"

"Woof, woof." And his lips settled softly on her cheek, a simple human-to-human contact that left her wanting more.

She sighed and made a belated attempt to wiggle away. Her body and nerves might welcome his touch but her head shouted, *Danger!* "I know it's silly. It's something my mom taught me when I was little. It kind of stuck."

"I think it's cute."

She went still. "I'm not cute. I'm not a pixie. And we're not going to be lovers. You need to let me go." One of them needed to be smart about this.

His arms tightened, pulled her back the few inches she'd gained. "Tell me about the storms."

"There's nothing to tell!"

His silence was a patient demand.

"What's to like about them? They're angry and destructive."

"A storm is cleansing. It can be loud, yes, but it takes the old and washes it clean."

She thought about that. "Destruction is not cleansing."

"It can be. If something is rotten or breaking, it's better to come down in a storm than under a person's weight. You might have to finish the cleanup but life is fresher once you're done."

"I doubt people who have lost their homes to a hurricane or tornado would agree with you."

"Hurricanes and tornadoes are different. This is a simple summer thunderstorm. Nothing to get so worked up over."

"I know." She lay with her cheek pressed against her hand. She should move away, put space and distance between them. But she didn't. Couldn't. Having strong arms surrounding her gave her a sense of belonging she hadn't experienced in way too long. It didn't even matter that it was all in her head. Her body had control right now. With a soft sigh she surrendered to his will and her body's demand.

"It's not even my phobia. It's my mother's that she passed on to me." She blamed the kiss for loosening her resolve. Hard to keep her wits about her with the heat of his kiss on her cheek.

"How'd she do that?"

"She hates storms. They don't scare her, though, they make her cry."

"Why?"

"She was only seventeen when she got pregnant with me. My dad tried to step up and they got married, even though he was barely eightteen. My mom is very high maintenance. Her dad always gave her everything she wanted. Took care of things for her. She expected my dad to do the same. She was too demanding and he finally left. It was during a storm that he took off and never came back. She was left pregnant and alone."

"So she cries when it rains."

"Yes." Lindsay had pieced the story together through the years. She loved her mother; she was fun and free-spirited. But Lindsay also recognized her faults; it had been a matter of self-preservation.

"Her dislike of storms comes from sadness."

She nodded, her hair brushing over his chin. She'd never talked to anyone about this.

"But your jumpiness suggests a fear-based reaction."

A shiver racked her body and she curled in on herself. Everything in her tightened, shutting down on a dark memory. She wanted to tell him it was none of his business, but then he might let her go and she wasn't ready to give up the cocoon of his embrace.

His arms tightened around her and his lips slid over her cheek, giving her the courage to answer.

"It's a lingering unease leftover from childhood. It's distressing to hear your mother cry and know there's nothing you can do to help."

"It seems the mother should be comforting the child, not the other way around."

"She's more sensitive than I am."

A tender touch tucked her hair behind her ear, softly trailed down the side of her neck. "Just because you're tough doesn't mean you don't need reassurance now and again."

She relaxed under the gentle attention. Though she rejected the truth in his words.

"This storm caught me when I was tired. I'm sorry I disturbed you. I usually put my earbuds in but I left my phone in the Land Rover."

"Ah, a sensible solution. I should have known." He shifted behind her, leaving her feeling chilled and alone. And then his weight settled against her again and earbuds entered her ears. "You're stuck with my playlist, but maybe it'll help you sleep."

She smiled and wrapped her hand around his. "Thank you."

His fingers squeezed hers.

She felt the tension drain away. Now she had the music, she'd be okay. She no longer needed the comfort of his arms.

Her eyes closed. In a minute she'd pull away. There was danger in staying too close to him. Already her body recognized his, which made it all too easy for him to hold sway over her. She needed to stay strong, to stay distant...

The last thing she knew was the feel of his lips on her cheek.

CHAPTER FIVE

LINDSAY WOKE JUST before eight with the earbuds still in her ears. The tunes had stopped. She felt around for the phone but came up with the end of the earbuds instead. Her hand hadn't encountered a hard male body, but the stillness of the room had already told her Zach was out and about.

She threw back the covers and her feet hit the floor, her toes curling in her socks against the chill of the hardwood. Padding to the window, she pushed back the drapes to a world awash in sunshine. The ground was still wet but the greenery and rock fences had a just-scrubbed brightness to them.

Or was that Zach's influence on her?

A peek down the hall showed the bathroom was free so she quickly grabbed her things and made a mad dash to claim it. Aware others may be in need of the facilities she kept it short and soon returned to the room to dress and put on her makeup.

Before going downstairs, she packed her things so she'd be ready to leave when a car arrived. In spite of Zach's comfort and kindness last night, or maybe because of it, she fully intended to make her break from him today.

The heavenly scent of coffee greeted her in the dining room. Some fellow occupants of the B and B were seated at the long wooden table, including Zach. Cheerful greetings came her way as she moved through the room.

"Breakfast is buffet style this morning as there're so many of us." A gray-haired gentleman pointed with his fork toward the buffet she'd passed.

"Henry, don't use your utensils to point." An equally

gray-haired woman pushed his hand down. "They'll think we have no manners." She smiled at Lindsay with a mouth full of crooked teeth. "That handsome husband of yours made you a cup of coffee he was about to take upstairs. I'm glad you could join us. I'm happy to meet up with some fellow Americans. We're Wes and Viv Graham from Iowa and the folks there on the end are Frank and Diane Murphy from Oregon."

"Nice to meet you all." She sent Zach a questioning look at the husband comment and received a shrug in reply. Right. She'd get him for that. Hopefully they wouldn't be there long enough for it to be an issue. She backtracked to the buffet.

Croissants, sausage, bacon, quartered oranges and some cappuccino. No eggs. She took a couple of pieces of bacon, one sausage and a few orange wedges.

"I was just about to come wake you." Zach appeared beside her and took her plate. "I've arranged for alternate transportation and it'll be here in about half an hour. How'd you sleep?"

Huh. If he was leaving in half an hour maybe she'd stick with him, after all. It would take her longer than that to get her phone. "I slept well, thank you." Truly thanks to him.

"You're going to want one of these." He placed a croissant on her plate. "It's called a *cornetto*. There's a wonderful jam inside."

He took off for his seat, leaving her to follow. Their audience watched with avid curiosity. At their end of the table, Lindsay smoothed her hand across his shoulders. "Thank you, sweetie." She kissed him softly, lingering over his taste for a beat longer than she intended to, then slid into the chair around the corner to his right.

She pressed her lips together. Okay, that bit of payback totally backfired. But playing it through to the end, she glanced shyly down the table. "I'm sorry. We don't mean to be rude. Newlyweds." She rolled her eyes as if that explained everything.

A pleased smile bloomed on Diane's face. "Oh, my dear, don't mind us old folks. Congratulations. You two enjoy yourselves." She turned to her husband. "Frank do you remember on our honeymoon when we—"

"Well done." Zach pushed her coffee toward her. "But that's the first and last time you ever call me sweetie."

She flashed him a provocative look. "We'll see."

Let him stew on that. He was the one to say they'd be lovers, after all.

"Be nice to me or I'll take your *cornetto*."

"I don't think so." She picked up the horn-shaped pastry and bit in. Chewed. Savored. "Oh, my dog."

"I told you so." Satisfaction stamped his features as he leaned back in his straight-backed chair.

"This is wonderful." She pointed at the jam-filled roll. "We have to have these at the wedding."

"We're a long way from Monte Calanetti."

"Oh, I'm aware." Censure met unrepentance. "Tell me again why we're in Caprese and not Monte Calanetti?"

"An errand for the prince."

She waited for more. It didn't come.

"I took care of it this morning. I'm ready to go when the new transportation gets here."

That was a relief. She finished the last of her *cornetto* with a regretful sigh and a swipe of her tongue over her thumb. "Maybe not these exact rolls but definitely *cornettos*."

"I'm all for it, but I suggest you discuss that with Christina."

She nodded, eyeing him speculatively through another bite. "How well do you know Christina?"

"Not well." He glanced down, snagged one of her orange wedges. "I met her once. Theirs has been a long-distance relationship."

"She seems really nice. And she showed a lot of enthusiasm when we first started planning, but she's cooled off lately."

"Really?" That brought his head up. "Do you think she's having second thoughts?"

Lindsay gave a half shrug. "Very few brides make it to the altar without suffering a few nerves along the way. It's probably nothing. Or nothing to do with the wedding, anyway."

"Tony's been off, too. He got me to come all this way a month in advance of the wedding, but now it feels like he's avoiding me."

"I'm sure they both have a lot on their plates right now." So much for the reassurances she'd been hoping for. The fact Zach had noticed something off, too, gave her some concerns. "I'll know more after my appointment with Christina, which was supposed to be this afternoon. I'll have to reschedule. Oh, that reminds me. I need to get my phone out of the Land Rover."

"Sorry, I forgot." Zach reached around and pulled something from his back pocket. He set her phone on the table. "I had Luigi bring it by this morning."

"Thanks." She picked it up, felt the warmth of the glass and metal against her flesh and tried to disengage from the fact it had absorbed the heat from his hot bum.

A loud whopping sound overhead steadily got louder. Everyone looked up. Then, in an unchoreographed move, they all stood and rushed to the back terrace. Lindsay, with Zach on her heels, brought up the rear.

As she stepped out onto the cobblestone patio, a helicopter carefully maneuvered in the air, preparing to land in the large farmyard.

Zach watched Lindsay's face as the big bird neared the

ground, knew by the pop of her eyes exactly when she spied the royal insignia on the door. She turned to stare at him as the inn occupants wandered forward to examine the helicopter and talk to the pilot.

Zach surveyed the royal conveyance with a smirk. "Our new transportation."

"You have got to be kidding me."

He liked the look of awe in her eyes. Much better than the fear she'd tried so hard to hide the night before. There was something more to her dislike of storms than a leftover agitation from her mother's distress. Something she wasn't willing to share, or maybe something she didn't fully remember.

He wished he could have done more than just lend her his earbuds.

"It's good to have friends in high places. When I told Tony you were concerned about missing your appointment with Christina, he insisted on putting the helicopter at my disposal in assisting you for the duration."

Actually, Zach had suggested it; still Tony jumped at the chance to accommodate Christina. Forget bending over backward, Tony was doing flips to give Christina the wedding of her dreams. Because he knew their lives were going to suck.

For Zach's part, he figured the sooner he got to Christina, the sooner he could talk sense into her. They'd only met once, but Tony lauded her with being a sensible, caring person. Surely she saw the error in what they were about to do.

He could only hope she'd listen to reason and end things now. Then he and the wedding planner could spend the next month exploring the wonders of Tuscany.

Shock had her staring wide-eyed at the big machine. "I have a helicopter for the next month?"

"I have a helicopter until after the wedding. The pilot takes his orders from me."

"Ah. But you're here to help me." She rubbed her hands together. "So, I have my very own helicopter for the next month. Oh, this is going to make things so much easier."

"I'm glad you're happy." And glad he'd be able to keep tabs on her. Things were falling nicely into place. "I told him I had designs on his wedding planner and I needed something to impress her."

All wonder dropped away in a heartbeat.

His little pixie turned fierce, getting right up in his space.

"Listen to me, Mr. Sullivan." Her blue-diamond eyes pinned him to the spot. "You may not think much of what I do, but it's very important to me, to your friends and, in the case of this wedding, to this country. I was starting to like you, but mess with my business and you won't like me."

Dog, she was beautiful. She may be tiny but she worked that chin and those eyes. He'd never wanted to kiss a woman more in his life. Defensive, yes, but not just for herself. She honestly cared about Tony and Christina. And the blasted country.

He did like her. More than he should. He'd have to be careful not to damage her in his rescue mission.

"Tony is why I'm here. Ms. Reeves. I promise you, I'm going to do everything in my power to make sure this turns out right for him."

"Okay, then." Her posture relaxed slightly. "As long as we understand each other."

"Understand this." He wrapped his hands around her elbows, lifted her to her toes and slanted his mouth over hers.

She stiffened against him for the briefest moment, in the next all her luscious softness melted into him. She opened her mouth to his and the world dropped away. The sparkling-clean farmyard, chattering Midwest tourists and his majesty's royal helicopter disappeared from his radar.

He'd meant the kiss to be a distraction, to focus her on his mythical seduction and away from his actual plan to change Tony's mind about marrying Christina. And vice versa.

But all he knew in that moment, all he wanted to know, was the heated touch of the pixie coming apart in his arms. He wrapped her close, angling the kiss to a new depth. She tasted of berry jam and spicy woman. Her essence called to him, addled his senses until he craved nothing more than to sweep her into his arms and carry her up to their room.

Her arms were linked around his neck and he'd dragged her up his body so they were pressed together mouth to mouth, chest to chest, loins to loins. It wasn't enough. It was too much.

Someone patted him on the arm. "You young ones need to take that upstairs."

The world came crashing back. Zach slowly broke off the kiss. He lifted his head, opened his eyes. Passion-drenched pools of blue looked back at him. Her gaze moved to his mouth. A heavy sigh shifted her breasts against his chest. She looked back at him and blinked.

"You should put me down now."

Yes, he should. The kiss had gotten way out of control and he needed to rein it in. "I don't want to. Christina will understand if we're an hour late."

What was he saying? *Get a grip, Sullivan.*

"I won't." She pushed against him. "This was a mistake. And it won't happen again."

"Why not?" he demanded because that's what he'd want to know if he were seriously pursuing her, which he wasn't. She was too sweet, too genuine for him. He needed someone who knew the rules of non-commitment.

Still, when he set her on her feet, he took satisfaction in the fact he had to steady her for a moment.

"Because I'm a professional. Because you are the best man."

"And you have a policy. You're the boss, you can change policy."

"Not a good idea." She straightened her shirt, smoothing the fabric over her hips. "I have the policy for a reason. I'm the wedding planner. I'm not here to have fun. I'm here to work. You—" she swept him with a glance "—would be a distraction when I need all my wits about me."

"Signor..." The pilot approached. "If you desire to stick to your flight plan, we should leave within the next fifteen minutes."

"Thank you."

"May I assist with the luggage?"

Glad to have this scene wrapping to a close, Zach met her gaze. "Are you ready?"

"I am." She stepped back, composed herself. "I just need to grab my luggage and the wedding dress." She headed into the house. "Do you think they'd mind if I took a few *cornettos* to go?"

Grinning, he followed her inside. He best be careful or this woman was going to turn him inside out.

Lindsay loved traveling by helicopter. She'd been a little nervous to start out with, afraid the heights might get to her. Nope. Whizzing through the air above the scenic vista gave her a thrill.

The helicopter flew over a meadow that looked like gold velvet. She pointed. "It's beautiful. What crop is that?"

"No crop, *signorina.*" The pilot's voice came over her headphones. "Sunflowers."

"Sunflowers," she breathed. She'd never seen a whole field of the big, cheerful flowers.

Zach tapped the pilot on the shoulder and he took them down and did a wide loop so she actually saw the flowers. She'd told Zach she wasn't there to have fun, but, oh, she was.

That didn't mean she could throw caution to the wind and jump into a summer fling. Her blood still thrummed from his embrace. It would have been so easy to let him seduce her. Except she couldn't. She needed to grow a spine, put him in his place. The problem was she melted as soon as he touched her.

If she was honest, the physical attraction wasn't what worried her. She liked him. Way too much for her peace of mind. That made the physical all the more tempting. She wanted love in her life but this was the wrong time, wrong place, wrong man.

Restraint came at a cost, but she wouldn't jeopardize everything she'd built on an overload of hormones. She just needed to resist him for a few weeks and then she'd be back in Hollywood and he'd be back in Silicon Valley.

Zach pointed out the palace as they flew over Voti, Halencia's capital city and Christina's home. The big, yellow palace presented a majestic silhouette with its square shape and the round battlement towers at the corners. The notched alternate crenels screamed castle. The building had a strong, regal presence set on a shallow cliff side overlooking the sea on one side and the sprawling city of Voti on the other.

One of the towers had been converted into a heliport.

"Are we landing at the palace?" She spoke into the microphone attached to the headphones.

"Yes." Zach nodded.

"So I'll get a chance to meet Prince Antonio?"

Now he shook his head. "Sorry, he's in meetings all day. We'll be going straight down and out to a car waiting for us. We'll be just in time for your one-thirty appointment with Christina."

The helicopter made a wide turn then started its descent. Lindsay experienced her first anxious moments, seeing the land rush up to meet her. Without thinking, she reached out and grabbed Zach's hand.

His warm grip wrapped around her fingers and gave a squeeze. She instantly relaxed, feeling grounded. Putting her stringent, no-fraternizing policy aside for a moment, she smiled at him. He'd been gentle and kind last night and was supportive now. No doubt he'd hate the description, but he was a genuinely good guy.

Even though she was essentially a stranger to him, Zach had gone over and beyond the call of duty.

She longed to see some of the interior of the palace, but a palace attendant met them and a very modern elevator took them straight down to the ground level. The attendant led them through a ten-foot portico, which he explained was the width of the castle walls.

Wow, Lindsay mouthed. Seriously, she felt like a little girl at Disneyland. She was so busy trying to see everything at once she nearly tripped over her own feet.

Zach grasped her elbow. Steadied her. "Careful, Tinkerbell."

Caught gawking. But she couldn't care. This was amazing. "We're in a castle. Couldn't I be Cinderella?"

He released her to tug on her straight ponytail. "No changing up now. Tinkerbell is a pixie, right?"

"She's a fairy. And you need to stop. I'm not that short."

"You're a little bitty thing. With lots of spunk. Nothing bad about that."

She rolled her eyes. "If you say so." They exited onto

a round driveway where a car and driver waited. She grabbed Zach's arm to stop him. "Listen, you don't need to come to my appointment with Christina. I can promise you'll be monumentally bored. If you stay here, you may get a few minutes to visit with Antonio."

"I want to come. It'll be good to see Christina again and to let her know Antonio isn't shirking his groom duties." He waved the driver off and held the door open for her himself. "Besides, I'm not hanging around hours just to get a few minutes of Tony's time. We'll connect soon enough."

She should go through her notes on the ride through Voti to be prepared for the appointment. Should, but wouldn't. The city was so charming, not a high-rise to be seen, and the buildings were bunched closely together, creating narrow lanes. The warmth of the earth tones and red-tiled roofs was like an architectural hug. She loved the bursts of color in hanging planters. And the odd little plazas they'd drive through that all had lovely little fountains.

Christina worked not far from the palace. All too soon the car pulled to a stop in front of a three-story building. Lovely, black, wrought-iron gates opened into a cobble-stoned courtyard.

"Zach, Ms. Reeves, welcome." The driver must have called ahead because Christina stepped forward to greet them.

She was tall—Lindsay's notes read five nine and her subtle heels added a few inches to that—and stunning with creamy, olive skin and thick reddish-brown hair sleeked back in a French twist. She wore a fitted suit in cobalt blue.

Standing between her and Zach, Lindsay did feel short.

"Christina." Zach wrapped her hand in both of his. "You haven't changed a bit in four years."

"You flatter me," she said in perfect English, her accent charming. She led them through the courtyard and up a curving wrought-iron staircase to an office on the second floor. "We both know that's not true. Thank goodness. I was barely out of school and quite shy."

"And soon you'll be the Queen of Halencia."

Christina's eyelashes flickered and she looked down as she waved them into seats. "I prefer to focus on one thing at a time. First there is the wedding."

"Of course."

"Thank you, Ms. Reeves, for coming so early to assist in the preparations. I originally intended to continue with the foundation on a part-time basis in their offices here in Halencia, but the prince's advisors have convinced me I'll be quite busy. It would be unfair to the foundation to hold a position and not be here to help. It is such a worthy endeavor. I would not want to hamper it in any way."

"It's important work. I'm sure, as the queen, your interest will be quite beneficial, so you'll still be of help."

"That's kind of you to say." Christina inclined her head.

A regal gesture if Lindsay had ever seen one. Maybe she'd been practicing.

Lindsay waved toward the open window. "You have a lovely view of the palace from here. It must be amazing to sit here and see your future beckoning for you."

Christina's smile slipped a little. "Yes. Quite amazing."

"It's a lot to think about, isn't it?" Zach spoke softly. "All that you're giving up. All that you're taking on?"

Appalled at the questions that were sure to rattle the most confident of brides let alone one showing a slight nervousness, Lindsay sent him a quelling glance.

"I am at your disposal to assist in any way I can," she advised her bride.

"You have been wonderful. My mind is just everywhere these days. I hope you do not mind taking on the bulk of the arrangements?"

"Of course. If we can just make some final decisions, I

can take care of everything. Your attendants are all set, the dresses have been received and a first fitting completed. I just need to know your final thoughts on the flowers, the total head count and whether you want to do indoors or outdoors for the reception. I have some sketches for you to look at." She passed a slim portfolio across the desk. "The palace wants to use the royal photographer, but I know some truly gifted wedding photographers if you decide you want a specialist."

"I am sure the royal photographer will be fine. These are marvelous drawings, Ms. Reeves. Any of these settings will be wonderful."

"Lindsay." She gently corrected the soon-to-be princess, who seemed near tears as she looked at the reception scenes. Lindsay could tell she wasn't going to get much more from the woman. "Every wedding should be special. What can I do to make your day special?"

"You have done so much already. I like the outdoors. I remember playing in the palazzo courtyard, pretending it was a palace. It seems appropriate."

"Outdoors is a lovely choice. Regarding flowers, we passed a meadow of sunflowers on our way here today. Gold is one of the royal colors you listed. I wondered—"

"Sunflowers! Yes, I would love that. And roses, I think. You seem to know what I want better than I do."

"I've done this for a long time. I'll get the final head count from the palace contact. We've covered almost everything. But we never addressed if they do the traditional 'something old, something new, something borrowed, something blue' here in Halencia or if you even want to play along?"

"What is this tradition?" A frown furrowed her delicate brow.

"It's just a fun tradition that originated in England. It

represents continuity, promise of the future, borrowed happiness and love, purity and fidelity."

"It sounds quite lovely. But I do not have any of these things."

"The fun is in getting them. In America the items are often offered by friends and family. If you share you're doing this, you'll get everything you need and it will all have special meaning for you."

"I know of something old." She tapped a finger against her desk. "Yes, I would like to have it for the wedding. It is a brooch that has been in my father's family for many years. It is said that those who wore the brooch at their wedding enjoyed many happy years together. Yes. I must have the brooch."

"Sounds perfect." Pleased to get a positive reaction and some enthusiasm from the bride, Lindsay made a note in her tablet.

"But I do not know where the brooch is." Sadness drained the brief spark of light. "The women of my generation have not chosen to go with the old tradition. Do you think you can help me find it?" Christine's eyes pleaded with Lindsay. "My grandmother or Aunt Pia might know who had it last."

Goodness, Lindsay never liked to say no to a bride, but she couldn't see how her schedule would accommodate hours on the phone tracking down a lost family jewel.

"Sure, we'll be happy to locate it for you."

Zach stole her opportunity to respond. But, sure, it was a good way to keep him occupied and out of her hair.

"We're talking a few phone calls, right?"

Christina shook her head. "The older generation of women in my family are very traditional. They will not talk of such things to a stranger over the phone. And they will not talk to you alone, Zach." She reached for a pen and paper. "I will write a letter you can take with you. *Grazie*, both of you."

Oh, Zach, what had he got them into? The hope in Christina's eyes prevented Lindsay from protesting time constraints.

"I wish I could give you more time but with learning the workings of the palace, I am a bit overwhelmed." Christina handed Lindsay the letter she'd written. "With the two of you helping, I feel so much better."

"I'm glad." Lindsay tucked the letter into her tote.

"Lindsay, do you mind if I have a moment alone with Christina?" Zach made the quiet demand and tension instantly radiated from his companion.

"Of course." Lindsay stood and offered her hand to Christina. "I'll keep you apprised of the arrangements."

"Thank you." Christina used both hands to convey her urgency. "And the progress in locating the brooch."

"Absolutely." Lindsay smiled and turned away. With her back to Christina, Lindsay narrowed her eyes at him and mouthed the words, "Do not upset the bride."

He maintained an impassive demeanor. "I'll be along in a moment."

Though Christina watched him expectantly, he waited for the distinct click of the door closing before he addressed her.

"I hope you'll forgive my concern, but I noticed you seem unsettled."

"I have much on my mind."

"I understand. But I also know the circumstances of your…relationship with Antonio." The situation warranted discretion on so many levels. "And I wonder if you're having second thoughts?"

Her chin lifted in a defensive gesture. "No."

"Perhaps you should."

Surprise showed before she composed her features

into a calm facade. "I can assure you I have considered the matter thoroughly. Did Antonio send you here to test me?"

"No. Tony has asked me to be his advocate in all things wedding related. I take my responsibilities seriously and when I look at this situation, I have to wonder what the two of you are thinking. Marriage is a binding, hopefully lifelong, commitment. The two of you barely know each other. No one would blame you if you changed your mind. Least of all Tony. He knows how much you've already sacrificed for your country."

Her shoulders went back. "Has he changed his mind?"

It would be so easy to lie. To destroy the engagement with a bit of misdirection that resulted in an endless loop of he said, she said. But he had some honor. The decision to end it must be hers, Antonio's or theirs together.

"No. He's determined to see this through. He's very grateful to you."

She nodded as if his words affirmed something for her. "Thank you for your concern. There is much to adjust to, but I will honor my promise. In little over a month, I will marry Prince Antonio."

CHAPTER SIX

LINDSAY WAS STILL puzzling over what Zach felt compelled to talk to Christina about in private as she climbed to her room on the third floor of Hotel de la Calanetti, a lovely boutique hotel situated on a hillside overlooking Monte Calanetti's central courtyard.

Considering his opinion of lavish weddings and how unsettled Christina came across, leaving them alone together made Lindsay's left eyebrow tick. He better not have caused trouble.

In retrospect she wished she'd waited to say goodbye to Christina until after he'd spoken to her. Then Lindsay might have learned what the discussion had been about. Or maybe not. The other woman's natural poise hid a lot. Lindsay had been unable to tell if the woman was upset when she'd walked them out.

Holding the garment bag draped over her arm, Lindsay stepped aside so the hotel manager's teenage son, Mario, could unlock the door.

"Signorina." He ducked his head in a shy move and gestured for her to precede him.

She stepped in to a comfortable, refined room furnished with nice 1800s furniture. Thankfully there was a private bathroom. One large window allowed sunshine to flow in and provided a delightful view of the village and town center.

But it was tiny; smaller than the room at the farmhouse. Though this room included a desk, which she was happy to see, and a comfortable chair, she barely had space to walk around the double bed.

She tipped Mario—who'd lugged her suitcases up the three flights—with some change and a smile.

"Grazie, signorina." He rewarded her with a bashful grin and raced away.

The garment bag took up the entire closet to the point she had to bump it shut with her hip. She'd hoped to leave the dress with Christina, but the bride had nixed that plan. The queen had made a reservation with a favorite *modiste* in Milan and Christina had asked Lindsay to hold on to the dress and bring it to the fitting.

So of course that was what she'd do. And apparently everything else.

When Christina had walked them out, she'd given Lindsay a brief hug and whispered, "I trust you to finish it. Please make the prince proud."

Lindsay got the message. She was on her own for the final push. Luckily her assistant would be arriving in a few days.

Hands on her hips Lindsay surveyed her room. It was lovely. And if she were here on vacation it would be perfect. But where was she going to work?

The desk for computer work was the least of her needs. She'd shipped five boxes of pre-wedding paraphernalia to the hotel. Upon check-in, Signora Eva had eagerly informed Lindsay the boxes had arrived and she'd be sending them up shortly.

Lindsay puffed out a breath that lifted her bangs. She thought longingly of the hillside villa Zach had pointed out as they'd flown over it. He had the whole place to himself. He probably had a room he could donate to the cause. Unfortunately he'd constantly be around. Talking to her. Distracting her. Tempting her.

Better to avoid that trap if she could.

She lifted her suitcase onto the bed and started unpacking. When she finished, she'd walk down to the town center to get a feel for the small city. She may have to find office space; possibly something off the town courtyard would be pleasant and close. In the meantime, she'd ask Signora Eva to hold on to the boxes.

Dressed in beige linen shorts and a cream, sleeveless tunic, Lindsay strolled down the hill. There was no sidewalk, just the ancient cobblestoned street. Charming but not the easiest to walk on.

A young man zipped by her on a scooter, followed closely by his female companion. Lindsay watched them until they turned a corner and vanished from view. She hadn't heard from the car-rental company yet. Monte Cala-netti was a lovely little city, but not small enough she could do all her business by foot.

The zippy little scooter looked promising. It wouldn't hold anything, but she could have things delivered. But where? Not the hotel. She'd get claustrophobic after a day.

She reached the city center; not a courtyard, but a plaza. Oh, it was lovely. In the center an old fountain bubbled merrily, drawing Lindsay forward. Businesses ringed the plaza, many with hanging pots of flowers. It was bright and colorful and had probably looked much the same a hundred or even five hundred years ago.

Well, minus the cars, of course.

History in Tuscany wasn't something that needed to be brought to mind. The past surrounded you wherever you went, influenced your very thoughts. Already Lindsay was contemplating how she could make it a part of the wedding.

"Buon giorno, signorina," a male voice greeted her. "May I assist you in finding your way?"

She swung around to confront a large, barrel-chested man with a full head of black hair dusted gray on the sides. His bushy mustache was more gray than black. Friendly brown eyes waited patiently for her assessment.

"Hello." She smiled. "I'm just wandering." She waved her hand around. "I'm spellbound by the beauty of Monte Calanetti. You must be so proud the royal wedding will be performed here."

"Indeed we are. I am Alonso Costa, mayor of this fair city. I can assure you we have much to offer those who stay here. Amatucci's is one of the best boutique vineyards in the world, and Mancini's restaurant is superb. I fully expect Raffaele to earn an Italian Good Food Award this year. What is your interest, *signorina*? I will direct you to the best."

Oh, she was sure he could. She liked him instantly. He'd be a great source to help her.

"It's nice to meet you, Alonso, I'm Lindsay Reeves and I'd like to learn more about your beautiful city. Would you like to join me for coffee?"

White teeth flashed under the heavy bush of his mustache. "I would be most delighted, *signorina*. The café has a lovely cappuccino."

"Sounds wonderful." She allowed him to escort her across the plaza to an outdoor table at the café. He went inside and returned with two cappuccinos and some biscotti. She began to wonder if they had a gym in town. All this wonderful food, she'd be needing one soon.

She introduced herself more fully to the mayor and he proved a font of information. As she'd expected the media, both print and electronic, had already landed heavily in Monte Calanetti.

Alonso rubbed his chin when she asked after office space. "I will ask around. But I must warn you most available space has already been rented or reserved. The wedding has proved quite prosperous for the townspeople. Many have rented out spare rooms to house the paparazzi or provide work space as you have requested."

He named a figure a family had asked for the rental of their one-car garage and her mouth dropped open.

"Si," He nodded at her reaction. "It is crazy. But the press, they bid against each other to get the space."

"Well, it's more than I can afford. I'll have to figure out something else."

The empty chair next to Lindsay scraped back and Zach joined them at the table. He laid one arm along the back of her chair while holding his other hand out to Alonso. "Zach Sullivan. I've rented the De Luca villa."

"Ah, the best man." Alonso shook hands. "A palace representative provided a list of VIPs who would be visiting the area for the wedding. Your name is on the top."

Zach grinned. "It's good to know Tony has his priorities straight."

The casual reference to the prince impressed the mayor. He puffed up a bit as he gave Zach the same rundown about the town he'd given her. Except he offered to arrange a tour of the vineyard and make reservations at the restaurant. With great effort she restrained an eye roll.

"Tell me about the fountain," she asked to redirect the conversation.

Alonso gave her a bright smile. "The legend is that if you toss a coin and it lands in the clamshell you will get your wish. We recently learned that the sculptor of the nymph was Alberto Burano. The fact that the nymph wore a cloak caught the attention of an art historian. She recognized Burano's style and researched the fountain and Burano until she linked the two."

"That's amazing. And brings more value to the fountain and the city. Do you know anything more about the legend?"

"Actually, Lucia's search inspired me to do one of my own and I found that nymphs are known to be sensual creatures of nature, capricious in spirit living among humans but distant from them so when one presents an offering, such as the clamshell, it means the nymph has found true love and the offering is a gift of equal love."

"It's a lovely legend of unselfishness and love." The romance of it appealed to Lindsay.

"But does it work?" Zach questioned.

"Before I did the research I would have said half the time. Now, when I think back to the stories I've heard, success always involved matters of the heart. I believe when the coin lands in the clamshell it activates the gift and the wish is granted when true love is involved."

Zach quirked one dark eyebrow. "You're a romantic, Mr. Mayor."

Alonso smiled and shrugged in a very Italian gesture. "This is what I have observed. Does it make me a romantic to believe in the legend? Maybe so. But the tourists like it."

"I'm sure they do," Lindsay agreed. "Who doesn't like the thought of true love? Wouldn't it be cool to have a replica of the fountain at the reception?"

"*Si*. There is a mason in town that makes small replicas he sells to tourists. I'll give you his number. He might be able to make something bigger."

"That would be great. Thanks."

The mayor's cell phone rang. "Excuse me." He checked the display. "I must take this call. It has been a pleasure to meet you both. *Il caffè* is my treat today."

"Oh, no," Lindsay protested. "I invited you."

"And I am pleased you did. Allow me to welcome you both to Monte Calanetti with this small offering. You can reward me by thinking of local resources when planning this illustrious wedding."

"I already planned to do so."

"Ah—" he made a show of bowing over her hand "—a woman who is both beautiful and clever. You are obviously the right person for the job."

"You flatter me, Alonso. But I must be truthful. The bride insists that I use local goods and people whenever I can."

"Molto bene." He nodded, his expression proud. "Already our princess looks after the people. But I think maybe you would do this anyway, *si*?"

"I've found that local talent is often the best."

"Si, si. As I say, a clever woman. *Buona giornata.* Good day to you both. Ms. Reeves, I will get back to you with a referral. *Ciao."* He made his exit, stopping to yell something inside the café. Then with a salute the mayor hurried across the square.

"I thought the French were supposed to be the flirts of Europe," Zach mused.

"I liked him."

"Of course. He was practically drooling over you. Clever woman."

She laughed and batted her lashes. "Don't forget beautiful."

His eyes locked on hers, the whiskey depths lit with heat. "How can I when you're sitting right next to me?"

Held captive by his gaze, by a quick and wicked fantasy, it took a beat to compose herself. She cleared her throat as she chased the tail of the topic. Oh, yeah, the mayor. "You can tell he cares about his town and his people. I respect that. Excuse me."

She grabbed her purse and made her escape. Whew, the man was potent.

"Where are we going?" He slid into stride next to her.

And apparently hard to shake.

"We are not going anywhere." She reached the fountain and began to circle the stone feature, making the second answer unnecessary.

"I thought I made it clear, I'm here to assist you."

She flashed him a "yeah, right" glance.

"I appreciate the offer, but my assistant will be arriving at the end of the week." She continued circling.

"What are you doing?"

"I'm checking out the fountain, choosing the best place to throw a coin." The fountain was round, about twelve feet wide with a rock formation rising from slightly off center to a height between seven and eight feet. The cloaked nymph, reclined across two rocks from which the water flowed, reached forward, displaying one nude breast as she offered the clamshell to the side of the rushing water so some of it ran over the stone dish. If you threw too far to the left, the flow of water would wash your chance away, too far to the right and an over-cropping of rock would block the coin.

"You're going to make a wish? For true love? I thought your schedule didn't allow for such things."

"It doesn't." He was right about that. "It's not for me."

"For who then? Your mother?"

"Now there's a thought. But…no." Unfortunately she didn't know if her mother would recognize true love if she found it. She was so focused on the high, she rarely made it past the first few bumps. Even true love required an effort to make it work. "I'm making a wish for Antonio and Christina."

He stopped following her and planted his hands on his hips. "Why? They're already headed for the altar. They don't need the nymph's help."

"Really?" she challenged him. "You're that sure of them?"

His expression remained set. "I think fate should be allowed to take its course."

"And I think it needs a little help." She dug out her coin purse. Hopefully American coins worked as well as euros. Choosing a spot a little to the left because she was right-handed, she tossed her coin. Too light. It fell well short of the clamshell. She tried again. This one went over the top. A third got swept away by the water. "Dang it. That one was in."

"You're not going to make it in. It's set up to defeat you."

"Hey, no advice from the galley." Maybe a nickel? Oh, yeah, that had a nice heft. "What did you talk to Christina about earlier?"

"If I'd wanted you to know, I wouldn't have asked you to leave."

"Tell me anyway." The nickel bounced off the rock.

"No. Try a little twist at the end."

"I'd share with you," she pointed out as she tossed her last nickel. And missed.

"It's none of your business."

She fisted the dime she was about to throw and faced him. "Wrong. I'm here to plan the royal wedding, which makes the bride very much my business. She was already unsettled. And I know you're not a big fan of lavish weddings. I need to know if you upset her."

"I didn't upset her," he said too easily.

"Good. Great. So, tell me, what did you talk about?"

He just lifted a dark eyebrow at her.

"Seriously, I need to know. Just because she didn't look upset doesn't mean she wasn't."

"You're being a nutcase."

"And it'll all go away if you just tell me."

"Okay." He shoved his hands into his pockets. "I picked up on her uneasiness, as well. I asked her if she was having second thoughts."

"Zach!"

"What? This is my best friend. If she's going to bolt, now would be the time to speak up. Not when he's standing at the altar."

"I told you, all brides go through a bit of nerves. Unless you're the M-O-B, pointing out their shakiness only makes it worse. Even then it can be iffy."

His features went blank. "M-O-B?"

"Mother of the bride."

"Oh. She's probably the last person Christina would confide in."

"Why do you say that?"

"My impression is the two aren't particularly close."

"Hmm. Good to know." Lindsay had already noted Christina's reluctance to include her mother in the planning.

Mrs. Rose made her displeasure quite well known, which brought Mr. Rose out to play. Lucky for Lindsay the palace official had taken over dealing with the Roses.

"All the more reason to show Christina support rather than undermine her confidence," Lindsay advised Zach.

"Rest easy. She assured me she would be marrying Tony."

"Okay." She read his eyes and nodded. "Good. Thanks." She turned back to the fountain. "My last coin. What kind of twist?"

"You're still going to make a wish? I just told you Christina's fine."

"I want more than fine. I want true love."

"You do know most political marriages aren't based on love." Something in his tone had her swinging back to him. The late-afternoon sun slanted across his face, casting his grim features into light and shadow.

"Yes," she said softly, "but is that what you want for your friend?"

He moved closer, brushing her ponytail behind her shoulder. "So what is your wish?"

"I'm wishing for true love and happiness for the bride and groom." With the words, she pulled her arm back. As it moved forward Zach cupped her hand and, as she released the coin, gave it a little twist.

The dime flew through the air and plopped with a splash right in the middle of the clamshell.

"We did it!" Lindsay clapped her hands then threw her arms around Zach's neck and kissed his cheek. "Thank you."

He claimed a quick kiss then set her aside. "Don't celebrate yet. We still need to see if it works. Which should only take—what?—the next fifty years."

"Nope." Flustered from the kiss, Lindsay stepped back shifting her attention from him to the fountain. What had he said? Oh, yeah. How did it work? "Now we have faith."

The first attempt to find the brooch was a bust.

Lindsay tried insisting she could handle finding the brooch herself. It was something she could do while she waited for her assistant to arrive and figured out her work space situation. And she needed a break from Zach, especially after the kiss at the fountain. His casual caresses were becoming too common and were definitely too distracting for her peace of mind.

A little distance between them would be a good thing.

Unfortunately, as he pointed out, Christina's grandmother lived in a tiny house in a village halfway between Monte Calanetti and Voti, and Lindsay didn't have transportation without him. A new rental hadn't showed up and the helicopter flew at his discretion. Plus, he'd offered to interpret for her. Since Mona didn't speak much English and Lindsay didn't speak much Italian, she was stuck.

Mona Rose was small with white hair, glasses and lots of pip. She greeted them warmly as Christina had called to say they would be coming. Lindsay sat on a floral-print couch with crocheted lace doilies on the arms while Zach lounged in a matching rocking chair.

Mona served them hibiscus tea and lemon cake while she chatted with Zach.

Lindsay smiled and sipped. After a few minutes of listening, she discreetly kicked Zach in the foot.

He promptly got the clue. "She's very pleased Christina wishes to wear the brooch. She wore the brooch for her wedding and had many happy years with her Benito. Her daughter, Cira, chose not to wear the brooch and now she's divorced with two children."

"I'm sorry to hear that." Lindsay accepted a plate of cake. "Does she know where the brooch is?"

Zach conveyed the question.

Mona tapped her chin as she stared out the window. After a moment she took a sip of her tea and spoke. "Sophia, my youngest sister, I think was last to wear *le broccia*." She shook her head and switched to Italian.

Zach translated. "Pia is her older sister. Her daughter was the last to get married. She didn't wear the brooch, either, but Mona thinks Pia may have it."

"Grazie." Lindsay directed her comments to Mona, smiling to hide her disappointment. She was hoping this chore could be done.

"Would you be willing to do a quick look through your things while we're here? Just to be on the safe side."

Zach translated both the question and Mona's answer.

"Si. I will look. Christina is a good girl. And Antonio, he is good for Halencia. But they will both need much luck."

The next morning Lindsay struggled to get ready while shuffling around five large boxes. When she'd returned to the hotel last night, all five boxes had been delivered to her room. As predicted, she'd had a hard time getting around the bed. She'd actually had to climb over it to get to the bathroom.

When she'd asked about it at the front desk, Signora Eva apologized but explained a delivery of provisions had forced her to reclaim the space she'd been using to store Lindsay's boxes. That had meant the boxes needed to be delivered to Lindsay's room. This morning she'd managed to arrange them so she had a small aisle around the bed, but she had to suck in a breath to get through.

The thought of unpacking everything in this limited space made her cringe. She'd be tripping over her samples every time she turned around.

Frustrated, she left the room for some breakfast. Later she wanted to view the palazzo and chapel where the wedding and reception would take place. But she hoped to rent a scooter before making the trip to the other side of town.

If any were still available.

The press truly had descended. On her way to breakfast she fended off two requests for exclusive shots of the wedding dress. She informed them the dress was under lock and key at the palace and suffered no remorse for her lie.

When Signora Eva came by to refill her coffee, Lindsay asked if she knew of any place she might rent for a work space and received much the same response as she'd gotten from the mayor.

She was processing that news when her cell rang.

With a sinking heart she listened to her assistant advise her she wouldn't be joining her in Halencia, after all. While Mary gushed on about the part she'd landed in a situation comedy all Lindsay could think about was how she'd manage without an assistant.

Lindsay needed to be out in the field a lot. She counted on her assistant to keep track of all the details of a wedding, do follow up and advise Lindsay of any problems. She'd quickly become bogged down if she had to take on the extra work.

Because she cared about Mary, Lindsay mustered the enthusiasm to wish her well. But as soon as she hung up she had a mini meltdown. Stomping over to the sideboard, she plopped an oversize muffin onto her plate and returned to her seat, her mind churning over her lack of options...

As Lindsay made the hike up the hill to Zach's villa she contemplated the obvious answer to her space problem. Much as she preferred to avoid Zach, after two short days she seriously considered asking him for help.

Her hesitation wasn't worry over his answer. He'd been ordered to assist her and he genuinely seemed to take his duty seriously.

The problem would be in dealing with him.

From the air, the villa had looked vast enough to provide a small corner for her without causing her to trip over him at every turn. But she wouldn't know until she saw the inside, which is what had prompted this little trip.

She wiped her brow with the back of her hand. Only eight in the morning and already the day had some heat to it. The blue, cloudless sky offered little relief from the relentless sun. But it also meant no humidity.

"Good morning, partner." Zach's voice floated on the air.

She paused and shaded her eyes to seek him out. He stood on a terrace of his rented villa. The big, stone building rested right up against the old protective wall that ringed the city. From this vantage point it looked huge. Three stories high, the bottom floor created the terrace where Zach stood. The top floor was a pergola with windows on all sides.

"Good morning." She waved.

"You missed the street." He gestured for her to backtrack a bit. "It's a narrow drive right by the pink house."

She followed his directions, turning at the pink house, and there he was coming to greet her. He wore khaki shorts and a blue cotton shirt untucked. The sleeves were rolled to expose his muscular forearms. He looked cool, calm and competent.

How she envied him.

The trees thinned as they neared the villa. He took her

hand and led her down a steep set of steps and a walkway along the side of the house. When they rounded the corner, her breath caught in her throat.

The small city spread out below them, a backdrop to the green lawn that covered the hillside. Oak, olive and pine trees provided shade and privacy. To her right a table and chairs sat under a covered patio, the ivy-covered trellis lending it a grotto effect while a stone path led to a gazebo housing white wicker furniture.

To the far side rosebushes lined a path leading to an infinity pool.

Forget the palazzo. This would make a beautiful setting for a wedding. Well, if you weren't a royal prince.

She took pride in the large, lavish weddings she'd planned for hip and rising celebrities, but she took joy in putting together weddings that were cozy gatherings. Yup, give her intimate and tranquil over pomp and circumstance any day of the week.

"Come up with me." A spiral wrought-iron staircase took them to the terrace he'd been standing on when he'd hailed her. She followed his tight butt up the steps.

Good dog, he was fine. His body rivaled any sight she'd seen today. Even the view from the terrace that provided a panoramic vista of everything she'd seen.

"Impressed yet?" Zach asked behind her left ear.

"I passed impressed before I reached the pool."

"I had my coffee out here this morning. I don't think I've ever spent a more peaceful moment."

"I'm jealous." She stepped away from the heat of his body. She needed her wits about her when she presented her proposition. His assertion they'd be lovers haunted her thoughts. And dreams.

Oh, she was a weak, weak woman in her dreams.

As heat flooded her cheeks she focused on the view

rather than his features. "I'm afraid I'm about to disrupt your peace."

"Pixie, just looking at you disrupts my peace. In the best possible way." He punctuated the remark by tracing the armhole of her sleeveless peach-and-white polka dot shirt, the backs of his fingers feathering over sensitive flesh.

She shivered, shaking a finger at him as she created distance between them. "No touching."

He grinned, again unrepentant. "What brings you by today?"

"I wondered if you wanted to go to the cake tasting with me." She tossed out her excuse for the spy mission. Men liked cake, right?

As soon as the words left her mouth, she thought better of her desperate plan. If she worked here, it would be more of his charming flirtation and subtle caresses until she gave in and let him have his wicked way with her. Or she stopped the madness by seducing him on the double lounge down by the pool. Enticing as both scenarios were, neither was acceptable.

"You know…never mind. I've already taken advantage of your generosity. Enjoy your peace. I can handle this on my own." She turned for the stairs. "I'll catch you later."

The chemistry between them nearly struck sparks in the air. The force of the pull buzzed over her skin like a low-level electrical current. She had it banked at the moment, but the right word or look and it would flare to life in a heartbeat.

Her best bet was to walk away and find another solution to her problem. One that didn't tempt her to break her sensible rules and put her company at risk. She purposely brought Kevin to mind, remembered the pain and humiliation of his betrayal and recalled the looks of pity and disapproval on the faces of her friends and colleagues.

She'd never willingly put herself in that position ever again.

"Cake." Zach caught her gently by the elbow. "You can't tease me with cake and then walk away. It's one of the few chores regarding this wedding gig I'd actually enjoy."

She studied him for a moment before replying. He met her stare straight-on, no hint of flirting in his steady regard. She appreciated his sincerity but still she hesitated.

"Okay. You're in. But we have to go now. I have an appointment to view the palazzo this afternoon. Has the rental company replaced your car yet?"

"No. I have my assistant following up on it. Do we need the helicopter?"

She shook her head. "The bakery is in town." She supposed she'd have to follow up on her own rental now. Pulling out her phone, she made a note. "But it's hot out. My plan is to rent a scooter."

A big grin brought out a boyishness in his features. "You don't have to rent a scooter. There are a couple downstairs in the garage along with something else you might find useful."

"What?"

"Come see." He strode over to a French door and stepped inside.

Trailing behind him, she admired the interior almost as much as the exterior. The bedroom they moved through displayed the comfort and luxury of a five-star hotel. Downstairs it became apparent the villa had gone through a modern update. The lounge, dining room and gourmet kitchen opened onto each other via large archways, creating an open-concept format while exposed beams and stone floors retained the old world charm of a Tuscan villa.

Oh, yeah, she could work here. Too bad it was a no-go.

Off the kitchen Zach opened a door and went down a

half flight of stairs to the garage. He flipped a light and she grinned at what she saw. A sporty black golf cart with a large cargo box in the back filled half the space. On the far side were two red scooters.

"Sweet. This will work nicely."

"Dibs on the cart."

She lifted her eyebrows at him. "What are you, ten?"

"No, I'm six-four. I'd look foolish trying to ride the scooter."

Running her gaze over the full length of him, she admired the subtle muscles and sheer brawn of his wide shoulders. She saw his point. He'd look as though he were riding a child's toy.

He grunted. "Work with me here, Lindsay. You can't tell me no touching and then look at me like that."

"Sorry," she muttered. She claimed the passenger seat. Caught.

Turned out wedding planning could be quite tasty. Zach finished the last bite of his sample of the white amaretto cake with the vanilla bean buttercream icing. And way more complicated than it needed to be.

The baker, a reed-thin woman with a big smile and tired eyes, had six samples set out for them when they'd arrived at the quaint little shop on a cobblestoned street just off the plaza. She'd dusted her hands on her pink ruffled apron and explained what each sample was.

Lindsay explained Christina had already chosen the style and colors for the cake; their job was to pick out the flavors for the three different layers. It took him five minutes to pick his three favorites. Lindsay agreed with two but not the third. He was happy to let her have her preference, but...no. The baker brought out six more samples, which were all acceptable.

The fact was they couldn't go wrong whatever choice

they made. There was no reason this appointment needed to be an hour long. But Lindsay insisted the flavors be compatible.

They were finally done and he was finishing off the samples of his favorites while Lindsay completed the order with the baker up at the counter.

He'd be taking a back seat on the hands-on stuff from now on. He was a stickler for attention to detail, but efficiency had its place, too.

The little bell over the door rang as two men strolled in, one tall and bald, the other round and brown-haired. They eyed the goods on display and Zach heard a British slant to their accent.

He knew immediately when they realized who Lindsay was. They closed in on her, obviously trying to see the plans for the cake. Their interest marked them as two of the media horde invading the town.

Lindsay politely asked them to step back.

Baldy moved back a few inches but Brownie made no move to honor her request.

Zach's gaze narrowed on the two, waiting to see how Lindsay handled herself. His little pixie had a feisty side. She wouldn't appreciate his interference. And this may well blow over. All press weren't bad, but he knew money could make people do things they'd never usually contemplate.

Ignoring the looming goons, Lindsay wrapped up her business and turned toward him. The media brigade blocked her exit, demanding details about the cake, pestering her for pictures. She tried to push past them but they went shoulder to shoulder, hemming her in.

In an instant Zach crossed the room.

"You're going to want to let her by."

"Wait your turn." Brownie dismissed him. "Come on, sweetcakes, show us something."

Sweetcakes?

"It's always my turn." Zach placed a hand on either man's shoulder and shoved them apart.

They whirled on him like a mismatched tag team.

"Back up," Brownie snarled at Zach's chest. And then he slowly lifted his gaze to Zach's. Even Baldy had to look up.

Zach rolled his thick shoulders. That's all it usually took. Sure enough, both men took a large step back.

"Ms. Reeves is with me." He infused the quiet words with a bite of menace. "I won't be pleased if I see you bothering her again."

"Hey, no disrespect." Baldy quickly made his exit. Brownie clenched his jaw and slowly followed.

"Thank you." Lindsay appeared at his side. "Those two were more aggressive than most."

"Are you okay?" He pulled her into his arms. "Do you put up with that often?" He couldn't tolerate the thought of her being hassled by those media thugs on her own.

"All the time." For a moment she stood stiffly, but with a sigh she melted against him. "One of the guys at my hotel offered me a hundred-thousand dollars for a picture of the wedding dress, which means the tabloids are probably willing to pay a million for it."

"That explains why you've lugged it halfway across the world."

"I said it was locked up at the palace. But for a million dollars, I don't doubt someone might try to check out my room anyway."

That did it. He may not support this wedding, but he had his limits. He wouldn't put his plan, or Tony's happiness, before Lindsay's safety. The thought of her vulnerable on her own at the hotel and someone forcing their way into her room sent a primitive wave of rage blasting through him. He had to fix this.

"You should give up your room at the hotel and stay with me at the villa. It would be safer for you."

CHAPTER SEVEN

"Uh, no." Lindsay pushed away from the safety of his arms. Yes, she'd been spooked by the menacing media jerks, but was Zach totally insane? "That is not an option." She even thought better of asking for work space at the villa. "This—" she waved between the two of them, indicating the chemistry they shared "—makes it a bad idea."

"Even I'm picking up on what a big deal this is for the press." He led her back to their table. "It didn't really strike me at first. I'm used to photographers hanging around hawking at Antonio for a picture. Some of them can be unscrupulous in their bid for a shot." He sat back crossing his arms over his chest his gaze intent, focused on her, on the problem. She had a sudden, clear vision of what he'd look like sitting at his desk. "It's the only solution that makes sense."

She sent him a droll stare. "You're just saying that to get in my pants."

"Not so."

The bite in the denial sent embarrassed heat rushing through her.

"Yes, I want in your pants, but not at the expense of your safety."

She blinked at him, her emotions taking a moment to catch up with her hearing. Obviously she'd touched a nerve.

"Okay."

"Excellent." Satisfied, he leaned forward in his chair. "It's settled. You'll move into the villa. We'll find a secure spot for the dress and you can choose a room for yourself and one of the spare rooms for your office. Or you can use the sunroom if you prefer."

"No. Wait." Panicked, she made a sharp cut-off gesture with her hand. "I was acknowledging your comment not agreeing to move in. We need to talk about this."

"We just did."

"Yes, and I appreciate your putting my safety ahead of your libido, but what does that mean? I've told you how I feel about maintaining a professional distance with all members of the wedding party, especially the best man."

A raised eyebrow mocked her. "I remember."

She gritted her teeth. "Well, you're a touchy-feely guy and I can't deal with that in a professional relationship."

A stunned expression flashed across his well-defined features but was quickly replaced with a contemplative mask.

"You have my promise I'll try to keep my hands to myself."

"The problem with that sentence is the word *try*."

He ran a hand over the back of his neck, kneading the muscles and nerves as if to relieve tension, studying her the whole time. Then he flexed his shoulders and faced her.

"Here's the deal. I'm not a touchy-feely guy. Not normally. I go after what I want, but I respect boundaries and I can handle being told no."

Yeah, like that happened.

"For some reason it's different with you. I like my hands on you, like the touch and taste of you to the degree it's instinctive to seek it."

OMD. That is so hot.

"So, yes. I promise to *try*."

She gulped. "Okay."

His eyes flashed dark fire. "Is that okay you'll stay or—"

"Yes. Okay, I'll move in." It may be insane to move in

with him, but she would feel safer. Plus, it solved her work problem. "But I'm keeping my room at the hotel. Space is already at a premium here in Monte Calanetti and I need a place I can retr—uh…go to if things don't work out."

"Fair enough. And as a gesture of my commitment, I'll pay for the room since you won't be using it."

"That's not necessary."

"It is to me. I'll feel better with you at the villa, and I want you to know you can trust me."

She slowly nodded. "Okay. I'll go pack."

"I had your boxes delivered up here, but if you choose this space, you'll need a proper desk. It has a bar and a billiard table, but that's it."

"I don't need anything new," Lindsay protested.

"I doubt the owners will object to us leaving behind an extra piece of furniture."

"That's not the point." He'd warned her that the space lacked a desk or table for her laptop. But, seriously, she didn't see the problem; she sat with it in her lap half the time.

"Pixie." He stopped in the upper hallway and swung to face her. His hand lifted to touch but he caught himself and curled the fingers into a fist that he let drop to his side. "Didn't you look at the numbers? The government contract will lift me to billionaire status. I can afford a desk."

He opened a door she'd thought was a linen closet. It revealed a staircase of stone steps. His hand gestured for her go ahead of him.

"First of all—" she paused in front of him "—congratulations."

A pleased smile lit his eyes. The simple expression of joy made her glad she'd put that first.

She got the feeling he received very little positive reinforcement in his personal life. The business world recognized and respected his genius, and his employees obviously appreciated his success and most likely his work ethic. But as an only child whose parents ignored his personal business interests in favor of their own agenda for him to join his father in politics, who did he have that mattered to tell him job well done?

She shook the thought away. He was not a poor, unfortunate child, but an intelligent, successful man.

And he'd hate her pity.

"Second—" she started up the stairs "—it's not for you to buy me a desk."

"The duties of a best man are unlimited. But you could be right. Do you want me to call Tony and ask him? Because I can pretty much guarantee his response will be, 'If the wedding planner needs a desk then buy her a desk. And don't bother me with such trivial things.'"

Aggrieved, she rolled her eyes, making sure he saw as she rounded the bend in the stairs. "Please, even if he blew off the request that easily, he wouldn't add that last bit."

"Not only would he say it, Pixie, that was the clean version. Tony doesn't have a whole lot of patience these days."

"He must be dealing with a lot—oh, I love, love, *love* this."

She strolled into the middle of the bright room and did a slow turn. The room was a long octagon. Three walls were made of glass and windows, two others were of stone and one held a fireplace. The last was half stone, the other half was a stained-glass mural of a Tuscan hillside; a bar with brown-cushioned stools ran almost the full length of the wall. At the far end there was a door. She checked it out and found it opened onto another spiral staircase that led to the terrace below.

"A separate entrance."

"Yes, I'll give you a set of keys. When your assistant gets here, she can still have access if we're gone."

"That'd be great but my assistant won't be coming."

"What happened?"

"My practical, poised, ever-efficient assistant finally landed a part in a sitcom."

"Ah, the joy of proprietorship in Hollywood."

Still feeling deserted, Lindsay nodded. "It's the third time it's happened to me. Of course, I'm thrilled for her. But seriously? Worst timing ever."

"Hey, listen. I'm the first to admit this wedding stuff is not my thing, but I'll help where I can."

"Thanks, but you've done enough by offering me this space. I'll finally be able to put up my wedding board. And the help I need involves a hundred little things, well below your pay grade." She really couldn't see him playing secretary. And she may appreciate the space and assistance, but the last thing she needed was to have him constantly underfoot.

"There's no help for it. I'll have to hire someone local. Maybe Alonso knows someone he can recommend. On the plus side, it will be good to have someone who knows the area and the people, who speaks the language and knows the cost of things."

"Alonso will know someone. In the meantime, I'm sticking with you. I'll get a locksmith in to reinforce the locks on all the doors."

She wanted to protest the need for him to shadow her. Instead she nodded, knowing he was reacting out of concern for her. And she was happy to have the extra security for the dress. It might seem a bother for something they'd only have for another week, but she'd be more comfortable knowing the villa was secure.

She strolled further into the room. In soft beige and sage green, the furniture looked sturdy and comfortable. A U-shaped couch invited her to sit and enjoy the amazing view. The billiard table Zach had mentioned was on the right and her boxes were stacked on the green felt. Past it was the fireplace wall with a bookshelf that offered a wide selection of reading material. Another door hid a bathroom.

The ceiling was high, the beams exposed, and a large fan circulated the air in the room.

There were only two low-slung tables. One in front of the large couch and one between the swivel chairs near the fireplace.

"Oh, yeah, I can work here. No hardship at all."

She'd totally make do.

Hands on his hips, Zach surveyed the room. "You'll need a desk." He repeated his earlier decree. "And you mentioned a wedding board. Is that a whiteboard?"

"A whiteboard would be nice, too. My wedding board is usually a corkboard. I need to be able to tack things to it."

He had his phone in his hands and was making notes. She sighed, knowing there'd be no shaking him until she hired an assistant. In one sense it was reassuring to know she wasn't on her own, but it made her plan to avoid him a no-go. It was almost as if fate were working against her.

"I guess we have our shopping list, then. What do you want to do now? Unpack your boxes? You said earlier that you wanted to check out the palazzo."

"Yes. The boxes can wait." Better to have the boards when she went to do that, anyway. "But, honestly, there's no need for you to accompany me. Stay. Enjoy your day."

"I'm coming with you."

Of course he was. At this point, it was easier to agree than to argue. "Fine. Let me call Louisa and remind her I'm coming then we can go."

"Who's Louisa?"

"The owner of the palazzo. We've spoken a couple of times. She seems nice. Did you hear they discovered a fresco when they were restoring the chapel?"

"No. That's quite a discovery. It has to add to the property value."

"You are such a guy."

"Pixie, were you in any doubt?"

"Hello, Louisa, it's so nice to finally meet you. Thank you for allowing us to tour the property today." Lindsay greeted the owner of the palazzo.

It surprised Zach to see Louisa was an American. The two women were close to the same age but dissimilar in every other way. Louisa topped Lindsay by four or five inches and wore her white-blond hair in a messy knot on top of her head. Her willowy frame and restrained posture gave her a brittle appearance.

Funny, she held no attraction for him because she fit his type to a tee: long, lithe, and blond. Sure he recognized she was a beautiful woman, but she appeared almost fragile next Lindsay's vibrancy.

"Louisa, I have to say I'm a little concerned. I thought the renovation would be further along." Lindsay swept her hand out to indicate the overgrown vegetation and construction paraphernalia strewed through the courtyard and surrounding grounds.

"I can see why you'd be confused." Louisa's smile was composed. "But we're actually right on schedule. They've just completed the interior restoration. The construction crew will be back today to finish clearing out their equipment and trash. The next step is the landscapers, but I was actually thinking of hiring some men from town first, to just clear all this out."

"That might be a good idea," Lindsay agreed. "Just level it and start fresh."

"Exactly. I can see some rosebushes, lavender and a few wild sunflowers. But it's so overgrown it's hard to know if they'd be worth saving if we took the time and effort to clear the weeds around them."

Lindsay nodded as the other woman talked. "I think you have the right idea."

Zach enjoyed watching them interact. He liked how Lindsay's ponytail bobbed as she talked and the way the sunshine picked up golden highlights in her hair.

He almost forgot his purpose in shadowing her every move.

Mostly because it was against his nature to be covert, to be less than helpful. Case in point: this morning. When he saw Lindsay being intimidated by the press, he jumped right into fix-it mode and invited her to move into the spacious villa. And he'd provided her with a prime workspace. Hell, he fully intended to get her a desk.

All of which went against his prime objective of keeping Antonio from a life of misery. With that thought Zach took out his phone and texted his friend, tagging him for a meeting time.

Right now his biggest problem was the blurring line between his mock flirtation with Lindsay and his honest reactions. There'd been too much truth in his arguments to get her to stay at the villa. She was too comfortable to be around, too soft to the touch, too easy to imagine in his bed.

And too dangerous to succumb to.

He hadn't felt this way about a woman since…ever. And he wasn't going there.

From here on out he was back on his game.

"Thanks for talking it through with me." Louisa folded her arms in front of her. "I'm very grateful to the monarchy for doing the renovation of the palazzo and chapel. I certainly couldn't have afforded anything this elaborate all at once. Probably never, come to that. But it's been a pretty intense process. It's good to have someone to discuss a decision with."

"I bet." Lindsay grinned. "Call on me anytime. I'm great at discussion."

"I can see you are." A friendly sparkle entered Louisa's light blue eyes. "And probably pretty good at decisions, too."

Lindsay rocked on her heals. "Yeah, it's kind of part of the job description."

The composed smile held a little more warmth as Louisa gestured to the chapel. "Shall we do a walk-through? I'm afraid we'll have to make this fairly quick. I have an appointment in Florence tomorrow. I'm driving over tonight so I'll be there in the morning. I've booked passage on the two o'clock ferry."

"That's fine. Today I just want to get a feel for the place and take some pictures so I know what I'm working with. And—oh, this is beautiful." Lindsay surveyed the interior of the chapel with a mix of wonder and calculation on her face. "So charming with the arched windows and the dark wood pews. I can come back on another day to get actual measurements and check out the lighting. I love how the jewel colors flow over the stone tiles from the stained-glass windows. Christina has chosen an afternoon wedding and evening reception. She wants to have it outdoors, so the landscaping will be important."

"I won't be able to hire the workers to clear the grounds until I return from Florence," Louisa informed her, "but I'll make it a priority when I get back."

"Why don't I handle that for you?" Zach offered, seeing an opportunity to cause a few days' delay. He'd simply tell the workers to be careful to preserve any original flowers. "I'll talk to the mayor to get some referrals."

"Thank you. I appreciate it. They did a wonderful job with the restoration," Louisa stated. "It was quite a mess in here. Stones were missing, the stained-glass windows were broken and some of the walls had wood covering them. Here's the fresco that was uncovered." Louisa moved to a shallow alcove and Zach followed Lindsay over.

He understood her gasp. The ancient painting of Madonna and child took his breath away. The colors were vibrant, the detail exquisite. It was almost magnetic—the pull of the fresco, from the pinky tones of Jesus's skin and the color of Mary's dark blue robe, to the white and yellow of the brilliant beam of light encasing them and the greens of the surrounding countryside bright with orange and red flowers. The details were so exact, every brush stroke so evident, it seemed it could have been painted a week ago rather than five hundred years.

"Look at the love on their faces." Lindsay breathed. "The artist caught the perfect expression of Mary's unconditional love for her child and Baby Jesus's childlike wonder and awe for his mother. It shows the full bond between mother and child. This will certainly add to the ambience of the wedding."

With the beauty and love inherent in the fresco, Zach could see how she'd think so. But with his friend's future and happiness at risk, he couldn't take that chance.

Zach surprised Lindsay with his patience and insight the next day as they toured four nurseries. She had a whole list of requirements from bouquets and boutonnieres to centerpieces and garlands and more.

Lindsay planned to use roses for the groomsmen, sunflowers over linen chair covers for the reception and a combination of the two for everything else.

To bring about a sense of intimacy in the courtyard and to define the separate areas for eating and dancing, she planned to have rustic scaffolding erected. Lights, flowers and silk drapery would blend rustic with elegance to create a sense of old and new. She actually appreciated Zach's male point of view and his logistical input.

The helicopter came in handy as they buzzed around the countryside. Deciding on the second vendor she spoke with, Lindsay asked to return to the nursery to put in her order. Zach made no argument. He simply directed the pilot and helped her aboard.

Zach waited patiently in an anteroom of the magnificent palace. He stood at the terrace doors overlooking a section of the rose garden. Curved benches spaced several feet apart created a circle around a marble fountain of a Roman goddess.

Lindsay would love it. He had to hand it to her, that woman worked. He could practically hear her discourse on what a lovely venue the rose garden would be for a wedding, how the circle represented the ring and the ring represented the commitment made between bride and groom, who once joined together there became no beginning and no end, just the unity of their bond.

"Yeah, right."

"Talking to yourself, *amico mio*?" a gruff voice said before a hand clapped on his shoulder.

"Just keeping myself company waiting for you."

"I'm glad you came." Tony pulled Zach into the hug he'd learned to endure through the years. Tony was a demonstrative man, how could he not be with such passionate parents?

"Yeah, well, it became clear if I wanted to see you, I'd have to come to you."

"I only have thirty minutes. I wish I had more time to give you. Hell, I wish we were at Clancy's eating wings, drinking beer and catching a game."

"We could be there in fourteen hours," Zach said, hoping it would be that easy.

Tony laughed. "I'm tempted." He opened the terrace door and stepped outside. To the left stood a table with comfortable chairs. And a bucket of beers on ice.

"What, no chicken wings?"

"They are on the way."

Zach sat across from his friend and leaned back in his chair. Tony looked tired. And harassed. Zach knew Tony had to be busy for him to put Zach off. They were as close as brothers, too close for the other man to brush him aside.

"How are things going with the wedding?" Tony asked.

"Let's just say I could tell you in excruciating detail and leave it at that."

Tony grinned. "Thanks, bro. I mean that."

"Only for you," Zach assured him. "How are things going here?"

"Slowly." Tony grabbed a beer and opened it. "Everyone has a different opinion of how the monarchy should be run."

"And you have to learn the worst-case scenario for each before you'll make a determination," Zach stated, knowing that's how his friend operated. In working security protocols he liked to work backward to make sure the worst never happened.

"It doesn't help that I constantly have to address some question or concern about the wedding or coronation. It's a lot to juggle."

"So maybe you should put the wedding off." Zach took the opportunity presented to him. "Get the monarchy stabilized first and then revisit the idea of marriage when you can choose someone for yourself."

"Are you kidding me?" Tony laughed again. "Instead of cheering me, the people would be rioting in the streets. I think they want this wedding more than anything else."

"Because it's a Cinderella story?"

Tony shrugged. "Because I've made them wait so long."

"Because you never intended to marry Christina."

"Shush." Tony glanced around the terrace. "We won't speak of that here."

"Someone needs to speak of it before it's too late to stop it."

"That time is long gone, my friend. Christina will make a good queen. The people love her."

"They don't know her any better than you do. She's been off in Africa."

"Taking care of sick children. It plays well. Ah, the chicken wings. *Grazie*, Edmondo."

The servant bowed and retreated.

Zach quirked a brow at his friend. Tony shrugged and they both reached for a chicken wing.

After a moment Tony sighed. "Man, I needed this." He upended his beer, drinking the last. "I don't know anything about running a country, Zach."

"You know plenty. You've been training for this your whole life. Even while living in California," Zach reminded him.

"That's different. I always planned to hand over control to a republic, but I'm not sure that's what the people want. They are all behind this wedding and I can't let them down. I just need to do the opposite of what my dad would do and I'll be doing a better job than has been done."

"A little harsh, don't you think?"

"No." Tony shook his head and reached for another beer. "I love my parents, but their relationship is messed up. I don't ever want to love anyone so much it messes with my head. Better a business arrangement than a volatile, emotional mess."

Zach plucked a bottle of beer from the bucket, knowing he'd gotten as far as he was going to get tonight. He reached out and clicked bottles with Tony. "To the monarchy."

Tony's statement about a business arrangement only made Zach more determined to see him freed from a loveless marriage. Because his friend was wrong. At least a volatile, emotional mess inferred someone cared. You didn't get that guarantee with a business arrangement. What you got was a cold, lonely life.

CHAPTER EIGHT

WHAT A DIFFERENCE a week made. As she flew through
the air on the way to Milan, Lindsay thought about all
she'd accomplished since her last flight in the helicopter.
She had her wedding board up and she'd made contact
with all the local vendors she'd lined up before coming to
Halencia, confirming plans and reevaluating as necessary.

She'd talked to the landscapers and she had an appointment at the end of the week to meet at the palazzo to go
over her needs for the wedding and reception. On the
mayor's recommendation, Zach had hired a crew to clean
up the palazzo and chapel grounds. They should be well
done by the time she met with the landscapers.

Yesterday she'd hired an assistant. Serena was twenty-
two, fresh out of university and eager to assist in any way
she could with the royal wedding. Lindsay worried a little
over the girl's age, knowing she'd have to be strong enough
to say no to outrageous offers for inside information about
the wedding, and mature enough to know when she was
being played. But Serena was Mayor Alonso's daughter
and she had his glib tongue and a no-nonsense attitude
that convinced Lindsay she could handle the job.

Plus, she just plain liked the young woman.

She'd gone a little googly-eyed over Zach but, seriously, who wouldn't? It was a fact of life she'd have to
put up with.

"We are coming up on Milano," the pilot announced.

Lindsay leaned forward to get a view of the northern
city. Two prominent pieces of architecture caught the eye.
A very modern building of glass and metal that twisted
well into the air and an ancient cathedral dramatically

topped with a forest of spires. Both buildings were stunningly impressive.

She glanced at Zach and found his gaze on her. Smiling, she gestured at the view. "It's spectacular."

"It is, indeed," he agreed without looking away from her.

She turned her attention back to the view, pretending his focus on her didn't send the blood rushing through her veins.

He'd kept to his promise not to touch her. Well, mostly. He didn't play with her hair or take her hand, but he stayed bumping-elbows close wherever they went. And he still liked to put his hand in the small of her back whenever he directed her into or out of a building or room.

Serena had asked if they were together, so Lindsay knew the townspeople were speculating about their relationship. She'd given Serena a firm no in response and hoped the word got out about the true state of things.

They landed at a heliport on a mid-rise building not far from the Duomo di Milano. Downstairs a car was waiting to take them to a shop along Via Monte Napoleone. Lindsay checked her tablet to give Zach the address.

She looked forward to handing the dress over to Christina and the queen's seamstress. Providing security for the gown had proved more stressful than she'd anticipated. Having it off her shoulders would allow her to focus on the many other elements of the wedding demanding her attention.

"There it is. Signora Russo's. Christina and the queen are meeting us there. I already spoke to Signora Russo about the damage to the beading. She said she's a master seamstress and she would fix it."

"I'm glad to hear it."

A valet took the car and she and Zach were escorted inside. An attendant took the garment bag and led them to a plush fitting suite. A large, round couch in a soft ivory with a high back topped by an extravagant flower arrangement graced the middle of the room.

The bride and queen stood speaking with a petite, ageless woman in a stylish black suit. Lindsay walked across the room with Zach to join them.

Christina made the introductions. It might have been Lindsay's imagination, but the other woman seemed quite relieved to see them.

"Zachary!" exclaimed Her Royal Highness Valentina de l'Accardi, Queen of Halencia when she saw Zach. "As handsome as ever." She glided forward and kissed him on both cheeks. "*Mio caro*, thank you for helping Antonio. He is so busy. Many, many meetings. We do not even see him at the palace."

"Valentina." Zach bent over her hand. "You are ever youthful. I thought for a moment Elena was here."

"Zachary!" Valentina swatted his forearm and giggled. Yes, the matriarch of Halencia giggled. And flushed a pretty rose. "Such a charming boy. Be careful, Ms. Reeves, this one knows what a woman wants to hear, be alert that he does not steal your heart."

"Yes. I've noticed he's a bit of a flirt."

"*Si*, a flirt." Warm brown eyes met hers with a seriousness her lighthearted greeting belied. The woman clasped her hand and patted it. "I am so pleased you were able to come to Halencia to plan Antonio and Christina's wedding. I wanted only the best for them."

"Now, you flatter me." Lindsay squeezed the queen's hand before releasing her and stepping back. "It is I who is privileged to be here. And to be here in Signora Russo's shop. I may have to steal a moment to shop for my own dress for the wedding."

"Oh, you must. My friend will take the best care of you. Giana, Ms. Reeves needs a dress. Charge it to my account. It shall be my treat for all her hard work."

Appalled, Lindsay protested. "Your Highness, I cannot—"

"I insist." The queen waved her objection aside. "I only wish I could stay and help you shop. And see Christina in her gown!" She sighed with much drama. "Regretfully, I must leave. One of Antonio's many meetings draws me away. Christina—" Valentina moved to the bride's side and Christina bowed to receive a kiss on the cheek. "Worry not. Giana has made many women look like a princess. She will do her *magia* and make you a *bella* bride."

For an instant Christina seemed to freeze, but in a blink it passed and she bowed her head. "*Grazie*, Your Highness."

"But you, Christina, will be a real princess. And that demands something special from a woman. The reward is something special in return." She picked up an ornate, medium-size box from the couch and slowly lifted the lid. A glimmering tiara rested on a bed of white velvet.

Christina put a hand to her throat. "Valentina."

"I wore this when I married Antonio's father. It must stay in my family, but you would honor me if you wore it when you marry my son."

Tears glistened in Christina's eyes. "It's beautiful." Diamonds and sapphires swirled together in gradually bigger scrolls until they overlapped in the front, creating a heart. "It's too much."

"Nonsense. A princess needs a tiara," Valentina insisted. "It would please me very much."

Christina sent Lindsay a pleading look. What should she do?

Lindsay gave a small shrug. "It's something borrowed and something blue."

"Oh, my." Christina gave a small laugh. "You said the items would come."

"I must go." Valentina handed the box to Christina.

"Try it on with your dress and veil, you will see. A security officer will stay behind to collect it until the wedding."

"Valentina." Christina gripped the other woman's hand. *"Grazie."*

"Ciao, my dears." With a wave of her fingers, the queen breezed out the door.

Immediately the room felt as if a switch had been flipped and the energy turned off.

Giana Russo excused herself and followed behind Valentina.

Christina sighed, her gaze clinging to Zach. "And I'm supposed to follow that?"

Lindsay's gut tightened. She'd soothed many a nervous bride. But a nervous queen-to-be? That was out of her league. She sent Zach a pleading look.

He didn't hesitate. He went to Christina and wrapped her in a warm hug. "She's a force of nature, no denying that. Everyone likes Valentina. She's fun and vivacious." He stepped back at the perfect moment. "But what Halencia needs now is warm and constant. And that's you."

"Grazie, Zach." Christina's shoulders relaxed with his words. "I am glad you came today."

"Of course. Hey, listen. I'm sorry for sitting on your dress. I'll pay for all the repairs and alterations."

"You sat on my dress?" Christina's surprise showed on her face. "Lindsay said some beading came loose during the travel."

"With a little help from my butt." He glanced at Lindsay over his shoulder, gratitude warming his whiskey eyes. "She seems to think Signora Russo can do *magia* and fix it."

"Si, si. I can fix." Giana blew back into the room. An attendant followed behind and carried Christina's beautiful gown into one of the dressing rooms. "I have looked

at the damage. It is not so bad. A little re-stitching will solve everything."

"Nonna!" A little girl ran into the room. Adorable, with big brown eyes and a cap of short, wild curls, she clutched a bright pink stuffed dog under arm. She came to a stop when she spotted three strangers with her grandmother.

"Ah, Lucette. *Scusa il bambina.*" Giana tried to pick up the toddler but she squealed and ducked behind Christina. "My apologies. We had a small emergency and I was recruited to babysit. My daughter should be here shortly to get her. Lucette, come to Nonna."

"Oh, she's no trouble. *Ciao*, Lucette." Christina bent at the knees so she was on the same level as the little girl, who stared at her with big, beautiful eyes. "What's your doggy's name?"

Lucette giggled and held out the dog. She jabbered a mouthful of words that made no sense to Lindsay at all. She looked at Zach but he shook his head, indicating he didn't understand the words, either.

"What a lovely name." Christina apparently made the dog's name out or pretended to. She chatted with the child for another few minutes, making the girl laugh. From her ease with the little one, it was obvious Christina loved children. Her gentleness and genuine interest delighted Giana's granddaughter until a harried assistant hurried into the room and swept the girl up.

"Scusa." The young assistant bobbed her head and left with the little girl.

Giana sighed. "Such excitement today. Are you ready, Signorina Rose, to try on your dress?"

Christina nodded. She and Giana disappeared into one of the dressing rooms.

Lindsay and Zach looked at each other.

"Do we stay or go?" Zach asked.

"I'm going to stay until she comes out." Lindsay sat

facing the occupied dressing room. "She may want company for the whole appointment. You can go if you want. I'm sure she'd understand."

"I'll wait to see how long you're going to be." He settled next to her. Way too close. His scent reached her, sensual and male, distracting her so she almost missed his question. "Have you ever come close to being the bride?"

"Not really." She smoothed the crease in her pale beige pants. "The one time I even contemplated it, I found out the relationship existed more in my imagination than in reality."

Interest sparked behind his intelligent gaze.

"How about you?" She tried to sidetrack him.

"Once," he admitted. "How do you get to marriage in your imagination? You're too levelheaded to make up what's not there."

"Thanks for that." She uncrossed and then re-crossed her legs, creating distance between them on the couch though her new position had her facing him. "He was my high school sweetheart. We got split up during our senior year when his parents moved away."

"That's tough."

She chanced a quick peek at him through her lashes to see if he truly understood or was simply saying what he thought she wanted to hear. The intensity in his regard showed an avid interest, encouraging her to go on.

"It was tough. We just understood each other. I lost my best friend as well as my boyfriend." The crease on her right leg got the same smoothing action as her left. "I always felt he was the one who got away."

"But you reconnected."

"We did. When the royal wedding was announced last year, he saw a piece where it mentioned I was the event planner, so he looked me up in Hollywood."

"And you had fonder memories of him than he had for you?"

"You could say that." The gentle way he delivered the comment made it safe to look at him as she answered. "I was so surprised and happy to see him. My mom, too. She's always on me to find a man. At first it was as though Kevin and I'd never been apart." Because of their past connection, he'd skipped right under her shields. "We were having lots of fun just hanging out and catching up. But I was so busy. Especially after word I'd been chosen to handle Antonio's wedding started to get around.

"Kevin was a freelance writer, so his schedule was flexible and he offered to help. I didn't want to take advantage, but I wanted to be with him. I let him tend bar at a few of the smaller events. That went well, so he started pushing to work the weddings."

"This is where the but comes in?"

Lindsay nodded, went back to plucking at her crease. Zach's hand settled over hers, stilling the nervous motion.

She calmed under his touch. Under the sympathy in his eyes.

It still hurt to recall what a fool she'd been.

"First I got a warning from one of my vendors. He didn't know we were involved and he said I should keep an eye on the new bartender. He'd seen him outside with one of the guests."

"Bastard."

"It gets worse. And it's my own fault."

"How is it your fault when he's the one cheating?"

Good question. Too bad she didn't have a good answer.

"Because I let him charm me. When I asked him about what the vendor had seen, he didn't get defensive or act guilty. He had a story ready that the woman told him she was feeling sick so he'd walked her outside, hoping fresh air would help. I had no reason not to believe him. It explained what the vendor saw and…Kevin could be very solicitous."

"But it happened again."

Her head bobbed; perfect representation for the bobble-head she'd been.

"He tried to explain that one away, too. But I was starting to wise up. I should have ended it then." But that ideal from the past lingered in her heart, overriding the urging of her head. "Before things started going south, I'd been invited to a big wedding of a studio head and asked Kevin to go with me. I didn't want to go alone and I wasn't working so I thought it would be okay." She blinked back tears. "I should have known what he wanted. The clues were there."

"He was using you."

"Oh, yeah. He always wanted to know who everyone was. I thought he was just starstruck by the movers and shakers of Hollywood. The truth was he had a script he was shopping. I found him messing around with a well-known producer."

"Male or female?"

That surprised a bark of laughter from her; the moment of levity easing her rising tension. "Female. But thanks for that perspective. I guess it could have been worse."

"Bad enough. He hurt you."

"Yes. But only because I saw what I wanted to see."

"The possibility of a wedding for the wedding planner?"

"How is it you can see me so clearly?" she demanded.

It was uncanny how he saw straight to her soul. She hadn't been half as sad at losing Kevin as she had been to lose a boyfriend with marriage potential. She wanted what she gave to all her clients. A lovely wedding, in a spectacular venue, with friends and family surrounding her as she pledged her love. She longed for it with all her heart.

Kevin had stolen that from her. He'd given her hope, dangled the reality within her reach, only to yank it away. He was a user with no real affection or respect for her.

He'd seduced her for her contacts. And, yeah, that hurt. Her pride had taken a huge hit and the experience had left her more relationship-shy than ever. But it had taken less than a week for her to recognize it was more work-related than personal. He could have damaged her reputation. She'd worked twice as hard since the breakup to make sure it didn't happen again.

And she shored up her defenses to keep from letting anyone close enough to use her again. Or hurt her.

"Because it's all right here." Zach responded to the question about seeing her so clearly by stroking his thumb over her cheek. "There's no deception in you, Lindsay. You're open and giving and articulate."

"You're saying I'm an open book. How flattering." Not.

"I'm saying there's no artifice in you. When you interact with someone, they know they're getting the real you—straightforward good or bad. Do you know what a gift that is? To know you can trust what's being presented to you without having to weigh it for possible loopholes and hidden agendas?"

"Politics," she said dismissively.

"School. Business. Friends. Dates." He ran down a list. Then, too restless to sit, he rose to pace. "For as far back as I can remember I've known not to take anything at face value. My nannies used to praise me for being a good kid then lie about my behavior to get a raise."

"That's terrible." What a sad lesson for a child to learn. "You said you almost got close to a wedding. What happened? Is it what put you off big, fancy weddings?"

"It never got that far." He fell silent and fingered a wisp of lace edging a floor-length veil. Then he moved to one glittering with diamonds and, finally, to one of lace and the opalescence of pearls.

As the silence lengthened, she knew an answer wasn't coming. And then he surprised her.

"Luckily I learned before it was too late that it wasn't me she wanted but the Sullivan name." The lack of emotion in his reply spoke volumes.

He didn't add more. He didn't have to. After a childhood of indifference, he'd fallen for a woman only to learn she had more interest in his family name than in the man who carried that name.

Lindsay felt his pain. Shockingly so. Meaning he was getting under her skin. That shouldn't be happening; her shields were firmly in place. Zach just refused to acknowledge them. And he was getting to her.

She wanted to know more, to ask what happened, but she'd been wrong to get so personal. They weren't on a date. They were working. She had no right to dig into his past when she insisted theirs was a professional relationship.

Yet she was disappointed. She rarely talked about herself, never exposed her heart like that. And he'd responded, obviously reluctant to share but reciprocating just the same. How unfair that life should send her this man when all her attention needed to be focused on her job.

He lifted the lace-and-pearl veil and carried it to her.

"What are you doing?" she breathed.

Pulling her to her feet, he turned her and carefully inserted the combs of the veil in her hair. The exquisite lace flowed around her, making her feel like a bride even in a sleeveless beige-linen pant suit.

"Imaging you as a bride." His breath whispered over her temple. "What would you choose for yourself, Lindsay?"

"I'm like you," she said as he led her toward a three-way mirror. Why was she letting him do this? "I want small, intimate."

"But with all the trimmings?"

"Of course. Oh, my." The pearls on the lace gave it a glow. He'd placed the veil just under her upswept bun. The lace caressed her arms as it fell down her back in an elegant waterfall of tulle and lace and pearls. It had such presence it made her beige pantsuit appear bridal.

The picture in the mirror stole her breath. Made her longing for what eluded her come rushing back.

She'd hoped coming to Tuscany, managing the royal wedding, would help her get her wedding mojo back. Peering into the mirror she realized that would only happen when she opened herself to love again. Sweat broke out on her upper lip at the very notion of being that vulnerable.

"I love the pearls against your sunshine-brown hair." Zach brushed the veil behind her shoulder and met her gaze in the mirror. "You're going to make a beautiful bride."

With him standing beside her in his dress shirt and black pants the reflection came too close to that of a bride and groom. Her heels brought her up to his shoulder. They actually looked quite stunning together.

She swallowed hard and took a giant step backward, reaching up at the same time to remove the veil. She was in so much trouble.

"I'm the planner, not the bride," she declared. "I don't have time to play make-believe." Handing him the veil, she retreated to the couch and her purse. Time to put fanciful thoughts aside and call Christina's aunt to set up an appointment on their way home.

Because she'd liked the image in the mirror way too much for her peace of mind.

Just Lindsay's luck. Christina's aunt Pia couldn't meet with them until five in the evening. She ran through her current to-do list in her head, looking for something she could check off.

"Oh, no, you don't." Zach tugged on her ponytail. "You've worked nonstop this past week. We are due some rest and relaxation. We're in the lovely city of Milan. I say we play tourist."

Okay, there were worse ways to spend the afternoon than wandering the streets with a handsome man on her arm.

Lunch at an open café on the Naviglio Grande—a narrow canal with origins in the 1100s used to transport the heavy marble to the middle of the city where the Duomo di Milano was being built—was a true delight. As was strolling along the canal afterward and checking out the antique stores and open-air vendors.

A lovely candleholder at a glassblower's stall caught her eye. How perfect for the reception tables. They had a flat bottom and five-inch glass petals spiked all the way around to create a floral look. The piece had presence but was short enough to converse over without being in the way. And she loved that it came in so many colors. She wanted the one with spiking gold petals. It reminded her of sunflowers.

"I'd like to order two hundred, but I need them within two weeks. Can you do that?" The young artist's eyes popped wide.

"Si. Si," he eagerly assured her. "I have ready."

"Why so many?" Zach asked. "And don't you already have candleholders with the royal crest on them?"

"Yes, but I think the clear glass bowls etched with the royal crest will sit nicely right in the middle of these and be absolutely gorgeous with a candle inside. A win-win." She got a beautiful, unique presentation that was both fragile and bold, and the palace got their staid, boring candleholders used.

"That's pretty genius." He applauded her.

"It's my job to mix the styles and needs of the bride and groom into a beautiful event that's appealing to them individually and as a couple."

"I'm learning there's more to this wedding planning stuff than I ever would have believed."

"Yeah. I'll convert you yet."

"Now, that's just crazy talk."

She sent him a chiding glance. "I want two hundred because I want plenty for my reception tables, but I also think the candleholders will make good gifts for the guests. What do you think, best man? Christina has pretty much left the decisions up to me and you're Antonio's stand-in. Do you think this would make a good gift for the guests to take away?"

He blinked at her for a moment, clearly surprised to have his opinion sought. He rubbed his chin as he contemplated the candleholder she held. "It's a pretty sophisticated crowd, but, yeah. Each piece is unique. That will appeal to the guests while the piece will also act as a reminder of the event."

"Then it will have served its purpose."

She turned back to the vendor. "In two weeks," she repeated, needing to know his excitement wasn't overriding his capabilities.

"*Si, si…due* weeks. I work night and day."

Given he would be working with heat and glass, she wasn't sure that was a good idea. She made a note in her tablet to check on his progress in a week. If he wasn't going to make it, she'd adjust her order to cover the tables only. And just give the royal crest candleholders away as a gift. But she really hoped he could pull it off.

She gave him her card with her email, asked him to send her a purchase order and advised him he'd have to sign a confidentiality agreement. His hand shook as he took the card, but he nodded frantically and handed Zach the package containing the sample she'd bought.

Zach made the next purchase. A Ferrari California T convertible. She thought they were just window shopping when he dragged her to the dealership. There was no denying the cars were sexy beasts. And it seemed the height of luxury to have the showroom on the fifth floor.

Even when Zach started talking stats and amenities, she blew it off. Nobody walked into a Ferrari dealership and walked out with a car. Or they shouldn't. It was a serious investment and required serious thought.

But Zach stood, hands on hips, surveying the slick car and nodding his head to whatever the salesman was saying. The portly man spoke English with such a thick accent she didn't know how Zach understood him.

"What color?" Zach asked her.

Her turn to blink at him in surprise at having her opinion sought. "What?"

"What color do you like better? The red or the black?"

"Are you insane? You can't just walk in here and buy a car."

"I'm pretty sure I can."

"But—"

"I've been thinking of buying one," he confessed. "I'm stoked at the idea of buying it here in Italy, from the original dealership. And it'll be nice to have a car since the rental company hasn't replaced the Land Rover yet."

She eyed the beautiful, sleek cars. "They'll probably have it replaced before they can deliver one of these."

"Pixie, they could have a car ready in an hour. But they have one downstairs with all the amenities I want. I could drive it back to Monte Calanetti if I wanted."

"Oh, my dog. You're serious about this."

He grinned, flashing his dimple and looking younger and as satisfied as a teenaged boy getting his first car.

"It's the California T series. I have to have one, right? I deserve something for closing the government deal. What color?" he demanded again.

Okay, she got it. He sought a physical treat for recent accomplishments because he wasn't getting any emotional accolades. Who could blame him? Not her.

"Indeed you do." Adjusting her mood to his, she glanced around the show room. "You don't want red or black. Too cliché."

"I'd use the word classic."

"I like that pretty blue. It reminds me of the sea around Halencia. If you're taking a souvenir home, it should represent where you've been."

"The blue." His inclined his head, his brown eyes reflecting his appreciation of her comeback. "Hmm." He strolled over to look it over better. "I'm not really looking for pretty."

"Is rockin' a better adjective? More masculine? We can use that if you prefer, because it's a rockin' pretty blue."

"I like rockin'."

"But do you like the blue?"

"I do. Though the classics are nice, too."

"They're cliché for a reason."

"Signora." The salesman flinched, unable to stay silent any longer. *"Per favore,* not say cliché."

"Scusa," she apologized, sending Zach an unrepentant smirk.

He said something in Italian to the salesman, who nodded and stepped away.

"I have to do this," he said, lifting her chin on his finger and lowering his mouth to cover hers as if he couldn't wait another moment to taste her.

CHAPTER NINE

THE FLAVOR OF him filled her senses. Oh. Just, oh.

She should protest, step away, remind him of their professional status. She did none of those things. Instead she melted against him, lifting her arms around his neck.

How she'd missed his touch. She thrilled at his hands on her waist pulling her closer, at his body pressed to hers from mouth to knees, the two of them fitting together like cogs and grooves. This was more dangerous than watching their reflection in the mirror at Signora Russo's. By far.

Didn't matter. She sank into sensation as she opened to him. More than she should in a Ferrari dealership. Or maybe not. They were hot cars, after all.

A throat clearing loudly announced the return of the salesman.

Zach lifted his head, nipped her lower lip.

"Hold on." She ducked her head against him, turning away from the salesman.

"What are you doing?" He spoke gently and cradled her head. Perfect.

"Saving you some money. Tell our friend over there that you're sorry, but I'm totally embarrassed and want to leave."

He rattled off a few words of Italian. Predictably the salesman protested.

She pushed at Zach, making a show of wanting to leave. "Tell him you'll have to buy the car when you get back to the States because we're leaving Milan tonight and probably won't make it back here."

While he conveyed her message, she grabbed his hand

and began pulling him toward the exit, carefully avoiding the salesman's gaze.

The salesman responded in a conciliatory tone, his voice growing closer as he spoke.

"He just dropped the price by ten thousand dollars," Zach advised her.

She frantically shook her head and, holding his hand in both of hers, she bracketed his arm and buried her face in his shoulder. "Let's see if we can get him to twenty. Shake your head sadly, put your arm around me and head for the elevator."

"You know I can afford the car."

"So not the point."

"What was the point again?"

"Trust me. He's not going to let you walk away."

He sighed, then she felt the movement of his head and his arm came around her. She leaned into him as they walked toward the elevator.

"I can't believe I'm leaving here without a car."

"You can always order it online and have them deliver it. If he lets you walk away."

"You owe me dinner for this."

They got all the way to the elevator before the salesman hailed Zach. He rushed over, all jovial and solicitous, giving his spiel as he approached. The elevator doors opened just as he arrived next to them. The man opened his arms wide in a gesture that welcomed Zach to consider what a good deal was being offered.

Zach nodded. *"Si, avete un affare."*

"You took the offer?"

"I have. And you're invited to visit the gift shop and pick out a gift while I finalize things here."

"Oh. Nice touch. Okay, you can buy the car." She stepped into the elevator. "Don't be long."

Thirty minutes later he collected her from the gift shop

and they headed out. On the street he pulled her into his arms and gave her a long, hard kiss. Then he draped his arm around her shoulders and started walking.

"That's the most fun I've had in a long time."

"How much?"

"For twenty-five thousand less than quoted."

"Aha! So you owe me dinner."

"You have skills, Pixie."

"I have a few tricks. I'm always working with a budget whether it's five hundred dollars or five million, so I've learned to negotiate for my job. I enjoy the challenge. You have money. You're used to buying what you want without worrying about the cost."

"I've negotiated for my business."

"But that's different, isn't it? You're on the sales side then, demanding value for services. When it comes to buying—"

"I want the best regardless of price. It's how I was raised."

"You were fortunate." As soon as the words left her mouth she remembered what he'd said about people in his life always having an agenda even when he was a young child and how his parents brushed aside his success to make demands of him. Money didn't make up for everything. She quickly changed the subject.

"So, are you driving home? Am I visiting Christina's aunt on my own?"

"I'm going with you. I went with the blue car, which needed modified for some of the upgrades I wanted. They'll be delivering the car in a couple of days. We have an hour before we need to meet the helicopter. Do you want to go see the cathedral?"

He was right. Today had been fun. She couldn't remember when she'd last let go and played for a day. She liked playing tourist. Wanted it to continue.

She sighed, knowing she needed to rein them in. A bell kept pinging in her brain, warning her to stop the foolishness, reminding her of the danger of surrendering to his charm. Hadn't she already rehashed all this with herself at the fitting?

Yes, and she knew what she risked if she continued to let her emotions rule her actions.

Yet she still reached up and tangled her fingers with his at her shoulder.

"It'll be rushed, but it sounds like fun."

"Okay, let's go." He stepped to the curb and waved down a taxi. "At least we'll get to see it. And if we really want to see more, we can plan a day when we can come back and do a full tour."

Her heart soared at the way he linked them into the future.

She deserved this time. Work always came first and because the nature of it was so party central she experienced a faux sense of having an active social life. For too long she'd suppressed her loneliness. Just this once she'd let loose and enjoy the history and charm of an ancient city in the company of a gorgeous man totally focused on her.

Sliding into the back of the cab, she smiled when Zach linked their hands. And sighed when he leaned in for a kiss.

Tomorrow could take care of itself.

Zach in a Speedo was a piece of art.

He swam once or twice a day. She remembered from her research that he'd met Antonio on the Harvard swim team. Obviously he still enjoyed the water. And she enjoyed him.

Funny how his swims always seemed to coincide with her need for a break. Uh-huh, a girl was allowed her illusions.

And she could look as long as she didn't touch.

The man was grace in motion. Watching that long, tanned, toned body move through the water gave her a jolt that rivaled caffeine. It was one fine view in a villa full of spectacular views and it made Lindsay's mouth water with want.

Now that she knew how it felt to brush up against that fine body, she longed for more. But she was back in the real world so she turned away from the sight of Zach striding confident and wet from the pool.

She took a sip from her soda, needing the wet and the cool. And drained it before she was through. Leaving the empty can on the bar she joined her assistant at the lovely oak table Zach had purchased for her use.

She pulled up her email and sent Christina a message to let her know they were still on the hunt for the brooch. As Christina had warned her Aunt Pia had been leery about talking to them, but with Christina's note she'd finally softened. She'd given the brooch to her daughter, but the younger woman hadn't worn it for her wedding, either. Pia had called her daughter while they were there and she couldn't recall what had happened to the brooch. Pia suggested Sophia might know.

Lindsay would be meeting with Sophia tomorrow, two weeks from the wedding.

"Serena, can you call and remind Louisa that Zach and I will be meeting the landscapers at the palazzo this morning."

The two of them were set to leave in a few minutes and she needed work to help her get the visual of his nearly nude body out of her head.

"Already done. And I sent the information to the glassblower as you requested. He already confirmed delivery for a week before the wedding."

"Excellent."

Serena turned out to be a godsend. She looked cool and competent in blue jeans and a crisp white tee, her long black hair slicked back in a ponytail that nearly reached her waist. And she was every bit as efficient as she appeared.

"Let's put it on the calendar to check with him in a few days to be sure he's on schedule. If I have to find another gift, I'd rather know sooner than later."

"*Si*, I put a note on your calendar."

"Perfect."

They went over a few other items, scratching off two on the to-do list and adding three. "The palace rep is supposed to take care of ordering the table and chairs, but can you call to make sure they have and confirm what they've ordered."

Her brown eyes rounded. "You want me to check the palace's work?"

"Yes. There's no room for misunderstandings. I need to know every detail is covered."

The girl nodded. "*Si*, I will call them."

"Good. I know this may be a hard concept for you, Serena, but until this wedding is over, your first loyalty is to me. It's my job to give the prince and Christina a beautiful wedding that will represent the house of L'Accardi well. You have no idea how many errors I've found by following up on details handled by other people. Some have been innocent mistakes, but others were outright sabotage."

"That's terrible!"

Lindsay nodded. "If I hadn't caught the mistakes, intentional or otherwise, not only would the bride and groom have been disappointed and possibly embarrassed, but my reputation would have suffered badly."

"*Si*. I will check every detail."

"*Grazie*. And don't forget to find a nice, understated dress for the occasion. Something in light blue."

Serena's brown eyes rounded even bigger than before. "I am to attend the royal wedding?" It was a near squeak.

"You'll be working it with me, yes."

"Oh, my goodness! I have to shop!"

Lindsay smiled. "After you check on the table and chairs."

"*Si.*" Serena nodded, her eagerness offset by a desperate look in her eyes.

"And bring me the receipt. It's a work expense."

Relief flooded the girl's features. "*Grazie.*"

"Are you ready to go?" A deep male voice filled the room.

Zach stood in the doorway to the house, thankfully fully dressed in jeans and a brown T-shirt that matched his eyes.

"Ready." Lindsay grabbed her purse and dropped her tablet inside. "Let's go."

The wind whipped through her hair as Zach drove them across town in the golf cart. He pulled straight into the drive.

Two things struck her right away. Louisa was in the middle of a heated discussion on her doorstep. Her opponent towered over her smaller frame. He had dark hair, broad shoulders and a wicked-fine profile.

And second, construction paraphernalia had been cleared away but the grounds were only a quarter cleared.

"What the heck, Zach?" Lindsay demanded as she climbed out of the golf cart. "I thought you hired someone to clean this all out."

"I did and I take full responsibility for the mess-up. I hired the crew the mayor recommended and I told them to clear out all the weeds but to save the original plants."

"No, no, no. Everything was supposed to be cleared out."

He grimaced. "I'm hearing that now, at the time I was answering a text from my office. I got it wrong. I'm sorry."

"They didn't even do what you asked." She stomped forward, scanning the dry brush and overgrown ground cover. "The landscaping team is going to be here any minute. The construction team is scheduled to start the day after they're done. This needed to be done already."

This couldn't be happening. She'd had everything planned down to the last minute. There were acres to clear. The whole property needed to be in shape, not just the area around the chapel and palazzo.

"Lindsay, I'm sorry."

Lindsay swung around to Louisa. The other woman stood huddled into herself, the tall man she'd been arguing with at her side.

"This is my fault," Louisa said. "I've been distracted the past few days. I should have noticed the grounds weren't being cleared out like they should be."

"No. It's mine. I should have been checking on the progress." Follow up on every detail. Hadn't she just pressed that fact home with Serena? She'd been the one to drop the ball.

"Placing blame does no good." Zach refused to play the role of dunce. He'd made this mess. It was up to him to clean it up. "We need to focus on a solution."

"He's right." Hands on his hips, the tall man Louisa had been arguing with surveyed the grounds. "You must be Lindsay Reeves, the wedding planner. Nico Amatucci." He held out his hand as he introduced himself. "I own the vineyard next door."

"Right." She shook his hand, appreciated the firm grip. "We're serving your wine at the reception. I've sampled some. It's very good."

"Zach Sullivan, best man." Zach inserted his hand between the two of them, not caring for the admiration in

Amatucci's gaze as it ran over Lindsay. Some distance between the two suited Zach fine.

No way was Zach letting the other man play hero while he chafed under the restraint of his plan. It didn't help that his gut roiled with guilt at seeing Lindsay so upset.

He was making her work harder than she needed to on the most important event of her career. Watching her blame herself for something he'd done didn't sit well, no matter how well-intentioned his plan had been.

Especially when he had nothing to show for it.

Neither Tony nor Christina showed any signs of backing out of the wedding. The two of them had managed to distance themselves from what went on in Monte Calanetti so any delays Lindsay suffered were mere blips on their radars.

Zach had only managed one meeting with Tony, but whenever he broached the topic on their hurried calls, Tony shut him down. Christina did the same when Zach got a few minutes alone with her at the fitting, though he had to give her points for being much more polite about it.

"I'm not sure how this happened." Zach gritted his teeth as he played his part for his audience of three. "I was telling Lindsay I hired the crew Mayor Alonso recommended. He mentioned the owner had just broken up with his girl, but I didn't figure that signified."

"Are you talking about Fabio?" Nico ran his hand through his dark hair. "He gets *molto* messed up when he and Terre are fighting, and he is no good for anything."

"I need to call him, get him out here." Lindsay took out her tablet. "This needs to be finished today. If he can't get it done, I need to get someone who can."

"Let me talk to him, *signorina*," Nico offered, his tone grim. "His girl is *incinta*. Fabio needs the work. I will make sure it gets done."

Lindsay hesitated then slowly nodded.

Seeing the despair in her indomitable blue eyes shredded Zach. He decided right then to stop messing with her. Why should she suffer for Tony and Christine's stubbornness?

She shouldn't.

No more than he should be forced to play the fool.

The trip to Milan rated as one of the best days of his life. He'd enjoyed spending time with Lindsay, more than anyone he could remember in a long time. She was smart and fun, and too restrained, which challenged him to loosen her up. And she constantly surprised him. He marveled at her performance at the Ferrari dealership.

Her ex had given her enough grief. Zach wouldn't add to it.

He'd still try talking sense into the couple. For all the good it would do him. But no more messing with the wedding.

"Fabio's going to need help getting this all done," Zach announced, feeling the need to fix the problem. "Who else can we get to help?"

"I can call my men over to lend a hand for a few hours," Nico offered.

"Thanks, that's a start. I'm going to call the mayor."

"I'll help," Louisa stated. "It'll feel good to get outside and do some physical labor for a change."

Zach lifted his brow at that. The temperature topped eighty and the palazzo was in a valley. There was little in the way of a breeze to offset the mugginess from the clouds overhead.

"It is too hot for you," Nico told her bluntly. "You will stay inside."

Wrong move, buddy. Zach watched the storm brew in the palazzo owner's light blue eyes. She was almost guaranteed to work harder and longer than she would have if the other man had kept his mouth shut. But her offer gave him an idea.

"No," Louisa informed Nico, her chin notched up, "I will not. I'm partially responsible for this situation and I want to help."

"Me, too," Lindsay piped in. "Louisa, do you have an extra pair of gloves? We can get started while Nico contacts Fabio."

"I do. I have a scarf, too. You'll want to put your hair up."

The women wandered off. Nico glared after them. "She never listens."

Zach cleared his throat and clapped Nico on the shoulder. "My man, let me give you some advice. Rather than order a woman about, it's better to make her think it's her idea to start with."

Nico grimaced. "I know this. But she drives me… *pazzo*."

"Crazy? I know the feeling. Perhaps when she starts to weary you can casually mention how thirsty the workers look and she'll go inside to provide refreshments."

"You misunderstand. There is nothing between us," Nico clarified with more emphasis than necessary. "As there is between you and Ms. Reeves."

"If you asked her, she would say there is nothing between us, either."

Nico scowled.

Zach laughed. "You should call me Zach, as we'll be working together." And they got to work.

The whole town came out to help. Or so it seemed. The mayor arrived shortly after a remorseful Fabio. Alonso didn't ask what needed to be done. He wore khaki pants and an old denim shirt with the sleeves rolled up to his elbows. He picked up a shovel and got to work.

Lindsay called Serena and she showed up with a few

friends, four of Nico's men arrived in a pickup, including his brother Angelo. Eva's son, Mario, and a pack of early teens pitched in. The barber closed his shop to help. And on and on it went. Even the landscaping crew joined in, helping to haul debris and refuse away.

Everyone was happy and laughing.

At some point Lindsay was introduced to Vincenzo Alberti, the director of tourism. When she expressed her gratitude, he explained that the whole town was proud the royal wedding was happening there. That they wanted their city to be represented well and that they were all excited to be a part of it in some way.

Lindsay wiped at the sweat on forehead with a towel she'd tucked into her waistband and surveyed their progress. Another hour should see it done. A good thing as it would be dark not long after.

She was hot and sticky, tired and sore. And hungry.

She imagined everyone else was, too. But no one was leaving. They all meant to see it finished. Nico and Louisa had put their animosity aside to coordinate the workers' efforts.

"Almost done." Zach appeared beside her, his tanned and muscular chest on full display. As had many of the men, he'd ditched his shirt somewhere along the way.

She resisted the urge to run her palm down his sweaty abs. More than once she'd caught herself admiring the flex and flow of muscle and tendon under smooth flesh. Dark and tanned, he fit right in with the Halencians. Fit and toned, he matched the laborers pace for pace.

He was poetry in motion and she had a hard time keeping her attention fixed on her chore. Especially with him standing in front of her.

"I'm amazed by the support we got from everyone." Rather than look at him she watched the landscapers fill their truck with bags of weeds. "I wish there was something we could do for them."

"I was thinking the same thing." He took her towel and wiped the back of her neck, sending tingles down her spine where his fingers trailed over her skin. "I thought about hosting a party at the villa, but I prefer to reward everyone now, so I asked Alonso for a suggestion. He mentioned Mancini's. I called and talked to the owner. Raffaele Mancini said he'd open up the patio for us and put a nice meal together."

"'Nice' is the operative word there, champ. Mancini's is catering the wedding. Eva also told me about Mancini's as an option for an upscale meal. I'm not sure I can afford that."

"I'm covering it."

"You don't have to do that."

"I insist. I feel this is mostly my fault. Paying for dinner is a small enough thing to do. Plus, Mancini heard about what happened and apologized for not making it over here to help out. So he's giving us a discount."

The spirit of this town just kept amazing her.

"Shall we start passing the word? Mancini's at eight. That'll give Raffaele time to cook. And the rest of us time to clean up."

Dinner turned into a party. When Lindsay stepped inside, assisted by Zach's hand at the small of her back, she got pulled into a big hug by the maître d', who was a curvy blonde with bright gray eyes and a smile so big she beamed.

"Hello. Welcome to Mancini's." Surprisingly the bubbly blonde was American. Then she announced why she was so excited, "Winner of the Italian Good Food Award!"

"Wow." Lindsay knew the award was on par with the

Michelin Star in France. "Congratulations. That's fantastic."

Zach echoed her. "Raffaele didn't mention it when I spoke to him earlier."

"We just heard an hour ago. You must be Lindsay Reeves and Zach Sullivan, the wedding planner and best man. I'm Daniella, Rafe's fiancée. We have the patio all set up for you. Some people have already started to arrive. You'll have to excuse us if we're a little giddy tonight. We're over the top about the award."

"As you should be," Zach said easily. "I hope you, Raffaele and the staff can join us later for a congratulatory toast."

That smile flashed again. "I'm sure that can be arranged. I'll tell Rafe."

The patio was enclosed but the large windows were wide open, letting in the cool evening air. Wine bottles hung from the overhead beams along with green ivy. Red-checked tablecloths covered two large picnic tables that seated twenty each and three round tables at the far end.

A couple of extra chairs were needed, but everyone shuffled around so everyone got seated. Alonso arranged it so he and Vincenzo sat with Lindsay and Zach along with Nico and Louisa.

Raffaele had "thrown together" a steak Florentine for them that melted in Lindsay's mouth. She was definitely putting it on the wedding menu.

She wondered if Raffaele knew how to make *cornettos*.

"I'm exhausted," Louisa told Lindsay toward the end of the delicious meal when they had the table to themselves. "But it's a good tired."

"It's the same for me." Lindsay sipped her wine. "We accomplished a lot today. The landscapers will start tomorrow and the owner assured me they would make up the lost time."

"That's great. I'm glad we were able to get it done for you."

"I'm so impressed with the townspeople. How they rallied together to help out and were so cheerful even working in the heat and mugginess."

"Well, they're all enjoying dinner. This was a nice gesture."

"Zach's the one to thank. But we were happy to do it. Everyone worked so hard. I can tell you I've decided to order some big fans for the wedding and reception. I want the guests to be comfortable."

Louisa clinked her wineglass against Lindsay's. "I like the way you think. I'm sorry I dropped the ball."

"Don't sweat it. You worked as hard as anyone today." Lindsay eyed Zach talking with Nico, Alonso and a couple of other men near the bar. "And I know how easy it is to get distracted."

"Are the two of you involved?" Louisa asked.

Lindsay's gaze whipped back to her fellow American.

"There's a…tension between the two of you," the woman explained.

"He'd like there to be." Lindsay rolled the stem of her wineglass between her fingers, watched the liquid swirl as her thoughts ran over the past two weeks. "But I need to stay focused on the job. As today clearly proved."

"He can't take his eyes off you."

"And Nico keeps you in his sights. Is there something between the two of you? You seemed to be arguing this morning."

"We're always arguing." Louisa's gaze flicked over the man in question. Her expression remained as composed as always, but there was no hiding the yearning in her pale eyes. "That is why it's good there's nothing between us."

A loud cheer went through the patio. Lindsay glanced around to see Rafe and Danielle had joined the party. Another round of cheers sounded as waiters flowed through the room with trays of champagne glasses.

Alonso grabbed a flute and held it high. "*Primo*, a huge *grazie* to Raffaele and Mancini's for hosting us tonight on such short notice. And for the wonderful meal he provided." More cheers. "*Secondo*, we are all excited to be here to share in the joyous news of Mancini's receiving the Good Food Award!" He held his glass high. "We had no doubts, *amico mio*, none at all. *Complimenti!*"

"*Complimenti!*" The crowd clapped and cheered, lifting their glasses and sipping.

Rafe stood on a chair. "*Grazie, grazie*. I am happy so many of my friends could be here to share this with me tonight. Business picked up when Mancini's was chosen to feed the royal wedding guests. Now, we have the Good Food Award the tourists will come even more. Monte Calanetti is on the map!"

A roar of approval rose to the roof.

"Nice touch, sharing his success with the citizens." Zach slid into his seat. "Classy."

"Raffaele is good people," Louisa affirmed. "I'm going to congratulate him on my way out. Good night. Zach, thank you for dinner."

"My pleasure."

Louisa walked away, leaving Lindsay and Zach alone together. He picked up her hand. "You look tired."

"I am." Too tired to fight over possession of her hand. She really needed to tell him the day in Milan had been a mistake and they needed to regroup to where they'd been before the trip. But every touch weakened her resolve.

"I'm sorry I messed up." There was a quality to his voice she couldn't quite pinpoint. She dismissed it as fatigue and the fact he probably didn't have to apologize for his work effort very often. Like never.

"You thought you were hiring the best crew," she reminded him. "And, you know, I really enjoyed today, getting to know more of the local people, seeing how they all rallied around each other to help. It was an inspiring experience. As you said before, too often people are all about their own agendas. Today reinforced my view of humanity."

"Sometimes those agendas can be well-meaning." Again his tone was off.

"You mean like Fabio obsessing over his girl and their baby? I get that, but look at how many lives he impacted by not honoring his contract. Yes, I enjoyed the day, but the landscaper is still going to have to make up lost time, and I lost a whole day. Life is so much easier when people are up front with each other."

He brought her hand to his mouth and kissed her knuckles. "Let's go home and soak our aches away in the Jacuzzi."

Oh, goodness, that sounded wonderful.

And dangerous.

She'd promised herself she'd get her head on straight today, put her infatuation aside and focus on the job. It was the smart thing to do. All he wanted was a summer fling. She had only to recall how he'd clammed up after she'd shared her humiliating history with Kevin to realize his interest was strictly physical.

And still she tangled her fingers with his. "Let's go."

CHAPTER TEN

AFTER THE INTENSE heat of the day, the balmy softness of the night air caressed Lindsay's shoulders with the perfect touch of cool. The rest of her, submerged in the hot, roiling water of the spa, thanked her for her foolish decision.

"I really did need this." She rolled her neck, stretching the tendons.

Strong hands turned her and began to work at the tightness in her shoulders. "So much stress."

The low timbre of Zach's voice made her whole body clench in need. She tried to shift away, but he easily held her in place.

"I never would have thought a wedding would be so much work."

She bit her bottom lip to suppress a moan, not wanting to encourage him. "Why, because it's just a big party? It's more than that, you know. It's two people creating a life together. That requires the meshing of many moving parts. The bride and groom, family members, attendants and, in this case, palace representatives and dignitaries. And that's just on the day. Before that there's flowers, food, wine, cake, photographers, seating in the chapel, setting up for the reception. Seating arrangements. Thank you, once again, for your help with that. I got the final approval from the palace today."

"My pleasure."

There was that tone again. She glanced at him over her shoulder. "You stopped listening after family members, didn't you?"

"You caught me." He let her float away a bit before turning her so she faced him.

"What's up with you?" She brushed the damp hair off his furrowed brow. "You've been slightly off all night."

"Today was my fault."

So that was it. Zach was so laid-back with her she sometimes forgot he ran a multibillion-dollar company. He was used to being in control and being right.

"We already talked about this. Stop feeling guilty."

"You know how I feel about large weddings."

"So what? You deliberately hired someone you knew couldn't do the job? You're just feeling bad because you're a problem solver and today it took a lot of people to fix the problem. It's okay. You repaid them all with a very nice dinner. And they all got to celebrate Mancini's award with Raffaele. I didn't hear a single gripe from anyone today, so cut yourself some slack."

"It's not that. I can't help but think Tony and Christina are making a mistake."

"So you subconsciously sabotaged the cleanup?"

He looked away, staring out at the lights of Monte Calanetti. "Something like that. They barely know each other."

"They've been engaged for four years."

"And he's lived in America the whole time."

This was really tearing him up. So often since they'd met he'd been there for her when she'd needed him. She wished she had the magic words that would ease his concerns.

"They have no business getting married."

"Zach—" she rubbed his arm, hoping to soothe "—that's not for you to say."

"They're going to end up hating each other." The vehemence in his voice reinforced his distress. "I watched it happen to my parents. I can't stand to watch it happen to a man I think of as my brother."

She cupped his cheek, made him look at her. "No matter how much we love someone, we can't make their decisions for them. We wouldn't welcome them doing so for us and we owe them the same respect."

He sighed then pulled her into his lap, nuzzling the hair behind her ear. She wrapped her arms around him and hugged him tight. His arms enfolded her and they sat there for a while just enjoying the closeness of each other.

"She threw me over for my father."

Lindsay went still. "Who?"

"The woman I once got close to marrying."

"Oh, Zach." She tightened her grip on him and turning her head slightly, kissing him on the hard pec she rested against. "I'm so sorry."

"We met in college. My name didn't intimidate her, which was a real turn-on. It seemed all the girls I met were supplicants or too afraid to talk to me. Julia was a political science major. She said that was to appease her parents, that her real love was her minor, which were arts and humanities."

"She targeted you."

"Oh, yeah, she played me. Right from the beginning." He suddenly rose with her in his arms. "It's time to get out."

"I suppose we should." Her arms ringed his neck as he climbed out. She longed to hear more but had the sense if she pushed, he'd close down on her. So she kept it light-hearted. "I'm starting to prune."

He claimed her lips in a desperate kiss, holding her high against him as he devoured her mouth. His passion seduced her body just as his vulnerability touched her heart.

He carried her to the cabana where they'd left their towels. He released her legs and let her slide down his body. In her bare feet he towered over her, a dark shadow silhouetted by the nearly full moon. It took him a mere second to bridge the distance before his mouth was on hers again, hot and unsettling.

The right touch and she'd be lost to reason. From the reaction of his body to hers she knew he felt the same.

But he'd started his story and if she let this moment slip away, she may never hear the full tale.

She pulled back, leaning her brow on his damp chest while she caught her breath. "Tell me."

His hands tightened on her and then his chest lifted in a deep breath. He reached for her towel and wrapped it around her before grabbing his own.

She slid onto the double lounge and patted the cushion beside her. He joined her and pulled her into his arms so her back was to his front and the vista of Monte Calanetti spread out before them.

"She showed disinterest to catch my attention. And when I finally got her to go out with me, we just clicked so smoothly. We enjoyed all the same things. Had some of the same friends. She made me feel like she saw me, Zach Sullivan, as more than the son of William Sullivan. I reached the point where I was contemplating marriage. So I took her home to meet the parents. She was so excited. For the first time she asked me why I wasn't studying political science."

"With your family background, you'd think she'd ask that fairly early in the relationship."

"Yes, you'd think. I explained that I wanted nothing to do with politics. That technology was my passion. And I told her what she could expect with my parents. How they married to connect two politically powerful families and how they spent more time with others than with each other."

"And she went after your father."

"She barely spoke to me for the rest of the flight. I thought she was mulling it over, feared I'd put her off."

"You just gave her a new target." She held him tighter.

"She assumed because I grew up surrounded by politics

that I didn't need to study it. And when I let her know I had no interest in it, and revealed my father liked to play discreetly, she went for the big guns. I caught them kissing in his study."

"I'm so sorry. I know how debilitating it is to walk in on a scene like that. The shock, the embarrassment, the betrayal. But I can't imagine how much worse it must hurt for her to be with your father."

With a double betrayal of this magnitude in his past, she kind of got why he didn't like big weddings. And why he was concerned for his friend.

"I just wanted out of there. My dad stopped me and said she'd be the one leaving. She'd come on to him, surprised him with the kiss. He wasn't interested. After she stormed off, he told me he may not be the best husband, but he'd never put a woman before his son."

"Well, that was good, to know he didn't betray you. Still, it's not something you can unsee."

He rested his head against hers, letting her know he sympathized with her, too. "It meant a lot. It's the single incident in my life I can look back on and know he put me first."

Wow, how sad was that? And yet when she looked at her own life, she couldn't find one instance that stood out like that. The difference was that her mom may put herself first, but Lindsay knew her mother loved her. From what Zach described, his folks rarely displayed affection.

She rolled her head against his chest, letting him know she understood his pain.

"So you've never gotten close to marriage since?"

"No. I've never met a woman I could see myself with five years from now let alone fifty. I don't ever want to end up like my folks. I want someone who will knock me off my feet."

"Good for you. That's what you should want. Hearing you say that about five years down the line, I realize I didn't have that with Kevin, either. I could see myself in a nice house with a couple of kids, but Kevin wasn't in the picture."

"I can see you in my future."

Her heart raced at his words and she had to swallow twice before she could answer. "Do you now?"

"Yes, all the way to tomorrow. I got a call from the dealership. The Ferrari will be here by nine. I thought we could drive to Sophia's."

She bit her lip, waffling a tad because she'd lost so much time today it was hard to justify the drive when the helicopter did the job so fast. Still she didn't want to make him feel even guiltier about today's events.

And, truly, how often did she get the chance to drive through the Halencia countryside in a Ferrari convertible with a handsome billionaire by her side?

This was probably a once-in-a-lifetime adventure. So why not stop fighting the inevitable and let the billionaire seduce her? She only had him for another couple of weeks. Less, really. She didn't want to look back and regret not knowing him fully.

Because she was very much afraid she'd be looking back a lot.

"Do I get to drive?"

"A little pixie like you? I don't think so." He laughed, his body shaking with the sound. The good cheer was wonderful to hear after his earlier despair.

"Come on. We both know it's not the size that matters, but what you do with it." His laughter shook her some more. "I feel I earned the opportunity to drive it at least once."

"We'll see."

"Oh, I'm driving." She snuggled into him. "I can tell it's going to be a lucky day."

"Yeah? How?"

"Well, if you're going to get lucky tonight, it seems only fair I get lucky tomorrow."

He picked her up as if she was no bigger than the pixie he called her and set her in his lap. Using the edge of his hand he tipped her face up to his and kissed her softly.

"Am I getting lucky? What about your strict policies?"

She brushed his hair back, enjoying the feel of the silky strands running through her fingers. "I should stay strong, but you are just too tempting, Mr. Sullivan."

He leaned forward and nipped her bottom lip. "I like the sound of that, Ms. Reeves. Shall we start with a bath in the claw-foot tub?"

How did he know she'd been dying to soak in that tub? It was a modern version of the old classic and could easily hold the two of them. She'd just been waiting for him to be gone long enough to slip into the master bathroom.

Something was still off with him. Why else suggest walking back to the house and risk her coming to her senses? Seated as she was in his lap, there was no doubting his desire for her. Maybe his attempts at humor hadn't quite rid him of his funk in talking about his near miss with wedded bliss.

Unwilling to risk him coming to his senses, she leaned into him, looped her arms around his neck and pressed her lips to his. "Why don't we start here?"

He needed no other prompting. He rolled her so she lay under him. Her head was cradled in one big hand holding her in place for his kiss that belied the fierceness of his embrace by being tender. He cherished her with his mouth; seducing her with soft thrusts and gentle licks until she melted in his arms.

He pulled back, his face unreadable in the darkness of the cabana. A finger traced slowly down the line of her jaw.

"I don't want to hurt you," he said, his breath warm against her skin.

"Then don't," she responded and pulled him back to her.

There were no more words after that, her mind too absorbed with sensation to put coherent thoughts together. The balmy night and towels served to dry them for the most part but she found a few stray drops of water on his side and he shivered when she traced her fingers through the drops, trailing the wet across his smooth skin.

It thrilled her to know her touch affected him as strongly as his did her. He stirred her with his gentleness, but he ignited her when his mouth became more insistent, his touch more demanding. She arched into him, seeking all he had to give.

He grinned against her mouth, assuring her he'd take care of her. A moment later her bikini top slipped away and he lavished attention on the exposed flesh. Her nipple puckered from the rush of heat on damp skin. And the agile use of his tongue.

Wanting nothing between them, she wiggled out of the rest of her suit and pushed at his. Despite her efforts, the damp cloth clung to him.

"Off." She panted against his mouth.

He pushed it down and off without leaving her side. She admired his efficiency almost as much as she admired his form. He was so beautiful she would have liked to see him but he felt too good in her arms for her to regret anything.

Especially when his mouth and fingers did such wicked things to her.

She felt more alive, more energized, more female than any other time in her life.

Being outside made it a hedonistic experience. The night breeze caressed heated skin, while the scent of roses perfumed the air. The rush of emotion compelled her to reach for the moon that hung so heavy in the sky.

Her senses reeled from an overload of sensation. He made her want, made her sizzle, made her mind spin.

When he joined them with an urgency that revealed he was as engaged as she was, she was excited to know she moved him, too. It made her bolder, braver, more determined to drive him insane with pleasure. She loved when he hissed through his teeth, when he kissed her as if he'd never get enough.

When he lost control.

When the connection they shared took her to a whole new level.

Never had she felt so close to another person, in body, in spirit, in heart. He lifted her higher, higher until together they soared through the stars and she shattered in the glow of the moon.

And later, after they roused and he led her to the house for a warm soak in the claw-foot tub and then landed in the comfort of his bed for a repeat performance, she knew for her this was more than two bodies seeking each other in the night.

Somewhere along the way, she'd fallen in love with the best man.

Lindsay stared out the window of the passenger seat in the Ferrari, brooding to the point where the beautiful countryside flew by unnoticed.

She'd had such a lovely morning with Zach. Waking snuggled in his arms, she'd waited for the regret to hit. But no remorse surfaced. She loved Zach. Being in his arms is where she wanted to be.

That would change when she had to walk away. In the meantime she'd make the most of every moment with him.

Watching him put the new Ferrari through its paces on

the trip to Aunt Sophia's pleased her on a visceral level. Seeing his joy, absorbing his laughter, listening to him explain what made his new toy so special. His happiness made her happy, too.

The return trip was much more subdued, with Zach as quiet as she was.

Christina's aunt Sophia was a lovely woman, but a bit unorganized. Pia had called her, so she knew why they were there. She was so happy Christina wanted to wear the pin. Sophia had worn the brooch and she and her husband were still happily married after thirty-nine years.

Lindsay got her hopes up because Sophia seemed certain she had the brooch somewhere, but she'd already looked through her personal jewelry so she thought she must have stored it in the attic with other family heirlooms. Bad knees kept her from doing the search herself so she'd invited Lindsay and Zach to look all they'd like.

Luckily the attic was clean. And airy, once Zach opened the windows. But there was a lot to look through. She found a standing jewelry hutch and thought for sure the brooch would be there. Unfortunately not. Nor was it in any of the boxes or trunks they'd searched. In the end they'd left empty-handed.

"You okay?" Zach reached over and claimed her hand. "You did everything you could to find the brooch."

"I know." She summoned a wan smile, grateful for his support. "I just hate to disappoint the bride. Especially Christina. I've never had a bride disassociate herself so completely from the process so close to the wedding. It's almost as if she's afraid to invest too much of herself into the wedding."

"She's dealing with a lot."

"I get that. That is why I really wanted to find the brooch." With a sigh she turned back to the window. "It's the one thing she seemed to latch onto. It kills me not to be able to find it for her."

The car slowed and then he pulled to the side of the road. She looked at him. "What's wrong? Is it something to do with the car?"

"I needed to do this."

He cupped her face in his hands and kissed her softly. Then not so softly. Slightly breathless she blinked at him when he lifted his head.

"Much better." He slicked his thumb over her bottom lip.

He surprised her by getting out of the car and walking around the hood. He opened her door and helped her out. She looked around and saw nothing but green rolling hills for miles.

"What are we doing?"

"Well, I'm going to be riding. And you are going to be driving."

"Really?" Squealing in excitement she threw herself into his arms. "Thank you. Thank you. Thank you." She peppered his face with kisses between each word.

"Wait." He caught her around the waist when she would have run for the driver's seat. "You do know how to drive a stick, right?"

"I do, yes." This time she pulled his head down to kiss him with all the love in her heart. She knew he was doing this to distract her from her funk, which made the gesture all the more special because he'd categorically refused to let her drive earlier. "I'll take care with your new baby."

He groaned but released her.

She practically danced her way to the driver's seat. Of course she had to have the roof down. That took all of fourteen seconds. Too cool. He took her through where everything was and she pushed the ignition.

Grinning, she said, "Put your seat belt on, lover."

And she put the car in gear.

Grave misgivings hounded Zach as he stared down at the crystal bauble in his hand. Two hearts entwined side by side. Christina's lucky brooch. He'd given up on finding it, given up on sabotaging the wedding, but he'd opened a small tapestry box in one of the trunks in Sophia's attic and there it was. Tarnished, with a few crystals missing, but unmistakable nonetheless.

He'd had no plan when he'd taken it, but for one bright moment he saw a light at the end of the tunnel of Tony's train-wreck plan to marry a woman he didn't love. Without the brooch might Christina back out of the wedding?

With no more thought than that he'd pocketed the trinket.

Now as he clutched it, he realized what he'd done. Christina wasn't backing out. Tony wasn't listening to Zach's appeals to rethink the madness. And Lindsay would freak if she ever learned he'd taken it. On every level professional, friends, lovers, she'd see it as a betrayal.

How could she not when that's what it felt like to him?

He wished he'd never seen it. Never taken it. Never risked everything he'd come to care so much about. Hell, he'd invested so much time in this wedding, even he cared about it being a success.

If only Tony wasn't the victim in all this.

It killed Zach to stand aside while his best friend set himself up for such a big fail. But there was no going back now. It didn't matter that the brooch was not wearable. Didn't matter that he had regrets. The damage was done.

He thought back to the conversation they'd had in the car on the way back from Sophia's. With the brooch burning a hole in his pocket he'd voiced his concerns for Tony and Lindsay had warned him interference never paid off.

"Do you know how many weddings there are where someone doesn't think it's a good idea for some reason?" she'd asked him. "The timing's not right, someone's too young, someone's too old, their ages are too far apart. They don't know what they're doing. She's all wrong for him. He's too good for her. Every one. Show me a wedding and there will be a dissenter in the crowd somewhere."

"They couldn't all be wrong."

"Oh, yeah. Some of them were spot-on. But has it ever worked out well when they try to intervene? No. Because it's not their decision to make. The heart wants what the heart wants."

"What if it isn't love?" he'd demanded.

"Then the situation that brought them together wants what it wants. If the couple is consenting adults, then it's their decision to make."

He heard the message. Understood that a marriage was between the man and woman involved. Still, it was hard to swallow when he knew this was a wedding that was never meant to be.

Glancing around, he looked for a place to stash the piece. Spying a likely spot, he buried it deep. After the wedding, he'd find a way to return the brooch to the Rose family.

In the meantime it was time he got on board and supported his friend.

"Hey," Lindsay called out to Zach where he still sat sipping coffee on the terrace. "I'm doing laundry today. I'm going to grab your stuff."

She went into his walk-in closet and gathered up the items in the hamper. There wasn't that much and she could easily handle it with her things. Something thumped to the floor as Zach filled the doorway.

A crystal brooch, two hearts entwined side-by-side, lay on the brown-and-rust rug.

Heart racing, she blinked once then again, hoping—
no, praying—the view would change. Of course it didn't.
Christina's brooch lay on the floor at her feet.

It had been hidden in Zach's dirty laundry. Because it
was his dirty secret.

Pain bigger than anything she'd ever suffered tore
through her heart.

"Lindsay." He stepped into the room that had seemed
so big a moment ago but was now tiny and airless.

"You found the brooch." As if it might bite, she backed
away from it. A heavy ball of dread lodged in her gut.

"Let me explain." He reached for her.

She pulled away from him.

"What's to explain? You kept it from me. Hid it." Rather
than look at him, she stared down at the crystal pin. The
silver was tarnished, a few crystals were missing; a beautiful piece ravished by time. It would need to be repaired
before it could be worn again.

She lifted anguished eyes to his. "You lied to me."

"I didn't lie," he denied. "I just didn't reveal I'd found
it."

"How is that not lying when our whole purpose for
being there was to find the brooch?"

"You have to understand, I just want the two of them
to stop and think about what they're doing. A lucky pin
is a joke." He bent and picked it up. "This is a bandage at
the best and a crutch at the very least."

"I understand perfectly." Her stomach roiled as nausea
hit. She circled to the left, wanting out of the closet without touching him. "You haven't been helping me at all.
You've been using your position as best man to spy on the
wedding preparations. Oh, oh." As realization dawned, she
retreated from him. When her back hit the wall she sank
and wrapped her arms around her knees.

"It was your fault. I thought you were confessing because you felt bad. But it was your fault. You knew exactly what you were doing when you hired Fabio—or had a good idea, anyway. It was all you."

He went down on his haunches in front of her. She shrank away from him.

"Lindsay, this wasn't about you. You were never meant to get hurt."

She closed her eyes to block him out. "Go away."

"You have to listen to me."

"I can't believe anything you say."

"Antonio is a good guy. Always thinking of others. He's kept up with his duties while working in America. He's invested in a lot of businesses here, supported charities. Now he's giving up his life to be king, devoting his life to his country. He deserves to be happy. He has the right to choose his own wife."

"It's his life, Zach. He made his decision. He trusted you." She swallowed around the lump in her throat. "I trusted you."

"You don't understand" He rolled forward onto his knees. And still he loomed over her. "There's more at play here."

"I don't want to understand. I just want you to go away."

I can't." He sounded as if he had a mouth full of glass shards. "Not until I fix this."

"You can't fix this." She shook her head sadly. These past few days with him had been so perfect; a paradise of working and living together. Finding time to escape for a drive or some loving.

But it had been a fool's paradise.

"There's no undoing what's been done."

"There has to be." He reached for her.

She flinched from him.

His hand curled into a fist and fell to his side. "After the deal with the palazzo grounds I stopped. I saw how upset you were and I couldn't be responsible for that. You were never meant to get hurt."

"Stop saying that. What did you expect to happen when a wedding I was planning fell apart at the seams?" How could he possibly believe she'd come out of the situation unscathed if the prince called off the wedding? She was right in the middle of it. Especially with all the little things that had gone wrong. Starting with him sitting on the wedding gown.

Oh, God.

Had he sat on the dress on purpose? Had he known even then who she was and planned to use her all along?

"No, of course not," he responded, revealing she'd spoken aloud. "I had this idea before I left home." He rubbed the back of his head in frustration. "I didn't know who you were when I boarded the plane. This wasn't about you. It was about saving Tony from a lifetime of misery. The wedding planner got paid either way. But I got the opportunity to save him."

Fury drove her to her feet. "You think I'm worried about getting paid? Damn you." She stormed from the closet, not stopping until she reached her room. Yanking her suitcase from where she'd stored it, she opened it on the bed and began dumping in clothes.

Of course he followed her. For such a smart man, he knew how to do stupid real well.

"Do you think I work for a paycheck? Is that all your work is to you? I bet not." She emptied the drawers into the case and went for her shoes. "I take pride in my work."

The shoes didn't fit. She forced herself to stop and fold. She would not come back here. She went into the bathroom and grabbed what toiletries she'd left down here. She clenched her teeth when she thought of the items now occupying space in the master bathroom. He could have them. No way was she going back in that room.

He still stood in the doorway when she returned to her room. His shoulders drooped and his features were haggard. He looked as though he'd lost something precious.

Good. He'd pulled her heart from her chest and stomped on it. Let him suffer.

"I take satisfaction in giving the bride and groom something special, a day they can look back on with pride and happiness."

She closed the suitcase, pushed on the lid a couple of times to mash it down and then started zipping.

"There's more involved than arranging the flowers and cuing the music." With her suitcase closed, she yanked it from the bed and pulled up the handle. Finally she lifted her chin and faced Zach. "But then, I know you don't put much value in what I do. I really should have listened when you said you hate big weddings."

"Lindsay, no—"

"What did you say?" She talked right over his protest. "Oh, yeah, the couple needs to distract the crowd because they're marrying for something other than love."

"Don't do this. Don't leave. I didn't mean you."

"Oh, and let's not forget, love is a myth best left to romance novels."

He groaned.

"No, it's good this happened. Foolish me. I believed I was falling in love. It's so good to know it's just a myth. In a couple of days I'm sure I'll be fine."

She passed him in the doorway, making certain not to touch him. "But you should know there's nothing fake about what I do. I put my heart and soul into my weddings. And the couple doesn't walk away empty-handed. I make memories, Zach. I intend to give Antonio and Christina a spectacular wedding to look back on."

She turned her back on him and walked out. "Stay out of my way."

CHAPTER ELEVEN

AFTER SEVERAL DAYS of brooding, of waffling between righteous indignation and hating himself for the pain he'd caused Lindsay, Zach finally came to the conclusion the first was really no justification for the second.

She still used the sunroom as her workshop, but mostly Serena worked there and when Lindsay did come by, she kept the doors locked; a clear signal for him to stay out.

As he had for the past two evenings, he sat in the shadows of the patio, waiting to catch her when she left for the day. Hoping today she'd talk to him. He hadn't seen her at all yesterday and his chest ached with missing her.

In such a short time she'd burrowed her way into his affections. Watching her work fascinated him; the way she gathered a few odd items together and made something beautiful. Her expression when she concentrated was so fierce it was almost a scowl. Many times he'd wanted to run his thumb over the bow between her brows to see if her creative thoughts might transmit to him and show him what had her so enthralled.

He missed her wit, her laughter, the way she gave him a bad time.

Steps sounded on the spiral staircase and he surged to his feet, meeting her as she reached the patio level. The sun was setting behind her, casting her in a golden glow. Strands of her hair shimmered as a light breeze tossed them playfully around. In juxtaposition her blue eyes were guarded and the skin was pulled taut across her cheeks.

She made to walk by him and he caught her elbow in a light hold.

"Won't you talk to me for a minute?"

She didn't look at him. But she didn't pull away, either. "There's nothing more to say between us."

"There is." He ran his thumb over the delicate skin of her inner elbow. Touching her fed something that had been deprived the past few days. Still, he forced himself to release her. "I tried to explain, but I failed to apologize. I'm sorry, Lindsay. I didn't think hard enough about how this would affect you. I never meant to devalue what you do."

Her shoulders squared and she half turned toward him. "But you don't value it. You've seen the effort involved, you can respect that. But you don't see the value in a beautiful wedding because you see it as the prelude to a flawed marriage."

"In this case, yes."

She sighed. "Zach, I've heard you talk about your parents enough to know what growing up with them must have been like. And I know you love Antonio, that he's probably closer to you than anyone. Mix that with your dislike of big, fancy weddings, and I'm sure this has been hell for you."

"I meant well," he avowed, grateful she saw what motivated him. "I can't stand the thought of him making this mistake, of him being miserable for the rest of his life. But Tony isn't rational when it comes to Halencia."

"Why? Because he refuses to see things your way?" She shook her head, the disappointment in her eyes almost harder to take than the hurt it replaced. "I think that's a good thing. I think a king should be willing to sacrifice for his country. Considering what his parents have put this country through, I think that's exactly what Halencia needs right now. And I think as his friend and best man, you should start showing him some support."

Hearing it broken down like that made him pause and rethink. Hadn't he had the same thought just days ago?

She took the opportunity to walk away. "I understand

why you want to save Antonio. What I can't forgive is your willingness to sacrifice me to get it."

Unable to take anymore, Zack texted Tony.

Need to see you. I've messed up bad. You may want a new best man.

After sending the message, Tony wandered down to the pool to wait for the helicopter to arrive on the wide lawn they'd been using as a landing area. It would be at least an hour, but he had no desire to sit in the house so full of memories.

He stared at the pool and remembered the night he made love to Lindsay.

He couldn't regret it. Wouldn't.

Having her come alive in his arms was one of the high points in his life. He'd connected with her more closely than with any other woman he could recall. Her honest re-actions and giving nature seduced him every bit as much as the silky feel of her skin and hair, the sweet taste of her mouth, the soft moans of her desire.

The few days he'd had her by his side had given him a brief glimpse into what the future could hold.

He wanted to scoff at the notion. To discount it as an indicator he'd been on one wild trip to Tuscany. But the truth was he could all too easily see her in his life. Not just here in Halencia but back in the States, as well.

And it scared the hell out of him.

The only thing that scared him more was the thought of losing her from his life altogether.

He knew the biggest betrayal for her was the intimacy they'd shared while she believed he'd been using her. But that's not what happened. He'd wanted Lindsay before he'd known she was the wedding planner. His attraction for her was completely disassociated from what she did.

Or so he'd thought.

Now he knew better. What she did was a part of who she was. She'd spoken of being disillusioned with her job. Her impassioned speech calling him to task for thinking a paycheck would suffice if the wedding fell apart proved she wasn't as lost as she'd feared. She'd been shaken because she let herself get caught up with Kevin and he'd used her.

It sickened Zach to realize he'd done the same thing.

Time to make it right.

The whoop, whoop, whoop of the helicopter sounded in the distance and grew louder. Finally. In another hour or so he'd see Tony, apologize for the mess he'd made of everything and put this whole fiasco behind him.

Being so close to Lindsay but parted from her drove him insane. He wanted to stay and fix it, but she needed to be here. He didn't. Hell, Tony probably wouldn't want him here when he learned what Zach had done.

He'd go back to the States and wait for her to come home. Then he'd find her and apologize again. No justifications, just a straight-up apology.

Ready to have this done, he strolled toward the helicopter. As he got closer he was surprised to see the pilot headed toward him. And then he knew.

"Tony." He broadened his stride and met his friend in a hug. "You came."

"Si, amico mio." Unselfconscious in showing emotion, Tony gave Zach a hard squeeze then stepped back to clap him on the arm. "Your text sounded serious."

"I've messed up."

"So you said. We must fix whatever you have done. I do not care to have anyone else for my best man."

"You haven't heard what I've done yet."

Tony had given up so much to support his country, would he be able to forgive Zach for messing in his affairs?

He couldn't lose both Lindsay and Antonio. Why hadn't he thought with his head instead of his heart?

"This sounds ominous." By mutual consent they headed toward the house. "You are my brother, Zach. You have seen how far I will go for my sibling. There is nothing you can do that will change my love for you. I need someone I can trust at my back during this wedding."

Zach walked at his friend's side. They were passing near the pool when Tony stopped. He looked longingly at the pool.

"Ah, the water looks good. I have not been swimming since I got to Halencia."

"You want to swim?" Zach grabbed his shirt at the back of the neck and pulled it off over his head. "It's as good a place to talk as any."

He stripped down and dove in. As soon as the water embraced him, he struck out, arm overhead, legs kicking, arm overhead, kick, again and again. He needed the physical exertion to empty his mind of everything but the tracking of laps and the knowledge Tony matched him pace for pace.

Tony tapped his shoulder when they reached fifty. "Let's hit the spa."

Zach slicked a hand over his face and hair and nodded.

In one big surge, he propelled himself up and out of the pool. He walked to the controls for the spa and flicked the switch to generate the jets. After grabbing a couple of towels from a storage ottoman and tossing them on the end of a lounger near the spa, he hit the mini fridge for a couple sodas and joined his friend, sighing as the hot water engulfed him.

"Grazie." Tony took a big swig and closed his blue eyes on a groan as he let his head fall back. "You don't know how good this feels. Hey, I know you're working with the

palace liaison on the bachelor party but can we do it here? Keep it tight and quiet."

"Sure. How about poker, cigars and a nice, aged whiskey?"

"Perfect." Tony laughed. "Now, tell me what's up."

Zach did, he laid it all out, not bothering to spare himself. "The good news is you'll still have a beautiful wedding, but I think I should go."

"It's not like you to run, Zach."

He barked a harsh laugh. "None of this is like me."

"True. You actually let her drive your new car?"

Zach eyed his friend still laying back and letting the jets pound him with bubbles. "Focus, dude. I almost wrecked your wedding."

"But you didn't." Tony straightened and spread his arms along the edge of the spa. He nailed Zach with an intent stare. "You messed up your life instead. You care about Ms. Reeves."

He got a little sick every time he thought about never seeing her again. But that wasn't something he was willing to share.

"She's a good person. And she's really worked hard to give you and Christina an event to be proud of. She found these cool candleholders that merge your two styles—"

"Stop." Tony held up a dripping hand. "I'm going to stop you right there. Dude, you're spouting wedding drivel. Obviously you're in love."

"Shut up." Zach cursed and threw his empty soda can at his friend's head. "You know I don't do love."

"I know you have a big heart or you wouldn't care so much about my future. You deserve to be happy, my friend, and I think the wedding planner makes you happy."

How easily Tony read him. Zach had been happier here in Halencia than as far back as he could remember.

But he'd ruined any chance of finishing the trip in the same vein.

"You deserve happiness, too. That's all I really wanted when I started this mess."

"I appreciate that you want me to be happy. But this is something I have to do. To be honest, the thought of a love match would terrify me. Watching the roller coaster that has been my parents' marriage cured me of that. I will be happy to have a peaceful arrangement with a woman I can admire and respect who will stand by my side and represent my country. Like your Lindsay, Christina is a good woman. We will find our way. You need to do the same."

His Lindsay. That sounded good.

"My being here hurts her. It's best if I leave and let her do her job."

"You mean it's easier. Well, forget it. You're my best man and I'm not letting you off the hook. Relationships take work, Zach."

That's what Lindsay said when she was talking about her mother's many marriages.

"If you care for this woman, and it appears you do, you need to fight for her. Apologize."

"I did. She didn't want to hear it."

Tony cocked a sardonic eyebrow. "Apologize again."

Zach nodded. "Right."

"Tell her you love her."

Love. Zach held his friend's gaze for a long moment, letting unfamiliar emotions—confusion, fear, sadness, exhilaration, joy, hope—rush through him. And finally he nodded. "Right."

A knock sounded at Lindsay's door. She ignored it. Now she was back at the hotel she was fair game for the press who thought nothing about knocking on her door at all hours. So pushy.

Another bang on the door.

She kept her attention on her schedule for the next week. Circled in red at the end of the week was *the* day. The wedding.

The rehearsal was in two days, four days in advance of the actual event because it was the only day everyone could get together. She'd have to see Zach, deal with him. As long as he didn't start apologizing again, she'd be fine.

She knew he'd meant well, that he loved Antonio like a brother. She even admired how far he was willing to go to ensure his friend's happiness.

But she couldn't tolerate the fact that she was acceptable collateral damage.

Why did men find her so dispensable?

She was fairly smart, had a good sense of humor. She worked hard; if anything, too hard. She was honest, kind, punctual. Okay, she wasn't model beautiful, but she wasn't hideous, either.

So what made her so unlovable?

More knocking. Ugh, these guys were relentless.

"Signorina? Signorina?" Mario called out. "Are you there? Mama says you should come."

Oh, gosh. She'd left the poor kid standing out there. Lindsay set her tablet aside and rushed to the door.

"Signorina." Mario greeted her anxiously. "Someone is here to see you. Mama says you must come."

Lindsay gritted her teeth. Zach. Why couldn't he leave her be? "Can you tell him I'm busy?"

His eyes grew big and he frantically shook his head. "No, *signorina*. You must come."

She'd never seen the boy so agitated. Fine, she'd just go tell Zach, once more, to leave her alone. Mario led her downstairs to a room she hadn't seen before. A man stood looking out on the rose garden.

"Zach you need to stop— Oh, sorry." She came to an

abrupt halt when the man turned. Not Zach. "Oh, goodness. Prince Antonio. Your Highness."

Should she curtsy? Why hadn't she practiced curtsying?

"Ms. Reeves, thank you for seeing me." He spoke in slightly accented English and had the bluest eyes she'd ever seen. They twinkled as he took her hand and bowed over it in a gesture only the European did well. "I hope you are not thinking of curtsying. It is entirely unnecessary."

His charm and humor put her instantly at ease. That ability, along with his dark, good looks and the sharp intelligence in those incredible eyes, would serve him well as King of Halencia. She wondered if they'd approached him about running for president.

"You're here to plead his case, aren't you?" Why else would the prince seek her out? He'd showed little to no interest in the wedding plans, even through his advocate.

Anger heated her blood. How dare Zach put her in this position? What could the prince think but that she allowed her personal business to interfere with his wedding preparations? Showing no interest and having none were two different things.

This whole situation just got worse and worse.

"I am." Prince Antonio indicated she should sit.

She perched on the edge of a beige sofa. The prince sat adjacent to her in a matching recliner.

"Your Highness, I can assure you the plans for the wedding are on schedule. And, of course, I will continue to work with Zach as your representative, but anything beyond working together is over. He should not have involved you."

"Please, call me Tony."

Yeah, that wasn't going to happen.

"You are obviously important to Zach and he is important to me, so we should be friendly, *si*?"

She meant to nod; a silent, polite gesture to indicate she heard him. But her head shook back and forth, the denial too instinctive.

"He does not know I am here."

That got her attention. "He didn't send you?"

"No. In fact he planned to leave Halencia, to concede the field to you, as it were. He wanted to make it easier on you."

"Oh." What did she make of that? He was supposed to be best man. Of course he'd have to tell the prince if he planned to leave. Had he already left? Was that why Antonio was here, to tell her she'd be working with a new best man?

Her heart clenched at the thought of never seeing Zach again. The sense of loss cut through the anger and hurt like a sword through butter.

"But he is my best friend. I do not want another for my best man."

"Oh." Huge relief lifted the word up. The feeling of being reprieved was totally inappropriate. He'd used and betrayed her. That hadn't changed. Just as her foolish love for him hadn't changed. It was those softer feelings that tried to sway her now.

Too bad she'd learned she couldn't trust those feelings.

"I have never seen Zach so enamored of a woman. Is it true he let you drive his car?"

She nodded. And she knew why. In piecing things together she figured that must be the trip where Zach had found the pin. She'd been brooding on the trip back and he'd felt guilty.

As he should.

The prince laughed, drawing her attention.

"He really does have it bad. I wish I could have been here to watch this courtship."

"There's been no courtship, Your Highness. Far from

it." She'd stayed strong for two weeks. Why, oh, why had she let his vulnerability get to her? Because she'd fallen for him. Her mom was fond of saying you couldn't control who you fell in love with. Lindsay always considered that a tad convenient.

Turned out it wasn't convenient at all.

"Antonio," he insisted. "I am hoping I can persuade you to cut him some slack. I am quite annoyed with him myself, but I understand what drove him. Zach is not used to having people in his life that matter to him. He is a numbers man. He would have calculated the risk factors and figured those associated with you were tolerable. If the wedding was called off, you would still get paid."

"So he said, but there's more than a paycheck involved here. There's my reputation, as well."

"Which would not suffer if I or Christina called off the wedding."

"It would if it was due to a jinxed wedding, which I can only speculate is what he hoped to achieve."

"Was it such a bad thing he did? Fighting for my happiness?"

"That's not fair." She chided him with her gaze but had to look away as tears welled. She had to clear her throat before speaking. "People don't use the people that matter to them."

Something close to sadness came and went in his blue eyes. "Yes, we do. We are just more up front about it. Zach told me you have the brooch."

It took a second for her brain to switch gears "Yes. It's in my room. It's damaged so I haven't mentioned we found it to Christina yet."

"This is good. If you please, I'd like to take it with me to see if I can get it repaired in time for the wedding."

"Of course. I'll go get it." She quickly made the trip

to her room and returned to hand him the antique piece. "It's really a lovely design."

"Yes, two hearts entwined side by side." Expression thoughtful, he ran his thumb over the crystals. "You can see why it represents true love and longevity."

"Indeed. I hope you are able to get it repaired in time. More, I hope it brings you and Christina much happiness."

"*Grazie*, Ms. Reeves. I can see why Zach has fallen for you. I think you will be good for him."

She sighed on a helpless shrug. "Your Highness."

"Antonio." He bent and kissed her cheek. "As you think about his sins, I wish for you to consider something, as well."

Cautious, she asked, "What's that?"

"Zach does not let anyone drive his cars."

She opened her mouth on a protest.

He stopped her with a raised hand. "Not even me."

She blinked at him as his words sank in, biting her tongue to hold back another ineffective "Oh."

He nodded. "Zach told you of Julia?"

She inclined her head in acknowledgment.

"Ah. Another sign of his affection for you. He does not talk about himself easily. He does not speak of Julia at all. He thought he should have known, that he should have seen through her avarice to her true motives. He's never been as open or as giving since. Until now."

Antonio stepped to the door. "Please do not tell Christina of the brooch. I do not want her to be disappointed if it is not ready in time." With a bow of his head, he took his leave.

Lindsay continued to look at where he'd been. She wrapped her arms around herself, needing to hold on to something. Because everything she believed had just been shaken up.

The Prince of Halencia had come to see her, to plead

Zach's case after he'd tried to sabotage Antonio's wedding. How mixed up was that? If Antonio could overlook Zach's craziness, could—should—Lindsay?

Hurt and anger gripped her in unrelenting talons, digging deep, tearing holes in her soul. She wanted to think this would let up after a couple of weeks of nursing the hurt as it had with Kevin, but this went deeper, stung harder.

What she felt for Kevin had been make-believe; more in her head than anything else. What she felt for Zach came from the heart. And it hadn't stopped just because he'd hurt her. The wrenching sickness in her gut when Antonio'd said Zach planned to leave proved that.

Seeking fresh air, she slipped out of the house and into the dark garden. Lights from the house showed her the way to a path that led to the back of the garden where a bench sat beside a tinkling fountain.

The earthy scent of imminent rain hung in the air. Lindsay looked up. No stars confirmed clouds were overhead.

Great. A storm. Just what she needed.

But it wasn't fear or an uneasiness that took control of her head. Memories of being stuck in Zach's car and staying with him at the farmhouse B and B in Caprese bombarded her.

He'd held her, a stranger, because she was afraid. He'd listened to her sad tale of being scared because her mother always cried during storms. The truth was her father left during a storm and deep down in her child's psyche, she'd feared her mother would leave, too, and Lindsay would be all alone.

Antonio had asked if Zach's fighting for his happiness was such a bad thing.

And the answer was no. She understood Zach's motivation. He'd grown up a victim of his parents' political alliance and the trip to see them en route to Halencia probably trigged the need to intervene on Antonio's behalf.

If this were just the summer fling she'd convinced herself she could handle, she'd forgive him and move on.

But she loved him.

She dipped her fingers in the fountain and swirled the water around. It was still warm from the heat of the day.

She missed the villa. Missed sharing coffee with Zach in the morning seated out on the terrace watching the city come alive down below. She missed his sharp mind and dry humor and his total ignorance of all things wedding-related.

But most of all she missed the way he held her, as if she were the most precious thing in his world.

And that's what she couldn't forgive.

He'd made her believe she mattered. And it had all been a lie.

She'd never been put first before.

Her dad had walked out before she even knew him. And her mother loved her. But Lindsay had always known her mother's wants and needs came first. Even when it was just Lindsay, work came first.

For a few magical days Zach had made her feel as if she was his everything. It showed in the way he'd touched her and by the heat in his eyes. It was in the deference and care he'd demonstrated, the affection and tenderness.

Maybe it was a facade he assumed and that's how he treated all the women in his life—the thought sliced through her brain like shards of broken glass—but it felt real to her. And she couldn't—wouldn't—accept less just to finish out a summer fling.

No more settling. She'd done that with Kevin and learned her lesson. She'd been willing to settle for a fling with Zach because she'd sensed how good it would be between them. And she'd been right. But she loved him, and a fling was no longer enough. She needed honesty, respect and a willingness to put your partner first.

How often had she watched her mother's relationships fall apart because a little work was involved? Her mom was so used to being the center of her world she didn't see that sometimes she needed to make her husband feel he was the center of her world.

Antonio inferred Zach cared for her. He made it sound as if Zach had planned to leave to make things easier for her. More likely he'd wanted out of this whole gig. But there was the bit about letting her drive his car when he never let anyone drive his cars, not even the man he thought of as his brother.

No. Just stop. She pushed the wistful thinking aside as she headed inside. His actions told the story. He didn't love her. He'd proved that when he'd put his friend before her.

Zach had said he liked storms, for him they washed things clean, made them shiny and new, allowing new growth. A good metaphor for him. He was the storm that allowed her to put the horror of Kevin's betrayal behind her. But would her heart survived the tsunami Zach had left in his wake?

CHAPTER TWELVE

TWO DAYS LATER Lindsay walked with Serena toward the Palazzo di Comparino chapel. The rehearsal started in twenty minutes. Nothing was going right today. She should be totally focused on damage control and all she could think about was the fact she'd be seeing Zach in a few minutes.

Her mind and heart played a mad game of table tennis over him. One moment she was strong and resolute in holding out for what she deserved. The next she was sure she deserved him, that his actions proved he cared deeply for the people in his life and she wanted to be one of those people.

"You just got an email from Christina confirming she will not make it to the rehearsal." Serena jogged to keep up.

Lindsay came to a full stop, causing Serena to backtrack. "What about Antonio?"

"He is still delayed at the palace, but he is trying to get here."

"Okay, we're talking a good two hours. Let me call Raffaele to see if he can move dinner up." Before the big blowup between them, she'd suggested to Zach that he host the rehearsal dinner at the villa. With her taking care of the details, he'd been happy to agree.

It was a no-brainer to put Mancini's in charge of the food. Still moving dinner up an hour would be a challenge. But so worth it if it allowed if at least one of the bridal couple to make it to the rehearsal.

"The prince's email said we should start without him."

"Wonderful. Zach will have to act as the groom and can you play the part of Christina?"

"Oh, Lindsay, I am sorry, but I cannot."

"Sure you can. I know these are high-profile people, but all you have to do is walk slowly down the aisle. No biggie."

"No, remember, Papa and I are meeting the glassblower to pick up the last delivery of candleholders. I have to leave in half an hour."

"Oh, yeah, that's tonight. Well, of course. Why should anything workout tonight?"

"Perhaps Papa can go on his own?" Serena made the offer hesitantly. Generous of her since Lindsay knew the two were looking forward to the road trip. A little father-daughter time before Serena went back to school.

"No, you go. I know this trip means a lot to you. I'll work something out."

"You could play the bride," Serena suggested.

"Uh, no. Thanks, but I have to keep things moving." So not a good idea. The very notion of walking down the aisle to Zach in groom mode messed with her head.

And her heart.

The elderly priest had other ideas. He looked like a monk of days gone by and he held her hand and patted the back ever so gently. He spoke softly, listened carefully, and totally took over the rehearsal. Everything must be just so.

He explained what was going to happen, who was going to go where, who stood, who sat, who would leave first and who would follow. He was quite thorough.

Because she found her gaze repeatedly finding Zach, who looked gorgeous in a white shirt and dark sports jacket, Lindsay ran her gaze over the participants. Everyone listened respectfully. Even Queen Valentina and the king, who sat holding hands. Apparently they were in an "on again" phase of their relationship.

The chapel looked lovely. A rainbow of colors fell through the stained-glass windows and standing candle-holders in white wrought-iron lined the walls from the back to the front and across the altar, illuminating the small interior. For the wedding they would be connected with garlands of sunflowers and roses.

And from what she observed, the palace photographer seemed to be doing a good job. He was the only extra person in the room. Serena had quietly made her departure during the priest's soliloquy.

"Come, come." The priest raised his cupped hands as if lifting a baby high. "Let us all take our places. You, young man—" he patted Zach on the shoulder "—will play the part of the groom. And you, *signorina*—" he looked at Lindsay "—will be our bride today."

No, no, no.

Pasting on a serene smile, she politely refused. "I'm sorry, Father, I really need to observe and take notes to ensure a smooth ceremony the day of the wedding."

"*Si, si.* You will observe as the bride. Come, stand here." He motioned to his right.

Zach stood tall and broad on the priest's left.

She swallowed hard and shook her head. She couldn't do it. She couldn't pretend to be Zach's bride when she longed for the truth of the position with all her broken heart.

"Perhaps Elena can play the bride?" she suggested. Hoped.

"Oh, no. Elena has her own role to play as the maid of honor. You are needed, *signorina*. Come."

There was no protesting after that. Plus, others would begin to make note if she made any more of a scene. Clenching her teeth together, she moved forward, holding her tablet in front of her like a shield, looking everywhere but at Zach.

She was fine while the priest directed the action from the altar, but when he stepped away to help people find their spots, Zach narrowed the distance between them by a step then two.

"Please don't start anything here," she implored.

"I'm not." He put his hands in his pockets and rocked on his heels. "How have you been?"

"We should listen to the Father."

"I've missed you."

"Zach, I can't do this here."

"You have to give me something, Lindsay. You asked me to stay away and I have."

She narrowed her eyes at him. "You've texted me several times every day." Crazy things, thoughtful things, odd facts about himself. She'd wanted to delete them without reading them, but she'd read every one, came to look forward to them, especially those that revealed something about him.

"I needed some link to you. I'm afraid I'm addicted."

"You're not going to charm me, Zach." She frantically searched out the priest. When was this show going to get on the road? When she looked back, Zach was closer still.

He bent over her. "You smell so good. Do you miss me at all?"

"Every minute of every day." Her hand went to her mouth. Oh, my dog. Did she just say that out loud?

"Lindsay—"

"The priest is calling me." Heart racing, she escaped to the back of the chapel where the wedding party congregated. The priest nodded when she appeared, as if he'd been waiting for her.

"*Si, si.* We will start with the procession. Just as I described. *Signorina*, you will be last with Signor Rose."

Lindsay took her place by the robust man who made no

effort to disguise his disapproval of Christina's absence. She wasn't Lindsay's favorite person at the moment, either.

Oh, gosh, instead of settling, her heart raced harder. Zach stood at the altar waiting for her to come to him. It felt too real. And, sweet merciful heavens, she wished it were real.

It mattered what he'd done. Yes, he'd meant well. And no, he hadn't known her when he initiated his plan. But it mattered.

The procession began to move. She closed her eyes and stepped forward. Her foot slipped on the uneven ground, so, okay, that wasn't going to work. She opened her eyes and concentrated on the smooth stones of the chapel floor.

He had apologized. And he'd honored her request to stay away. But he hadn't let her forget him, or the time they'd spent together.

Had that been him fighting for her? Or was that wishful thinking?

Suddenly, Mr. Rose stopped and Zach's strong, tanned hand came into view. She fought the urge to put her hands behind her back. All eyes were on her, on them, but this was for Antonio and Christina's wedding. Nobody cared about her or Zach; they didn't care that touching him would be a huge mistake.

She hated how her hand shook as she placed it in his.

He set her hand on his arm and led her to stand in front of the priest. And then he covered her hand with his warm hold and leaned close to whisper, "No need to be nervous. I'm right here by your side."

For some odd reason she actually found his promise reassuring. Facing the priest, not so much.

"Well done, well done." He motioned for the wedding party to be seated. "Lindsay, Zach, if you will face each other. Next I will begin the ceremony. I'll share a few words and then we'll go through the exit procession."

Lindsay turned to face Zach and he took both her hands in each of his. It was the most surreal moment of her life.

The priest began. "Today is a glorious day which the Lord hath made, as today both of you are blessed with God's greatest of all gifts, the gift of abiding love and devotion between a man and woman. All present here today, and those here in heart, wish both of you all the joy, happiness and success the world has to offer—"

"Stop. I can't do this." Lindsay tried to pull away. This hurt too much.

"Lindsay, it's okay." Zach's voice was calm and steady. His hold remained sure and strong as he moved to shield her from the audience. "Father, may we have a moment?"

"Of course, my son." The priest bowed and moved away.

"Breathe, Lindsay. It's going to be okay." Zach leaned over her. "I felt it, too. How right those words were between you and me."

Lindsay clutched at Zach's hands, clinging to him as emotions raged through her heart and head.

"I can't do this. I'm sorry." Aware her behavior embarrassed both her and him, she lifted bleak eyes to meet his gaze. What she saw made the breath catch in her throat.

His eyes were unshielded and in the dark, whiskey depths shone a love so big and so deep it seemed to go on forever. She felt surrounded in a cushion of caring, lifted on a throne of adoration.

"Zach," she breathed.

"I love you, Lindsay." The words echoed everything his eyes already revealed.

Hope slowly swelled through her as her love surged to the surface eager for all his gaze offered. Already weakened, her self-preservation instincts began to crumble as unleashed longing filled her heart.

"I hurt you and I'm more sorry than I can say that I let the fears of my childhood control my common sense when it came to Tony's wedding. You opened my eyes to what I was doing and he hammered it home. But even when I finally accepted the truth and apologized, something still nagged at me, a sense of wrongness that grew rather than diminished."

Behind him she was aware of movement and whispers, reminding her they were not alone. But all she heard, all she saw, was Zach and the raw pain filling eyes that had been overflowing with love just moments ago.

"And then the truth came to me. I couldn't get past how my actions hurt you. I wronged you, not just by disrespecting what you do and by making you work harder, but by putting Tony's needs before yours. That's when I knew the happiness I take in your company and the joy that consumes me when I touch you is actually love."

Now his hands were tight on hers. She ran her thumbs softly over the whites of his knuckles. Everything he'd said was just what she'd longed to hear. She let the last of her concerns melt away.

"Zach." She squeezed his hands. "I love you, too."

Relief flooded his features and he rested his forehead against hers. "Thank God. Because this is bigger and more terrifying than anything I've ever known."

A laugh trilled out of her. "Yes. I'm glad to know I'm not alone."

"You'll never be alone again." He raised his head and his love rained down on her. "Watching you walk down that aisle to me felt more right than anything else in my life. I love you, Lindsay Reeves. Will you marry me?"

"Yes." No hesitation, no need to think. Her misery had come from that same sense of rightness. She longed to spend the rest of her life with this man. "I would love to marry you."

"Right now?" His brown gaze danced with love and mischief.

She blinked at him. "What?"

"Will you marry me right now, in this beautiful chapel we refashioned together?"

Her mind slowly grasped what he wanted, and then her heart soared with excited anticipation. Still, she couldn't get married without her mother. "What about our friends and family?"

"We can have a lavish ceremony back in the States. As big as you want. But I don't want to wait to claim you as mine. So I made sure everyone who truly matters is here."

He stepped back to reveal the chapel filled with people. She saw Louisa sandwiched between Nico and Vincenzo. Raffaele and Daniella sat next to Eva and Mario. Alonso and Serena were here instead of on the road. And many more of the townspeople she'd met and worked with over the past month filled the pews, including the King and Queen of Halencia.

And standing with the grinning priest was Prince Antonio and...her mother.

"Mom?"

"I knew you'd want her here." Zach's hand rested warm and familiar in the small of her back.

"You must have been planning this for days."

"It's the only thing that's kept me sane." He lifted her chin, his mouth settling on hers in restrained urgency. When he raised his head, his eyes gleamed with the heat of desire, the steadfastness of love. "Shall we do this?"

She nodded slowly. "Yes."

Her answer ignited a flurry of activity. Antonio stepped forward while her mother grabbed her hand and hustled her back down the aisle and out the door. In an instant she was in her mom's arms being hugged hard.

"I'm so happy for you, baby. Zach is a force of nature.

If he loves you anywhere near as much as his actions indicate, you will have a long and joyous marriage." She sighed. "For all my marriages, I've never had anyone look at me with so much love."

Lindsay was too excited to have her mother here to care that her special day had circled around to focus on her mom's feelings.

"I'm so glad you're here. You look beautiful." Her mom wore a lovely, pale green silk suit that went well with her upswept brown hair and green eyes. "And you're wrong. Matt looks at you like that. You've just been too focused on yourself to notice."

"Lindsay!" her mother protested, but a speculative glint entered her eyes. "I'll let that slide. We need to get you ready."

"I think I'm as ready as we have time for." Lindsay glanced down at her flowing ivory dress that came to just below her knees in the front and to her ankles in the back and knew she'd been set up. Serena had insisted the dress was perfect for today; business moving into party mode. Of everything she owned this would have been her choice for an impromptu wedding gown.

"Oh, we have time for a few special touches." Darlene pulled Lindsay around the side of the chapel where a full-length, gold-framed mirror leaned against the side of the building, next to it was a garment rack with a flow of tulle over one end and a stack of shelves hanging from the other.

"Something old." From the shelves her mother lifted out a set of pearl-and-sapphire earrings.

"Grandma's earrings." Darlene had worn them for her first wedding and Lindsay recalled saying wistfully she'd wear them at her wedding someday. Her mother had remembered. Her hands shook a little as she put them on.

"Something new." A beaded belt and matching shoes adorned in pearls and crystals shimmered in the late-afternoon sun. While Lindsay traded her sandals for the high-heeled pumps, Darlene stepped behind her and clipped it into place at her waist. They both fit perfectly.

"Something borrowed." Mom smiled. "I saved this because you loved it so much." The tulle turned out to be a full-length veil scalloped on the edges in delicate pearl-infused embroidery. "Close your eyes and face the mirror."

Lindsay's heart expanded; she hadn't realized her mother had been paying such close attention to her reactions through the years. She closed her eyes against a well of tears while Darlene fussed with the veil and the lovely floral hair clip that went with it.

Next she felt a rouge brush dust over her cheeks and some gloss being dabbed on her lips. A tissue caught an escaping tear.

"You can open your eyes."

Lindsay did and was amazed to find a beautiful bride staring back at her. "Mom."

"You're stunning, baby."

Lindsay nodded. She felt stunning and ready to begin her life with Zach.

"Let's go. Your man is waiting."

Rounding the corner of the chapel, she spied the replica of the fountain from the plaza and thought of the wish she'd made with Zach. The wish for true love had been meant for Antonio and Christina. Lindsay supposed she'd been pushing it to make a wish for another couple, but she couldn't be disappointed that fate had chosen to grant true love to her and Zach.

This time when she walked down the aisle her mother escorted her and Lindsay's heart swelled with joy as her gaze locked with Zach's. He'd changed into the suit he'd been wearing when they'd met and she loved the symbolism of the gesture. He knew her so well.

There was no shaking as she placed her hand in his,

just a surety of purpose, a promise to always be there for him. The warmth and steadiness of his grip was the same as it had been earlier and she recognized he'd always be her rock. She suddenly realized something she'd missed when taking in the surprise he'd given her.

"What about your parents?" she whispered.

"They couldn't make it."

"I'm sorry." And angry. His parents didn't deserve him.

"Pixie—" he cupped her cheek "—you're all the family I need."

Her throat closed on a swell of emotion. She swallowed and pledged. "I love you."

"I can't wait for you to be my wife."

"Ahem." Antonio placed his hand on Zach's shoulder. "The priest is waiting."

"Right." Love and anticipation bright in his gaze, he gave the nod. "We're ready, Father."

"We are gathered together on this glorious day which the Lord hath made, to witness the joining of Zachary Sullivan and Lindsay Reeves, who have been blessed with God's greatest of all gifts, the gift of abiding love and devotion between a man and woman…"

* * * * *

"How have you been?" he asked.

Pregnant.

The word was on the tip of Kayla's tongue because, of course, that reality had been at the forefront of her mind since the little plus sign had appeared on the test she'd bought at the pharmacy in Kalispell. But she didn't dare say it aloud, because she knew he couldn't understand when he didn't even remember sleeping with her.

"Fine," she said instead. "And you?"

"Fine," he echoed.

She nodded.

An awkward silence followed.

"I wanted to call you," he said, dropping his voice to ensure that his words wouldn't be overheard by any passersby. "There were so many times I thought about picking up the phone, just because I was thinking about you."

Her heart, already racing, accelerated even more. "You were thinking about me?"

"I haven't stopped thinking about you since we danced at the wedding."

Since we danced?

That was what Trey remembered about that night? She didn't know whether to laugh or cry.

* * *

**Montana Mavericks:
What Happened at the Wedding?**
A weekend Rust Creek Falls will never forget!

MERRY CHRISTMAS
BABY MAVERICK!

BY
BRENDA HARLEN

Published in Great Britain 2015
by Mills & Boon, an imprint of Harlequin (UK) Limited,
Eton House, 18-24 Paradise Road, Richmond, Surrey, TW9 1SR

© 2015 Harlequin Books S.A.

Special thanks and acknowledgement to Brenda Harlen for her contribution to Montana Mavericks: What Happened at the Wedding? continuity.

ISBN: 978-0-263-25189-0

23-1215

Harlequin (UK) Limited's policy is to use papers that are natural, renewable and recyclable products and made from wood grown in sustainable forests. The logging and manufacturing processes conform to the legal environmental regulations of the country of origin.

Printed and bound in Spain
by CPI, Barcelona

Brenda Harlen is a former attorney who once had the privilege of appearing before the Supreme Court of Canada. The practice of law taught her a lot about the world and reinforced her determination to become a writer—because in fiction, she could promise a happy ending! Now she is an award-winning, national best-selling author of more than thirty titles for Mills & Boon. You can keep up-to-date with Brenda on Facebook and Twitter or through her website, www.brendaharlen.com.

For loyal readers of all the Montana Mavericks
series, from Whitehorn to Thunder Canyon
and Rust Creek Falls.

This book is also dedicated to Robin Harlen
(May 8, 1943–December 20, 2014)—
a wonderful father-in-law to me and granddad
to my children. He would be pleased to know that
I finished this book on schedule.

Prologue

Fourth of July

Trey Strickland did a double take when he first spotted Kayla Dalton at the wedding of local rancher Braden Traub to Jennifer MacCallum of Whitehorn.

Although Trey was only visiting from Thunder Canyon, his family had lived in Rust Creek Falls for a number of years while he was growing up. His best friend during that time was Derek Dalton, who had two older brothers, Eli and Jonah, and two younger sisters, twins Kristen and Kayla.

Trey remembered Kayla as a pretty girl with a quiet demeanor and a shy smile, but she'd grown up—and then some. She was no longer a pretty girl, but a beautiful woman with long, silky brown hair, sparkling blue eyes and distinctly feminine curves. Looking at her now, he couldn't help but notice the lean, shapely legs showcased by the short hem of her blue sundress, the tiny waist encircled by a narrow belt, the sweetly rounded breasts hugged by the bodice…and his mouth actually went dry.

She was stunning, sexy and incredibly tempting. Unfortunately, she was still his friend's little sister, which meant that she was off-limits to him.

But apparently, Kayla was unaware of that fact, because after hovering on the other side of the wooden dance floor that had been erected in the park for the occasion, she set down her cup of punch and made her way around the perimeter of the crowd.

She had a purposeful stride—and surprisingly long legs for such a little thing—and he enjoyed watching her move. He was pleased when she came to a stop beside him, looking up at him with determination and just a little bit of trepidation glinting in her beautiful blue eyes.

"Hello, Trey."

He inclined his head in acknowledgment of her greeting. "Kayla."

For some reason, his use of her name seemed to take her aback. "How did you know it was me?"

"I haven't been gone from Rust Creek Falls *that* long," he chided gently.

Soft pink color filled her cheeks. "I meant—how did you know I was Kayla and not Kristen?"

"I'm not sure," he admitted. But the truth was, he'd never had any trouble telling his friend's twin sisters apart. Although identical in appearance, their personalities were completely different, and he'd always had a soft spot for the shyer twin.

Thankfully, she didn't press for more of an explanation, turning her attention back to the dance floor instead. "They look good together, don't they?"

He followed her gaze to the bride and groom, nodded. They chatted a little bit more about the wedding and various other things. A couple of older women circulated through the crowd, carrying cups of wedding punch to distribute to the guests. The beverage was refreshingly cold, so he lifted a couple of cups from the tray and handed one to Kayla.

When they finished their drinks and set the empty cups aside, he turned to her and asked, "Would you like to dance?"

She seemed surprised by the question and hesitated for a moment before nodding. "Yes, I would."

Of course, that was the moment the tempo of the music changed from a quick, boot-stomping tune to a soft, seductive melody. Then Kayla stepped into his arms, and the intoxicating effect of her soft curves against him shot through his veins like the most potent whiskey.

A strand of her hair had come loose from the fancy twist at the back of her head and it fluttered in the breeze, tickling his throat. The scent of her skin teased his nostrils, stirring his blood and clouding his brain. He tried to think logically about the situation—just because she was an attractive woman and he was attracted didn't mean he had to act on the feeling. But damn, it was hard to remember all the reasons why he needed to resist when she fit so perfectly against him.

As the song began to wind down, he guided her to the edge of the dance floor, then through the crowd of people mingling, until they were in the shadows of the pavilion.

"I thought, for a moment, you were going to drag me all the way to your room at the boarding house," Kayla teased.

The idea was more than a little tempting. "I might have," he said. "If I thought you would let me."

She held his gaze for a long minute then nodded slowly. "I would let you."

The promise in her eyes echoed her words. Still, he

hesitated, because this was Kayla—*Derek's sister*—and she was off-limits. But she was so tempting and pretty, and with her chin tipped up, he could see the reflection of the stars in her eyes. Dazzling. Seductive. Irresistible.

He gave in to the desire churning through him and lowered his head to kiss her.

And she kissed him back.

As her lips moved beneath his, she swayed into him. The soft press of her sweet body set his own on fire. He wrapped his arms around her, pulling her closer as he deepened the kiss. She met the searching thrust of his tongue with her own, not just responding to his demands but making her own. Apparently, sweet, shy Kayla Dalton wasn't as sweet and shy as he'd always believed—a stunning realization that further fanned the flames of his desire.

He wanted her—desperately and immediately. And the way she was molded to him, he would bet the ranch that she wanted him, too. A suspicion that was further confirmed when he started to ease his mouth away and she whimpered a soft protest, pressing closer.

"Maybe we should continue this somewhere a little more private," he suggested.

"More private sounds good," she agreed without hesitation.

He took her hand, linking their fingers together, and led her away.

Chapter One

Kayla walked out of the specialty bath shop with another bag to add to the half dozen she already carried and a feeling of satisfaction. It was only the first of December, and she was almost finished with her Christmas shopping. She'd definitely earned a hot chocolate.

Making her way toward the center court of the mall, she passed a long line of children and toddlers impatiently tugging on the hands of parents and grandparents, along with babies sleeping in carriers or snuggled in loving arms. At the end of the line was their destination: Santa.

She paused to watch as a new mom and dad approached the jolly man in the red suit, sitting on opposite sides of him after gently setting their sleeping baby girl—probably not more than a few months old—in his arms. Then the baby opened her eyes, took one look at the stranger and let out an earsplitting scream of disapproval.

While the parents fussed, trying to calm their infant daughter so the impatient photographer could snap a "First

Christmas with Santa" picture, Kayla was suddenly struck by the realization that she might be doing the same thing next Christmas.

Except that there wouldn't be a daddy in her picture, an extra set of hands to help console their unhappy baby. Kayla was on her own. Unmarried. Alone. A soon-to-be single mother who was absolutely terrified about that fact.

She'd always been logical and levelheaded, not the type of woman who acted impulsively or recklessly. Not until the Fourth of July, when she'd accepted Trey's invitation to go back to his room. One cup of wedding punch had helped rekindle her schoolgirl fantasies about the man who had been her brother's best friend. Then one dance had led to one kiss—and one impulsive decision to one unplanned pregnancy.

She owed it to Trey to tell him that their night together had resulted in a baby, but she didn't know how to break the news when he apparently didn't even remember that they'd been together. Even now, five months later, that humiliation made her cheeks burn.

She wasn't at all promiscuous. In fact, Trey was the first man she'd had sex with in three years and only the second in all of her twenty-five years. But Trey had also been drinking the wedding punch that was later rumored to have been spiked with something, and his memory of events after they got back to his room at the boarding house was a little hazy. Kayla had been relieved—and just a little insulted—when he left Rust Creek Falls to return to Thunder Canyon a few weeks later without another word to her about what had happened between them.

But she knew that he would be back again. Trey no longer lived in Rust Creek Falls but his grandparents—Gene and Melba Strickland—still did, and he returned two or three times every year to visit them. It was inevitable that their paths would cross when he came back, and she'd have to tell him about their baby when he did.

Until then, she was grateful that she'd managed to keep her pregnancy a secret from almost everyone else. Even now, only her sister, Kristen, knew the truth. Thankfully, she'd only just started to show, and the cold Montana weather gave her the perfect excuse to don big flannel shirts or bulky sweaters that easily covered the slight curve of her belly.

Regardless of the circumstances of conception, she was happy about the baby and excited about impending motherhood. It was only the "single" part that scared her. And although her family would likely disapprove of the situation, she was confident they would ultimately support her and love her child as much as she did.

The tiny life stirred inside her, making her smile. She loved her baby so much already, so much more than she would have imagined possible, but she had no illusions that Trey would be as happy about the situation. Especially considering that he didn't even remember getting naked and tangling up the sheets with her.

She pushed those worries aside for another day and entered the line in the café. After perusing the menu for several minutes, she decided on a peppermint hot chocolate with extra whipped cream, chocolate drizzle and candy-cane sprinkles. She'd been careful not to overindulge, conscious of having to disguise every pound she put on, but she couldn't hide her pregnancy forever—probably not even for much longer.

Which, of course, introduced another dilemma—how could she tell anyone else about the baby when she hadn't even told the baby's father? And what if he denied that it was his?

The sweet beverage she'd sipped suddenly left a bad taste in her mouth as she considered the possibility.

A denial from Trey would devastate her, but she knew that she had to be prepared for it. If he didn't remember sleeping with her, why would he believe he was the father of her child?

"It really is a small world, isn't it?"

Kayla started at the question that interrupted her thoughts, her face flaming as she glanced up to see Trey's grandmother standing beside her table with a steaming cup of coffee in her hands. Not that Melba Strickland could possibly know what she'd been thinking, but Kayla couldn't help but feel unnerved by the other woman's unexpected presence.

She forced a smile. "Yes, it is," she agreed.

"Do you mind if I join you?"

"Of course not." There weren't many empty chairs in the café, and it seemed silly for each of them to sit alone as if they were strangers. Especially considering that Kayla had known the Stricklands for as long as she could remember.

Melba and Gene were good people, if a little old-fashioned. Or maybe it was just that they were old—probably in their late seventies or early eighties, she guessed, because no one seemed to know for sure. Regardless, their boarding house was a popular place for people looking for long-term accommodations in Rust Creek Falls—so long as they didn't mind abiding by Melba's strict rules, which included a ban on overnight visitors. An explicit prohibition that Kayla and Trey had ignored on the Fourth of July.

"Goodness, this place is bustling." Melba pulled back the empty chair and settled into it. "The whole mall, I mean. It's only the first of December, and the stores are packed. It's as if everyone in Kalispell has decided to go shopping today."

"Everyone in Kalispell and half of Rust Creek Falls," Kayla agreed.

The older woman chuckled. "Looks like you got an early start," she noted, glancing at the shopping bags beneath the table.

"Very early," Kayla agreed, scooping up some whipped cream and licking it off the spoon.

"I love everything about Christmas," Melba confided. "The shopping and wrapping, decorating and baking. But mostly I love the time we spend with family and friends."

"Are you going to have a full house over the holidays this year?" Kayla asked.

"I hope so," the older woman said. "We've had Claire, Levi and Bekka with us since August, and Claire's sisters have hinted that they might head this way for Christmas, which would be great. I so love having the kids around."

Kayla smiled because she knew the *kids* referred to— Bekka excluded—were all adults.

They chatted some more about holiday traditions and family plans, then Melba glanced at the clock on the wall. "Goodness—" her eyes grew wide "—is that the time? I've only got three hours until I'm meeting Gene for dinner, and all I've bought is a cup of coffee."

"Mr. Strickland came into the city with you?"

The older woman nodded. "We've got tickets to see *A Christmas Carol* tonight."

"I'm sure you'll enjoy it," Kayla said. "The whole cast— especially Belle—is fabulous."

Melba smiled at her mention of the character played on the stage by Kayla's sister. "Not that you're biased at all," she said with a wink.

"Well, maybe a little." Her sister had always loved the

theater, but she'd been away from it for a lot of years before deciding to audition for the holiday production in Kalispell. The part of Scrooge's former fiancée wasn't a major role, but it was an opportunity for Kristen to get back on stage, and she was loving every minute of it.

In support of her sister, Kayla had signed on to help behind the scenes. She'd been surprised to discover how much she enjoyed the work—and grateful that keeping busy allowed her to pretend her whole life wasn't about to change.

"Lissa and Gage saw it last week and said the costumes were spectacular."

"I had fun working on them," she acknowledged.

"But you have no desire to wear them onstage?"

"None at all."

"You know, Kristen's ease at playing different roles has some people wondering if she might be the Rust Creek Rambler."

Kayla frowned. "You're kidding."

"Of course, I wouldn't expect you to betray your sister if she is the author of the gossip column."

"She's not," Kayla said firmly.

"I'm sure you would know—they say twins have no secrets from one another," Melba said. "Besides, she's been so busy with the play—and now with her new fiancé—when would she have time to write it?"

"I'm a little surprised there's been so much recent interest in uncovering the identity of the anonymous author, when the column has been around for almost three years now."

"Three and a half," Melba corrected, proving Kayla's point. "I suspect interest has piqued because some people think the Rambler is responsible for spiking the punch at the wedding."

Kayla gasped. "Why would they think that?"

"The events of that night have certainly provided a lot of fodder for the column over the past few months," the older woman pointed out. "It almost makes sense that whoever is writing it might want to help generate some juicy stories."

"That's a scary thought."

"Isn't it?" Melba finished her coffee and set her cup down. "The Rambler also noted that you were up close and personal with my grandson, Trey, on the dance floor at Braden and Jennifer's wedding."

Kayla had long ago accepted that in order to ensure no one ever suspected she was the Rambler, it was necessary to drop her own name into the column every once in a while. Since her turn on the dance floor with Trey hadn't gone unnoticed, the Rambler would be expected to comment on it. As for *up close and personal*—that hadn't come until later, and she had no intention of confiding *that* truth to Trey's grandmother.

Instead, she lifted her cup to her lips—only to discover that it was empty. She set it down again. "We danced," she admitted.

"That's all?" Melba sounded almost disappointed.

"That's all," Kayla echoed, her cheeks flushing. She'd never been a very good liar, and lying to Trey's grandmother—her own baby's great-grandmother—wasn't easy, even if it was necessary.

The older woman sighed. "I've been hoping for a long time that Trey would find a special someone to settle down with. If I had my choice, that special someone would live in Rust Creek Falls, so that he'd want to come back home here—or at least visit more often."

"Maybe he already has someone special in Thunder Canyon," she suggested, aiming for a casual tone.

"I'm sure he would have told me if he did," Melba said. "I know he sees girls, but he's never been serious about any of them. No one except Lana."

"Lana?" she echoed.

Melba's brow furrowed. "Maybe you don't know about Lana. I guess Jerry and Barbara had already moved away from Rust Creek Falls before Trey met her."

Kayla hadn't considered that the father of her baby might be involved with someone else—or that he might even have been in a relationship when he was visiting in the summer. Thinking about the possibility now made her feel sick. She honestly didn't think Trey was that kind of guy—but the reality was that neither of them had been thinking very clearly the night of the wedding.

"Anyway, he met Lana at some small local rodeo, where she won the division championship for barrel racing," the other woman continued. "I think it was actually her horse that caught his eye before she did, but it wasn't too long after that they were inseparable.

"They were together for almost two years, and apparently Trey had even started looking at engagement rings. And then—" Melba shook her head "—Lana was out on her horse, just enjoying a leisurely trail ride, when the animal got spooked by something and threw her."

Kayla winced, already anticipating how the story would end.

"She sustained some pretty serious injuries, and died five days later. She was only twenty-three years old."

"Trey must have been devastated," Kayla said softly, her heart aching for his loss.

"He was," Melba agreed. "We were all saddened by her death—and so worried about him. But then, when I heard that he was dancing with you at the wedding, well,

I have to admit, I let myself hope it was a sign that his heart was healed."

"It was just a dance," she said again.

"Maybe it was," Melba acknowledged, as she pushed her chair away from the table. "And maybe there will be something more when you see him again."

"Did you leave any presents in the mall for anyone else to buy?" Kristen teased, as she helped her sister cart her parcels and packages into the sprawling log house they'd grown up in.

The Circle D Ranch, located on the north side of town, was still home to Kayla, but her twin had moved out a few weeks earlier, into a century-old Victorian home that their brother Jonah had bought after the flood for the purposes of rehabbing and reselling. Since Kristen had started working at the theater in Kalispell, this house, on the south edge of town and close to the highway, had significantly cut down her commuting time—and given her a taste of the independence she'd been craving.

"Only a few," Kayla warned her, dumping her armload of packages onto her bed.

"That one looks interesting," her sister said, reaching for the bag from the bath shop.

Kayla slapped her hand away. "No snooping."

"Then it *is* for me," Kristen deduced.

"You'll find out at Christmas—unless you try to peek again, in which case it's going back to the store."

"I won't peek," her sister promised. "But speaking of shopping, I was thinking that you should plan a trip to Thunder Canyon to check out the stores there."

Kayla gestured to the assortment of bags. "Does it look like I need to check out any more stores?"

Kristen rolled her eyes. "You and I know that your

shopping is done—or very nearly, but no one else needs to
know that. And shopping is only a cover story, anyway—
your *real* purpose would be to see Trey and *finally* tell him
about the secret you've been keeping for far too long."

Just the idea of seeing Trey again made Kayla's tummy
tighten in knots of apprehension and her heart pound with
anticipation. Thoughts of Trey had always had that effect
on her; his actual presence was even more potent.

She *really* liked him—in fact, she'd had a major crush
on him for a lot of years when she was younger. Then
his family had moved away, and her infatuated heart had
moved on. Until the next time he came back to Rust Creek
Falls, and all it would take was a smile or a wave and she
would be swooning again.

But still, her infatuation had been nothing more than a
harmless fantasy—until the night of the wedding. Being
with Trey had stirred all those old feelings up again and
even now there was, admittedly, a part of her that hoped
he'd be thrilled by the news of a baby, sweep her into his
arms, declare that he'd always loved her and wanted to
marry her so they could raise their child together.

Unfortunately, the reality was that five months had
passed since the night they'd spent together, and she hadn't
heard a single word from him after he'd gone back to
Thunder Canyon.

She'd been pathetically smitten and easily seduced, and
he'd been so drunk he didn't even remember being with
her. Of course, another and even more damning possibility was that he *did* remember but was only pretending
not to because he was ashamed by what had happened—
a possibility that did not bode well for the conversation
they needed to have.

"I know I have to talk to Trey," she acknowledged to

her sister now. "But I can't just show up in Thunder Canyon to tell him that I'm having his baby."

"Why not?" Kristen demanded.

"Because."

"You've been making excuses for months," her sister pointed out. "And you don't have many more left—excuses *or* months."

"Do you think I don't realize that?"

Kristen threw her hands up. "I don't know what you realize. I never thought you'd keep your pregnancy a secret for so long—not from me or the rest of your family, and especially not from the baby's father.

"I've tried to be understanding and supportive," her sister continued. "But if you don't tell him, *I* will."

Kayla knew it wasn't an idle threat. "But how can I tell Trey that he's going to be a father when he doesn't even remember having sex with me?"

Kristen frowned. "What are you talking about?"

"When I saw Trey—later the next day—he said that his memory of the night before was hazy."

"A lot of people had blank patches after drinking that spiked punch."

She nodded. "But Trey's mind had apparently blanked out the whole part about getting naked with me."

"Okay, that might make the conversation a little awkward," Kristen acknowledged.

"You think?"

Her sister ignored her sarcasm. "But awkward or not, you have to get it over with. I'd say sooner rather than later, but it's already later."

"I know," Kayla agreed.

"So…shopping trip to Thunder Canyon?" Kristen prompted.

"Three hundred miles is a long way to go to pick up

a few gifts—don't you think Mom and Dad will be suspicious?"

"I think Mom and Dad should be the least of your worries right now."

Kristen was right, of course. Her sister always had a way of cutting to the heart of the matter. "Will you go with me?"

"If I had two consecutive days off from the theater, I would, but it's just not possible right now."

She nodded.

"And no," Kristen spoke up before Kayla could say anything more. "That does not give you an excuse to wait until after the holidays to make the trip."

"I know," she grumbled, because she had, of course, been thinking exactly that—and her sister knew her well enough to know it.

"So when are you going?" Kristen demanded.

"I'll keep you posted. I have to get to the paper."

RUST CREEK RAMBLINGS: THE LA LAWYER TAKES A BRIDE

Yes, folks, it's official: attorney to the stars Ryan Roarke is off the market after being firmly lassoed by a local cowgirl! So what's the next order of business for the California lawyer? Filing for a change of venue in order to keep his boots firmly planted on Montana soil and close to his beautiful bride-to-be, Kristen Dalton. No details are available yet on a date for the impending nuptials, but the good people of Rust Creek Falls can rest assured that they will know as soon as the Rambler does…

Chapter Two

Trey Strickland had been happily living near and working at the Thunder Canyon Resort for several years now, but he never passed up an opportunity to visit his grandparents in Rust Creek Falls. His family had lived in the small town for nearly a decade while he was growing up, and he still had good friends there and always enjoyed catching up with them again.

Now it was December and he hadn't been back since the summer. And whenever he thought of that visit, he thought of Kayla Dalton. Truth be told, he thought of Kayla at other times, too—and that was one of the reasons he'd forced himself to stay away for so long.

He'd slept with his best friend's little sister.

And he didn't regret it.

Unfortunately, he wasn't sure he could say the same about Kayla based on her demeanor toward him the next day. She'd pretended nothing had happened between them, so he'd followed her lead.

He suspected that they'd both acted out of character as a result of being under the influence of the wedding punch. According to his grandmother, the police now believed the fruity concoction had been spiked and were trying to determine who had done so and why.

Trey's initial reaction to the news had been shock, followed quickly by relief that there was a credible explanation for his own reckless behavior that night. But whatever had been in the punch, the remnants of it had long since been purged from his system, yet thoughts and memories of Kayla continued to tease his mind.

As he navigated the familiar route from Thunder Canyon to Rust Creek Falls, his mind wandered. He was looking forward to spending the holidays with his grandparents, but he was mostly focused on the anticipation of seeing Kayla again, and the closer he got to his destination, the more prominent she figured in his thoughts.

He'd had a great time with her at the wedding. Prior to that night, they hadn't exchanged more than a few dozen words over the past several years, so he'd been surprised to discover that she was smart and witty and fun. She was the kind of woman he enjoyed spending time with, and he hoped he would get to spend more time with her when he was in town.

But first he owed her an apology, which he would have delivered the very next morning except that his brain had still been enveloped in some kind of fog that had prevented him from remembering exactly what had happened after the wedding.

He didn't usually drink to excess. Sure, he enjoyed hanging out with his buddies and having a few beers, but he'd long outgrown the desire to get drunk and suffer the consequences the next morning. But whatever had been in that wedding punch, it hadn't given any hint of its incredible potency...

It was morning.

The bright sunlight slipping past the edges of the curtains told him that much. The only other fact that registered in his brain was that he was dying. Or at least he felt as if he was. The pain in his head was so absolutely excruciating, he was certain it was going to fall right off his body—and there was a part of him that wished it would.

In a desperate attempt to numb the torturous agony, he downed a handful of aspirin with a half gallon of water then managed to sit upright without wincing.

The quiet knock on his door echoed like a thunderclap in his head before his grandmother entered. She clucked her tongue in disapproval when she came into his room and threw the curtains wide, the sunlight stabbing through his eyeballs like hot knives.

"Get up and out of bed," she told him. "It's laundry day and I need your sheets."

He pulled the covers up over his head. "My sheets are busy right now."

"You should be, too. Your grandfather could use a hand cleaning out the shed."

He tried to nod, but even that was painful. "Give me half an hour."

He showered and dressed then turned his attention to the bed because, as his grandmother was fond of reminding him, it wasn't a hotel and she wasn't his maid. So he untucked one corner and pulled them off the bed. There was a quiet clunk as something fell free of the sheet and onto the floor.

An earring?

He slowly bent down to retrieve the sparkly teardrop, his mind immediately flashing back to the night before, when he'd stood beside Kayla Dalton on the edge of the dance floor and noticed the pretty earrings that hung from her ears.

Kayla Dalton?

He curled his fingers around the delicate bauble and sank onto the edge of the mattress as other images flashed through his mind, like snapshots with no real connection to any particular time and place. He rubbed his fingers against his temples as he tried to recall what had happened, but his brain refused to cooperate. He'd danced with Kayla—he was sure he remembered dancing with her. And then...

He frowned as he struggled to put the disjointed pieces together. She'd looked so beautiful in the moonlight, and she'd smelled really good. And her lips had looked so temptingly soft. He'd wanted to kiss her, but he didn't think he would have made that kind of move. Because as beautiful and tempting as she was, she was still Derek's sister.

But when he closed his eyes, he could almost feel the yielding of her sweet mouth beneath his, the softness of her feminine curves against his body. Since he'd never had a very good imagination, he could only conclude that the kiss had really happened.

And in order for her earring to end up in his bed—well, he had to assume that Kayla had been there, too.

And what did it say about him that he didn't even remember? Of course, it was entirely possible that they'd gotten into bed together and both passed out. Not something to be particularly proud of but, under the circumstances, probably the best possible scenario.

He tucked the earring in his pocket and finished stripping the bed, shaking out the sheets and pillowcases to ensure there weren't any other hidden treasures inside. Thankfully, there were not. Then he saw the cor-

ner of something peeking out from beneath the bed—and scooped up an empty condom wrapper.

He closed his eyes and swore.

The idea that he'd slept with Kayla Dalton had barely sunk into his brain when he saw her later that day.

She'd been polite and friendly, if a little reserved, and she'd given absolutely no indication that anything had happened between them, making him doubt all of his own conclusions about the night before.

It had taken a long time for his memories of that night to come into focus, for him to remember.

And now that those memories were clear, he was determined to talk to Kayla about what happened that night—and where they would go from here.

Kayla was on her way to the newspaper office when she spotted Trey's truck parked outside the community center.

She'd heard that he was coming back to Rust Creek Falls for the holidays, but she wasn't ready to face him. Not yet. There were still three weeks until Christmas. Why was he here already? She needed more time to plan and prepare, to figure out what to say, how to share the news that she knew would turn his whole world upside down.

The back of his truck was filled with boxes and the doors to the building were open. She'd heard that last year's gift drive for the troops was being affiliated with Thunder Canyon's Presents for Patriots this year, and she suspected that the boxes were linked to that effort.

"Kayla—hi."

She didn't need to look up to know it was Trey who was speaking. It wasn't just that she'd recognized his voice, it was that her heart was racing the way it always did whenever she was near him.

But she glanced up, her gaze skimming at least six feet

from his well-worn cowboy boots to his deep green eyes, and managed a smile. "Hi, Trey."

"This is a pleasant surprise," he said, flashing an easy grin that suggested he was genuinely happy to see her.

Which didn't really make any sense. She not only hadn't seen the guy in four months, she hadn't spoken a single word to him in that time, either. There had been no exchange of emails or text messages or any communication at all. Not that she'd expected any, but her infatuated heart had dared to hope—and been sorely wounded as a result of that silly hope.

"How have you been?" he asked.

Pregnant.

The word was on the tip of her tongue because, of course, that reality had been at the forefront of her mind since she'd seen the little plus sign in the window of the test. But she didn't dare say it aloud, because she knew he couldn't understand the relevance of the information when he didn't even remember sleeping with her.

"Fine," she said instead. "And you?"

"Fine," he echoed.

She nodded.

An awkward silence followed, which they both tried to break at the same time.

"Well, I should—"

"Maybe I could—"

Then they both stopped talking again.

"What were you going to say?" Trey asked her.

"Just that I should be going—I'm on my way to the newspaper office."

"Do you work there?"

She nodded. "I'm a copy editor."

"Oh."

And that seemed to exhaust that topic of conversation.

"It was good to see you, Trey."

"You, too."

She started past him, relieved that this first and undeniably awkward encounter was over. Her heart was pounding and her stomach was a mass of knots, but she'd managed to exchange a few words with him without bursting into tears or otherwise falling to pieces. A good first step, she decided.

"Kayla—wait."

And with those two words, her opportunity to flee with her dignity intact was threatened.

Since she hadn't moved far enough away to be able to pretend that she hadn't heard him, she reluctantly turned back.

He took a step closer.

"I wanted to call you," he said, dropping his voice to ensure that his words wouldn't be overheard by any passersby. "There were so many times I thought about picking up the phone, just because I was thinking about you."

Her heart, already racing, accelerated even more. "You were thinking about me?"

"I haven't stopped thinking about you since we danced at the wedding."

Since we danced?

That was what he remembered about that night?

She didn't know whether to laugh or cry. Under other circumstances, it might have been flattering to think that a few minutes in his arms had made such a lasting impression. Under her current circumstances, the lack of any impression of what had come afterward was hurtful and humiliating.

"I really do have to go. My boss is expecting me."

"What are you doing later?"

She frowned. "Tonight?"

"Sure."

"I'm going to the movies with Natalie Crawford."

"Oh."

He sounded so sincerely disappointed, she wanted to cancel her plans and agree to anything he wanted. Except that kind of thinking was responsible for her current predicament.

"Well, I guess I'll see you around," she said.

He held her gaze for another minute before he nodded. "Count on it."

She walked away, knowing that she already did and cursing the traitorous yearning of her heart.

Trey helped finish unloading the truck, then headed over to the boarding house. He arrived just as his grandmother was slicing into an enormous roast, and the tantalizing aroma made his mouth water.

"Mmm, something smells good."

Melba set down her utensils and wiped her hands on a towel before she crossed the room to envelop him in a warm hug. "I was hoping you'd be here in time for dinner."

"I'd tell you that I ignored the speed limit to make sure of it, but my grandmother would probably disapprove," he teased.

"She certainly would," Melba agreed sternly.

"In time for dinner but not in time to mash the potatoes," Claire said, as she finished her assigned task.

His grandmother let him go and turned him over to his cousin, who hugged him tight.

He tipped her chin up to look into her brown eyes. "Everything good?"

"Everything's great," she assured him, her radiant smile confirming the words.

"Levi?" he prompted, referring to the husband she'd briefly separated from in the summer.

"In the front parlor, playing with Bekka."

"It's so much fun to have a child in the house again," their grandmother said. "I can't wait for there to be a dozen more."

"Don't count on me to add another dozen," Claire warned. "I have my hands full with one."

"At least you've given me one," Melba noted, with a pointed glance in Trey's direction.

He moved to the sink and washed his hands. "What can I do to help with dinner?" he asked, desperate to change the topic of conversation.

"You can get down the pitcher for the gravy." Melba gestured to a cupboard far over her head. "Then round up the rest of the family."

Trey retrieved the pitcher, then gratefully escaped from the kitchen. Of course, he should have expected the conversation would circle back to the topic of marriage and babies during the meal.

"So what's been going on in town since I've been gone?" he asked, scooping up a forkful of the potatoes Claire had mashed.

"Goodness, I don't know where to begin," his grandmother said. "Oh—the Santa Claus parade was last weekend and the Dalton girl got engaged."

The potatoes he'd just swallowed dropped to the bottom of his stomach like a ball of lead. "Kayla?"

His grandmother shook her head. "Her sister, Kristen." Trey exhaled slowly.

He didn't know why he'd immediately assumed Kayla, maybe because he'd seen her so recently and had been thinking about her for so long, but the thought of her with another man—*engaged* to another man—had hit him like a physical jab.

He'd been away from Rust Creek Falls for months—it wasn't just possible but likely that Kayla had gone out with other guys during that time. And why shouldn't she? They'd spent one night together—they didn't have a relationship.

And even if they did, he wasn't looking to fall in love and get married. So why did the idea of her being with another man make him a little bit crazy?

"Who'd she get engaged to?" he asked, picking up the thread of the conversation again.

"Maggie Roarke's brother, Ryan," Claire said.

Trey didn't know Ryan Roarke, but he worked with his brother, Shane, at the Thunder Canyon Resort. And he knew that their sister had moved to Rust Creek Falls the previous year. "Maggie's the new lawyer in town—the one married to Jesse Crawford?"

His grandmother nodded. "She gave up her fancy office in LA to make a life here with Jesse, because they were in love."

"I thought it was because he knocked her up," Gene interjected.

Melba wagged her fork at her husband. "They were in love," she insisted.

"And five months after they got married, they had a baby," Gene told him.

His wife sniffed—likely as much in disapproval of the fact as her husband's recitation of gossip. "What matters is that they're together now and a family with their little girl."

"Speaking of little girls," Trey said, looking at his cousin's daughter seated across from him in her high chair. "I can't get over how much this one has grown in the past few months."

"Like a weed," Levi confirmed, ruffling the soft hair on the top of his daughter's head.

Bekka looked up at him, her big blue eyes wide and adoring.

"No doubt that one's a daddy's girl," Claire noted.

Her husband just grinned.

"Speaking of Kayla Dalton," his grandmother said.

"Who was speaking of Kayla Dalton?" Gene asked.

"Trey was," Melba said.

"We were talking about Bekka."

"Earlier," Melba clarified. "When I mentioned the Dalton girl got engaged, he asked if it was Kayla."

"Hers was just the first name that came to mind," Trey hastened to explain.

"And I wonder why that was," his grandmother mused.

"Probably because he was up close and personal with her at Braden and Jennifer's wedding," Claire teased.

"Anyway," Melba interjected. "I was wondering if you were going to see Kayla while you're in town."

"I already did," he admitted. "She walked by the community center when we were unloading the truck."

His grandmother shook her head as she began to stack the empty plates. "I meant, are you going to go out with her?"

"Melba," her husband said warningly.

"What? Is there something wrong with wanting my grandson to spend time with a nice girl?"

Claire pushed away from the table to help clear it.

"Kayla is a nice girl," Trey confirmed. "But if you've got matchmaking on your mind, you're going to be disappointed—I'm not looking to settle down yet, not with anybody."

"And even if he was, Kayla is hardly his type," Claire noted.

Levi's brows lifted. "Trey has a type?"

"Well, if he did, it wouldn't be the shy wallflower type," his wife said.

"Still waters run deep," their grandmother noted.

"What's that supposed to mean?" Trey asked warily.

"It means that there's a lot more to that girl than most people realize," Melba said, setting an enormous apple pie on the table.

Claire brought in the dessert plates and forks.

"And ice cream," her grandmother said. "Bekka's going to want some ice cream."

"I think Bekka wants her bath and bed more than she wants ice cream," Claire said, noting her daughter's drooping eyelids.

"Goodness, she's falling asleep in her chair."

"My fault," Levi said, pushing his chair away from the table and lifting his daughter from hers. "She missed her nap today when I took her to story time at the library."

"Didn't I tell you to put her down as soon as you got back?" Claire asked.

"You did," he confirmed. "But every time I put her in her crib, she started to fuss."

"Why don't you give in to me whenever I fuss?" his wife wanted to know.

He kissed her softly. "Are you saying I don't?"

"Not *all* the time," she said, a small smile on her lips as they headed out of the dining room.

"I guess they've worked things out," Trey mused, stabbing his fork into the generous slab of pie his grandmother set in front of him.

"I really think they have," Melba confirmed. "There will still be bumps in the road—no relationship is ever without them—but over the past few months, they've proven that they are committed to one another and their family."

"If the kid doesn't want ice cream, no one else gets ice cream?" Gene grumbled, frowning at his naked pie.

"You don't need ice cream," his wife told him.

"You didn't need those new gloves you came home with when you were out Christmas shopping last week, but you bought them anyway."

Trey fought against a smile as he got up to get the ice cream. His grandparents' bickering was as familiar to him as the boarding house. They were both strong-willed and stubborn but, even after almost sixty years of marriage, there was an obvious affection between them that warmed his heart.

After they'd finished dessert, his grandmother asked, "So what are your plans for the evening?"

"Do they still show movies at the high school on Fridays?" Trey had spent more than a few evenings in the gymnasium, hanging with his friends or snuggling up to a pretty girl beneath banners that declared, "Go Grizzlies!" and had some fond memories of movie nights at the high school.

"Friday *and* Saturday nights now," she told him.

"Two movie nights a week?" he teased. "And people say there's nothing to do in Rust Creek Falls."

His grandmother narrowed her gaze. "We might not have all the fancy shops and services like Thunder Canyon, but we've got everything we need."

"You're right," he said. "I shouldn't have implied that this town was lacking in any way—especially when two of my favorite people in the world live here."

She swatted him away with her tea towel. "Go on with you now. Take a shower, put on a nice shirt and get out of here."

Trey did as he was told, not only to please his grandmother but because it occurred to him that the high school was likely where Kayla and Natalie were headed.

Chapter Three

Kayla gazed critically at her reflection in the mirror and sighed as she tugged her favorite Henley-style shirt over her head again and relegated it to the too-tight pile. The nine pounds she'd gained were wreaking havoc with her wardrobe.

Of course, it didn't help that most of the styles were slim-fitting and she was no longer slim. Not that she was fat or even visibly pregnant, but it was apparent that she'd put on some weight, and covering her body in oversize garments at least let her disguise the fact that the weight was all in her belly.

She picked up the Henley again, pulled it on, then put on a burgundy-and-navy plaid shirt over the top. Deciding that would work, she fixed her ponytail, dabbed on some lip gloss and grabbed her keys.

"Where are you going tonight?" her mother asked when Kayla came down the stairs.

She'd mentioned her plans at dinner—when she'd asked her dad if she could take his truck into town—but her mother obviously hadn't been paying attention. Ever since Ryan put a ring on Kristen's finger, her mother had been daydreaming about the wedding.

"I'm meeting Natalie at the high school," she said again. "We're going to see *A Christmas Story* tonight."

"Is it just the two of you going?" her mother pressed.

"No, I'm sure there will be lots of other people there."

"Really, Kayla, I don't know why you can't just give a simple answer to a simple question," Rita chided.

"Sorry," she said automatically. "And yes—it's just me and Natalie tonight. We're not sneaking out to meet boys behind the school."

"Your turn will come."

"My turn for what?" She was baffled by the uncharacteristically gentle tone as much as the words.

"To meet somebody."

"I'm not worried about meeting somebody or not meeting somebody," she assured her mother.

"I had sisters, too," Rita said. "I know it's hard when exciting things are happening in their lives and not your own."

"I'm happy for Kristen, Mom. Genuinely and sincerely."

"Well, of course you are," she agreed. "But that doesn't mean you can't be a little envious, too." A career wife and mother, Rita couldn't imagine her daughters wanting anything else.

She'd been appalled by Kristen's desire to study theater—worried about her daughter associating with unsavory movie people. She'd been so relieved when her youngest child graduated and moved back home to teach drama. Unfortunately, Kristen had faced numerous roadblocks in her efforts to get a high school production off the ground, causing her to turn her attention to the community theater in Kalispell.

Kayla was actually surprised their mother had approved of Kristen's engagement to a Hollywood lawyer. But Ryan had fallen in love with Montana as well as Kristen and was planning to give up his LA practice—as his sister, Maggie, had done just last year when she moved to Rust Creek Falls to marry Jesse Crawford.

But, of course, now that Kristen and Ryan were engaged, it was only natural—to Rita's way of thinking—that Kayla would want the same thing. Her mother would be shocked to learn that her other daughter's life was already winding down a very different path.

"Getting out tonight will be good for you," Rita said to Kayla now. "Who knows? You might even meet someone at the movies."

Meet someone? Ha! She already knew everyone in Rust Creek Falls, and even if she did meet someone new and interesting who actually asked her to go out on a date with him, there was no way she could say yes. Because there was no way she could start a romance with another man while she was carrying Trey's baby.

And no way could she be interested in anyone else when she was still hopelessly infatuated with the father of her child.

"I'm meeting Natalie," she said again. Then, before her mother could say anything else to continue the excruciating conversation, Kayla kissed her cheek. "Don't wait up."

When Kayla arrived, Natalie was standing outside the main doors, her hands stuffed into the pockets of her coat, her feet—tucked into a sleek pair of high-heeled boots that looked more fashionable than warm—kicking the soft snow.

"Am I late?" Kayla asked.

"No, I was probably early," Natalie admitted. "I needed to get out of the house and away from all the talk about weddings."

She nodded her understanding as she reached for the door handle. Natalie's brother had also recently gotten engaged. "When are Brad and Margot getting married?"

"That was one of the topics of discussion. Of course, Brad was married before, so he just wants whatever Margot wants. But Margot lost her mother almost three years ago, and her father's been AWOL since the infamous poker game, so as much as she's excited about starting a life with my brother, I think it's hard for her to be excited about the wedding, and I don't think my mother's being very sensitive about that."

"Believe me, I understand about insensitive mothers," Kayla told her friend.

They paid their admission at the table set up in the foyer for that purpose then made their way toward the gymnasium.

"I always get such a creepy feeling of déjà vu when I'm in here," her friend admitted.

"I know what you mean," Kayla agreed. "It doesn't help that Mrs. Newman—" their freshman physical education teacher "—works at the concession stand."

Natalie nodded her agreement. "Even when I count out the exact change for her, she gives me that perpetual look of disapproval, like I've just told her I forgot my gym clothes."

Kayla laughed. She was glad she'd let her friend drag her out tonight. Not that much dragging was required. Kayla had been feeling in a bit of a funk and had happily accepted Natalie's invitation. Of course, it didn't hurt that

A Christmas Story was one of her all-time favorite holiday movies.

"Oh, look," she said, pointing to the poster advertising a different feature for Saturday night. "We could come back tomorrow for *The Santa Clause*."

"Well, I'm free," Natalie admitted. "Which tells a pretty sad tale about my life."

"Actually, I'm not," Kayla realized.

"Hot date?"

"Ha. I'm helping out at the theater in Kalispell tomorrow night."

"Well, even working in the city has to be more exciting than a night off in this town," Natalie said. Then she stopped dead in her tracks. "Oh. My. God."

"What?" Kayla demanded, as alarmed by her friend's whispered exclamation as the way Natalie's fingers dug into her arm.

"Trey Strickland is here."

Her heart leaped and crashed against her ribs as she turned in the direction her friend was looking.

Yep, it was him.

Not that she really believed Natalie might have been mistaken, but she'd hoped. After a four-month absence, she'd now run into him twice within hours of his return to town. Whether his appearance here was a coincidence or bad luck, it was an obvious sign to Kayla that she wouldn't be able to avoid him while he was in Rust Creek Falls.

Natalie waved a hand in front of her face, fanning herself as she kept her attention fixed on the ginger-haired, broad-shouldered cowboy. "That man is *so* incredibly yummy."

Kayla had always thought so, too—even before she'd experienced the joy of being held in his arms, kissed by his lips, pleasured by his body. But she had no intention of sharing any of that with her friend, who she hadn't realized harbored her own crush on the same man. "Should we get popcorn?" she asked instead.

"I'd rather have man candy," Natalie said dreamily.

Kayla pulled a ten-dollar bill out of the pocket of her too-tight jeans and tried to ignore the reason her favorite denim—and all of her other clothes—were fitting so snugly in recent days. "I'm going for popcorn."

"Can you grab me a soda, too?" Natalie asked, her gaze still riveted on the sexy cowboy as he made his way toward the gym doors.

"Sure."

"I'll go find seats," her friend said, following Trey.

Kayla just sighed and joined the line for concessions. She couldn't blame her friend for being interested, especially when she'd never told Natalie what had happened with Trey on the Fourth of July, but that didn't mean she wanted to be around while the other woman made a play for him.

When she entered the gymnasium with the drinks and popcorn, she found Natalie in conversation with Trey. Though her instinct was to turn in the opposite direction, she forced her feet to move toward them.

Trey's gaze shifted to her and his lips curved. "Hi, again."

"Hi," she echoed his greeting, glancing around. "Are you here with someone?"

Please, let him be here with someone.

But the universe ignored her plea, and Trey shook his head.

"Why don't you join us?" Natalie invited, patting the empty chair on her left.

"I think I will," he said, just as an elderly couple moved toward the two vacant seats beside Natalie.

Trey stepped back, relinquishing the spot she had offered to him. Kayla didn't even have time to exhale a sigh of relief before he moved to the empty seat on the other side of *her*.

She was secretly relieved that her friend's obvious maneuverings had been thwarted, but she didn't know how she would manage to focus on the screen and forget that he was sitting right beside her for the next ninety-four minutes.

In fact, she didn't even make it through four minutes, because she couldn't take a breath without inhaling his clean, masculine scent. She couldn't shift in her seat without brushing against him. And she couldn't stop thinking about the fact that her naked body had been entwined with his.

She forced her attention back to the screen, to the crowd gathered around the window of Higbee's Department Store to marvel at the display of mechanized electronic joy and, of course, Ralphie, wide-eyed and slack-jawed as he fixated on "the holy grail of Christmas gifts—the Red Ryder two hundred shot range model air rifle."

"Are you going to share that popcorn?" Trey whispered close to her ear.

"I am sharing it," she said. "With Natalie."

But deeply ingrained good manners had her shifting the bag to offer it to him.

"Thanks." He dipped his hand inside.

She tried to keep her attention on the movie, but it was no use. Even Ralphie's entertaining antics weren't capable of distracting her from Trey's presence. It was as if every nerve ending in her body was attuned to his nearness.

It probably didn't help that they were in the high school—the setting of so many of her youthful fantasies. So many times she'd stood at her locker and watched him walk past with a group of friends, her heart racing as she waited for him to turn and look at her. So many times she'd witnessed him snuggled up to a cheerleader on the bleachers, and she'd imagined that she was that cheerleader.

Back then, she would have given almost anything to be in the circle of his arms. She would have given almost anything to have him just smile at her. She'd been so seriously and pathetically infatuated that just an acknowledgment of her presence would have fueled her fantasies for days, weeks, months.

When his family had moved away from Rust Creek Falls, she'd cried her heart out. But even then, she'd continued to daydream, imagining that he would come back one day, unable to live without her. She might have been shy and quiet, but deep inside, she was capable of all the usual teenage melodrama—and more.

Sitting beside him now, in the darkened gym, was a schoolgirl fantasy come to life. But he wasn't just sitting in the chair beside her, he was so close that his thigh was pressed against hers. And when he reached into the bag of popcorn she was holding, his fingertips trailed deliberately over the back of her hand.

At least she assumed it was deliberate, because he didn't pull his hand away, even when her breath made an audible catch in her throat.

Natalie glanced at her questioningly.

She cleared her throat, as if there was something stuck in it, and picked up her soda.

She felt a flutter in her tummy that she dismissed as butterflies—a far too usual occurrence when she was around Trey. Then she realized it was their baby—the baby he didn't know about—and her eyes inexplicably filled with tears.

You have to tell him.

The words echoed in the back of her mind, an unending reel of admonishment, the voice of her own conscience in tandem with her sister's.

He has a right to know.

You-have-to-tell-him-he-has-a-right-to-know-you-have-to-tell-him-he-has-a-right-to-know-you-have-to—

"Excuse me," she whispered, thrusting the bag of popcorn at Trey and slipping out of her seat to escape from the gymnasium.

The bright lights of the hallway blinded her for a moment, so that she didn't know which way to turn. She'd spent four years in these halls, but suddenly she couldn't remember the way to the girls' bathroom.

She leaned back against the wall for a minute to get her bearings, then made her way across the hall. Thankfully, the facility was empty, and she slipped into the nearest stall, locked the door, sat down on the closed toilet seat and let the tears fall.

In recent weeks, her emotions had been out of control. She'd been tearing up over the silliest things—a quick glimpse of an elderly couple holding hands, the sight of a mother pushing her child in a stroller, even coffee commercials on TV could start the waterworks. Crying in public bathrooms hadn't exactly become a habit, but this wasn't the first time for her, either.

No, the first time had been three months earlier. After purchasing a pregnancy test from an out-of-the-way pharmacy in Kalispell, she'd driven to the shopping center and taken her package into the bathroom. Because no way could she risk taking the test home, into her parents' house, and then disposing of it—regardless of the result—with the rest of the family's trash.

She remembered every minute of that day clearly. The way her fingers had trembled as she tore open the box, how the words had blurred in front of her eyes as she read and re-read the instructions to make sure she did everything correctly.

After she'd managed to perform the test as indicated, she'd put the stick aside—on the back of the toilet—and counted down the seconds on her watch. When the time was up, she picked up the stick again and looked in the little window, the tears no longer blurring her eyes but sliding freely down her cheeks.

She hadn't bothered to brush them away. She couldn't have stopped them if she'd tried. Never, in all of her twenty-five years, had she imagined being in this situation. Pregnant. Unmarried.

Alone.

She was stunned and scared and completely overwhelmed.

And she was angry. At both herself and Trey for being careless. She didn't know what he'd been thinking, but she'd been so caught up in the moment that she'd forgotten all about protection until he was inside of her. Realization seemed to have dawned on him at the same time, because he'd immediately pulled out of her, apologizing to her, promising that he didn't have unprotected sex—ever.

Then he'd found a condom and covered himself with it before he joined their bodies together again. She didn't know if it was that brief moment of unprotected penetration that had resulted in her pregnancy, or if it was just a statistical reality—if she was one of the two percent of women who was going to be a mommy because condoms were only ninety-eight percent effective in preventing pregnancy.

Of course, the reason didn't matter as much as the reality: she was pregnant. She didn't tell anyone because she didn't know what to say. She didn't know how she felt about the situation—because it was easier to think about her pregnancy as a situation than a baby.

She found an obstetrician in Kalispell—because there was no way she could risk seeing a local doctor—and then, eighteen weeks into her pregnancy, she had an ultrasound.

Everything changed for her then. Looking at the monitor, seeing the image of her unborn child inside of her, made the existence of that child suddenly and undeniably real. That was when she finally accepted that she wasn't just pregnant—the unexpected consequence of an impulsive night in Trey's bed—she was going to have a baby.

Trey's baby.

And in that moment, when she first saw the tiny heart beating, she fell in love with their child.

But he still didn't have a clue about the consequences of the night they'd spent together—or possibly even that they had spent the night together— and she'd resolved to tell him as soon as possible. He had a right to know about their baby. She didn't know how he would respond to the news, but she knew that he needed to hear it.

Of course, at the time of her ultrasound, he'd been in Thunder Canyon, three hundred miles away. So she'd decided to wait until he came back to Rust Creek Falls. And another three-and-a-half weeks had passed. Now he was here—not just in town but in the same building. And she had no more excuses.

She had to tell him about their baby.

She pulled a handful of toilet paper from the roll and wiped at the wet streaks on her cheeks. The tiny life inside her stirred again. She laid a hand on the slight curve of her tummy.

I've always tried to do what I think is best for you, even when I don't know what that is. And I'm scared, because I don't know how your daddy's going to react to the news that he's going to be a daddy. I will *tell him. I promise, I* will. *But I'm not going to walk into the high school gym in the middle of movie night and make a public announcement, so you're going to have to be patient a little longer.*

Of course, there was no way the baby could hear the words of reassurance that were audible only inside of her head, but the flutters inside her belly settled.

"Everything okay?" Natalie whispered, when Kayla had returned to her seat inside the darkened gym.

She nodded. "My phone was vibrating, so I went outside to take the call."

Lying didn't come easily to her, but it was easier with her gaze riveted on the movie screen. Thankfully, Natalie accepted her explanation without any further questions.

When the credits finally rolled, people began to stand up and stack their chairs. Trey solicitously took both Kayla's and Natalie's along with his own.

"I'm sorry," Kayla said to her friend, taking advantage of his absence to apologize—although she wasn't really sorry.

"For what?"

"Because I know you wanted to sit next to him."

Natalie waved away the apology. "*I* should be sorry," she said. "When I invited him to join us, I completely forgot that you two were together at the wedding—"

"We weren't together," Kayla was quick to interject.

"Even the Rust Creek Rambler saw the two of you on the dance floor."

"One dance doesn't equal together."

"Well, even if that's true—" and her friend's tone warned Kayla that she wasn't convinced it was "—I'm getting the impression that Trey is hoping for something more."

She shook her head. "You're imagining things."

"I am *not* imagining the way he's looking at you," Natalie said, her gaze shifting beyond her friend.

Kayla didn't know what to say to that. She didn't know how—or even if—Trey was looking at her because she was deliberately avoiding looking at him, afraid that any kind of eye contact would somehow give away all of her secrets to him.

"Which means I have to find myself a different cowboy," Natalie decided.

"Do you have anyone specific in mind?" Kayla asked, happy to shift the conversation away from Trey—and especially talk of the two of them being together at the wedding.

"I'm willing to consider all possibilities," Natalie said. "And since it's still pretty early, why don't we go to the Ace in the Hole to grab a drink?"

She shuddered at the thought. "Because that place on a Friday night is a bad idea."

The local bar and grill was more than a little rough around the edges at the best of times—and a Friday night was never the best of times as the cowboys who worked so hard during the week on the local ranches believed in partying just as hard on the weekends. As a result, it wasn't unusual for tempers to flare and fists to fly, and Kayla had no interest in that kind of drama tonight.

Natalie sighed. "You're right—how about a hot chocolate instead?"

That offer was definitely more tempting. Though Kayla hadn't experienced many cravings, and thankfully nothing too unusual, the baby had definitely shown signs in recent weeks of having a sweet tooth, and she knew that hot chocolate would satisfy that craving. But, "I thought you had to open up the store in the morning."

Natalie waved a hand dismissively. "Morning is a long time away."

"Hot chocolate sounds good," she admitted.

"It tastes even better," Trey said from behind her.

Kayla thought he'd left the gym after helping to stack the chairs, but apparently that had been wishful thinking on her part.

"But where can you get hot chocolate in town at this time of night?" he asked.

"Daisy's," Natalie told him. "It's open late now, with an expanded beverage menu and pastries to encourage people to stay in town rather than heading to the city."

"I always did like their hot chocolate," Trey said. "Do you mind if I join you?"

"Of course not," Natalie said, buttoning up her coat as they exited the gym.

They said "hello" to various townspeople as they passed them in the halls, stopping on the way to chat with some other friends from high school. A few guys invited Trey to go for a beer at the Ace in the Hole, but he told them that he already had plans. When they finally made their escape, Natalie pulled her phone out of her pocket and frowned at the time displayed on the screen. "I didn't realize it was getting to be so late."

Kayla narrowed her gaze on her friend, wondering how it had gone from "still pretty early" to "so late" in the space of ten minutes.

"I think I should skip the hot chocolate tonight," Natalie decided. "I have to be up early to open the store in the morning."

"You were the one who suggested it," Kayla pointed out.

"I know," her friend agreed. "And I hate to bail, but there's no reason that you and Trey can't go without me."

Kayla glanced at Trey. "Wouldn't you rather go to the Ace in the Hole with your friends than to Daisy's with me?"

"Let me see—reminiscing about high school football with a bunch of washed-up jocks or making conversation with a pretty girl?" He winked at her. "It seems like a no-brainer to me."

"Great," Natalie said, a little too enthusiastically.

Then she leaned in to give Kayla a quick hug and whisper in her ear. "I'll call you tomorrow to hear all of the juicy details, so make sure there *are* some juicy details."

Chapter Four

"She's not very subtle, is she?" Trey asked Kayla, after her friend had gone.

"Not at all," she agreed. "And if you want to skip the hot chocolate—"

"I don't want to skip the hot chocolate," he told her.

"Okay."

It was one little word—barely two syllables—which made it hard for him to read her tone to know what she was thinking. But her spine was stiff and her hands stuffed deep in the pockets of her jacket, clear indications that she was neither behind her friend's machinations nor pleased by them.

"Do *you* want to skip the hot chocolate?" he asked her.

Her hesitation was so brief it was barely noticeable before she replied, "I never say no to hot chocolate."

Despite her words, he suspected that she wanted to but couldn't think of a way to graciously extricate herself from the situation that had been set up by her friend.

Was she avoiding him? Was she uneasy because of what had happened between them in the summer? He couldn't blame her if she was, especially since they hadn't ever talked about that night. Not since that first day, anyway, before he'd had a chance to really remember what happened.

He didn't want her to feel uncomfortable around him. Aside from the fact that her brother was one of his best friends, Rust Creek Falls was a small town, and it was inevitable that they would bump into one another. For that reason alone, they needed to clear the air between them.

"I'd offer to drive, but I walked over," he told her.

His grandparents' boarding house being centrally located, there wasn't anything in the town that wasn't within walking distance. Which included Daisy's Donuts, only a block over from the high school.

"We'll go in my truck," she said, because driving was preferable to walking even that short distance in the frigid temperatures that prevailed in Montana in December.

She unlocked the doors with the electronic key fob, and he followed her to the driver's side and opened the door to help her in. It was a big truck, and she had to step up onto the running board first. He cupped her elbow, to ensure she didn't lose her balance, and she murmured a quiet "Thanks."

By the time he'd buckled himself into the passenger side, she had the truck in gear. Either she was really craving hot chocolate or she didn't want to be alone with him for a minute longer than necessary. He suspected it was the latter.

He wasn't sure if she was sending mixed signals or if he was just having trouble deciphering them. When he'd stepped out of the community center earlier that afternoon and saw her walking past, he'd been sincerely pleased to see her. His blood had immediately heated and his heart had pounded hard and fast inside his chest. And he'd thought that she was happy to see him, too.

In that first moment, when their eyes had met, he was sure there had been a spark in her blue gaze and a smile on her lips. Then her smile had faltered, as if she wasn't sure that she should be happy to see him. Which confirmed to him that they needed to talk about the Fourth of July.

As she parked in front of Daisy's Donuts, he realized this probably wasn't the place to do so. Not unless they wanted to announce their secret to all of Rust Creek Falls, which he was fairly certain neither of them did.

"Why don't you grab a table while I get our drinks?" he suggested.

"Okay," she agreed.

"Any special requests?" He glanced at the board. "Dark chocolate? White chocolate? Peppermint? Caramel?"

"Regular," she said. "With extra whipped cream."

"You got it."

He decided to have the same and added a couple of gingerbread cookies to the order, too.

"I thought you might be hungry," he told her, setting the plate of cookies between them. "Considering that I ate all of your popcorn."

"I'm not hungry," she said, accepting the mug he slid across the table to her. "But I love gingerbread cookies. My mother used to make a ton of them at Christmastime, but there were never any left when company came over because Kristen and I used to sneak down to the kitchen and eat all of them."

"You said she used to make them," he noted. "She doesn't anymore?"

"She makes us do it now. She decided that since we eat most of them anyway, we should know how to make them."

He nudged the plate toward her, silently urging her to take a cookie. She broke the leg off one, popped it into her mouth.

"Good?"

She nodded.

"My grandmother used to make gingerbread houses— one for each of the grandkids to decorate. When I think back, she must have spent a fortune on candy, and we ate more than we put on the buildings." He broke a piece off the other cookie, sampled it. "I wonder if she'd make one for me this year, if I asked."

"I'm sure she'd make anything you wanted," Kayla said.

"What makes you say that?" he asked curiously.

"Three words." She broke off the gingerbread boy's other leg. "Vanilla almond fudge."

He smiled, thinking of the plate he'd found on his bedside table—neatly wrapped in plastic and tied with a bow. "She does spoil me," he admitted.

Kayla smiled back, and their eyes held for a brief second before she quickly dropped her gaze away.

The group of teenagers who had been sitting nearby got up from their table, put on their coats, hats and gloves and headed out the door. There were still other customers around, but no one close enough that he needed to worry about their conversation being overheard.

"Did I do something wrong?"

She looked up again. "What are you talking about?"

"I'm not sure," he admitted. "But I get the feeling that you're not very happy to see me back in town."

She sipped her cocoa and shrugged. "Your coming back doesn't have anything to do with me."

"Maybe it does," he said. "Because I haven't stopped thinking about you since I left Rust Creek Falls in the summer."

She blinked. "You haven't?"

"I haven't," he confirmed, holding her gaze.

"Oh."

He waited a beat, but she didn't say anything more. "It would be nice to hear that you've thought about me, too…if you have."

She glanced away, color filling her cheeks. "I have."

"And the night of the wedding?" he prompted.

He watched, intrigued, as the pink in her cheeks deepened.

"You mean the night we were both drinking the spiked punch?" she asked.

"Is that the only reason you started talking to me that night?"

"Probably," she admitted. "I mean—I would have wanted to talk to you, but I wouldn't have had the nerve to start a conversation."

"And the kiss? Was that because of the punch, too?"

"*You* kissed *me*," she said indignantly.

"You kissed back pretty good," he told her.

She remained silent, probably because she couldn't deny it.

"And then you went back to my room with me," he prompted further.

She nodded slowly, almost reluctantly.

"Are you sorry that you did?"

She kept her gaze averted from his, but she shook her head.

"I'm not sorry, either," he told her. "The only thing I regret is that it took me so long to remember what happened."

"Lots of people had memory lapses after that night— because of the punch," she said.

"Do you really think that what happened between us only happened because of the punch?"

"Don't you?"

He frowned at her question. "I don't know how drunk *you* were, but I can assure you, there isn't enough alcohol in the world to make me get naked with a woman I'm not attracted to."

Her perfectly arched brows drew together. "You were attracted…to me?"

"Why do you find that so hard to believe?"

"I'm the quiet one. Kristen's the pretty one."

"You're identical twins."

She lifted a shoulder. "You seem to be able to tell us apart."

"There are some subtle differences," he acknowledged. "Your eyes are a little bit darker, your bottom lip is just a little bit fuller and you have a mole on the top of your left earlobe."

"I never would have guessed you were so observant," she said, blushing a little.

"I didn't realize how much I observed you," he admitted. "Are you worried now that I'm a stalker?"

She shook her head. "No, I'm not worried you're a stalker."

"Then you should trust me when I say that you're a beautiful woman, Kayla. Beautiful, sweet, smart and sexy."

"Sexy?"

"*Incredibly* sexy," he assured her.

She folded her arms over her chest. "Is *that* what this is about?"

"What?" he asked warily.

"You figure that since I fell into your bed so easily that

night, I'd be eager to do so again. Is that the real reason you wanted to see me?"

He held up his hands as his head spun with the effort of following her convoluted logic. "Whoa! Wait a minute."

"*You* wait a minute," she said. "I'm not so pathetic that I'm willing to go home with any guy who says a few kind words to me."

His jaw dropped. "*What* are you talking about?"

"I'm talking about your apparent effort to lure me back into your bed."

"*I* didn't lure you the first time," he reminded her. "*You* were the one who approached me at the wedding. *You* were the one who rubbed your body against mine on the dance floor. And *you* were the one who said you'd go back to my room with me."

She dropped her face into her hands. "Ohmygod—I did do all of that, didn't I? It was all my fault."

Her reaction seemed a little extreme to him, but she sounded so distraught, he couldn't help wanting to console her. "I'm not sure there's any need to assign blame," he said. "Especially considering that I didn't object to any of it."

"I really am pathetic."

He reached across the table and pulled her hands away from her face. "No, you're not."

"I am," she insisted. "I had such a crush on you in high school."

"You did?"

"And you didn't even know I existed."

"I knew you existed," he said. "But you were Derek's little sister."

She nodded. "And I guess…when you asked me to dance… I got caught up in the high school fantasy again."

"You had fantasies about me?" He was intrigued by the possibility.

"You played the starring role in all of my romantic dreams."

"I'm flattered," he told her sincerely. "But why are you telling me this now?"

Why was *she telling him this*? Kayla asked herself the same question.

Because she was nervous, and she always babbled when she was nervous. Of course, now that she'd confided in him about her schoolgirl crush, she could add *mortified* to the list of emotions that were clouding her brain.

"I'm trying to explain…and apologize."

"I don't want an apology."

"But I threw myself at you," she said miserably.

And, as a result of her actions, she was now pregnant with his baby. Which was what she was trying to work up to telling him, but she was sure that when she did, he would hate her—and she really didn't want him to hate her.

"It wasn't like that at all," he assured her. "And even if it was, I was happy to catch you."

"I don't usually…do what I did that night."

Trey was quiet for a minute before he finally said, "It seems obvious that you think that night was a mistake, and your brother would undoubtedly agree—after he pounded on me for taking advantage of you. And while I'm sorry you feel that way, I have no intention of telling anyone about what happened between us, if that's what you're worried about. As far as I'm concerned, it will be our little secret, okay?"

His speech left her speechless. The words that Kayla had been struggling to put together into a coherent sentence faded from her mind. Tears clogged her throat, burned her eyes, as she shook her head.

"I'm not sure that's possible," she admitted.

"You told somebody about that night?" he guessed.

She nodded. "My sister."

"Oh." He considered for a minute, then let out a weary sigh. "Well, I'm sure you can trust your sister to keep your secrets. Unless…"

"Unless what?"

"I've heard some speculation that she's the Rust Creek Rambler," he admitted.

"She's not."

"You're sure?"

"I'm sure," she confirmed. "If she was the Rambler, I would know."

"Then our secret is safe," he said again.

She thought about the baby she carried, the tiny life that was even now fluttering in her belly. She'd managed to keep her pregnancy a secret from everyone—even her own family—for months. But she'd put on nine pounds already, and the bulky sweaters she'd been wearing wouldn't hide the baby bump for much longer.

You have to tell Trey.

She opened her mouth to do so when her cousin, Caleb, came in with his wife, Mallory. They waved a greeting across the room before stepping up to the counter to order their drinks.

When they took their beverages to the table behind Kayla and Trey, she knew that the opportunity to tell him about her pregnancy had slipped away.

RUST CREEK RAMBLINGS: LIGHTS! CAMERAS! ACTIVIST!

Lily Dalton, the town's littlest matchmaker (though

certainly not the only one!) has turned her talents toward a new vocation: acting. But when the sign-up sheet was posted for auditions for the elementary school's production of *The Nutcracker*, the precocious third-grader refused to succumb to gender stereotypes. Uninterested in the traditional female parts, she insisted on auditioning for the title role—and won! The revised tale will undoubtedly be the highlight of this year's holiday pageant...

"I can't believe I had to hear about your date with Trey Strickland from Natalie Crawford," Kristen grumbled. "Why didn't you tell me?"

"It wasn't a date," Kayla pointed out. "And I didn't have a chance to tell you, because this is the first time you've been home since Friday night."

"You could have called or texted."

She could have, of course, but she hadn't been ready to talk to her sister about it. The shock of seeing Trey so unexpectedly had churned up all kinds of emotions, and she needed some time to sift through them before she could talk about them. Unfortunately, the thirty-six hours that had passed since then still hadn't been nearly enough.

"It wasn't that big a deal," she hedged.

Kristen's brows lifted. "The father of your baby is back in town—I think that's a pretty big deal."

Kayla pushed her bedroom door closed. "Can you please keep your voice down?"

"Everyone is downstairs having breakfast."

"Which is where we should be, too," Kayla said. "And if we don't go down, Mom's going to come up here looking for us."

"We'll go down in a minute," Kristen said. "I want

to know how many times you've seen Trey since he got back."

"Once."

Her sister's gaze narrowed.

"Okay, twice," she acknowledged. "But they were both the same day."

"Did you tell him?"

"No."

"Why not?"

"Because I didn't know how."

"It's only two words—I'm pregnant."

Kristen made it sound so easy, as if Kayla was making it harder than it needed to be. And maybe she was. But she was the one who had to find the right time and place to say those two words, and she didn't appreciate being bullied by her sister.

She blinked back the tears that threatened. "And on that note, I'm going down for breakfast."

Kristen reached out and touched her arm, halting her departure.

"I'm sorry," she said softly, sincerely. "It's just that I can see how this is tearing you up inside, and it's going to continue tearing you up until you find a way to tell Trey—and that's not good for you or the baby."

"I know," she admitted.

"Besides, I saw an adorable little bib the other day that read, 'If you think I'm cute, you should see my aunt,' and I want to be able to buy things like that and bring them home for your baby."

Kayla managed a smile. "You're going to spoil this kid rotten before it's even born, aren't you?"

"I'm going to try," Kristen confirmed.

They left the room together, Kayla feeling confident

that whatever happened with Trey, her baby was going to be surrounded by the love and support of her family.

Trey decided that he wanted to see Kayla again more than he wanted to play it cool. Besides, what was the point in waiting a few days to call when it only wasted a few days of the short time that he was in town?

She answered the phone with a tentative hello—obviously not recognizing his number. But even hearing her voice say that one word was enough to make him smile.

"I was hoping to take you out for dinner tonight."

She paused. "Trey?"

"Yeah, it's me," he confirmed. "Are you free?"

"Oh. Um. Actually, I'm not," she said. "I'm on my way to Kalispell with my sister."

"What's in Kalispell?"

"*A Christmas Carol.*"

"Another movie?"

"No, the play. Kristen is Ebenezer Scrooge's fiancée, Belle."

"I didn't know Scrooge was married."

"He wasn't. She ended their relationship when she realized he loved money more than he loved her."

"I don't remember that part of the story," he admitted.

"Maybe you should buy a ticket to see it onstage, to refresh your memory."

"Would you go with me?"

"I've seen it a dozen times already from the wings."

"Is that a yes?"

She laughed softly. "No."

"Okay—what are you doing tomorrow?"

"I don't have any specific plans," she admitted.

"Can I take you out for lunch?"

She hesitated, and he wondered if she was searching for

another excuse to say no. And if she did, then he should finally take the hint and stop asking. He wasn't in the habit of chasing women, and he wasn't going to sacrifice his pride—and his relationship with Derek—to chase after his friend's little sister.

But when she finally responded, it was to say, "That would be nice."

"I'll pick you up at noon."

"I'll meet you," she said quickly.

"You don't want me coming to the ranch?" he guessed.

"I just don't think there's any reason for you to drive all the way out here just to turn around and drive back into town again," she said. "Especially when I have to stop by the newspaper office in the afternoon, anyway."

"Okay," he relented. "Where do you want to meet?"

"How about Daisy's again?"

He made a face that, of course, she couldn't see. But when he mentioned lunch, he was thinking a thick juicy burger or a rack of ribs from the Ace in the Hole. Sure, the donut shop did hot beverages and pastries, but he wanted a real meal. "Do they have much of a lunch menu?"

"I'm sure you'll find something that appeals to you."

He suspected she was right, though he wasn't thinking about the diner's menu.

"Okay, I'll see you at noon tomorrow."

He was smiling when he hung up the phone—then he turned and found his grandmother in his doorway.

"Who are you seeing at noon tomorrow?"

He could hardly take her to task for eavesdropping when he hadn't bothered to close his door. "A friend."

"A female friend, I'd guess, based on the smile on your face."

He focused his attention on the plate in her hands. "Is that sandwich for me?"

"You didn't come down to make anything for yourself, and I didn't want you messing up my kitchen after I'd cleaned it up."

He kissed her cheek. "Thank you."

"Do you have beverages?" Melba asked, glancing toward the mini-fridge in the corner of his room.

"I do," he confirmed. "And chips in the cabinet."

"Don't be getting crumbs all over," she admonished.

"I won't." And he knew where the broom was kept if he did.

She nodded. "Was that the Dalton girl you were talking to?"

"You don't give up, do you?"

"I should give up hoping that my grandson finds a nice girl to spend his life with?"

He held up his hands. "You're getting way ahead of me here," he told her. "I'm talking about lunch, not a lifetime commitment."

"Every relationship has to start somewhere," she said philosophically.

He knew she was right. He also knew it was far too soon to be thinking about anything long-term with Kayla Dalton. They hadn't even been on a real date, and he wasn't sure that their lunch plans even counted as such.

He really liked Kayla. He wasn't sure what it was about her that set her apart from so many other girls that he'd met and dated in recent years. He only knew that he wanted to spend time with her while he was in town and get to know her better.

And yes, he wanted to make love with her again when his brain wasn't clouded by alcohol. He wanted to know if her lips would taste as delicious as he remembered, if her skin would feel as soft beneath his hands, if her body would respond to his as it did in his dreams.

But he was prepared to take things slow this time, to enjoy every step of the journey without racing to the finish. And he was looking forward to lunch being that first step.

Chapter Five

Kayla was waiting for Trey outside the diner when he arrived. She'd dressed appropriately for the weather and looked cute all bundled up in a navy hip-length ski jacket with a knitted pink scarf wrapped around her throat and a matching hat on her head. Her legs were clad in dark denim, her feet tucked into dark brown cowboy boots.

"Busy place," he noted, opening the door for her so they could join the lineup of customers waiting to order at the counter.

"As I'm sure you're aware, dining options are pretty limited around here."

He was aware—and reassured to see a few local ranchers chowing down on hearty-looking sandwiches.

"It doesn't look as if the newlyweds regret their impulsive ceremony or intoxicated nuptials," Kayla noted, nodding toward a table where Will Clifton was sitting with his wife, Jordyn Leigh.

Trey had heard that the couple married on the Fourth of

July while under the influence of the wedding punch, but something about Kayla's choice of words struck a chord— as if he recognized the phrase *intoxicated nuptials* from somewhere.

"I heard a lot of people did crazy things under the influence of that punch," he said.

An elderly woman in a long, purple coat with an orange cap over her gray hair was standing ahead of them in line, and she turned back to face them now. "For some, the repercussions of that night are yet to be revealed."

Trey didn't know what to make of that cryptic comment, but Kayla's cheeks drained of all color.

"What was that about?" he whispered the question to her.

"I have no idea," she said.

"*Who* was that?"

"Winona Cobbs—a self-proclaimed psychic who moved here from Whitehorn a couple years back. Apparently, she used to run a place called the Stop 'N' Swap, but now she writes a nationally syndicated column, *Wisdom by Winona*."

"She's a little scary," he said. "Not just what she said, but the way she said it, as if she knows something that no one else does."

"Some people think she truly has a gift, others think she's a quack."

"What do you think?" he asked.

Kayla's expression was uneasy as she watched Winona settle at an empty table. "I think we should get our lunch to go."

"To go *where*?"

"We can eat in the park," she suggested.

"You want to eat outside?"

"It's a beautiful day," she pointed out.

"It's sunny," he acknowledged. "But the temperature is hovering just above freezing."

"I have a blanket in my car."

He'd been born and raised in Montana and was accustomed to working outside in various weather conditions, but even when the sun was shining, he didn't consider thirty-four degrees to be a beautiful day. But if Kayla could handle being outside, he wasn't going to wimp out.

He ordered a hot roast-beef sandwich platter with fries and slaw; Kayla opted for grilled turkey on a ciabatta bun with provolone and cranberry mayonnaise.

"To go," she told the server.

Trey glanced around the diner. "There are plenty of tables in here," he noted. "Are you sure you want to go to the park?"

"I'm sure."

He carried the bag of food and tray of hot drinks while she retrieved a thick wool blanket from her truck. It was a short walk to the park, where she spread the blanket over the bench seat for them, folding the end back across her lap when she was seated.

Maybe it wasn't exactly a beautiful day, but she looked beautiful in the sunlight. He didn't think she'd ever worn a lot of makeup, but she didn't need it. Those big blue eyes were mesmerizing even without any artificial enhancement; the soft, full lips naturally pink and tempting. She smelled sweet, like vanilla and brown sugar. The scent triggered a fresh wave of memories of the night they'd spent together and stirred his blood. Thankfully, his sheepskin-lined leather jacket was long enough to hide any evidence of his body's instinctive response.

He opened the bag and took out the food, unwrapping Kayla's sandwich so that she didn't have to take off her mittens before turning his attention to his own.

"Thanks."

"You're welcome."

That was the extent of their conversation for a few minutes while they both concentrated on eating. Trey had to admit, his roast beef was delicious. The meat was thinly sliced and piled high on a Kaiser then topped with gravy so piping hot, there was steam coming off his sandwich.

When the sandwich was gone, he turned his attention to the fries—thick wedges of crispy potato that were equally delicious. "Obviously, Daisy's Donuts has a lot more going for it than just donuts these days."

"I told you you'd find something you liked."

"So you did," he agreed.

A gust of wind blew her hair into her face. Kayla lifted a mittened hand to shove it away.

"Your hair looks different today," he noted.

"It's covered by a hat," she pointed out.

"Aside from that."

She shrugged. "I haven't had it cut in a while. It's probably longer than it was in the summer."

He wrapped a strand around his finger, tugged gently. "You wore it pinned up at the wedding."

She nodded.

He remembered taking the pins out of her hair and combing his fingers through the long, silky tresses. Of course, he didn't mention that part to her, because he knew that she was still a little embarrassed about what had happened that night.

"So you mentioned that your sister plays the part of Scrooge's fiancée in *A Christmas Carol,* but you didn't tell me what your role is."

"I work behind the scenes," she told him. "Helping out with costumes, scenery and props."

"So you don't have to be there for every performance?" he guessed.

"No. I usually work Wednesday and Thursday nights, and the occasional Saturday matinee."

"That's a pretty big commitment."

"Kristen does eight shows a week," she noted. "And Belle isn't a major part, but she's also the understudy for Mrs. Cratchit."

Once again, she'd deflected attention away from herself in favor of her twin. Trey noticed that she did that a lot. What he didn't know was if it was because she was proud of her sister or uncomfortable having any attention focused on herself.

Now that he thought about it, she'd always seemed content to hover in Kristen's shadow, but he didn't remember seeing much of her sister on the Fourth of July. "Was Kristen at the wedding?" he asked her now.

"Of course," Kayla responded. "Although she spent most of her time on the dance floor or with Ryan."

"I'm glad she was preoccupied," he said. "Because I don't think you would have approached me if you'd been hanging out with her."

"Probably not," she acknowledged. "But even without Kristen around, I wouldn't have approached you if I hadn't been drinking the spiked punch."

"Then I guess I should say thank you to whoever spiked the punch."

She narrowed her gaze on him, but the sparkle in her blue eyes assured him that she was only teasing when she said, "Maybe it was you."

"The police still haven't found the culprit?"

She shook her head. "No, and I'm not sure they ever will."

"What makes you say that?"

"It's been five months and there's no new evidence, no more leads to follow, no other witnesses to interview."

"What about Boyd Sullivan?" he asked, referring to the old man who had literally bet his ranch in a high-stakes poker game the night of the wedding.

"I'm sure they'd like to talk to him, if they could find him, but I doubt that he's responsible for spiking the punch when that's believed to be the reason he lost his home."

"Some pretty strange things happened that night," he acknowledged. "But it wasn't all bad, was it?"

Kayla knew he was asking about the time they'd spent together, and seeking reassurance that she had no regrets.

"No," she said in response to Trey's question. "It wasn't all bad."

But he didn't know that there were unexpected repercussions from that night, and she had to tell him. There probably wouldn't be a smoother segue into the topic or a more perfect opportunity. She opened her mouth to speak, but the words—those two simple words—stuck in her throat.

Because those two words would only be the beginning of their conversation. Once she told him about their baby, he'd have questions—*a lot* of questions. How could she explain to him how it had happened when she wasn't entirely sure herself? And how could she possibly justify remaining silent about the fact for so long?

"But you wish you hadn't gone back to my room with me?" he guessed.

"No. I just wish…"

"What do you wish?"

She shook her head. "I just want you to know that I don't usually do things like that. At least, I never have before."

He frowned. "You weren't a virgin."

She flushed. "I didn't mean that. I only meant that I've never had a one-night stand before."

"I didn't invite you back to my room with the plan that we would only spend one night together," he told her. "But the next morning, well, you know that I was a little hazy on the details. And you seemed to want to pretend it had never happened, so I decided to play along."

"I thought *you* didn't remember."

"I wouldn't—couldn't—forget making love with you," he told her.

"But you never even looked at me twice before that night."

"That's not true. The truth is, I was always careful not to get caught looking at you, because of my friendship with your brother." He crumpled up his sandwich wrapper, dropped it into the bag. "The punch didn't make me notice you—it only lessened my inhibitions around you."

"Really?"

"Really." He wiped his fingers on a paper napkin. "But maybe you only noticed me because of the punch."

"You know that's not true."

"That's right—the remnants of your high school crush meant I was irresistible to you," he teased.

"Maybe it was the punch," she teased back.

He grinned. "Well, now that you're not under the influence, what do you say to the two of us spending some time together, getting to know one another better?"

Under other circumstances, she would have said "absolutely." She wanted exactly what he was offering, but she knew any time they might have together was limited—not just because he would be returning to Thunder Canyon in the New Year, but because her baby bump was growing every day.

If you don't tell him, I will.

With Kristen's voice echoing in the back of her mind, Kayla opened her mouth to finally confess her secret. "Before you decide that you want—"

"I'm sorry," Trey said, as his cell phone rang. He pulled it out of his pocket, glanced at the screen. "My cousin, Claire."

He looked at her, as if for permission.

"Go ahead," she said, grateful for the reprieve—and then feeling guilty about being grateful.

He connected the call. "Hey, Claire."

Whatever his cousin said on the other end made him wince. "TMI." He shook his head as he listened some more. "So why are you calling me?" Then he sighed. "Okay, text me the details—but that 'favorite cousin' card is wearing pretty thin."

"Problem?" Kayla asked, when he disconnected.

"She wants me to pick up diapers. Apparently, she bought a supersize package at the box store in Kalispell yesterday, but she left them in the car and Levi has the car at work, Grandma's out getting her hair done, she doesn't trust Grandpa to buy the right size and she needs diapers *now.*"

"And you didn't even know diapers came in different sizes?" Kayla guessed.

"I never really thought about it," he admitted. "Except about two minutes ago and more in the context of 'thank God I don't have to think about stuff like that.'"   •

She frowned as she folded up the blanket. "Stuff like what?"

"Any and all of the paraphernalia associated with babies. I swear, you can hardly see the floor in Claire and Levi's room for all of the toys and crap strewn around."

Toys and crap.

Well, that was an enlightening turn of phrase. If she'd

been under any illusions that Trey might be excited about impending fatherhood, the phone call from his cousin had cleared them away.

Thank God I don't have to think about stuff like that.

His phone chimed and he glanced at the screen again. "She actually texted me a picture of the package, to make sure I get the right ones."

"Then I guess you'd better go get the diapers."

"I'm sorry," he said. "She really did sound desperate, although I'll spare you the details that she didn't spare me."

"I have to head over to the newspaper office, anyway," she reminded him. "Thanks for lunch."

"Wait." He caught her arm as she started to move away. "You were in the middle of saying something when Claire called."

She furrowed her brow, as if trying to remember, then shrugged. "I don't remember now."

Liar, liar.

She ignored the recriminations from her conscience as she headed back to her truck.

When she got to the newspaper office and glanced at her own phone, Kayla saw that she had three missed calls and four text messages—all from her sister.

She sat down behind her desk and finally called her back.

"What did he say?" Kristen demanded without preamble.

"Hi, Kristen. It's good to hear from you. I'm doing well, thanks for asking, and how are you?"

Her sister huffed out a breath. "We covered all of that when I talked to you earlier. Now tell me what he said."

"I didn't tell him," she admitted.

"How could you not tell him? Wasn't the whole purpose of your meeting with him today to tell him about your baby—*his* baby?"

"Yes, that was the purpose," she agreed. "And I was trying to come up with the right words to tell him what I needed to tell him."

"That you're pregnant with his child."

She sighed. "I'm aware of that fact."

"If you can't even say the words over the phone to me, there's no way you're going to be able to say them to Trey."

"I know," she admitted. "And those words are going to turn his whole world upside down."

"Probably a lot less than the baby that's going to come along in a few more months," Kristen pointed out reasonably.

"Not just a baby, but all the *toys and crap* that go along with a baby."

"What?"

She sighed. "Claire called and asked Trey to pick up diapers for her, and he went off on a little bit of a rant that made it pretty clear he isn't ready to be a father."

"Ready or not—he is going to be one."

"I know," she said again.

"The longer you wait, the harder it's going to be," her sister warned.

She knew it was true. And she knew that she'd already waited too long, but with Trey's disparaging remark ringing in her ears, the truth had lodged in her throat. So many times, she'd tried to imagine how he'd react to the news, but every time she played the scene out in her mind, the mental reel came to a dead stop after she told him about the baby. She simply could not imagine how he would respond. His comments today gave her a little bit of a hint, and not a good one.

"The baby's moving around a lot now," she admitted.

"The whole time I was with Trey today, I could feel little flutters, as if the baby was responding to the sound of his voice."

"Maybe he was," Kristen said. "Or maybe my nephew was kicking at you, reminding you to tell his father about his existence."

"I don't know if the baby's a boy or a girl," she reminded her sister.

"It's a boy," Kristen said. "And a little boy needs his father."

"What if…"

"What if what?"

But Kayla couldn't finish the thought. A single tear leaked out the corner of her eye—not that her sister could see, of course, but in true Kristen fashion, she didn't need to see her to know.

"Are you crying, sweetie?"

"No."

"Kayla," her sister prompted gently.

"One tear is not crying," she protested.

"It's going to be okay," Kristen said. "But only if you tell him."

"What if he doesn't want our baby?" she asked, her voice barely a whisper. "What if he hates me for getting pregnant?"

"You didn't get pregnant alone," her sister said indignantly. "And if he couldn't be responsible enough to make sure that didn't happen, he has to be responsible for the consequences."

RUST CREEK RAMBLINGS: BITS & BITES
The spectacularly refurbished Maverick Manor has been doing steady business since it opened its doors last December. Rumor has it the exquisite honey-

moon suite is in particular demand and has already been booked for the wedding night of dashing detective Russ Campbell to Rust Creek Falls's sexy spitfire waitress, Lani Dalton.

In other news, a truckload of our neighbors from Thunder Canyon recently rode into town bringing Presents for Patriots. The group included DJ and Allaire Traub with their pint-size son, Alex; Shane and Gianna Roarke, who will obviously be adding to their family very soon; Clayton and Antonia Traub, with children Bennett and Lucy in tow; and Trey Strickland, who is apparently planning to spend the holidays with his grandparents. Take my advice, single ladies, and slip a sprig of mistletoe in your pocket just in case you're lucky enough to cross paths with the handsome bachelor while he's in Rust Creek Falls!

Gene folded his newspaper and set it aside. "Better watch out," he told his grandson. "The Rambler announced your return to all of the eligible women in town."

"As if the news hadn't spread farther and faster through the grapevine already," Trey noted.

"Something wrong?" Melba asked him.

"Why would you think that?"

"You've been pushing those eggs around on your plate for five minutes without taking a bite."

He lifted a forkful to his mouth and tried not to make a face as he swallowed the cold eggs.

"I heard about your lunch with Kayla Dalton on Monday," Melba said.

He didn't bother to ask where she'd heard. In a town the size of Rust Creek Falls, everyone knew everyone else's business.

"In the park," she continued, shaking her head. "Why on earth would you take the girl to the park in December?"

"The park was Kayla's idea," he told her.

Melba frowned at that. "Really?"

"And it was a nice day."

"Nice enough, for this time of year," his grandmother agreed. "But hardly nice enough for a picnic."

"You should take her to Kalispell," Gene said.

"Why would I take her to Kalispell?" he asked warily.

"For a proper date."

He looked across the table at his grandfather. "*You're* giving *me* dating advice?"

"Somebody apparently has to," Melba pointed out. "Because lunch in the park in December is *not* a date."

He didn't bother reminding her again that it had been Kayla's idea—clearly nothing he said was going to change her opinion.

"You should take her somewhere nice," his grandmother continued.

"Speaking of going places," he said. "I'm heading to Kalispell this afternoon to do some Christmas shopping. Do you need me to pick up anything for you?"

"I was there to get my groceries yesterday," Melba said. "You should ask Kayla to go with you."

"Grandma," he said, with more than a hint of exasperation in his tone.

She held her hands up in mock surrender. "It was just a suggestion."

And because it was one he was tempted to follow, he instead got up and cleared his plate from the table, then headed out the door.

Chapter Six

The following night Kayla had volunteered to help with the wrapping of Presents for Patriots at the community center. She wasn't surprised to see Trey was also in attendance, but she deliberately took an empty seat at the table closest to the doors—far away from where he was seated.

She wasn't exactly avoiding him, but after the way they'd parted at the conclusion of their lunch date, she wasn't sure of the status between them. She knew that nothing he'd said or done absolved her of the responsibility of telling him about their baby, but she couldn't summon up any enthusiasm to do so. Instead, she chose a gift from the box beside the table and selected paper covered with green holly and berries to wrap it. There was Christmas music playing softly in the background and steady traffic from the wrapping tables to the refreshment area. The mood was generally festive, with people chatting with their neighbors and friends while they worked.

Despite the activity all around her, Kayla was conscious of Trey's presence. Several times when her gaze slid across the room, she found him looking at her, and the heat in his eyes suggested that he was remembering the night they'd spent together.

She was remembering, too. Even before she'd learned that she was carrying his child—an undeniable reminder of that night—she hadn't been able to forget. She'd had only one cup of the spiked punch—or maybe it was two. Just enough to overcome her innate shyness and lessen her inhibitions, not enough to interfere with her memories of that night.

That evening had been the realization of a longtime fantasy. She'd had a secret crush on him all through high school, but she'd never let herself actually believe that he could want her, too. But for a few hours that night, she hadn't doubted for a moment that he did. The way he'd looked at her, the way he'd kissed her and touched her, had assured her that what was happening between them was mutual.

But the next day, he hadn't remembered any of it.

Or so she'd believed for five months.

Now she knew that he knew, but he was prepared to act as if nothing had ever happened. Unfortunately for Kayla, that wasn't really an option.

"Instead of staring at her from across the room, you could go over and talk to her."

Shane Roarke's suggestion forced Trey to tear his gaze away from Kayla. He pulled another piece of tape from the roll and resumed his wrapping.

"What?" he asked, as if he didn't know what—or rather whom—his friend was talking about.

Shane shook his head. "You're not fooling anyone, Trey."

"I don't know what you're talking about," he said.

But of course it was a lie. He'd noticed her the minute she'd walked through the door. He'd watched her come in, her nose and cheeks pink from the cold, and waited for her to come over and take the empty seat beside him. Her eyes had flicked in his direction, and his heart had pounded in anticipation. Then, much to his disappointment, she'd turned the other way.

"I'm talking about the pretty brunette across the room. The one with the big blue eyes and the shy smile who keeps looking over at you almost as much as you're looking at her."

"She's looking at me?"

Shane glanced at his wife and shook his head. "Was I ever this pathetic?"

"No," Gianna smiled indulgently. "You were worse."

Her husband chuckled. "I probably was," he acknowledged, reaching over to cover the hand that his wife had splayed over her enormous belly. "But look at us now."

Trey did look at them, and he was surprised by the little tug of envy he felt. He never thought he wanted what his friend had—certainly he wasn't looking to add a wife and a kid to his life just yet. But maybe, at some future time down the road.

For now, however, he couldn't stop thinking about Kayla. He'd told her that they could forget what happened between them on the Fourth of July, but it was a lie. He hadn't stopped thinking about her since that night, and now that he was back in Rust Creek Falls, he was eager to spend some time with her and to rekindle the chemistry that had sparked between them five months earlier.

"And look at his corners," Gianna said, interrupting his musing.

Trey followed her pointing finger to the package in front of him. "What's wrong with my corners?"

"They're lumpy."

"Shane's corners weren't so great, either, until you started helping him," he pointed out.

"That's true," Gianna agreed, pushing back her chair. She came around the table to his side. "Come on."

He eyed her warily. "Where are we going?"

"To get you some help."

He looked across the table at his friend and coworker; Shane just shrugged. Trey reluctantly rose to his feet and let Gianna lead him away. His steps faltered when he realized where she was leading, but she only grabbed his arm and tugged him along until they were standing by Kayla's table.

"You look like you know what you're doing," Gianna said to her. "Maybe you could help Trey with his wrapping?"

Kayla's pretty blue eyes shifted between them. "Help—how?"

"Show him how to fold the ends of the paper, for starters. He's making a mess of everything."

"You'd think a man who trains horses could handle a roll of paper," Kayla noted.

"You'd think," Gianna agreed. "But he can't."

"But I can hear," Trey pointed out. "And you're talking about me as if I'm not here."

"Sit," Gianna said, nudging him into a chair.

He sat.

"Good luck," she said to Kayla before she went back to her husband.

"I'm sorry about this," Trey said.

"About what?"

"Gianna dragging me over here."

"Why did she?"

He shrugged. "Partly because I was making a mess of everything. Mostly because I was paying more attention to you than my assigned task."

Her cheeks flushed prettily. "I'm sure you weren't making a mess of everything."

"You haven't seen me wrap anything yet," he warned her.

She handed him a box. "Give it a go."

He let his fingertips brush against hers in the exchange, and smiled when she drew away quickly. He laid the present on the paper and cut it to size, then wrapped the paper around the box. He was doing okay until he got to the ends, where he couldn't figure out how to fold it.

"You really do suck at this," she confirmed, amused by the fact.

"I'm not good with the paper," he admitted. "But I'm a tape master."

Her lips twitched, just a little, and her brows lifted. "A tape master?"

He demonstrated, tearing off four short, neat pieces of tape onto the tips of each of his fingers, and then transferring them one by one to secure the seams of the paper.

"Not too bad," she allowed.

"I have other talents," he told her.

"What kind of talents?"

He tipped his head closer to her and lowered his voice suggestively. "Why don't we go for a drive when we're finished here and…talk…about those talents?"

"I have a better idea," she said. "I'll cut and wrap, and you tape."

Her tone was prim but the pulse point at the base of her

jaw was racing. Satisfied by this proof that she wasn't as unaffected as she wanted him to believe, he backed off. "That'll work," he agreed. "For now."

The system of shared labor did work well, and they chatted while they wrapped. Their conversation was mostly easy and casual, but every once in a while, he'd allow his hand to brush against hers, or his knee to bump hers beneath the table. And every time they touched, her breath would catch and her gaze would slide away, reassuring him that the feelings churning inside him weren't entirely one-sided.

"I'm always impressed by the generosity of people at this time of year," he noted. "Even those folks who don't have a lot to give manage to make a contribution."

"You're right," Kayla agreed. "The year of the flood, when so many local families were struggling, Nina started the Tree of Hope to ensure that everyone in town had a holiday meal and presents under their tree. The response of the community was overwhelming."

"Nina Crawford?"

Kayla nodded. "Actually, she's Nina Traub now."

He'd grown up knowing about the feud between the Crawfords and the Traubs, although no one seemed to know for sure what had caused the rift between the families. Regardless of the origins, the animosity had endured through generations and escalated further when Nathan Crawford and Colin Traub both ran for the vacant mayoral seat after the flood. How Nathan's sister had ended up married to Colin's brother was a mystery to a lot of people, but their union showed promise of being the first step toward mending the rift between the families.

"The Tree of Hope is just one example of how the people of Rust Creek Falls look out for one another," she continued.

"I don't think I ever realized how much they did until I saw the way everyone pitched in and worked together after the flood."

"We had a lot of help from our Thunder Canyon neighbors, too," she reminded him. "And the money and publicity that Lissa brought in through Bootstraps was invaluable."

He nodded. "But looking around the town, I don't think anyone who wasn't here to see the devastation would ever guess how badly the town was hit."

"We're doing okay now."

"Better than okay, from what I've heard, since Maverick Manor opened its doors."

"Nate and Callie have big plans for their place, but I don't think the Thunder Canyon Resort needs to worry about its clientele heading this way."

"Have you ever been to the resort?" Trey asked.

She shook her head.

"You should come for a visit sometime."

Kayla wasn't sure if his statement was a general comment or an invitation, so she kept her response equally vague. "I've thought about it," she said. "In fact, I had considered doing some Christmas shopping that way."

"I wish you had come to Thunder Canyon," he said. "It would have been nice to spend some time with you without our every step being examined under the microscope of public opinion."

"Such is life in a small town," she said, glancing at the door to see Kristen and Ryan enter the hall.

"I didn't think you were going to make it," Kayla said to her sister.

"We didn't, either," Kristen admitted. "And I was exhausted after our final performance this week, but we both wanted to help out."

"There's no shortage of help," Trey said. "But still plenty

to do—especially if you have more wrapping experience than I do."

"How long have you guys been here?" Kristen asked.

"When I arrived, around seven-thirty, Trey was already here," Kayla told her.

"Which means you both must be ready for a break," Kristen decided. "Why don't Ryan and I take over for a little while so that you and Trey can take a walk to stretch your legs and get some fresh air?"

"Isn't it a little cold outside for an evening stroll?"

"Not if you bundle up," Kristen said.

Trey glanced from Kristen to her sister and back again. "Why do you want us to go for a walk?"

"Because Kayla needs to talk to you."

He looked at Kayla. "Can't we talk here?"

"No," Kristen said firmly, leaving her fiancé looking as confused as Trey felt. "Kayla needs to speak with you *privately*."

He looked at Kayla; she glared at her sister then offered him a halfhearted shrug.

"O-kay," he decided, pushing his chair away from the table.

Kayla did the same, sliding her arms into the sleeves of the ski jacket she'd draped over her chair.

It was frigid outside, and she shoved her hands into the pockets and tucked her chin into the collar of her jacket.

"It's going to snow," Trey said, pulling on his gloves.

"It's December in Montana," she agreed. "The odds are definitely in favor of more white stuff."

He chuckled at that. "So where are we walking to?"

"There's really nowhere to go."

"Then maybe you should just tell me why your sister was so determined to get us out of the community center so we could talk."

"Because she doesn't know how to mind her own business," Kayla grumbled.

But she knew her sister was right—Trey needed to know about the baby. And she needed to be the one to tell him.

"That's a little cryptic," he noted.

"I told you that Kristen knows what happened the night of the wedding," she reminded him.

He nodded.

"Well, she thought I should talk to you about..."

"About?" he prompted.

But her attention had been snagged by the approach of another couple. "I didn't know Forrest and Angie were in town."

Trey turned to follow the direction of her gaze. "They're very involved with Presents for Patriots."

Kayla wasn't surprised by this revelation. Forrest was one of six sons born to Bob and Ellie Traub but the only one who had opted for a career in the military rather than on the family ranch. Three years earlier, he'd returned from Iraq with a severely injured leg and PTSD. He'd gone to Thunder Canyon for treatment and therapy at the hospital there—although there was speculation that he'd wanted to escape all of the attention of being a hometown hero even more than he wanted to fix his leg. It was in Thunder Canyon that he'd met and fallen in love with Angie Anderson, and it warmed Kayla's heart to see how sincerely happy and content Forrest was now that he'd found the right woman to share his life.

They chatted with the war veteran and his wife for a few minutes before they continued into the hall. When the doors closed behind them, Kayla braced herself to speak once again. Then Bennett and Lucy Traub raced out of the community center, followed closely by their parents, Clay and Antonia.

"This isn't the easiest place to have a conversation, is it?" Trey asked when the Traubs had moved on.

"Not tonight," she agreed.

"So maybe we should try something different," he suggested, and lowered his head to touch his mouth to hers.

He caught her off guard.

Kayla had been so preoccupied thinking about the conversation they weren't having that she didn't realize his intention until he was kissing her. And then her brain shut down completely as her body melted against his.

Trey wrapped his arms around her, holding her as close as their bulky outerwear would allow. She lifted her arms to link them behind his head, holding on to him as the world spun beneath her feet.

It was funny—they couldn't seem to have a two-minute conversation without being interrupted, but the kiss they shared went on and on, blissfully, endlessly. When Trey finally eased his lips from hers, they were both breathless.

"I wondered," he said.

"What did you wonder?"

"If your lips would taste as I remembered."

"Do they?"

"No," he said. "They taste even better."

She felt her cheeks flush despite the chilly air. "I thought you wanted to forget about that night."

"I'm not sorry about what happened between us in the summer. I just wish we hadn't rushed into bed."

"I'd guess that had more to do with the punch than either of us," she said.

"Or the chemistry between us."

"I thought the alcohol was responsible for the chemistry."

"Have you been drinking tonight?"

She flushed. "Of course not."

"Because from where I'm standing, that kiss we just shared proves the sparks between us are real, and I'd like to spend some time with you while I'm in town over the holidays, so that we can get to know one another better, and maybe see where the chemistry leads us."

"But you're only going to be in town for a few weeks," she reminded him—reminded both of them.

"Thunder Canyon isn't that far away."

"And I'm sure there's no shortage of women there."

"There's not," he agreed. "But I haven't stopped thinking about you since July. I haven't been out with another woman in all that time because I didn't want to go out with anyone else."

His words stirred hope in her heart. If he really meant what he was saying, maybe they could build a relationship—except that anything they started to build now would be on a foundation of lies, or at least omission.

Her baby—their baby—kicked inside her belly, a not-so-subtle reminder of that omission.

"Trey…"

"Just give us a chance," he urged.

"I want to," she admitted. "But—"

He touched his fingers to her lips. "It's enough that you're willing to give us a chance."

She shook her head. "There are things you don't know. Things you need to know."

"We've got time to find out everything we need to know about one another," he told her. "I don't want to rush anything."

And she let herself be persuaded, because it was easier than telling him the truth.

Or so she thought until she considered having to go back inside and face her sister. Because she knew Kristen would take one look at her and immediately know that she'd failed in her assigned task.

"We should probably get back inside before people start whispering and my grandparents read about our disappearance from the gift-wrapping in Rust Creek Ramblings."

"They won't read anything in the paper," she told him.

His brows lifted. "How can you be so certain?"

Kayla wasn't quite sure how to respond to that.

"Is that what your sister wanted you to tell me?"

"What?"

"That you're the Rust Creek Rambler."

She gasped, shocked as much by his casual delivery as the statement itself. "Why would you think that?"

"The first clue was your assurance that Kristen wasn't the Rust Creek Rambler. It occurred to me that the only way you could be so certain was if you knew the true identity of the Rambler. And then, when we saw Will and Jordyn Leigh at the diner, you made reference to their *intoxicated nuptials*—which was, coincidentally, the same phrase that was used in the 'Ramblings' column."

She was surprised that he'd figured it out. She'd been writing the column for three and a half years with no one, aside from the paper's editor, being aware of her identity.

"You're right," she admitted softly. "But no one else in town has ever shown any suspicion about me being the author of the column."

"Maybe because no one else has been paying close attention to you."

"Are you mad?"

"Why would I be mad?"

"Because I kept it from you."

"And everyone else in town."

She nodded.

"Actually, I'm more baffled—especially when I think

about what was written in Ramblings about the two of us dancing together at the wedding."

She shrugged. "Several people saw us together. If I'd ignored that, it would have been suspicious. By mentioning it in the column, it deflected attention away from me as the possible author."

"Clever," he noted. "So tell me, is your copy editing job real or just a cover?"

"It's real, but only part of what I do."

"You are full of surprises," he told her. "But I'm not sure why it mattered so much to your sister that you tell me about your secret occupation."

"Kristen's a big fan of open communication," she told him. "But I wouldn't be able to do my job if everyone knew that I was the Rambler, so I'd appreciate it if you didn't out me to the whole community."

"I think, if I'm going to keep such a big secret for you, I'm going to need something in return."

"What kind of something?" she asked warily.

"Help with my Christmas shopping?" he suggested.

She smiled. "You've got a deal."

Kayla hadn't seen Trey since their gift-wrapping at the community center. She'd been lying low on purpose—not just because she still hadn't figured out how to tell him about the baby, but because she wanted to be able to tell her sister that she hadn't seen him and, therefore, hadn't had a chance to tell him.

Apparently, she was a liar *and* a coward. And while she wasn't particularly proud of her behavior, she consoled herself with the assurance that these were desperate times.

Thursday afternoon she went into the newspaper office again to work on the Sunday edition of the paper and polish her own column. Unfortunately, the onset of winter meant that many residents were hunkered down indoors rather than creating and disseminating juicy headlines.

There were rumors that Alistair Warren had spent several hours with the widow next door during a recent storm—"much longer than it would take to fill her firebox with wood" she'd heard from one source—but Kayla didn't have much more than that for her column.

She considered mentioning that Trey Strickland had recently been spotted at Crawford's buying diapers, but putting his name into any context with babies hit a little too close to the secret she was keeping—and knew she couldn't continue to keep for much longer.

Already her mother was looking at her with that calculating gleam in her eye, as if she knew her daughter was hiding something from her. Kayla's father—always preoccupied with ranch business—probably wouldn't notice if she sat down at the breakfast table with a ring through her nose, but her mother had always had an uncanny sense when it came to every one of her five children.

Kayla wanted to share the news of her baby with her family. She wasn't particularly proud of the circumstances surrounding the conception, but she wasn't ashamed of her baby. And the further she progressed in her pregnancy, the more she wanted to talk to her mother about being a mother, about the changes her body was going through and the confusing array of emotions she was experiencing. She wanted to share her thoughts and feelings with someone who had been through what she was going through right now.

Kristen had been great—aside from the constant pressure to tell Trey—but her sister was so caught up in the excitement of being in love and planning her wedding, she couldn't imagine the doubts and fears that overwhelmed Kayla.

She so desperately wanted to do right by her baby, to give her child the life he or she deserved. Of course, Kristen kept insisting the baby was a he, despite the fact that the ultrasound photo gave nothing away.

Kayla opened the zippered pocket inside her purse and carefully removed that photo now. At the time it was taken, her baby had measured about five inches long and weighed around seven ounces.

"About the size of a bell pepper," the technician had said, to help Kayla put the numbers into perspective.

She'd also reassured the mother-to-be that baby had all the requisite parts—although the baby's positioning didn't reveal whether there were boy parts or girl parts—but it was the rapid beating of the tiny heart on the monitor that snagged Kayla's attention and filled her own heart.

She'd marveled at the baby's movements on the screen, but she hadn't been able to feel any of those movements inside her. Not until almost three weeks later.

She was much more attuned to the tiny flutters and kicks now. Of course, the baby seemed most active when she was trying to sleep at night, but she didn't mind. Alone in her room, she would put her hands on her belly and let herself think about the tiny person growing inside her.

Her doctor had suggested that she start looking into childbirth classes. Kayla understood the wisdom of this advice, but she didn't dare register for classes in Rust Creek Falls and she didn't know that she'd be able to get to Kalispell every week to commit to classes there. Although Kalispell was a much bigger city than Rust Creek Falls, her encounter with Melba Strickland at the shopping mall had reminded her that she couldn't count on anonymity there. Instead, she'd been reading everything she could find and had even been taking online classes about pregnancy and childbirth.

As she traced the outline of her baby's shape with her fingertip, she hoped her efforts were enough. She was so afraid of doing something wrong, of somehow screwing up this tiny, fragile life that was growing inside her.

She wanted to show the picture to Trey; she wanted to talk about her hopes and dreams for their child and share her fears. Mostly, she wanted him to want to be part of their child's life, because she didn't want to raise their child alone. She wanted her baby to have two parents.

The beep of her phone interrupted her thoughts. She carefully tucked the photo away again before checking the message from her sister.

I want it!

She opened the attachment to see what *it* was, and smiled at the picture of a multi-tiered wedding cake. Each stacked layer was elaborately decorated with a different white-on-white design: silhouettes of bucking broncos, cowboy boots, cowboy hats and horseshoes.

Despite the Western motif, it was elegant and unique—totally Kristen.

She texted back,

Luv it

Because she did. She didn't have a clue where her sister would find someone in their small town capable of re-creating such a work of art, but that was a practical worry for another day. Right now her sister was dreaming of her perfect day, and Kayla was happy to be drawn into the fantasy with her.

Kristen had asked Kayla to be her maid of honor, and she had, of course, accepted, but she needed to talk to her twin about the timing of the event and the likelihood that she would be a maid of *dis*honor. She didn't think Kristen would want to be upstaged on her wedding day by her hugely pregnant and unwed sister. As much as Kristen enjoyed the spotlight, Kayla didn't think she'd want the happiest day of her life tainted by that kind of scandal.

Upon receiving her reply, Kristen immediately called. "Are you sick and tired of hearing about the wedding?" she asked.

"Never," Kayla assured her sister.

"Then you won't mind if Mom and I drag you into Kalispell tomorrow to go shopping for my dress?"

"Are you kidding? I've been wondering when you'd finally get around to that." She knew that Ryan had offered to fly his fiancée out to California so that she could shop on Rodeo Drive in Beverly Hills, but the idea hadn't appealed to Kristen. Her twin was surprisingly traditional in a lot of ways—and very much a country girl.

"I've just been so busy with the play that I haven't had much free time," Kristen said now. "But June isn't that far away, so I figured I'd better make time to start preparing for the wedding."

"You've set a date, then?"

"June eleventh," her sister confirmed.

"Then I guess we'd better find you a dress."

Chapter Seven

When Trey saw Kayla's truck pull up in front of the boarding house, for a moment he thought—hoped—she had come into town to see him. When he saw her lift a small box out of the passenger seat of her vehicle, he was disappointed to realize she had another reason for being there.

He met her at the door and took the box from her. "What's this?"

"Your grandmother wanted a couple of jars of bread-and-butter pickles."

"She makes her own pickles."

Kayla shrugged. "Apparently, your grandfather was looking for something in the cellar and knocked over a shelf and she lost the last of hers."

He hadn't heard anything about such an incident—and he was pretty sure if his grandfather had truly engineered such a mishap, the whole town would have heard about it. More likely his grandmother had engineered the story to bring Kayla to the boarding house, and though he didn't approve of Melba's meddling, he wouldn't complain about the results.

"Did she happen to mention why she needed—" he glanced into the box "—half a dozen jars of pickles right now, today?"

"She spoke to my mother, not me. I'm just the delivery girl."

"Because I'm sure you didn't have anything better to do," he said dryly.

"Not according to my mother," she agreed.

"Do you have anything else on your schedule today?"

"No, but I figured, since I was coming into town, I would stop in at the newspaper office and try to get a head start on editing anything that has been submitted for the next edition."

"Or you could help me," he suggested.

"Help you with what?" she asked, a little warily.

"I've been tasked with finding the perfect Christmas tree for the main floor parlor."

"Perfect is a matter of interpretation when it comes to Christmas trees," she warned him.

"I figure as long as it's approximately the right height and shape, it's perfect."

Kayla *tsked* as she shook her head. "What kind of tree does your grandmother want?"

"A green one."

She laughed. "Well, that narrows your search to most of Montana."

He shrugged. "She didn't seem concerned about specifics so much as timing—it's only two weeks before Christmas, and she wants a tree in the parlor today."

"Where in the parlor?" Kayla pressed. "Does she want something slender that can be tucked into a corner? Or would she prefer a fuller shape that will become the centerpiece of the room?"

It was an effort to refrain from rolling his eyes. "I don't know. I just know that the tree is always in the corner—with stacks of presents piled underneath it on Christmas morning."

She smiled. "Everyone's a kid at Christmas, aren't they?"

"You don't get excited about presents?"

"Of course I do."

"So will you help me out with the tree?"

She pulled back the cuff of her jacket to look at the watch on her wrist. "Sure."

Twenty minutes later he pulled into the parking lot of a tree farm on the edge of town.

"I didn't expect it would be this busy in the middle of the day on a weekday," he commented.

"Two weeks," she reminded him.

However, most of the customers seemed to be examining precut trees, and although he knew that was the easier option, his grandmother had specifically requested a fresh-cut tree and had sent her husband out to the shed to get the bow saw for him.

They walked down the path, following the signs toward the "cut your own" section of the farm.

"Aside from green, what should I be looking for?" Trey asked Kayla.

"It depends on what matters most to you—scent, color, hardiness. Balsam fir smells lovely but they tend to be bulky around the bottom and take up a lot of space. The Scotch pine is probably the most common type of Christmas tree. Its bright green color is appealing, but the branches and needles tend to be quite stiff, making it more difficult—and painful—to decorate."

"You're not a fan," he guessed.

"They're pretty trees," she insisted. "But no, they wouldn't be my first choice."

"How do you know so much about Christmas trees?"

She shrugged. "Every year, from as far back as I can remember, we've trekked deep into the woods to cut down a tree, so I probably could have steered you in the right direction on the basis of that experience without necessarily knowing what was a spruce or a fir. The technical stuff I learned when I edited an article—'Choosing the Perfect Christmas Tree'—for the newspaper a couple of years back."

"You must get to read some interesting stuff in your job."

"I do," she agreed. "And not just in the "Ramblings" column."

"That doesn't count, anyway—you make that stuff up."

"I do not," she said indignantly. "I simply report facts that are brought to my attention."

"There's a fair amount of speculation in addition to the facts," he noted.

"Speculation about the facts, perhaps," she allowed.

He shook his head, but he was smiling when he paused beside a blue spruce. "What do you think of this one?"

She let her gaze run up the tall—extremely tall, in fact—trunk. "I think it's a beautiful tree for the town square but way too big for anyone's parlor."

He nodded in acknowledgment. "Who picks out the tree in your family?"

"Majority rules, but there's usually a lot of arguing before a final decision is made. My mom has a tendency to pick out a bigger tree than we have room for, which means my dad ends up muttering and cursing as he cuts down the trunk 'just another inch more' or trims some of the branches 'just on one side' so it'll end up sitting closer to the wall." She smiled a little at the memory. "My dad now carries a tape measure, so that he can show my mother that a tree isn't 'perfect' for an eight-foot room when it's actually eleven feet tall."

"I suspect my grandmother has had the opposite experience, because she made a point of telling me that the room has a twelve-foot ceiling and she doesn't want anything shorter than ten feet, preferably ten and a half."

"Did you bring a tape measure?"

He pulled it out of his pocket to show her.

"Did you bring a ladder so that you can measure up to ten feet?"

"It's in my other pocket."

She laughed.

He looked at her—at her cheeks pink from the cold, at the delicate white flakes of snow against her dark hair and at her eyes, as clear and blue as the sky, sparkling in the sun—and realized that he was in danger of falling hard and fast.

And in that moment, he didn't care.

He caught her hand, halting her in midstride. She tipped her head back to look up at him, and he lowered his head to touch his mouth to hers.

He kissed her softly, savoring the moment. He loved kissing her, loved the way her lips yielded and her body melted. He loved the quiet sounds she made deep in her throat.

But he wanted more than a few stolen kisses. He wanted to make love with her again, to enjoy not just the taste of her lips but the joining of their bodies. But he'd promised that they could take things slow this time, and he intended to keep that promise—even if it meant yet another cold shower when he got back to the boarding house.

When he finally eased his lips away, she looked as dazed as he felt. "What was that for?"

"Does there need to be a reason for me to kiss you?"

"I guess not," she admitted. "You just...surprised me."

He smiled at that. "You surprise me every time I see you."

"I do?"

"You do," he confirmed. "I always thought I knew you. You were Derek's sister, the shy twin, the quiet one. But I've realized there's a lot more to you than most people give you credit for."

"I am the shy twin, the quiet one."

He slid his arms around her, wanting to draw her nearer. "You're also smart and beautiful and passionate."

She put her hands on his chest, her arms locked to hold him at a distance. "Tree," she reminded him.

"They're not going anywhere," he noted.

"You say that now, but do you see that stump there?"

He followed the direction of her gaze. "Yeah."

"That might have been *your* perfect tree, but someone else got to it before you did."

"So I'll find another perfect tree."

"Do you think it will be that easy? That perfect trees just—"

"Grow like trees," he interjected drily.

Her lips curved. "Touché."

Half an hour later, they were headed back to the boarding house with a lovely tree tied down in the box of Trey's truck.

When they arrived, they found that Gene had carted out all of the decorations: lights and garland and ornaments.

"Looks like our work isn't done yet," he noted.

"I thought your grandmother usually let her guests help with the trimming of the tree."

"Apparently she stopped that a couple of years ago, when a three-year-old decided to throw some of her favorite ornaments rather than hang them. A few of them were mouth-blown glass that a cousin had brought back for her from Italy."

Kayla winced sympathetically.

"She has a story for every ornament on her tree," Trey told her. "And now a story for eight that aren't."

She tucked her hands behind her back. "Now I'm afraid to touch anything."

"You can touch me," Trey told her, with a suggestive wink. "I won't break."

Kayla laughed. "Let's focus on the tree," she responded, stepping out of his reach.

But Trey circled around the tree in the other direction and caught her against him. "Now I have to kiss you."

"Have to?" She lifted a brow. "Why?"

"Because you're standing under the mistletoe."

Kayla looked up, but there was no mistletoe hanging from the ceiling above her. There was, however, a sprig of the recognizable plant in Trey's hand, which he was holding above her head.

"That's cheating," she told him.

"I don't care," he said and touched his mouth to hers.

As Kayla melted into the kiss, her objections melted away.

The slamming of the back door returned her to her senses. "It's only two weeks until Christmas," she reminded him. "And your grandmother wants her tree up."

He sighed regretfully but released her so they could focus on the assigned task.

After leaving the boarding house, Kayla stopped at Crawford's to pick up a quart of milk for her mother. She was carrying the jug to the checkout counter when she saw Tara Jones, a third-grade teacher from the local elementary school.

"This is a lucky coincidence," the teacher said.

"Why's that?" she asked curiously.

"Our annual holiday pageant is in less than a week and we're way behind schedule with the costumes and scenery. I know it's a huge imposition," Tara said, "but we could really use your help."

"It's not an imposition at all," Kayla told her. "I'd be happy to pitch in."

"Thank you, thank you, thank you. We do have other volunteers who can assist you, but I think one of the biggest problems is that no one was willing to take the lead because they're not sure what they should be doing. But with your experience in the Kalispell theater, you should have them on track in no time."

"When do you need me?"

"Yesterday."

Kayla laughed.

"Okay, Monday would work," Tara relented. "Three o'clock?"

"I'll be there."

"And if you want to bring your beau, I'm sure no one would have any objections to an extra pair of hands."

She frowned. "What?"

"Come on, Kayla. Do you really think people haven't noticed that you've been spending a lot of time with Trey Strickland?"

"I wouldn't say it's a lot of time," she hedged.

"So you're not exclusive?"

She frowned at the question. "We're not even really dating—just hanging out together."

"Is that what you told the Rambler?"

"What?"

The other woman shrugged. "I just wondered how it is that everyone knows you and Trey have been hanging out, but that little tidbit has yet to make the gossip column of the local paper."

"Probably because it's not newsworthy."

"That's one theory," Tara agreed. "Another is that the Rambler is someone you know."

"Or maybe it's someone Trey knows," she countered.

"I guess that is another possibility. But you can bet if I was dating Trey Strickland, I'd shout it out from the headlines."

Trey was shoveling the walk that led to the steps of the boarding house when he heard someone say, "Hey, stranger."

He recognized his friend's voice before he turned and came face-to-face with Derek Dalton. The instinctive pleasure was quickly supplanted by guilt. Derek had been his best friend in high school and one of the first people he sought out whenever he returned to Rust Creek Falls, but he hadn't done so this time because he didn't know how to see Derek without feeling guilty about what had happened with Derek's sister. And now he had another reason to feel guilty, because he was dating Kayla behind her brother's back.

"What brings you into town?" Trey asked.

"I'm heading over to the Ace in the Hole for a beer and thought I'd see if you wanted to join me."

Trey had decided to tackle the shoveling while he waited for Kayla to respond to any of the three messages he'd left for her. Since that had yet to happen, he decided he'd look pretty pathetic sitting at home waiting for her to call.

"Let me finish up here and grab a quick shower," Trey said.

While he was doing that, Derek visited with Melba and

Gene, hanging out in their kitchen as he'd often done when he and Trey were teenagers.

Trey was quick in the shower, then he checked for messages on his phone again. *Nada.*

He pushed Kayla from his mind and headed out with her brother.

They climbed the rough-hewn wooden steps and opened the screen door beneath the oversize playing card—an ace of hearts—that blinked in neon red. Inside, a long wooden bar ran the length of one wall with a dozen bar stools facing the mirrored wall that reflected rows of glass bottles. Shania Twain was singing from the ancient Wurlitzer jukebox at the back of the room.

There was a small and rarely used dance floor in the middle of the room, surrounded by scarred wooden tables and ladder-back chairs. The floor was littered with peanut shells that crunched under their boots as they made their way to the bar, taking the last two empty stools. He nodded to Alex Monroe, foreman of the local lumber mill, who lifted his beer in acknowledgment.

Trey settled onto his stool and looked around. "This place hasn't changed at all, has it?"

"Isn't that part of its charm?"

"It has charm?"

Derek chuckled. "Don't let Rosey hear you say that."

"She still in charge of this place?"

"Claims it's the only relationship that ever worked out for her."

"Sounds like Rosey," Trey agreed.

The bartender delivered their drinks and they settled back, falling into familiar conversation about ranching and horses and life in Rust Creek Falls. They were on their second round of drinks when two girls in tight jeans and low-cut shirts squeezed up to the bar beside them on the pretext of wanting to order, but the flirtatious glances they sent toward Trey and Derek suggested they were looking for more than drinks.

The girls accepted their beverages from the bartender then headed toward an empty table, inviting Trey and Derek to join them.

"What do you say?" Derek asked, his gaze riveted on their swaying hips as the girls walked away.

Trey shook his head, not the least bit tempted.

"C'mon, buddy. You're supposed to be my wing man."

"Don't you ever get tired of women throwing themselves at you?"

Derek laughed. "That's funny."

Trey frowned.

"You weren't joking?"

"No," he said.

"You meet someone?"

"As a matter of fact, I did."

Derek obviously hadn't expected an affirmative response, but he shrugged it off, anyway. "So even if you've got a girl in Thunder Canyon, she wouldn't ever know about a meaningless hookup here."

He didn't correct his friend's assumption that he was seeing someone in Thunder Canyon. If he admitted that he was interested in a local girl, Derek would be full of questions—questions that Trey wasn't prepared to answer. So all he said was, "*I'd* know."

Derek shook his head. "She's really got her hooks into you, doesn't she?"

Trey frowned at the phrasing, but he'd recently started to admit—at least to himself—that it was probably true. "Your turn will come someday," he warned his friend.

"Maybe," Derek allowed, setting his empty bottle on the bar. "But that day is not today."

"Where are you going?" he demanded when Kayla's brother slid off his stool.

"When a girl gives me a 'come hither' glance, I come hither."

Trey just shook his head as he watched him walk away to join the two girls at the table they now occupied.

Even if Kayla did have her hooks in him, so to speak, he knew there were still obstacles to a relationship between them, and the geographical distance between Thunder Canyon and Rust Creek Falls was one of the biggest.

But that distance wasn't an issue right now, and he really wanted to see her. He slipped his phone out of his pocket and checked for messages. There were none.

He scrolled through his list of contacts, clicked on her name then the message icon. The blank white screen seemed blindingly bright in the dimly lit bar.

Just thinking abt u, wondering what u r doing...

There was no immediate reply. Of course not—whatever she was doing, she obviously wasn't sitting around waiting to hear from him.

He glanced over at the girls' table, where his friend was holding another bottle of beer. Derek caught his eye and waved him over, but Trey shook his head again. Then he tossed some money on the bar to pay for his drink and walked back to the boarding house.

Kayla didn't get Trey's message until the morning, and her heart fluttered inside her chest when she picked up her phone and saw his name on the screen. She clicked on the message icon.

Just thinking abt u, wondering what u r doing...

The time stamp indicated that he'd reached out to her at 10:28 pm.

Sorry—I was in the barn all night watching over a new litter of kittens.

He replied immediately.

Everything okay?

8 kittens, only 5 survived.

Tough night for you.

She hadn't expected his immediate and unquestioning understanding. It had been a tough night. Yeah, she'd grown up on a ranch and seen a lot of births and deaths, but it still hurt to lose an animal. She'd tried to keep the kittens warm with blankets and hot water bottles and her own body heat, but the three she'd lost had just been too small.

I'm sorry I didn't have a chance to call.

Me 2. I ended up @ the Ace with Derek.

She had enough secrets in her life, but she wasn't ready for the third degree from her family when they learned that she'd been hanging out with Trey Strickland, because they all knew that she'd had a huge crush on her brother's best friend in high school. And though she wasn't proud of her instinctive cringe, she had to ask.

You didn't say anything about us?

There r enough brawls there without giving your brother an excuse to hit me.

She exhaled a sigh of relief.

Good. I like your nose where it is.

Me 2. But now I'm wondering…r u ashamed of our relationship?

I'm just not sure what our relationship is.

Maybe we can work on figuring it out today.

Which was an undeniably tempting offer. She missed him more than she wanted to admit, conscious with each day that passed that he wasn't going to be in Rust Creek Falls for very long, and the time was quickly slipping away. Unfortunately, she knew that they wouldn't be able to figure out anything that day.

I'm on maid of honor duty today—looking for Kristen's wedding dress.

All day?

Knowing my sister, probably.

OK. I'll touch base with u 2morrow.

I'm at the theater 2morrow. But I'm free Tuesday.

Tuesday is too far away.

It was far away, and the fact that he thought so, too, put a smile on her face as she got ready to go shopping with the bride-to-be.

RUST CREEK RAMBLINGS: DECK THE COWBOY
Local cowboys have been showing their holiday spirit…or maybe it would be more accurate to say that Tommy Wheeler and Jared Winfree demonstrated the effect of imbibing *too many* holiday spirits after the men went a couple of rounds at the Ace in the Hole this past Friday night! Both were declared winners in the brawl and awarded a free night's accommodation in the sheriff's lockup as well as receiving a detailed bill for damages from everyone's favorite bar owner, Rosey Travern.

Chapter Eight

Kristen tried on at least a dozen different styles of wedding dresses—from long sleeves to strapless, slim-fitting to hoop skirts, simple taffeta to all-over lace decorated with tiny beads and crystals. And she looked stunning in each and every one. Even the layers and layers of ruffled organza that would have looked like an explosion of cotton candy on anyone else looked wonderful on Kristen.

"You must at least have a particular style in mind," Rita Dalton chided, when Kristen went back to the sample rack and selected four more completely different dresses again.

"I don't," the bride-to-be insisted. "But I think I'll know it when I see it."

But none of those four dresses seemed to be the right one, either. Rita moved away from the bridal gowns to peruse a more colorful rack of dresses.

"What do you think of this for your maid of honor?" she asked, lifting a hanger from the bar.

"Oh, I *love* the color," Kristen agreed, touching a hand

to the cornflower taffeta. "The blue is almost a perfect match to Kayla's eyes."

Kayla glanced at the dress. "It is pretty."

"You should try it on," Rita urged.

Her panicked gaze flew to her sister. Though Kristen understood the cause of her panic, she was at a loss to help her out of the sticky situation.

Rita looked at the tag. "This is a size six—perfect."

The dress wasn't only a size six, it was also very fitted, and there was no way Kayla could squeeze into the sample without revealing her baby bump.

"Today is about finding Kristen a dress," she reminded their mother.

"But if Kristen likes it and you like it, why can't we pick out your dress, too?"

"Because the bridesmaids' dresses should complement the bride's style—which means that there's no point in considering any options until she's chosen her dress."

"But look at this," Kristen said, coming to her rescue by holding up another outfit. "Doesn't it just scream 'mother-of-the-bride'?"

Rita glanced over, the irritated frown on her brow smoothing out when she saw the elegant sheath-style dress with bolero jacket that Kristen was holding.

Thank you, Kayla mouthed to her sister behind their mother's back.

"I'm not sure I want a dress that screams anything," Rita said. "But that is lovely."

Kristen shoved the dress into their mother's hands and steered her into the fitting room she'd recently vacated. They left the store thirty minutes later with a dress for the mother-of-the-bride but nothing for the bride herself.

"There's another bridal shop just down the street," Rita said.

"Can we go for lunch first?" Kristen asked. "I'm starving."

"Priorities," their mother chided. "June is only six months away, and you need a gown."

"I need to eat or I'm going to pass out in a puddle of taffeta."

Rita glanced at her watch. "All right—we'll go for a quick bite."

They found a familiar chain restaurant not too far away. Even before she looked at the menu, Kayla's mouth was watering for French fries and gravy, a lunchtime staple from high school that she hadn't craved in recent years— until she got pregnant. After a brief perusal of the menu, she set it aside.

"What are you having?" Kristen asked.

"The chicken club wrap and fries."

Her mother frowned. "French fries, Kayla?"

"What's wrong with French fries?" she asked, aware that she sounded more than a little defensive.

"Do you think I don't know the real reason you didn't want to try on that dress is that you're afraid you won't fit into a size six right now?"

"I've put on a few pounds," she admitted. "Not twenty." At least, not yet.

"It always starts with a few," her mother said, not unsympathetically.

"What starts with a few?"

"Emotional eating."

Kayla looked at Kristen, to see if her sister was having better luck following their mother's logic, but Kristen just shrugged.

"I understand that it's hard," Rita continued.

"What's hard?"

She glanced across the table at her other daughter. "You

and Kristen have always been close. You've always done so many things together. Now your sister is getting married, and you're afraid that you're going to be alone."

She opened her mouth to protest then decided that if that was the excuse her mother was willing to believe, why would she dissuade her?

"I'm going to wash up," Rita said. "If the server comes before I'm back, you can order the chicken Caesar for me."

"And people think I'm the only actress in the family," Kristen commented when their mother had gone.

"Am I really that pathetic?" Kayla wanted to know. "Do you think I'd ever be so devastated over the lack of a man in my life that I'd eat myself into a bigger dress size?"

"You're not pathetic at all," her sister said loyally. "And if Mom had seen you and Trey dancing at the wedding, she'd realize how far off base she is. Then again, if she'd seen you two dancing at the wedding, she might suspect the real reason you're craving French fries."

"She's right about the weight gain, though," Kayla admitted. "I'm up nine pounds already."

"And still wearing your skinny jeans." She lifted the hem of her sweater to show that the button was unfastened and the zipper half-undone.

"Wow—we're going to have to paint 'Goodyear' on you and float you up in the sky pretty soon."

"Sure, you're making jokes," Kayla said. "But at dinner Sunday night, when I said that yes, I would like some dessert, Mom cut me a sliver of lemon meringue pie that was so narrow, I could see through the filling."

"So tell her that you're pregnant," her sister advised. "I bet she'd let you have seconds of dessert if she knew you were eating for two."

"If she didn't drown the pie with her tears of disappointment and shame first. And then, of course, she'd demand to know who the father is—"

"And daddy would get out his shotgun," Kristen interjected.

She shook her head. "Definitely not a good scene."

"But probably inevitable," her sister said. "Which is why you have to tell Trey."

Kayla sighed. "I know."

The server came and they ordered their lunches—Kayla opting for a side salad rather than fries to appease her mother. Kristen chose the same sandwich as her sister but with the fries and gravy that Kayla wanted.

"When are you seeing Trey again?" Kristen asked when the waiter left them alone again.

"I don't know."

"You need to make a plan to see him," her sister insisted. "And you need to *tell him*."

"Tell who what?" Rita asked, returning to her seat at the table.

"I need to, uh, tell Derek that Midnight Shadow was favoring her right foreleg when I moved her out of her stall this morning."

"He won't be happy about that," their mother noted.

"Hopefully it isn't anything serious," Kristen said.

When their meals were delivered, talk shifted back to the wedding. Kayla ate her salad, silently promising the baby that she'd have something fatty and salty later, when she'd escaped from the eagle eye of her mother.

"What did you think of the dresses I tried on?" Kristen asked her sister, as she dragged a thick fry through the puddle of gravy on her plate. "And I want your honest opinion."

Kayla focused on her own plate and stabbed a cherry tomato with her fork. "I think they were all beautiful dresses and you looked stunning in each one."

"That's not very helpful," Kristen chided.

"Well, it's true. It's also true that I don't think any of them was the right dress for you."

"Why not?"

She chewed the tomato. "Because they were all too... designer."

Kristen wrinkled her nose. "What does that even mean?"

"It means that you're trying too hard to look like a Hollywood bride."

"Ryan lived and worked in Hollywood for a lot of years, surrounded by some of the world's most beautiful women," her sister pointed out. "I don't want to disappoint him on our wedding day."

"Think about what you just said," Kayla told her. "Yes, your fiancé was surrounded by beautiful women in Hollywood—but he didn't fall in love until he came to Montana and met *you*. So why would you want to be anything different than the woman he fell in love with?"

"I don't," Kristen said.

"Remember the first dress you looked at—the one you instinctively gravitated toward and then put back on the rack without trying it on because it was too simple?"

"The one with the little cap sleeves and the open back?"

Kayla nodded. "You need to go back and try it on."

"I will," Kristen decided, popping another French fry into her mouth. "Right after we finish lunch."

"How was shopping with your sister and your mother?" Trey asked Kayla, when he called the next morning.

She let out a deep sigh. "It was...an experience."

"Did Kristen find a dress?"

"I think it was about the thirty-fifth one she tried on, but yes, she finally found it."

"Does that mean you're free today?"

"It means I don't have to go shopping," she told him. "But I do have to bake Christmas cookies."

"Okay, what are you doing after that?"

"I'm probably going to be tied up in the kitchen most of the day," she told him.

He paused. "I was really hoping we could spend some time together."

She was hoping for the same thing, especially since she knew that Trey's time in Rust Creek Falls was limited. "Do you want to come over and help me make cookies?"

"I can't believe I'm actually saying this," he noted. "But yes, if that's the only way I can be with you, I do."

"You know where to find me."

"Will I find coffee there, too?"

"There will definitely be coffee," she assured him.

It wasn't until he pulled into the long drive of the Circle D Ranch that he considered the possible awkwardness of the situation if Derek was at the main house. Not that his friend's potential disapproval would have affected his decision to come, but he should have factored him into the equation and he hadn't. He hadn't thought about anything but how much he wanted to see Kayla.

When he got to the house, there was no sign of Derek— or anyone else other than Kayla. "Where is everyone?"

"My parents went to an equipment auction in Missoula, and my brothers are out doing whatever they do around the ranch."

"So no one will interrupt if I kiss you?"

"No one will interrupt," she promised.

He dipped his head toward her. "Mmm…you smell really good."

She laughed softly. "I think it's the cookies."

He nuzzled her throat, making her blood heat and her knees quiver. "No, it's definitely you."

"You smell good, too." She kissed him lightly. "And taste even better."

He drew her closer, kissed her longer and deeper—until the oven timer began to buzz.

Saved by the bell, Kayla thought, embarrassed to realize that she'd momentarily forgotten they were standing in the middle of her mother's kitchen, making out like teenagers.

"You said no one would interrupt," he reminded her.

"Mechanical timers excluded." She moved away from him to slide her hand into an oven mitt and take the pan out of the oven.

While she was doing that, he surveyed the ingredients, bowls and utensils spread out over the counter. "How many cookies do you plan to make?"

She gestured toward the counter. "The list is there."

He read aloud: "Pecan Sandies, Coconut Macaroons, Brownies, Peppermint Fudge, Sugar Cookies, Rocky Road Squares, Snowballs, Peanut Brittle, White Chocolate Chip Cookies with Macadamia Nuts and Dried Cherries." He glanced up. "You don't have a shorter name for that one?"

She shook her head.

"Well, I guess people would at least know what they're getting," he acknowledged. "As opposed to a snowball."

"Snowballs are one of my favorites," she told him. "Chopped dates, nuts and crispy rice cereal rolled in coconut."

"There's no gingerbread on the list."

"Kristen and I baked that last week."

"What are these?" he asked, pointing to a plate of cookies she'd baked earlier.

"Those are the Pecan Sandies."

"Can I try one?"

"Sure," she said.

He bit into the flaky pastry. "Mmm. This is good," he mumbled around a mouthful of cookie. "No wonder so many people put on weight over the holidays with these kinds of goodies to sample."

She froze with the spatula in hand, wondering if he was just making a casual comment or if he'd noticed the extra pounds she was carrying. She was wearing yoga pants and a shapeless top that disguised all of her curves, but especially the one of her belly.

"What can I do to help?" Trey asked. "Because if you don't give me a job, I'll just eat everything you make."

She chided herself for being paranoid and turned her attention back to the task at hand. "You can start by pouring yourself a cup of the coffee you wanted." She indicated the half-full carafe on the warmer. "Sugar is in the bowl above, milk and cream are in the fridge."

"Can I get you some?" he asked.

"No, I'm fine, thanks."

While he doctored his coffee, she measured out flour and sugar and cocoa powder.

"What are you making now?"

"Brownies."

"One of *my* favorites," he told her.

She laughed. "Did you skip breakfast?"

"As if my grandmother would let me," he chided, stealing another cookie.

She put a wooden spoon in his hand and steered him toward a pot on the stove containing the butter and chopped semisweet chocolate she'd measured earlier. She turned the burner on to medium-low. "Just keep stirring gently until the ingredients are melted and blended."

He sipped his coffee from one hand and stirred, as instructed, with the other. "I think I have a talent for this."

"Just so long as you keep your fingers out of it."

"I'll try to resist." He caught her as she moved past him and hauled her back for a quick kiss. "But only the chocolate."

"I'm going to have to send you out of the kitchen if you continue to distract me," she warned him.

"I like kissing you."

She felt her cheeks flush. "Stir."

He resumed stirring.

She had expected that Trey would end up being more of a hindrance than a help, but aside from stealing the occasional kiss at the most unexpected times, his presence really did help move things along quickly. He willingly measured, chopped and mixed as required and without complaint.

Rita called home just after two o'clock to tell Kayla that the auction was over and that they were going for dinner in Missoula and would be home late. It was only then that Kayla realized she hadn't given any thought to dinner—or lunch. She immediately apologized to Trey for not feeding him, which made him laugh, because he'd been steadily sampling the cookies and bars while they worked.

"But you're probably starving," he realized. "You haven't touched any of this."

"I had a brownie," she confessed.

"A whole brownie?"

"It's not that I'm not tempted," she admitted. "But most of this stuff would go straight to my hips."

His gaze slid over her body, slowly, appraisingly. "I don't think you need to worry."

Kayla half wished her mother could have been there to hear what he said, except that she wouldn't have invited him to help her with the baking if her mother had been home.

"But cookies probably aren't a very healthy dinner," he continued. "Do you want to go out to grab a bite?"

She should offer to cook something there so they could sit down and talk, but the truth was, after standing around in the kitchen most of the day, her feet and back were sore, and the idea of sitting down and letting someone else prepare a meal was irresistible. "I do," she decided.

Of course, going out with Trey meant giving up another opportunity to tell him about their baby, because she didn't dare whisper the word *pregnant* within earshot of anyone else in town. She might have control over what appeared in the Ramblings column, but the Rust Creek Falls grapevine had a life of its own.

They went to the Ace in the Hole. The bar wasn't one of Kayla's favorite places, but it did have a decent menu and wasn't usually too busy on a Sunday night.

It wasn't until they were seated in the restaurant that she thought to ask, "Your grandparents weren't expecting you home for dinner?"

"I called them while you were getting changed and told them that I was going out."

She didn't ask if he'd mentioned that he was going out with her—she wasn't sure she wanted to know. Whether or not Melba had deliberately called about the pickles to force her path to cross with Trey's, as he believed, she suspected it would be dangerous to encourage the older woman's matchmaking efforts.

Especially when she was worried enough about getting her own hopes up. Yes, she had to tell Trey about the baby, but she'd thought it might be easier if they knew one another a little better. But as they were getting to know one another, she was letting herself get caught up in the romance of being with him—talking and flirting and kissing. For a girl with extremely limited dating experience, he was a fantasy come to life. A fantasy that she knew would come crashing down around her when she told him that she was pregnant.

And she wasn't ready for that to happen. Not yet.

After their meal, Trey drove Kayla back to the Circle D.

He wasn't anxious to say good-night to her, but he could tell that she was tired. She'd been on her feet in the kitchen all day, having started her baking hours before he showed up, and was obviously ready for bed.

Of course, thinking about Kayla in bed stirred his memories and his blood and made him wish that she didn't still live in her parents' home—or that he wasn't staying with his grandparents.

He'd been back in town a little more than a week—barely nine days—but she'd been on his mind each and every one of those days. No one he knew would believe it if he told them that he'd spent the day in the kitchen with Kayla, but the truth was, he didn't care what they were doing so long as he was with her. And when he couldn't be with her, he was thinking about her.

Now that he knew her a little better, he wondered how he could have been so blind as to overlook her for so many years—even if she was his best friend's little sister. Because she was also a smart and interesting woman with hair as soft as the finest silk, eyes as blue as the Montana sky and a smile that could light up a room. And when she smiled at him, she made him feel like a superhero.

No other woman had ever made him feel that way. No other woman had ever made him feel as good as he felt when he was with her. He loved touching her and holding her and kissing her. In recent years he'd had a few relationships, but for some reason, those had been short on the simple things—like kissing and hand-holding.

He and Kayla had already made love, and he wanted to make love with her again, but for now, he was enjoying the kissing and hand-holding and just being with her.

He was also taking a lot of cold showers.

As enjoyable as it was to spend time with Kayla, she also got him stirred up. But he was determined not to rush into anything. Not this time. He wasn't a teenager anymore—or under the influence of spiked wedding punch—and he was determined to take things slow, to show Kayla that she was worth the time and effort.

Kayla didn't tell Trey that she'd been asked to help out at the elementary school, but when she showed up at the gymnasium at three o'clock, he was there, anyway. Of course, there were a lot of people there. With the pageant scheduled for the following weekend and much work still to do, the teachers had obviously tried to pull in as many extra hands as they could.

Apparently Trey had been asked to contribute his, as he was already hammering a set together, Natalie was working on costumes—and flirting with Gavin Everton, the new gym teacher—while Kayla was put to work painting scenery.

She felt perspiration bead on her face as she stretched to paint stars in the night sky. She was wearing leggings and an oversize flannel shirt, and while the bulky attire did a good job of disguising the extra pounds she was carrying, it also ratcheted up her internal temperature considerably.

She swiped a hand over her brow. "It's warm under these lights."

"Why don't you take off that flannel shirt?" Trey suggested.

"Because I'm only wearing a camisole underneath," Kayla told him.

He grinned. "And the problem?"

She waved her paintbrush at him. "Don't you have to go hammer something?"

He lifted the tool in acknowledgment and returned his attention to the set he was building.

On the pretext of retrieving a box of lace and ribbon, Natalie sidled over to her friend. "How do you resist jumping his bones?" she asked.

"It's not easy," Kayla admitted.

"So why don't you give in and share all the details with your friends who have no romantic prospects and need a vicarious thrill?"

"Because I want what Kristen has with Ryan," she admitted. "A happily-ever-after, not just a holiday fling."

"I want a happily-ever-after someday, too. But in the meantime, I'd settle for a little happy-right-now."

"Is that why you were chatting up the new gym teacher?"

Natalie's gaze shifted to the man in question. "He's cute," she acknowledged. "But not good fling material."

"How can you tell?"

"Residential address."

"What does that mean?"

"He lives in Rust Creek Falls, which means that a casual hookup could—and very likely would—result in awkward encounters after the fact."

"Or maybe a relationship," Kayla suggested.

Natalie shrugged. "Maybe. But the risk might be greater than the reward."

But when Gavin came over to ask Natalie for her help untangling the strings of candy garland that would line the path to the Land of Sweets, she happily walked away with him.

Over the next few hours, many more people came and went, giving a few hours of their time, including Paige Traub, Maggie Crawford, Cecelia Pritchett and Mallory Dalton. Both Paige and Maggie had young children, and as Kayla picked up on little bits and pieces of their conversation, she wished she didn't feel compelled to hide her pregnancy. She wanted to be free to join in their circle and listen to their experiences and advice.

Instead, she was on the outside, alone with her questions and fears. A soon-to-be single mother still afraid to tell even the father of her baby about the baby.

She capped the paint, dropped her brush into the bucket to be washed and wiped her hands on a rag.

Trey must have finished his assigned task, too, because he closed up the toolbox and made his way over to her. "My stomach's telling me that we worked past dinner."

"Your stomach would be right," she confirmed.

"Why don't we head over to the boarding house to see what my grandmother cooked up tonight?"

Kayla brushed her hands down the thighs of her paint-splattered pants and shook her head. "I'm not going anywhere dressed like this."

"I think you look beautiful."

She looked at him skeptically. "I think someone must have hit you in the head with your hammer."

He smiled as he wiped a smear of green paint off her cheek. "Do you really have no idea what you do to me?"

"What do I do to you?" she asked warily.

"You tangle me up in knots inside."

"I'm…sorry?" she said, uncertain how to respond to his admission.

"I don't need you to be sorry," he told her. "I need you to stop taking two steps back every time we take one step forward."

She frowned. "Is that what you think I'm doing?"

He looked pointedly at the floor so she could see that she had—literally—done exactly that.

He stepped forward again.

She forced herself to hold her ground.

"Good." He framed her face in his hands and, despite the presence of several other people still lingering in the gym, lowered his mouth to hers. "That's a start."

Chapter Nine

While Kayla seemed to be resisting Trey's efforts to get closer to her, he also knew she had a hard time saying no to anyone who asked for help. The elementary school production was a case in point. So instead of asking her if she wanted to take a trip into Kalispell to go shopping with him, an invitation that he suspected she would politely decline, he stopped by the ranch the next day and said to her, "I need your help."

Not surprisingly, she responded, "With what?"

"Christmas shopping."

"I'm sure you're perfectly capable of shopping."

"You'd think so," he acknowledged. "But the truth is, I suck at shopping even worse than I do at wrapping."

She managed a smile. "I'm not sure that's possible."

"It is," he insisted. "I never seem to know what to buy, and on the rare occasion that I have a good idea, I end up with the wrong size or color."

"That's why vendors introduced gift receipts."

"We had a deal," he said, reminding her of the bargain he'd extracted from her in exchange for keeping her identity as the Rust Creek Rambler a secret. Not that he would ever have betrayed her confidence, but he wasn't opposed to using the leverage she'd given him to spend more time with her. "And I'll buy you lunch."

She sighed. "You're right—we had a deal. You don't have to bribe me with lunch."

"You'll earn it," he promised, as she followed him out to his truck. "I have a couple of things for my grandparents, but I've just found out that Hadley and Tessa are coming to Rust Creek Falls for the holidays, and I don't have a clue where to start finding something for either of them."

"What about your parents and your brothers—are they coming, too?"

He shook his head. "Not this year."

"Isn't it strange, not being with your own parents for Christmas?"

"Not really," he said. "Because when we were kids, we were always at Grandma and Grandpa's. It would seem stranger to me not to be here."

"I guess that makes sense," she agreed. "Okay, tell me about the cousins you need to shop for."

"They're Claire's older sisters. Both of them live in Bozeman. Hadley is a twenty-nine-year-old veterinarian who never turns a stray away from her door. Tessa is a twenty-seven-year-old graphic designer and movie buff."

Half an hour later, they were at the shopping center. She moved with purpose and though she claimed not to have anything specific in mind, she assured him she would know when she found what she was looking for. Since he honestly didn't have a clue, he was content to let her lead the way.

For Hadley, she found a set of glass coasters with etched

paw prints that somehow managed to be both elegant and fun. For Tessa, she found a book of iconic movie posters that he knew his cousin would love. As they exited the bookstore, he couldn't help but be impressed by her efficiency.

"I bet you're one of those people who has all of her shopping and wrapping done by the first of December, aren't you?" Trey asked her.

"Not the first," she denied. "But I don't believe in leaving things to the last minute, either."

"It's still ten days before Christmas," he pointed out.

"Apparently, we have different opinions of what the last minute is."

"Apparently," he agreed. "So tell me—have you sent your letter to Santa yet?"

She shook her head. "I think the big guy's going to be kept busy enough meeting the demands of those under the age of ten."

"Is that how old you were when you stopped believing in Santa?"

"Who says I stopped believing in Santa?"

His brows lifted.

She shrugged. "Santa made Kristen's wish come true this year."

"Huh?"

So she told him about Ryan riding in the parade as Santa Claus and his subsequent proposal to her sister.

"My grandparents told me that she was engaged, but they didn't tell me how it happened."

"Well, that's how it happened," Kayla said.

"It was pretty quick, don't you think? I mean—they only met in the summer."

She shrugged. "I guess when you know, you know."

He wondered if that was true—if that was the real reason he hadn't stopped thinking about Kayla since the night they spent together. He'd never believed there was one woman who was the right woman for him—why would he want to narrow down his options when there were so many women in the world? But since the summer, he hadn't thought about anyone but Kayla; he hadn't wanted anyone but Kayla.

"Okay, so now that Hadley and Tessa are taken care of—what about Claire?"

"I've got that one covered," he told her. "Grandma and Grandpa have booked a weekend at the Thunder Canyon Resort for Claire and Levi, and I got Claire a gift certificate for the spa."

"She'll love that," Kayla said, sounding surprised by his insight and thoughtfulness.

"That's what my grandmother said when she suggested it."

She laughed, then stopped abruptly in front of the display window of a store called Christmas Memories. She tapped a finger on the glass. "Speaking of your grandmother."

His gaze followed to where she was pointing. "Um… that's a Christmas tree."

She rolled her eyes. "What's *on* the tree?" she prompted.

"Ornaments," he realized.

She nodded, already heading into the store.

There weren't just ornaments displayed on trees but boxes of them stacked high and baskets overflowing. There were classic ornaments and fun ornaments, sports-themed and movie-themed decorations, baubles that lit up or played music—or lit up *and* played music. And there was even a selection of imported mouth-blown glass ornaments.

She held up a delicate clear glass sphere with a gold angel figurine inside. "What do you think?"

"I think I'll be the favorite grandchild this Christmas," he told her, grinning. "She'll love it so much that she'll probably rearrange all of the other ornaments on the tree so that it's hanging front and center."

"I doubt she has that much time on her hands."

"You're right—she'll make my grandfather do it."

Kayla chuckled as he took the ornament to the register to pay for it.

"Now you're all done except for the wrapping," she told him, as they exited the store.

"Oh, yeah." He made a face. "I forgot about the wrapping part."

"Do you have paper? Bows?"

"My grandmother has all of that stuff."

"You can't wrap your grandmother's gift in paper that she bought," Kayla protested.

"Why not?"

"Because you can't."

"That's not a reason."

"Yes, it is," she insisted.

"Okay, so I'll pay for the gift-wrapping service down the hall for her gift and use her paper for the rest."

Kayla shook her head. "You can bring the gifts to the ranch and I'll help you wrap them."

"Really? You'll help me?"

"I'll fold your corners—you're in charge of the tape."

He didn't manage to avoid Derek at the Circle D later that day. When they got back from shopping, Kayla sent him to the kitchen to set up at the table while she went to get her wrapping supplies. His steps faltered when he saw his friend standing at the counter, filling his thermos with coffee from the carafe.

"What are you doing here?" Derek asked, his tone more curious than concerned.

He held up the bags of gifts in his hands. "Kayla offered to help me with my wrapping."

"When did she do that?"

"When we were shopping."

"My sister went shopping with you? How did that come about?"

"I asked her."

"Why?"

"Because I needed some help figuring out what to buy for my cousins." Although that was partly true, the real truth was that he'd used the shopping as an excuse to spend time with her, and he was deliberately tiptoeing around that fact. He didn't want to tiptoe around it—he didn't want to keep his relationship a secret from anyone, especially his best friend. "And because I like her."

Derek frowned. "What do you mean—you *like* her?"

"I mean she's smart and fun and I enjoy spending time with her."

"How much time have you been spending with her?" Kayla's brother wanted to know.

"As much as possible," he admitted.

"I thought you were seeing someone in Thunder Canyon."

"I only said I was seeing someone," Trey pointed out. "You assumed that someone was in Thunder Canyon."

Derek's scowl deepened. "Are you telling me that you're *dating* my sister?"

He nodded.

"Dammit, Trey. I thought we were friends."

"We are friends."

"You can't date a friend's sister—it makes everything awkward."

"I'm sorry."

"Sorry enough to back off?" Derek challenged.

"No," he replied without any hesitation.

"How long has this been going on?"

Trey thought back to the night of the wedding but decided that didn't count—or even if it did, he had no intention of mentioning it to Kayla's brother. "A couple of weeks."

Derek shook his head as he capped his thermos. "I suppose I should be glad you didn't hook up with the blonde that night we were at the bar," he said, and walked out the door.

"What blonde in the bar?"

He winced at the sound of Kayla's voice from behind him. "Heard that, did you?"

"And I'm still waiting for an explanation," she told him.

"I mentioned that I went to the Ace in the Hole with your brother last week," he reminded her.

She nodded.

"Well, there were a couple of girls who invited us to join them," he explained. "Derek went to their table. I went home."

"Why didn't you go to their table?" she asked, sounding—to his surprise—more curious than annoyed.

"Because," he said honestly, "I didn't—I don't—want to be with anyone but you."

Kayla was so confused.

Trey was saying and doing all of the right things to make her believe that he wanted a real relationship with her. He'd even told her brother that they were dating. But he was only in town for the holidays, after which he would be going back to Thunder Canyon, and he hadn't said a word about what would happen between them after that.

Did she want a long-distance relationship? Did long-distance relationships ever work or were they just extended breakups? What were their other options?

If Trey asked, she would move to Thunder Canyon to be with him. She wasn't a schoolgirl with a crush anymore but a woman with a woman's feelings and desires. And she wanted a life with Trey and their baby—the baby he still didn't know anything about.

"That didn't take as long as I thought," Trey said, when she'd affixed a bow to the final gift.

"Doesn't it feel good—to have your shopping and wrapping done?"

"I can think of something that would feel even better," he said, leaning across the table to brush his lips to hers. "Why don't we go down to the barn, saddle up a couple of horses and go for a ride?"

She wasn't sure whether she was relieved or disappointed by his suggestion. "Actually, I have to go into town."

"For what?"

"I've got some things to do at the newspaper office."

"We don't have to go out for very long," Trey said.

"I'm sorry, but I really don't know how much time I'm going to need. I probably should have gone into the office first thing, but I promised to help you."

"I didn't mean to impose on your time," he said, just a little stiffly.

"You didn't," she assured him, reaching across the table to touch his hand. "I *wanted* to help, but now I need to go into town."

She wasn't surprised that he looked disappointed. He was probably accustomed to spending several hours a day on horseback in addition to the several more that he spent training horses at the Thunder Canyon Resort, and he likely missed the exercise and the routine.

"But there's no reason you can't go down to the barn and ask Derek—or Eli—" she added, not certain of the status of things between her youngest brother and his friend "—to give you a mount to saddle up."

"I didn't want to ride as much as I wanted to ride with you," Trey told her.

"I'm sorry," she said again, and she meant it. Not just because she couldn't accept his invitation but because she couldn't tell him the real reason why.

"Okay, we'll do it another time," he said. "For today, why don't I give you a ride into town?"

"Then I'd need a ride back again," she pointed out.

"And I was hoping you wouldn't see through my nefarious plan."

"That was your nefarious plan? Don't you have better things to do than play chauffeur for me?"

"Actually, I don't," he said. "There's nothing I want more than to be with you."

"Then I will accept your offer," she agreed.

It didn't take her very long at all to read and edit the copy for the next edition of the paper, but Kayla lingered in the office to give credence to her claim that it was a major task. She felt guilty about lying to Trey—and she'd panicked when he mentioned riding.

She hadn't been on a horse in almost two months. She'd read a lot of conflicting advice about the safety of riding during pregnancy. Many doctors said a clear and unequivocal no. In Montana, though, where most kids were put on the back of a horse before they started kindergarten, doctors were a little less strict. Kayla's own doctor had assured her that while it was usually safe for a pregnant woman to ride during her first trimester, because the baby was small and adequately protected by the mother's pelvic bone, after twelve weeks, the risks to both mother and child were increased.

Kayla had decided that she wasn't willing to take the risk. She might not have planned to have a baby at this point in her life, but as soon as she became aware of the tiny life growing inside her, she'd been determined to do everything in her power to protect that life. Of course, it was a little awkward to invent new and credible excuses to explain why she wasn't participating in an activity she'd always loved, but the busyness of the holiday season had supplied her with many reasons.

She was sure she would love riding with Trey, because she enjoyed everything they did together. At the same time, it was hard to be with him with such a huge—and growing—secret between them. Contrary to what her sister believed, she *wanted* to tell him about their baby, but she knew that revelation would change everything. She was enjoying the flirting and kissing, and she wanted to bask in the glow of his attention just a little while longer.

Surely there wasn't anything wrong with that—was there?

"Did Grandma run out of coffee?" Trey asked, sitting down across from his grandfather at Daisy's Donuts.

"She wanted me out of the house," Gene said. "Something about a fancy tea for her girls. But what are you doing here?"

"I wasn't invited to the fancy tea for the girls, either."

His grandfather barked out a laugh. "I don't imagine you were—but I was more interested in why you aren't with a certain pretty lady who has been keeping you company of late."

Trey didn't see any point in pretending he didn't know who his grandfather was talking about. "Kayla had some things to do at the newspaper."

"I forgot she worked there," Gene said. "Things getting serious between you two?"

He tried not to squirm. "I don't know."

Gene's bushy white brows lifted. "What the hell kind of response is that?"

"An honest one," Trey told him.

"She's not the type of girl you toy with. She's the type you settle down with."

He shifted uneasily. "I'm not ready to settle down, Grandpa."

"Why not?"

"I'm only twenty-eight years old."

Gene nodded. "You're twenty-eight years old, you've got a good job and a solid future. Why wouldn't you want to add a wife and a family to that picture?"

"Because I like the picture exactly as it is right now."

"Sometimes we don't really know what we want until we've lost it," his grandfather warned.

"And sometimes people rush into things that they later regret," Trey countered. "Like Claire and Levi."

"What do you think they regret?"

"Getting married so young, having a baby so soon."

"Do you really think so?"

He couldn't believe his grandfather had to ask that question. "Claire was barely twenty-two when she got married, and then she had a baby less than a year after that."

"And she's thriving as a wife and mother."

"Was she thriving when she packed up her baby and left her husband?"

"She was frustrated," Gene acknowledged. "Being married isn't always easy, but even though they hit a rough patch, they're still together, aren't they? Not just committed to one another and the vows they exchanged, but actually happy together."

Trey couldn't deny that they seemed happy and devoted to one another and their little girl. But that didn't mean he was eager to head down the same path.

"And I couldn't help but notice that you seem happy with Kayla," his grandfather continued.

"I enjoy being with her," he agreed cautiously.

"What's going to happen when the holidays are over and you go back to Thunder Canyon?"

"I haven't thought that far ahead," he admitted.

"Well, maybe you should, because if you think a girl as pretty and sweet as Kayla Dalton will still be waiting around for you when you finally come back again next summer, you might find yourself in for a nasty surprise."

The possibility made him scowl. "If she finds someone else and wants to be with someone else, then that's her choice, isn't it?"

"It is," Gene agreed. "I just wanted to be sure that you could live with those consequences."

"Besides, she doesn't give the impression of a woman chomping at the bit for marriage."

"Maybe she's not. On the other hand, her twin sister just got engaged and is starting to plan her wedding. That kind of thing tends to make other women think about their own hopes and dreams." Gene pushed his empty cup away and stood up.

"Do you want a refill?" Trey asked.

His grandfather shook his head. "I'm going to head over to the feed store and catch up with the other old folks. You young people exasperate me."

Trey got himself another cup of coffee while he waited for Kayla to text him to say that she was finished at the newspaper. Daisy's seemed to do a pretty steady business throughout the day, and several people stopped by his table to say hi and exchange a few words. But mostly he was left alone, and he found himself thinking about what his grandfather had said.

If you think a girl as pretty and sweet as Kayla Dalton will still be waiting around for you...you might be in for a nasty surprise.

Gene was probably right. There wasn't any shortage of single men in Rust Creek Falls, and just because Kayla hadn't dated many of them in the past didn't mean that couldn't change. As a result of her naturally shy demeanor, she'd been overlooked by a lot of guys, but since he'd been spending time with her, he'd noticed the speculative looks she'd been getting from other cowboys. He suspected several of them were just waiting for Trey to go back to Thunder Canyon so they could make a move—and the thought of another man making a move on Kayla didn't sit well with him.

He'd never been the jealous type, but he hadn't exactly been thrilled to see Kayla hug some guy the night they were talking outside the community center. She'd introduced the guy as Dawson Landry and told Trey he'd worked in advertising at the *Gazette* before he moved to a bigger paper in Billings. Dawson then told her that he'd recently moved back to Rust Creek Falls and the *Gazette* because he realized he wasn't cut out for life in the big city.

It was a simple and indisputable fact that after his holidays were over, Trey would go back to Thunder Canyon. He had a job and a life there, and he was happy with both. But he was happier when he was with Kayla. And when he was gone, Dawson would still be around.

The realization made him uneasy. He'd meant what he'd said to his grandfather—there were a lot of things he wanted to see and do before he tied himself down. So why did the prospect of being tied to Kayla seem more intriguing than disconcerting?

RUST CREEK RAMBLINGS: MISSING IN ACTION...
OR GETTING SOME ACTION?
Architect Jonah Dalton and artist Vanessa Brent both seemed intent on putting down roots in this town when they married last year. But the happy couple, who lives in the stunning house built by Jonah himself on the Triple D Ranch, has dropped out of sight in recent days, fueling speculation about their whereabouts. Have they slipped out of town for a pre-holiday getaway? Or are they sticking closer to home and family—and working toward expanding their own? Only time will tell…unless the Rambler tells it first!

Chapter Ten

The Candlelight Walk was an event to which all the residents of Rust Creek Falls were invited, and most enjoyed taking part in at least some aspect of it. At one end of Main Street, members of city council distributed lighted candles that were then carried in a processional to the other end where a bonfire would be lit, refreshments served and carols sung.

"I don't remember this," Trey admitted as he walked beside Kayla, the flicker of hundreds of candles illuminating the dark night with a warm glow that moved slowly down the street toward the park.

"It's a fairly new Rust Creek Falls tradition," Kayla told him.

His brows lifted. "Isn't new tradition an oxymoron?"

"I guess it is," she agreed. "Maybe it would be more accurate to say it's a recent ceremonial event that the townspeople have embraced."

"The people of this town find more excuses to get together than anyone I've ever known."

She smiled as she looked around the crowd, recognizing so many familiar faces. "That's probably true. The flood was an eye-opener for all of us, a reminder that everything we take for granted can be taken away. Even those whose homes were spared weren't immune to the effects on the community. As a result, it brought everyone closer together."

He looked around, too, and saw Shane and Gianna heading in their direction. He lifted a hand to wave them over.

"I swear, Gianna looks more pregnant every time I see her," he commented to Kayla. His friend's wife was hugely pregnant—her baby bump plainly evident even beneath the heavy coat she wore.

"When is she due?"

"I have no idea."

"Don't you and Shane work together at the resort?"

"Sure, but I'm in the stables and he's in the kitchen, and guys don't talk about stuff like that."

She rolled her eyes as his friends drew nearer.

"I didn't realize you were still in town," Trey said. "Are you staying for Christmas?"

"We are," Shane confirmed. "With both my sister and brother here now, it seemed the easiest way to get the whole family together for the holidays. Even my parents are coming—they're flying in on the twenty-second and staying at Maverick Manor."

They talked some more about holiday plans, with Gianna admitting that she was already more excited about *next* Christmas, when they would be celebrating the occasion with their baby.

"Staying with Maggie and Jesse and witnessing first-hand the havoc a child can wreak, I'm not quite so eager," Shane admitted.

"Well, it's not as if you can change your mind now," his wife pointed out. Then, to Trey and Kayla. "Madeline has made both of us realize that you can't learn parenting from a book. No matter how much you think you know, a child will quickly prove you wrong."

"Of course, the child in question is my sister's daughter," Shane interjected. "Which might explain a lot."

Kayla smiled at that.

"You guys are going to be fabulous parents," Trey said.

"Do you think so?" Gianna asked, obviously seeking reassurance.

"Of course," he agreed.

"We're both so afraid that we're going to screw something up," she admitted.

"We're going to screw a lot of things up," Shane said. "We just have to hope that our child makes it to adulthood relatively unscathed."

His wife shook her head. "And he wonders why I worry."

"Right now I'm worried about getting you back to the house and off your feet."

"As if my belly wasn't big enough, my ankles are swelling, too," Gianna explained.

Kayla and Trey exchanged good-nights with the other couple, then moved away in the opposite direction.

"Are you okay?" Trey asked. "You seemed to get quiet all of a sudden."

"I was just thinking about Gianna and Shane," she told him.

"What about them?"

"Your assurance that they're going to be fabulous parents," she admitted. "Not that I disagree—I guess I'm just wondering how you can be so sure, how anyone can know how they'll deal with parenthood before they're actually faced with the reality of it."

"Maybe no one can know for sure, but the odds are in their favor because they love one another and their unborn baby."

She nodded, envying the other couple that. She agreed that their commitment and support were important factors in parenting—and wished that she could count on Trey for the same. Of course, she couldn't expect him to support her through the pregnancy and childbirth when he still didn't know that she was pregnant. "They're certainly excited about impending parenthood, notwithstanding the challenges," she noted.

"They've been married two and a half years and are ready to enter the next stage of their life together."

"Could you ever imagine yourself as excited about becoming a father as Shane is?" she asked, striving to keep her tone light and casual.

Trey's steps faltered anyway. "What kind of a question is that?"

She shrugged. "I'm just wondering whether you've ever thought about having kids of your own."

"Well, sure," he finally said. "Someday."

"Someday?"

"There's a lot I want to do before I'm hog-tied by the responsibilities of marriage and babies."

Hog-tied?

Kayla stopped in the middle of the street and turned to look at him. "Is that how you view a family—as something that ties you down and limits your opportunities?"

"I don't mean it as if it's a bad thing," he explained. "It's just not something I'm ready for right now. Especially when I look at my parents—married thirty-two years with five kids born within the first seven years of their marriage. No, I'm definitely not in any rush to go down that same path."

She nodded, pretending to understand, but inside she felt as if her fledgling hopes—and her fragile heart—had been crushed like a candy cane beneath the heel of his boot. There was no way she could be with a man who would feel tied down by her and their baby—no way she could even tell him about their baby now.

She'd had such high hopes for their relationship a few hours earlier. While they'd walked through the town, hand in hand, she'd let herself dream that they would always be together. When she saw Nate Crawford with Noelle perched on his shoulders, she'd imagined that would be Trey with their baby in a couple of years. But now that she knew how he really felt about the prospect of fatherhood, she knew she had to end their relationship before she got in any deeper.

"It's starting to snow," she noted. "Which means it's time for me to be heading home."

"It's only a few flakes," he pointed out. "And we haven't even roasted marshmallows on the bonfire yet."

"A few flakes is all it takes for my mother to worry."

"Well, we don't want that to happen," he said, guiding her to his truck.

She felt his hand on her back, even through the thick coat she wore, and felt tears sting her eyes as she accepted she would never feel his hands on her again. Whatever fantasies she'd spun about living happily-ever-after with this man and their baby weren't ever going to be.

He helped her up onto the passenger seat and she murmured her thanks.

"Are you sure everything's okay?" he asked her.

"I'm sure," she said. "I'm just really tired." And she was—not just physically but emotionally exhausted. Not eager to make any more conversation, she fiddled with the radio until she found a station playing Christmas music, then settled back in her seat, concentrating on the song and holding back the tears that burned her eyes.

Kayla jolted when the door opened and a blast of cold air slapped her face. "What—"

"You're home," Trey told her.

She blinked. "Did I fall asleep?"

"You did," he confirmed.

"I'm sorry."

"I should apologize to you for keeping you out past your bedtime."

She managed a wan smile. "It isn't really that late," she acknowledged. "I've just had so much on my mind— so many things still to be done before Christmas—that I probably haven't been getting enough sleep."

"Then I should let you get inside to bed," he said.

She nodded. "Thanks for the ride."

He didn't take the hint. Instead, he took her arm and guided her to the front door. "Will I see you tomorrow?"

"I don't know," she hedged, aware that she needed to start putting space between them. A lot of space. Three hundred miles would be a good start, but she knew that wouldn't happen until after Christmas.

And right now, Trey seemed more focused on eliminating the space between them. "I'll call you in the morning and we'll figure it out," he said.

Then he leaned in to kiss her, but before his lips touched hers, the porch light clicked on. He pulled back just as Rita Dalton poked her head out the front door.

"What are you two doing outside in this cold weather?" she chided. "Why don't you come on in for some of the hot chocolate I just took off the stove?"

"I'm sure Trey is anxious to get back to town before the snow gets any worse," Kayla told her mom.

"It's just a few flakes," he said again.

Rita smiled at him and stepped away from the door so that they could enter.

"It's so nice that you're here to spend the holidays with Melba and Gene," Rita commented to Trey, as she busied herself pouring the steaming liquid into mugs.

"There's nowhere I'd rather be," he admitted. "And spending time with Kayla has been an added bonus on this trip."

"I know she's been enjoying your company," Rita said. "Her happy glow has brightened up the whole house these past few days."

Kayla kept her gaze focused on the mug she held between her hands and resisted the urge to bang her head against the table.

Could her mother be any more obvious in her matchmaking efforts? And how would she react if Kayla told her that *happy glow* wasn't a consequence of Trey's company but his baby in her belly? Would her mother think the man sitting at her table and drinking hot chocolate was so wonderful if she knew he'd knocked up her daughter?

"Do you have any specific plans for tomorrow?" Rita asked him, setting a plate of cookies on the table.

"Not yet," Trey said, reaching over to touch Kayla's hand. "Although I was hoping to talk Kayla into taking a drive into Kalispell with me so we could go ice skating in Woodland Park."

"Oh, that sounds like fun—doesn't it, Kayla?"

"It does," she agreed. "But I've got to put the finishing touches on the sets for the elementary school holiday pageant tomorrow."

"But you've been working on those sets all week," her mother pointed out. "Surely you can take a day off."

"Actually, I can't. The pageant is tomorrow night."

"Well, maybe we can go skating the day after," Trey suggested.

"Maybe," she agreed.

Rita frowned at her daughter's noncommittal response before she turned her attention back to their guest. "Tell me about your plans for Christmas—is your grandmother cooking a big meal with all the trimmings?"

"Of course."

"She usually serves it around midday, doesn't she?"

"Everyone is expected to be seated at the table at one o'clock sharp," he confirmed.

"We don't eat until six," Rita said. "If you wanted to join us later in the day for another meal."

Kayla felt as if she was watching a train wreck in slow motion—she could see what was happening, but she was powerless to stop it. Not an hour after she'd vowed to put distance between herself and Trey as the first step toward ending their relationship, her mother had invited him to Christmas dinner. On the other hand, spending Christmas with a girlfriend's family was probably too much of a commitment, so she felt fairly confident that he would decline the invitation.

But just in case, she decided to nudge him in that direction. "Mom, you're talking about Christmas Day," she pointed out. "I'm sure whatever plans Trey has with his family will keep him busy throughout the afternoon."

"And if they don't, I'm just letting him know that he's welcome to come here," Rita replied.

"Thank you, Mrs. Dalton. I appreciate the invitation and I'll see what I can do."

"Well, I'll leave you two to finish your beverages," she said.

"Thanks for the hot chocolate and the cookies," Trey said.

Rita beamed at him. "Anytime, Trey."

The next night Kayla attended the holiday pageant at the elementary school. The night after that she was busy helping Nina and Natalie assign and wrap gifts from the Tree of Hope for the area's needy families. It was the day after that—Saturday—while Kayla was hiding out in her room after breakfast that her sister came in.

Kristen had been so busy with the theater and wedding plans that she hadn't been at the ranch very much over the past couple of weeks.

"Trey came to see me yesterday," Kristen announced without preamble.

Kayla's head whipped around in response to her sister's casual announcement. "Why?"

"Because he's trying to plan a special surprise for you and wanted my help."

"What kind of surprise?" she asked, both curious and wary.

Kristen rolled her eyes. "If I told you, it wouldn't be a surprise, would it?"

"Then why did you mention it?"

"Because he mentioned to me that you've been so busy he hasn't seen you since the night of the Candlelight Walk, and I know for a fact that you haven't been any busier than usual and certainly not too busy to spend time with Trey if you wanted to spend time with Trey."

"Okay, so I don't want to spend time with Trey," she acknowledged.

"I don't understand," Kristen said. "Everyone can see

that the man is head over heels for you, and I know how you feel about him, so why are you avoiding him now?"

"Because I finally realized that we want different things."

"What different things?"

"A family, for starters."

Kristen frowned.

So Kayla found herself telling her sister the whole story of that night, from the candle-lighting to their encounter with Gianna and Shane and Trey's subsequent denouncement of marriage and everything that went along with it.

"Wait a minute," Kristen said. "Are you telling me that Trey still doesn't know about the baby?"

"How could I tell him?"

"How could you not?" her sister demanded. "Kayla, the man has been spending every possible minute with you over the past couple of weeks—*everyone* knows he has feelings for you. Except, apparently, the Rust Creek Rambler."

Kayla's eyes filled with tears. "Even if he does have feelings for me, how can I be with a man who doesn't want our baby?"

Her sister was silent for a long moment. "You don't know that he doesn't want your baby," she finally said. "You're making an assumption based on his response to a vague and seemingly hypothetic question. You can't hold that response against him."

"He compared being married to being hog-tied."

"He's still the father of your baby." Kristen's tone was implacable. "And even if you think you can get through the holidays without him finding out about your pregnancy, what's going to happen afterward? What are you going to tell people when they want to know the identity of your baby's father? And even if you refuse to name him, what's going to happen when Trey comes back to Rust Creek Falls and sees you with a baby? Do you really believe he won't immediately know the child is his?"

"Maybe he won't," Kayla argued, albeit weakly. "Maybe he'll want to think it's someone else's baby so that he doesn't have to be tied down by the responsibilities of parenthood."

"There's no maybe," Kristen said. "Because you're going to tell him."

Kayla sighed, but she knew her sister was right.

And maybe her dreams had been crushed, but at least now she had no expectations. Trey had made his feelings clear, and she was going to tell him about the baby without any illusions that he would want to be part of their life, and she would make it clear that she didn't want or expect anything from him. She was simply doing him the courtesy of telling him that she was pregnant.

She was admittedly a little late with that courtesy, but she would tell him.

"Tonight?" Kristen prompted.

"I can't tonight," Kayla said. "Russell called this morning. He's down with the flu and asked me to fill in for him at the theater this afternoon."

"Then tomorrow," her sister said firmly.

"Tomorrow," she agreed.

But when the curtain fell after the matinee, Kayla found Trey waiting for her backstage, and her heart gave a jolt—of surprise and longing. And when he smiled at her, her knees went weak.

Despite what she'd said to her sister about their wanting different things, she couldn't deny that she still wanted Trey. She managed to smile back, though her stomach was a tangle of nerves and knots.

"What brings you to the Kalispell Theater?"

"I decided to take your advice and check out the play," he told her.

"What did you think?"

"I was impressed. I didn't expect a small theater production to be so good."

"The actors are all spectacular," Kayla agreed. "But Belle steals the show."

Trey chuckled. "Your sister does have a flair for the dramatic."

"Speaking of my sister, I'm supposed to meet her outside her dressing room. She's waiting to give me a ride home," she explained.

"Actually, she's not—Kristen knows that I'm here to kidnap you."

"Kidnap me?"

"Well, I'm not going to throw you over my shoulder and carry you off against your will, but I asked Kristen to help me figure out a way to spend some time with you, and this was the plan we came up with."

The *surprise* that her sister hadn't given her any details—or warning—about. "Are you going to tell me anything else about this plan?"

"You don't like surprises?" he guessed.

"I guess that would depend on the surprise."

"How does a romantic dinner and a luxury suite at a local B and B sound?"

"It sounds like you've thought of everything—except what I'm going to tell my parents about where I am."

"They think you're spending the night at your sister's place," he told her, taking her hand. "I just wanted us to have some time together—just the two of us—away from all of our well-meaning but nosy family and friends in Rust Creek Falls."

"It's a good plan," she said and resigned herself to the

fact that her promise to tell him about their baby *tomorrow* had been bumped forward to *tonight*.

Trey was having a hard time reading Kayla.

She was going through the motions, but her attention seemed to be a million miles away. The restaurant he took her to for dinner had been highly recommended for both its menu and ambience. The lighting was low, the music soft and the service impeccable. His meal was delicious, and Kayla assured him that hers was, too, but she pushed more food around on her plate than she ate, and although she responded appropriately, she didn't attempt to initiate any conversation.

Needless to say, by the time he pulled into the driveway of the bed-and-breakfast, he was certain that he'd made a mistake—he just wasn't sure where. Was it the surprise aspect that she objected to? Would she have preferred to be involved in the planning? Or was she worried about his expectations? Did she think that because he'd paid for the room and dinner he'd expect her to get naked to show her appreciation?

He suspected it might be the latter when he opened the door to their suite and she caught sight of the enormous bed that dominated the room. And yeah, when he'd made the reservation he'd hoped they might share that bed, but he knew there was a sofa bed in the sitting area if Kayla decided otherwise.

He guided her past the bed to the sofa and sat her down. "What's going on, Kayla? What did I do wrong? Because it seems obvious to me that there *was* something."

"You didn't do anything wrong," she said. "Not really. It's just that… I've come to the realization that we want different things."

"What are you talking about?"

"I want what Shane and Gianna have," she told him. "I want to fall in love and get married and have a family."

"So? I want those things, too."

"'Someday,'" she remembered.

"And when I think of that someday, I think I'd like it to be with you."

That announcement gave her pause. "You do?"

"I do," he assured her. "I'll admit the whole conversation threw me for a loop, and it's probably going to be a while before I'm ready for marriage and babies, but please don't give up on me—on us."

Then he held out his hand to her, and Kayla gasped when she saw her teardrop earring sparkling against his palm.

"Ohmygod. I can't believe…" Her words trailed off as her eyes filled with tears. "I thought I'd lost it forever."

"I've been carrying it around with me since July," he told her. "Waiting for the right time to give it back. I should have returned it sooner. I did plan to give it back to you the next day, but you seemed so embarrassed by what happened between us."

He'd been carrying it around with him? Why? Was it possible that night had meant as much to him as it had to her? Or was she reading too much into his words because she wanted his gesture to mean more than it did?

"I was embarrassed because I thought you didn't remember," she admitted.

"I was fuzzy on the details," he acknowledged. "But I knew it was your earring and how it ended up in my bed."

She lifted the delicate piece from his palm. "Thank you. It's not worth a lot of money, but it used to be my grandmother's and it means a lot to me."

"I have to admit, when I found it in my sheets, I felt a little bit like Prince Charming after the clock struck midnight—except I had an earring instead of a shoe."

She knew that accessories weren't the only difference between her life and that of the fairy-tale princess, and yet his claim of wanting a future with her gave her hope that her story with Trey might also have a happy ending. But she knew that wasn't possible until she was honest with him about what had happened at the beginning.

"Will you give me another chance?" he asked her.

She looked around the room, noting the flowers and candles, the bottle of champagne chilling on ice. He wouldn't have gone to so much effort if he didn't think she was worth it, but would he still think so if he knew the truth she'd kept from him for so long?

"There's something I have to tell you—something that's going to change everything."

"What are you talking about?"

"I should have told you a long time ago—I wanted to tell you. But I was afraid that it would change how you felt—"

"Nothing is going to change how I feel about you," Trey said. "I promise you that."

She shook her head. "Don't. Please, don't make promises you can't keep."

"I don't know what's going on here, but you're starting to scare me," he admitted. "So whatever it is, I wish you'd just tell me so that we can deal with it."

She buried her face in her hands. "I'm messing this up."

"What's wrong, Kayla? Are you—" He hesitated, as if he didn't even want to ask the question. "Are you sick?"

"No, I'm not sick." The words were little more than a whisper as she lifted tear-drenched eyes to his. "I'm pregnant."

Chapter Eleven

Trey took a step back. Actually, it was more of a stumble than a step, which probably wasn't surprising, considering that he felt as if the rug had been pulled right out from beneath him.

"What did you say?"

"I'm pregnant."

His gaze dropped to her stomach, hidden behind yet another oversize sweater. She smoothed a hand over the fabric to show the slight but unmistakable curve of her belly.

Holy crap—she really was pregnant.

His knees buckled, and he dropped to the edge of the sofa.

"When…how—" He shook his head at the ridiculousness of the latter question. "Is it…mine?"

She nodded.

His stomach tightened painfully. "So you're—" he mentally counted back to the wedding "—five months along?"

She nodded again.

"Five months," he said again, shock slowly giving way to fury. "You've kept your pregnancy from me for *five months*?"

Kayla winced at the anger in his tone. "I didn't realize I was pregnant until the beginning of October."

"October," he echoed. "So you've only kept it a secret for the past three months?"

"I haven't told anyone because I was waiting to tell you first."

"Really? Because I think if you wanted to tell me, you would have picked up a phone and called."

Her big blue eyes filled with tears. "You don't understand," she said, her tremulous voice imploring him to try.

"You're damn right I don't understand. If the baby you're carrying really is mine—"

She gasped. "How could you doubt it's true?"

"How can I doubt it?" he demanded incredulously. "How can I believe anything you've told me when you just admitted that you've deliberately kept your pregnancy a secret for three months?"

She lifted her chin. "You have every right to be angry, but you should know me well enough to know that I wouldn't lie about my baby's paternity. And I wouldn't have spent the past couple of weeks agonizing over how to tell you if the baby wasn't yours."

"I *am* angry," he confirmed. "And obviously I don't know you as well as I thought because I never would have imagined you'd keep something like this from me."

"Please, Trey," she said. "Listen to me. Give me a chance to explain."

"I'm listening," he said, but his tone was grim, and his attention was focused on the screen of the cell phone that he'd pulled out of his pocket. His thumbs moved rapidly over the keypad, then he skimmed through the information that appeared. "We can be married right away, without any waiting period required."

Her eyes widened. "You want to get married?"

"Under the circumstances, I can't see that what I want is relevant right now," he said.

"You don't *want* to get married," she realized, her gaze dropping away. "You're only trying to do the right thing."

"Of course I'm trying to do the right thing." He looked at his phone again. "Come on—there's an office in Kalispell where we can get a license."

"It's Saturday night, Trey."

"So?"

"So I doubt very much if the county clerk's office is open right now."

He scowled. "I didn't think about that."

"And even if it was open…I'm not going to marry you."

"Why not?" he demanded.

"Because it's not what you want."

"None of this is what I want," he admitted. "But we've only got a few more months until the baby is born, and there's no way any child of mine is going to be illegitimate."

"Illegitimate is only a label," she pointed out.

"And not a label I want applied to my child."

"I'm not going to marry you, Trey."

Something in her quiet but firm tone compelled him to look at her. The stubborn set of her shoulders and defiant tilt of her chin warned him that she was ready to battle over this, although he didn't understand why. "You don't have a choice in the matter."

"Of course I do," she countered. "You can't force me to marry you."

"Maybe I can't, but I'm willing to bet your father—and your brothers—can and will."

At that, some of her defiance faded, but she held firm. "They would probably encourage a legal union, under the circumstances," she acknowledged. "But they're hardly going to demand a shotgun wedding if it's not what I want."

"You're saying you don't want to marry me?"

Her gaze slid away, her eyes filling with fresh tears. "I don't want to marry you—not like this."

The words were like physical blows that left him reeling. He didn't understand why she was being so unreasonable. She was carrying his child, but she didn't want to marry him? Why the hell not? What had he done that she would deprive him of the opportunity to be a father to his child?

And how could he change her mind? Because he had no intention of accepting her decision as final. But he also knew that he couldn't talk to her about this anymore right now. There was no way they could have a rational conversation about anything when his emotions were so raw.

He turned blindly toward the door.

"Where are you going?"

"I don't know," he admitted.

"Please, Trey. Let's sit down and talk about this."

He shook his head, his fingers curling around the doorknob. "I can't talk right now. I need some time to try to get my head around this."

And then he was gone, and Kayla was alone.

She sank down onto the sofa, her heart aching, and put a hand on the curve of her belly. "I'm sorry, baby, but I guess it's just going to be you and me."

She wasn't really surprised. She'd always expected it would be like this. From the moment she'd realized she was pregnant, she'd anticipated that she would be on her own—a single mother raising her child alone.

Over the past couple of weeks, she'd let herself imagine that things could be different. Spending time with Trey, she'd got caught up in the fantasy, believing that they were a couple and, with their baby, could be a family.

Except that wasn't what he wanted. Not really. But he had asked her to marry him—and for one brief shining moment, the dream had been within her grasp.

And she'd let it slip through her fingers.

She heard the sound of his boots pounding on the steps, fading away as he moved farther away from her.

Would he have stayed if she'd agreed to marry him?

It was what she wanted, more than anything, to marry the man she loved, the father of her child. But she'd meant what she said—she couldn't do it. Not like this. Not because he was feeling responsible and trapped. Not without knowing that he loved her, too.

And right now she was pretty sure he hated her.

But she couldn't let him storm off with so much still unresolved between them. She understood that he needed time, that he needed to think. But she suspected that if she let him go now, she could lose him forever. No—it would be better for them to talk this through. It was her fault that they hadn't done so before now, but she wasn't willing to put off their conversation any longer.

She pushed herself off the sofa and turned quickly toward the door, determined to go after him.

But she'd barely risen to her feet when the room started to spin, then the floor rushed up to meet her.

Trey was beyond angry. He was thoroughly and sincerely pissed off—possibly at himself as much as at Kayla.

He felt like a complete idiot.

Pregnant.

Since *July*.

And she hadn't said a single word to him.

Not. One. Single. Word.

Worse—he'd been completely and frustratingly oblivious. Despite all the time he'd spent with her over the past few weeks, despite the numerous times he'd kissed her and the countless times he'd held her, he hadn't had a clue.

Her assurance that no one knew about her pregnancy didn't make him feel any less like an idiot. He should have wondered about her sudden preference for baggy clothes, her unwillingness to go horseback riding with him and her determination to keep him at a physical distance. But he hadn't, and the revelation of her pregnancy had completely blindsided him.

How was he going to share the happy news with his family? If it was, indeed, happy news. *A baby.* His head was still reeling, his mind trying to grasp not just the words but what they meant to him, to his life.

He yanked the steering wheel and pulled over to the side of the road. *Christ.* He was going to be a father. Him. And he was so completely unprepared for this his hands were shaking and his heart was pounding.

Have you ever thought about having kids?

Had it only been three days ago that she'd asked him that question, after they'd seen Shane and Gianna in town after the Candlelight Walk? At the time, he'd thought the question was out of the blue—now he knew differently. She'd been trying to figure out his feelings, anticipate his reaction to the news that he was going to be a father.

And what had he said? How had he responded to her question about whether he wanted to have kids? "Someday," he'd acknowledged. A lackluster response that he'd immediately followed with, "There's a lot I want to do before I'm hog-tied by the responsibilities of marriage and babies."

He dropped his head against the steering wheel.

He'd actually compared being married to being hog-tied—no wonder she hadn't replied with an announcement of her pregnancy and confetti in the air. He couldn't have screwed things up any worse if he'd actually tried.

And what was he supposed to do now?

He had no clue.

He was surprised by the sudden urge to want to talk to his father. Maybe that was normal for a man who'd just learned he was going to be a father himself, but he couldn't begin to imagine how that conversation might proceed. No doubt his father would be completely stunned—although perhaps not so much by the news of his impending fatherhood as the identity of the mommy-to-be. Because who would believe that sweet, shy Kayla Dalton had gotten naked with serial dater Trey Strickland?

When he thought about it, even he continued to be surprised by the events of that night. And especially the repercussions. Because one of his first clues that they'd done the deed was the condom wrapper he'd discovered on the floor beside the bed the next morning. Obviously they'd taken precautions to prevent exactly this scenario, and yet, it had happened. Condom companies advertised their product as ninety-eight percent effective, but the baby Kayla was now carrying proved that they'd beaten those odds.

Unless she was taking advantage of his memory lapse from that night to make him think—

No. As frustrated and angry and hurt as he was—and despite his own question to her—he knew that Kayla wouldn't lie about something like that. There was no doubt that she was pregnant or that it was his baby. She wouldn't have agonized over how and when to tell him if she was perpetrating some elaborate ruse.

She was pregnant.

More than five months pregnant.

With his child.

Nope—it didn't get any easier thinking it the second, third or even the tenth time, and he wasn't sure he'd be able to say it aloud to anyone else, especially his father. Would his parents be disappointed in him? He was sure they would accept and love their grandchild, but he didn't think they'd be particularly proud of his actions. Not in July and not now.

They would definitely expect him to do the right thing by his child—which meant marrying the child's mother. Surprisingly, the prospect of marriage didn't scare him half as much as impending fatherhood. But he knew Kayla was scared, too, and he realized that it really didn't matter who had said or done what on the Fourth of July or even in the time that had passed since then. What mattered was what they were going to do now—and they needed to figure that out together.

Now that he'd had a little bit of time to get his heart rate down to something approximating normal, he could acknowledge how difficult it must have been for her to face him and tell him that their impulsive actions that night had resulted in a pregnancy. Especially after he'd told her that he wasn't eager to be a father.

But was it really fair for her to judge him on a response he'd given when he'd assumed she was speaking hypothetically? Because the idea of a baby, without any context, would probably scare the hell out of any guy. Not that a real child was any less terrifying than a hypothetical one, but the idea of having a child with the woman he loved—because over the past couple of weeks, he'd gradually come to accept that he did love Kayla—was almost as exciting as it was terrifying.

Maybe he'd been a little high-handed in his assertion

that they needed to get married, but he did *want* to marry her. He *wanted* to be a father to their child.

Okay—there. He didn't feel like the vise around his chest was tightening. In fact, he could almost breathe again.

His first glimpse of that subtle curve beneath her sweater had thrown him for a loop, but the ability of the female body to grow and nurture another human being was amazing. And the realization that Kayla was carrying *his* baby was both awesome and humbling.

He wondered how big the baby was now, whether she could feel it moving. Would he be able to feel it kicking inside her? Suddenly, he wanted to.

He thought about his friend, Shane, how excited he was about his baby and how he was always touching his wife's swollen belly. Trey had been happy because his friend was happy, but he didn't really get it. Now—barely an hour after he'd learned that he was going to be a father—he finally did.

Gianna was due to give birth in early February which—Trey did a quick count on his fingers—was only a few months before what he estimated was Kayla's due date. It would be kind of cool for their kids to grow up together—except that might not happen if he wasn't able to convince Kayla to marry him.

Obviously, they still had a lot of details to work out. She had a home and a job in Rust Creek Falls, and he lived and worked in Thunder Canyon. If they were going to raise this child together—and he refused to consider any other possibility—they needed to be together.

The light snow that had been falling when he left the bed-and-breakfast had changed—the flakes were coming heavier and faster now, but he wasn't concerned. He had all-wheel drive and snow tires on his truck. What he didn't have was any particular destination in mind, so when he turned onto a street filled with shops, he decided to park and walk for a while.

He tucked his chin in the collar of his jacket and walked with his head down. The wind was sharp and cold but he didn't really notice—everything inside him felt numb. At the end of the block, he found himself standing outside a jewelry store, the front window display highlighting a selection of engagement rings.

He impulsively opened the door and stepped inside.

Apparently he wasn't the only one who had decided to ignore the inclement weather. There was a man about his own age looking at bangle-style bracelets, a woman browsing a selection of watches and an older gentleman perusing engagement rings with a much younger woman.

He found what he was looking for almost immediately. The vintage-style was similar to the earrings she'd been wearing the night of the wedding, and he knew the delicate design crusted with diamonds would suit her. The clerk, visibly pleased with the quick sale, wished him a Merry Christmas and happy engagement—Trey wasn't counting on either but he was going to give both his best effort.

The weight of the ring was heavy in his pocket as he considered how and when to propose to her again. He thought she would appreciate a traditional proposal, despite the fact—or maybe because—nothing else about their relationship had been traditional. From their first kiss at Braden and Jennifer's wedding, they'd followed their own timetable. They'd fallen into bed together before they'd even gone out on a date, and now she was pregnant and showed no indication of wanting to marry him. But he was determined to change her mind on that account.

He had to brush a couple of inches of snow off his windshield before he could pull out onto the road, which was also covered with snow. The driving wasn't difficult but it was slow, and he was eager to get back to the inn, back to Kayla.

He was ready to talk to her now, eager to tell her that he was happy about their baby. He was still scared, but he was excited, too, and he wanted to share all of his thoughts and feelings with her.

But when he got back to the bed-and-breakfast, she wasn't there.

He tried calling her cell, but there was no answer. He didn't know where she could have gone—she didn't have a vehicle. And he couldn't imagine that she would have ventured outside to go for a walk in this weather. He went back downstairs, to check with Jack and Eden Caffrey, the owners of the inn. It was then that he found their note.

Kayla had a little bit of a fainting spell, so we took her to the hospital to be checked out.

Now his heart was racing for a completely different reason.

"I really am fine," Kayla told Eden, who had been hovering over her since she found her guest sprawled on the floor of her third-floor guest room.

She'd tried to resist the woman's efforts to get her to go to the hospital, because she really did feel fine, but in the end, worry about her baby won out. Jack had driven the car while Eden sat in the back with Kayla, just to be sure everything was okay. And except for a few minutes while the doctor performed his exam and then to get Kayla a snack from the cafeteria, Eden had not left her side. Jack was there, too, but he was tucked into a chair in the corner, working in a crossword puzzle book he'd brought in from the car.

She glanced from Eden's worried face to the doctor's calm facade. "Please, Dr. Gaynor, tell them that I'm fine."

"She's fine." Her ob-gyn—who had conveniently been making rounds when Kayla was brought in to the hospital—echoed the words dutifully.

"And she can go home now," Kayla prompted hopefully.

The doctor smiled as she shook her head. "I'd prefer to keep an eye on you a little bit longer, just to ensure the slight cramping you experienced earlier has truly subsided."

She sighed as she turned her attention back to Eden. "I know you must be anxious to get back. Please don't feel as if you have to stay here with me. I can catch a cab back to the inn when the doctor finally okays it."

"We run a bed-and-breakfast," Eden reminded her. "And there are a lot of hours until breakfast."

"I'll be back to check on you in a little while," Dr. Gaynor said.

Trey entered the room as she was leaving.

Jack set his book and pencil aside and rose to his feet, offering his hand to the other man. "I see you got our note."

"I did," Trey confirmed. "Thank you for taking care of Kayla."

"Of course."

Kayla eyed Trey warily as he moved closer to the bed. He'd been so angry when he left, but she didn't hear any evidence of that in his voice now.

He touched his lips to her forehead, and the sweetness of the gesture made her throat tighten.

"How are you?"

She swallowed. "I'm okay."

"I'm so sorry I wasn't there."

"It's okay," she said, but she couldn't look at him when she said it. She understood why he'd been angry and upset, but she was still hurt by his abandonment of her. Reasonable or not, his walking away had felt like a rejection of not only her news but of herself and their child, too.

He turned to Eden and Jack again. "I'm so grateful you were there, and that you brought Kayla here."

"It's lucky that she knocked the lamp off the table when she fell, or we might not have known that she fainted."

"I'm not sure I really fainted," Kayla said. "I just felt dizzy for a minute."

"And didn't remember what had happened when I found you," Eden said. "Because you fainted."

"But I'm fine now," she insisted.

"The doctor wants to keep her a little longer, for observation," Eden told Trey, contradicting Kayla's statement.

"I'll stay with her," he told the couple.

"Then we'll get out of your way," Jack said.

"Any special requests for breakfast?" Eden asked Kayla.

She shook her head. "I'm sure whatever you have planned will be perfect."

"Drive safely," Trey said to Jack. "The snow is really blowing out there."

"My honey does everything slow and steady," Eden assured him, adding a saucy wink to punctuate her statement.

Jack shook his head. "We'll see you both in the morning," he said, putting his hand on his wife's back to guide her toward the door, quietly chiding her for "embarrassing the poor fellow."

"She did embarrass you, didn't she?" Kayla asked. "Your cheeks are actually red."

"It's cold and windy outside," he told her.

"They weren't that red when you walked in a few minutes ago."

"Okay," he acknowledged. "Now let's talk about you. Are you really okay?"

"How many times do I have to say it before people start believing it?"

"Maybe a hundred more."

She eyed him warily. "How are *you*?"

"I'm okay."

She lifted her brows; he smiled.

"What about…is the baby…okay?"

"The baby's fine. Apparently, he's well-cushioned in there."

"He?"

She shrugged. "Or she."

"You don't know?"

"I didn't want to know." She played with the plastic hospital bracelet on her wrist. "Do you want to know?"

"I don't mind being surprised."

Chapter Twelve

Kayla eyed him skeptically. "Really?"

"Okay—I know that's not what I was saying earlier," Trey acknowledged. "But I'm not sure I've ever been hit with a surprise of quite that magnitude before."

"I would hope not," she admitted, managing a small smile.

He reached for her hand, linked their fingers together. "I'm sorry."

She swallowed. "Sorry that I'm pregnant?"

"No." He squeezed her fingers. "I'm not sorry about the baby—I'm sorry that I was such an ass when you told me about the baby."

"And I'm sorry I waited so long to tell you."

"Why did you?"

"I was scared."

"Of me?"

She shook her head. "Of how you'd react."

"How did you think I'd react? Did you expect me to get mad and walk out?"

"That was one possible scenario—after you rejected the possibility that it was your baby."

He winced. "It was knee-jerk."

"I get that. But you should know that there wasn't any other possibility. What happened between us that night— I don't do things like that."

"I know."

Now it was her turn to wince. "I'm not sure if I should feel reassured or insulted."

He chuckled. "Rust Creek Falls is a small town," he reminded her. "You have a reputation for flying under the radar."

"Obviously, no one saw me do the walk of shame out of the boarding house the morning after Braden and Jennifer's wedding."

"Walk of shame? Because you spent the night with me?"

"Because I don't do things like that," she said again.

"I kind of hoped we'd do it again sometime."

"Like maybe this weekend?"

"Like maybe this weekend," he acknowledged. "But that isn't why I brought you here. I really did just want to spend some time with you away from all of the demands and distractions of our families."

"It was a sweet gesture."

He winced. "Sweet?"

She chuckled softly then sighed. "I really wanted to tell you," she insisted. "But every time I tried to lead into the conversation, something else came up."

"Nothing that was more important than what you weren't telling me," he pointed out.

She nodded, silently acknowledging his point. "The

first time was the day we had lunch—when Claire called and asked you to pick up diapers."

He did remember that his cousin's call had interrupted something Kayla started to say, and he winced when he remembered some of the things he'd said when he'd explained the errand request to Kayla. "Okay, I guess that one's on me."

"And then there was the night we were wrapping Presents for Patriots and you told me we had time to figure out everything we needed to know about one another."

"Only because I didn't know then that our time would be limited by the arrival of a bundle of joy."

"And then when we ran into Shane and Gianna after the Candlelight Walk."

"When I said that I wasn't looking to be a father anytime soon," he realized.

She nodded.

"You really should have just blurted out the news before I had a chance to make such an ass of myself."

"I'll keep that in mind if I ever find myself in this predicament again."

"You won't," he told her. "Our next baby—"

Whatever else he was going to say was interrupted by a knock at the door.

Kayla let out a breath—a sigh that was part relief and part frustration—when a technician pushed a trolley cart into the room.

"I'm Judy," she said. "Dr. Gaynor asked me to stop by so we could take a look at your baby."

Kayla's hand tightened on his. "Is something wrong?"

"There's no reason to think so," the technician assured her. "The doctor just wants to double-check before she releases you."

"Okay." But she didn't relinquish her viselike grip of Trey's hand.

Judy lifted the hem of Kayla's shirt and pushed down the top of her pants to expose the curve of her belly. She squirted the warm gel onto her tummy then spread it over her skin with the wand attached to the portable ultrasound machine.

A soft whooshing sounded, and the screen came to life, but Kayla found herself watching Trey, whose attention was riveted by the image that appeared.

"Is that…our baby?"

"That's our baby," she confirmed.

"It's…wow."

She understood exactly what he was feeling: the complete array of emotions that filled his heart. Awe. Joy. Fear.

She understood because it was the way she'd felt the first time she'd seen tangible evidence of the life growing inside her, not just the outline of the baby's head and torso or the little limbs flailing around, but the tiny heart inside her baby's chest that seemed to beat in tandem with her own.

"Everything looks great," Judy said. "Your baby is measuring right on target for twenty-four weeks."

"What does that mean?" Trey asked. "How big is he? Or she?" he hastened to add.

"Approximately eleven and a half inches long, probably weighing in at just under a pound—about the size of an ear of corn."

"Less than a pound?" Kayla wasn't happy. "I've gained more than ten, and you're telling me that less than one of that is my baby?"

The technician chuckled. "But all of it is necessary—there's also the placenta, amniotic fluid and various other factors that contribute to mother's weight gain during pregnancy."

"So it's not the hot chocolate with extra whipped cream?"

"It's not the hot chocolate," Judy promised. "Even with extra whipped cream." She continued to move the transducer over Kayla's belly. "You said 'he—or she'…did you want to know your baby's sex?"

Kayla looked at Trey. "Do you?"

"Do *you*?"

"I am a little curious," she admitted. "Especially because my sister seems convinced—on the basis of no scientific evidence whatsoever—that it's a boy."

Trey frowned at that but didn't comment, and Kayla realized he was probably unhappy to discover that her sister had known about the pregnancy before he did. But she wasn't going to explain or apologize—not in front of the ultrasound tech—and she was grateful that all he said to Judy was, "We'd like to know."

"The aunt-to-be is right," Judy told her. "It's a boy."

When Dr. Gaynor finally returned and approved Kayla's release, Trey insisted on bringing his truck right up to the exit doors of the hospital so that she didn't have to walk across the snowy ground to the parking lot. She appreciated his solicitousness, but she also knew his apparent acceptance of her pregnancy didn't mean anything was settled between them.

The earlier blizzard-like conditions had passed and the plows had already been out to clear the main roads, so the drive back to the bed-and-breakfast was quick and uneventful.

Throughout the short journey, her mind was so preoccupied with other things that she'd almost forgotten they weren't heading back to Rust Creek Falls. She knew that Trey would take her home if she asked, but she also knew that running away was a cowardly thing to do. They had to figure out their plans for the baby together so they could tell both of their families.

But back in their room at the inn, her gaze kept being drawn to the big bed at its center—the bed she'd hoped to share with Trey. The bed she still wanted to share with Trey, because apparently her active pregnancy hormones didn't care that there were unresolved issues so much as they remembered how much fun it had been to make a baby with this man and wanted to do the deed again.

She moved past the bed to the sitting area and lowered herself onto the edge of the sofa.

"Do you need anything?" Trey asked. "Are you hungry? You didn't eat very much at dinner."

She shook her head. "Eden got me some fries and gravy from the hospital cafeteria before you arrived."

"French fries and gravy?"

"Pregnant women have some strange cravings," she said, a little defensively.

"Anything else you've been wanting? Pickles? Ice cream? Pickles and ice cream?"

"No—at least, not at the same time," she assured him. "But if you're hungry, maybe Eden will let you sneak into the kitchen to make a sandwich."

She'd no sooner finished speaking when there was a knock on the door. Trey went to answer it and returned with a silver tray in his hands.

"Apparently Eden thought we might both be hungry," he said, setting down the tray set with a plate of cheeses and crackers, another of crudités and dip and a bowl of fresh fruit.

"They're both lovely people," Kayla said. "And this house is spectacular. How did you find it?"

He nodded. "Gage Christensen recommended it."

"You haven't stayed here before?"

"No." He selected a grape from the bowl, popped it into his mouth. "Did you think this was my usual rendezvous spot in Kalispell?"

She lifted a shoulder.

"I know I had a reputation in high school—and maybe for some years afterward—but I'm not that same guy anymore. And I didn't bring you here because there was a bed and none of our family within spitting distance. I brought you here because I wanted to give us a chance to reconnect without all the other craziness of our lives interfering."

"And the bed?" she prompted.

"I might have had hopes," he admitted. "But no expectations."

He plucked another grape from the bowl, offered it to her. She took the fruit from his fingertips, bit into it. The skin was crisp, the juice sweet. "Oh!"

"What is it?" Trey dropped the strawberry he'd selected. "What's wrong?"

"Nothing's wrong." She took his hand and laid it on the curve of her belly.

His brows drew together. "What…oh."

She knew then that he'd felt it, too, the subtle nudges against his palm that were evidence of their baby moving around inside her.

His lips curved and he shifted his hand to one side to make room for the other, splaying both of his palms against her belly. "Now I know why Shane's always touching Gianna's stomach."

The baby indulged him with a few moments of activity before settling again.

"It's fascinating," he said. "To know there's a tiny human being inside there. A baby. *Our* baby."

She smiled at the wonderment in his tone. "Our baby boy," she reminded him.

His hands moved from her belly to link with hers. "Do you know why I came back?"

"Hopefully because you didn't plan on returning to Rust Creek Falls with me stranded here."

"I didn't," he assured her. "But I meant why I came back when I did."

She shook her head. "Why did you come back when you did?"

"Because I realized that I love you."

For a moment, her heart actually stopped beating. Then it started racing. "You...what?"

"It kind of snuck up and surprised me, too," he admitted. "Maybe because I didn't ever expect to feel this way again. But it's true, Kayla. I love you."

She looked at their intertwined fingers and willed her heart to stop acting crazy for a minute so that she could think.

"This would be a great place to say that you love me, too," he prompted.

And she did love him. Maybe she always had. But she wasn't yet ready to put her heart on the line simply because he'd said the three little words she'd often dreamed he might one day say to her. Especially when she couldn't help but question the timing and his motives.

"I'm not sure that you're feeling what you think you're feeling," she said gently.

He scowled. "You don't believe I'm in love with you?"

"I think you *want* to believe you're in love with me because that would make the situation more acceptable to you."

"Kayla, there is nothing about this situation that is the least bit *un*acceptable to me."

"Six hours ago, the idea of being a husband and father totally freaked you out, and I understand that—"

"I'm not freaked out," he told her.

She lifted her brows.

"Okay, I *was* freaked out," he admitted. "Because the possibility that the one night we spent together might have created a baby never crossed my mind, and finding out not only that you were pregnant but more than five months pregnant was a little bit of a shock.

"But once I had some time to think about it—once my brain got past the holy-crap-I'm-going-to-be-a-father part and began to focus on the I'm-having-a-baby-with-Kayla part—I realized that I was okay with this."

"You're okay with it?" she echoed dubiously.

"I'm not explaining myself very well, am I?"

"I don't know," she admitted. "But if you're trying to reassure me, I'm not feeling very reassured."

"I wouldn't have planned for you to get pregnant that night," he said. "As I'm sure it wasn't in your plans, either."

"Definitely not," she agreed.

"But then I realized that if this had to happen—if a condom had to fail—I'm glad it was with you."

"That sounded…almost poetic," she decided, touched by the sincerity in his tone even more than his words.

"I want to be a father to our baby. I really do."

"I want that, too."

He was tempted to show her the ring right then and there, to prove how serious he was about wanting to be with her, but he suspected it was too soon to ask her again to marry him. If she needed some time to be sure of him and his feelings, he would give her that time.

Because the next time he proposed, he wasn't going to accept any answer but yes.

It wasn't really late, but it had been a long and emotionally draining day, and when Trey caught Kayla attempting to stifle a yawn, he said, "Why don't you go get changed and crawl into bed?"

"I don't have anything to change into," she realized.

"Your sister packed you a bag. I brought it up to the bedroom when I checked in before I went to the theater."

"I'm not sure I want to know what she packed for me," Kayla admitted, but she went into the other room to find out.

She was right to be suspicious. The silky short nightshirt and matching wrap certainly weren't from Kayla's closet, but since they were all she had, she put them on, then brushed her hair and cleaned her teeth.

When she was finished, she heard the television from the sitting area and saw that Trey was stretched out with his feet on the table and his eyes half-closed. She hesitated inside the doorway, and his eyes slowly opened and slid over her with a heated intensity that felt like a physical caress.

"I like what your sister packed," he murmured.

"This isn't mine," she blurted out.

"It looks good on you."

She tightened the belt around her waist, not realizing how the movement emphasized the curve of her belly until she saw his gaze drop and linger there.

"I think I understand your sudden affinity for shapeless clothing."

"I've gained ten and a half pounds already," she admitted.

"You're growing our baby."

"You didn't stumble over the words that time."

"I'm going to stumble," he told her. "This is all new territory for me."

"Me, too."

"But you've had a little bit more time to get used to the idea than me."

She didn't know if he'd intended the words as an accusation, but she couldn't help but interpret them as such, and she nodded in acknowledgment. "And more time to panic."

He'd been so shocked about the news of her pregnancy—and then so angry at her for keeping it from him—that he hadn't really considered how she'd felt, the gamut of emotions she must have experienced when she first suspected and then confirmed that she was going to have a baby. "Were you scared?"

"Terrified," she admitted without hesitation.

And she'd been alone.

But that had been her choice. She could have contacted him—could have shared her worries and her fears. Instead, she'd chosen to keep her pregnancy from everyone, including her baby's father.

"I didn't want to believe it was even possible," she said to him now. "I'd always thought I was so smart, that there really wasn't any such thing as an unplanned pregnancy anymore."

An understandable assumption considering that they'd taken precautions—and the reason for his own initial disbelief.

"I was so sure that my period was only late, but I went to a drugstore in Kalispell and bought a pregnancy test that I took into a public restroom. And I cried," she admitted softly. "I was so scared and confused. I couldn't do anything but cry."

He hated knowing that she'd been afraid and alone. Maybe she could have called him—*should* have called him—but he'd been three hundred miles away.

And maybe he should have shown some initiative and called her. Even if he'd had no reason to suspect there were any repercussions from the night they'd spent together, he should have kept in touch with her. By not doing so, he'd relegated their lovemaking to the status of a one-night stand.

"I'm sorry."

"I think we both need to stop saying that."

"I don't think I can say it enough," he said. "I totally screwed up. I should have—"

Determined to silence his self-recrimination, Kayla leaned forward and touched her lips to his.

Her kiss had the intended effect of halting his words, and the added benefit of clouding her own brain. Especially when he drew her closer and deepened the kiss, sliding his tongue between her lips to parry with her own.

Her hormones kicked into overdrive. She didn't know if it was a side effect of the pregnancy or just being with Trey, but she couldn't deny that she wanted him.

She slid her hands beneath his shirt, over the smooth skin and taut muscles. She felt his abs quiver beneath her touch. She wanted to feel his skin against hers, his body inside hers. She reached for the button of his jeans and was surprised—and disappointed—when he caught her wrist.

"I'm not sure that's a good idea," he told her.

"I disagree." She pressed her lips to his throat, just below his jaw, where his pulse was racing.

His hands gripped her hips. "You were just released from the hospital two hours ago."

"And when the doctor released me, she assured both of us that there were absolutely no restrictions on any physical activities."

"I'm sure she wasn't referring to…"

"To?" she prompted, amused by his inability to say the word *sex* aloud to her.

"Intimacy," he decided.

"I'm pretty sure she was," she countered. "Did you know that some women experience an increased sexual desire during pregnancy?"

"No, I…um…can't say that I did."

"And there are some women who become so hypersensitive they can't stand to be touched."

"I didn't…um…know that…either," he said, looking everywhere but at her.

"Of course, men have different responses to pregnancy, too. Some find their partners even more attractive and appealing…while others are completely turned off by the changes to her body," she said, attempting to withdraw from his embrace when he pointedly kept his gaze averted.

He let her pull back but not away. "And you think I'm turned off," he realized.

She shrugged. "You're not touching me."

"Only because I don't want to hurt you…or our baby."

"You won't," she assured him.

He drew her close again, so she couldn't possibly miss the evidence of his desire for her.

"I want you, Kayla. More than you could probably imagine."

"I don't know about that—I have a pretty good imagination," she told him. "And I want you, too."

"We were only naked together once before," he noted. "And as I recall, we were both fumbling around in the dark."

"I think we managed okay."

"This time, I want the lights on. I want to see you. And I want to take my time exploring every single inch of your sexy pregnant body," he told her.

"That sounds…promising."

"It is a promise."

Chapter Thirteen

He guided her through the doorway into the bedroom, over to the bed. He unfastened the knot at the front of her robe, parted the sides and then slid his hands over her belly and up. "Your breasts are fuller."

"I should have figured you'd notice that."

He grinned, unapologetic, as he brushed his thumbs over her nipples, through the silky fabric. She moaned softly.

"And more sensitive," he realized.

"Yes, but in a good way. You don't have to worry about touching me—I *want* you to touch me."

"I want to touch you." He pushed the robe off her shoulders, stroked his fingertips down her arms. "I am touching you."

Then he lifted the hem of her nightshirt and lowered his head so that he was kissing her. First one breast, then the other, softly, almost reverently. After he kissed the hollow between them, his mouth moved lower, to the swell of her belly.

He pulled back the covers on the bed and eased her down onto the mattress, stripping her nightshirt away in the process. She was completely naked now, and suddenly very self-conscious.

She wasn't sure how he would respond to her belly unveiled. It was one thing to look at the curve beneath the fabric of the clothes she was wearing and quite another to see the skin stretched taut and all kinds of tiny blue veins visible beneath the surface. But he didn't seem put off at all.

He stripped away his own clothes and set a small square packet on the table beside the bed.

"That's a little like closing the barn door after the horse has escaped, don't you think?" she asked.

His brow furrowed. "I guess it is," he acknowledged. "I wasn't thinking. It's just a habit."

She nodded. "I'm relieved to know it is."

"But since we're not worried about you getting pregnant, there's nothing else you need to worry about, either. I have a clean bill of health and I haven't been with anyone else since we were together."

"You haven't been with anyone else in six months?"

"I didn't want to be with anyone else—because I couldn't stop thinking about you," he told her, trailing his fingertips along the insides of her thighs, upward from her knees, silently urging her legs to part.

"I couldn't stop thinking about you, either," she admitted.

"I'm happy to hear it."

The first time they'd made love, there hadn't been much foreplay. There hadn't been any need. They'd both wanted the same thing, and she had no regrets about what happened between them that night. But she had to admit their lovemaking had been a little…she wouldn't say disappointing so much as quick.

Trey made up for it now. He took his time learning his way around her body, exploring with his hands and his lips, touching and teasing until she was so aroused she could hardly stand it. Her heart was pounding, her blood was pulsing and her body was aching, desperately straining toward the ultimate pinnacle of pleasure.

She was already close, so close, but she wanted him there with her. She wanted to feel his hard length driving into her. She shifted restlessly, lifting her hips off the bed, wordlessly seeking the fulfillment she knew he could give her. When he eased back and pushed her knees farther apart, she thought, *Yes—finally, yes.*

But apparently he wasn't as eager as she was for their bodies to join together. Instead, he lowered his head and pressed his lips to the inside of one thigh, then the other. A whimper—a tangle of frustration and need—caught in her throat as his thumbs brushed the curls at the apex of her legs.

"Is this okay?" he asked.

"Only if you're trying to make me crazy."

"I'm trying to satisfy that raging sexual desire you were telling me about."

"I didn't say it was raging," she denied, just a little primly.

He chuckled softly, then his lips were on her, nibbling and teasing, his tongue gently probing her feminine core.

"Okay…now it's raging," she admitted breathlessly.

And then it was spinning out of control.

Finally, he lowered himself over her, into her.

She closed her eyes, sighing with satisfaction as he filled her. Then he began to move, slow, deep strokes that touched her very center. Her desire was definitely raging now. He'd already given her so much pleasure, but he held back, resisting his own release until he felt her body convulse around him.

Afterward, he brushed her hair away from her face and touched his lips to her temple. "I love you, Kayla. I understand that you might need some time to believe it's true, but I hope you won't need too much time, because I'm anxious for us to build a life together."

I love you, too.

The words—his and her own—filled her heart to overflowing, but the words stuck in her throat.

She *did* love him, but until she was certain that his feelings were real and the declaration wasn't prompted by some overblown sense of chivalrous responsibility, she wasn't going to let herself trust that they were true.

Trey wasn't surprised when Kayla suggested that he could drop her off at her sister's place rather than take her home, and considering that he'd manufactured her sleepover at Kristen's house to explain her absence from the Circle D, it wasn't an unreasonable request. However, now that he knew about their baby, he didn't want to keep the news of her pregnancy from either of their families a moment longer.

Her parents were at the table, having just finished their midday meal, when they arrived. Rita immediately offered to fix a couple more plates, but Trey assured her they'd already eaten. He didn't tell her that they'd had a late breakfast at the lovely little inn in Kalispell where he'd spent the night with her daughter.

"You just missed Derek and Eli," Rita told Trey. "They were here for lunch but headed out to check the fence on the northern boundary of the property."

"That's too bad," he said, though truthfully, he was grateful. He was prepared to face Kayla's parents and share the news of her pregnancy, but he wasn't eager to witness her brother's response. Derek had been unhappy enough to learn that Trey was dating his sister; he wasn't sure what his friend would do if he knew she was pregnant.

"I'm sure they'll both catch up with you soon," Kayla said, her words sounding like an ominous warning.

"In the meantime," Trey said, refusing to be sidetracked from his purpose, "we wanted to share some news with both of you."

Rita glanced from him to her daughter and back again, her expression one of polite confusion. "What news is that?"

He glanced at Kayla, indicating that it was her turn to talk, hoping that her parents would accept the news more easily if it came from her lips.

She drew in a deep breath and tried to smile, but her lips wobbled rather than curved. "We're going to have a baby."

There was silence for a long moment before Rita finally spoke.

"You mean you're planning to have a baby sometime in the future?" she asked, clearly trying to understand a statement that made no sense to her because she had no idea of the history between Kayla and Trey.

"No, I mean I'm pregnant."

Charles set his coffee mug down on the table, hard, his grip on the handle so tight his knuckles were white. "You're the father?" he demanded of Trey.

"Yes, sir."

"I don't understand," Rita said. "How is this possible? Trey's only been in town a couple of weeks…and the two of you just started dating."

"It happened in the summer," Kayla admitted. "The baby's due in April."

Her mother's eyes shimmered with moisture. "I knew something was up with you, but I never imagined…oh, Kayla."

Her eyes filled, too. He knew she felt guilty for keeping her pregnancy a secret, and she probably felt as if she'd disappointed her parents. Beneath the table, he reached for her hand and squeezed it reassuringly.

"When's the wedding?" Charles wanted to know.

"We're still trying to figure that out," Trey said.

"What's to figure? You call a minister and set a date, and if you haven't already done so, it just means you're dragging your heels and I—"

"Daddy," Kayla interrupted. "I'm the one dragging my heels."

Charles frowned at his daughter. "You don't want to marry the father of your baby?"

"I don't want to get married for the wrong reasons."

"A baby is never a wrong reason," he insisted. "And if you did the deed with a man you don't love, that's no one's fault but your own."

A single tear slid down Kayla's cheek; she swiped it away.

"Don't you think that's a little harsh?" Rita asked.

"Reality's harsh," her husband replied.

"What's done is done," Kayla's mother said, attempting to be a voice of reason. Then, to her daughter, "Have you been seeing a doctor?"

"Yes, I've been seeing a doctor," Kayla assured her.

"And everything's okay?"

She nodded. "Everything's fine."

"Everything except that she's unmarried and pregnant," Charles grumbled.

* * *

"That wasn't so bad, was it?" Trey asked her.

"It wasn't exactly a walk in the park."

"True, but I half expected to be leaving with my backside full of buckshot so, in comparison, it wasn't so bad."

"I'm sorry that my father is pressuring you to marry me."

"You seem to have forgotten that I asked you first—that I *want* to marry you."

"You want to do the right thing," she reminded him.

"Yes, I do," he confirmed. "Lucky for me that the right thing also gives me what I want—a life with you and our child."

Now that Kayla had told her parents, it was time for Trey to tell his. But since he wouldn't be seeing them until after the New Year, he decided to face his grandparents first.

He found his grandmother in the kitchen, preparing the evening meal.

"Where is everyone?"

"Claire and Levi took Bekka for a walk, and your grandfather is in the garage trying to find replacement bulbs for the Christmas lights that he insists are packed away somewhere."

"How long has he been digging around in there?"

"Let's just say it would have been quicker for him to drive into Kalispell to buy new replacement bulbs." She looked up from the potatoes she was peeling. "Something on your mind?"

His grandmother's instincts were uncanny as usual and since he couldn't imagine an appropriate segue, he just blurted it out. "Kayla's pregnant."

"I don't believe it," she said sternly. "And you shouldn't

be spreading gossip about matters that aren't any of your business."

"It is my business," Trey told her. "It's my baby."

His grandmother put a hand to her heart. "You're joking."

He shook his head. "She's due in April. April ninth."

Melba silently counted on her fingers.

"It happened when I was here in the summer," he admitted.

"What happened in the summer?" his grandfather asked, stomping into the kitchen.

His grandmother looked at him, because it was his news to tell.

"I slept with Kayla Dalton," he admitted.

Gene winced. "Why do I need to know this?"

"Because she's pregnant."

"Didn't your father give you the talk?"

"Yes, he gave me the talk," Trey confirmed. "And you gave me the talk. And we were careful."

"Obviously not careful enough." Gene nodded to thank his wife for the coffee she set in front of him. "You're going to marry her."

It wasn't a question but a statement; Trey nodded, anyway. "As soon as I can get Kayla to agree."

"What do you mean? Why wouldn't she agree?"

Melba rolled her eyes at her husband. "Because he probably said 'we better get married' without any attempt at romance."

"Don't you think the time for romance is past?" Gene asked.

"The time for romance is never past," his wife insisted.

"I can do romance," Trey interjected, attempting to shift the attention back to the subject at hand and away from the argument he could sense was brewing between his grandparents.

"Of course you can," Melba agreed.

"Start by buying a ring," Gene advised. "That's the most important thing."

"Telling her you love her is the most important thing," his grandmother countered. "But only if it's true."

"It is. And I did."

"Then you should buy a ring."

"I did that, too."

"And she still said no?"

"I didn't have the ring when I asked," he admitted. "And I didn't know how I felt about her when I asked."

"And now she'll think you only said those words because of the baby."

"That's the root of the problem," Gene spoke up again. "Thinking."

"I beg your pardon?" his wife said.

"Young women these days overthink everything—and young men don't know when to take action."

"What do you suggest I do?" Trey wanted to know. "Throw her over my shoulder and cart her off to the preacher?"

"I don't know that your actions need to be that drastic," his grandfather allowed. "But I've got an idea."

Later that night, Kayla tracked her mother down in the laundry room. "I know you're disappointed in me, and I'm sorry," she said softly.

"I'm mostly disappointed that you didn't tell us about the baby sooner," Rita said, measuring soap into the dispenser and setting the machine to wash. "It might have been a lot of years ago, but I still remember how anxious and worried I was during my first pregnancy—actually frantic and paranoid might be more accurate. I needed reassurance about everything I was thinking and feeling and doing, and I relied so much on my mother for that advice and support."

"I wanted to tell you." Kayla picked up a T-shirt, still warm from the dryer, and began to fold it. "But I didn't think it was fair to tell anyone about the baby until I told the baby's father."

"I can understand that," her mother allowed. "I can't understand why it took you five months to do that."

"Because Trey had gone back to Thunder Canyon and it wasn't the kind of news I felt comfortable sharing over the phone." Especially after a drunken one-night stand— but, of course, she didn't share *that* part with her mother.

"So when did you finally tell him?"

She set the folded shirt aside and picked up another. "Yesterday."

Rita matched up a pair of socks. "Yesterday?"

She nodded.

"The man's been in town for more than two weeks," her mother pointed out.

She nodded again.

"Well, I can't say I know how awkward and difficult it must have been to share the news," Rita admitted. "And that's between the two of you."

Kayla continued to fold her father's T-shirts.

"You know, I wouldn't have made a big deal about the French fries if I'd known you were pregnant."

She managed a laugh. "I know, Mom."

Rita matched another pair of socks. "Trey Strickland… I never would have guessed."

"I really am sorry," Kayla said.

"I don't want you to be sorry—I want you to be happy."

"I've screwed everything up so badly, I'm not sure that's possible. Trey is so angry…and hurt."

"He wouldn't be so angry and hurt if he didn't care about you deeply," Rita told her.

Kayla considered that for a minute, wanting to believe it could be true and, at the same time, afraid to let herself hope.

"Do you care about him?" her mother prompted.

There was no point in denying her feelings any longer. "I love him."

Rita smiled. "I thought you did."

"I'm not sure that's a good thing," she admitted. "I can't separate what I want from what's best for both of us and our baby."

"It *is* a good thing," her mother insisted. "Because with love, all things are possible."

RUST CREEK RAMBLINGS: BITS & BITES
Lovely Manhattan transplant, Lissa Christensen, has been spending time with fellow newcomer and nurse, Callie Crawford—at the local medical clinic. Are the two friends catching up on local gossip…or is it possible that the sexy sheriff's wife is "in the family way"?

Kayla was relieved when she woke up on Christmas morning because it was the one day she could be fairly certain that her family would be too busy with other things to pressure her about the situation with Trey.

She appreciated that they were thinking about what was best for her and the baby, but what they didn't seem to understand was that she *wanted* to marry Trey—she just needed to know that it was what he wanted, too, and she couldn't shake the feeling that he had only proposed out of duty and obligation. Until she could be sure that he really wanted them to be a family, she couldn't say yes.

The door flew open and Kristen leaped onto Kayla's bed. "Merry Christmas, Sleepyhead."

She smiled at her twin, who had opted to sleep in her old room the night before so the sisters could celebrate Christmas morning together one last time. "Merry Christmas, Earlybird."

Kristen fell back on the mattress, so their heads were side by side on the pillow. "It's the end of an era, isn't it?"

Kayla nodded. "Next year, you'll wake up with your husband on Christmas morning."

"And you'll be celebrating your baby's first Christmas."

She nodded again. Although it was a full year away, she couldn't help wondering what the day would look like—when she and Trey would have an eight-month-old baby with whom to celebrate the holiday. But where would they be? And would they be together? Or would their baby be shuffled from one house to another from one year to the next?

"I understand why you turned down Trey's proposal," Kristen said to her now. "You didn't want to marry him for the sake of your baby. But maybe you shouldn't have looked at it that way."

"How should I have looked at it?"

"You could have focused on the fact that the man you love was asking you to marry him."

"But I don't just want to marry the man I love—I want to marry a man who loves me, too."

"And he does," Kristen said.

But Kayla wasn't so sure. Since the day after she'd told him about the baby—and after they'd told their respective families about the baby—he hadn't said another word about marriage or even hinted about wanting a life with her and their baby.

"What does he have to do to prove to you that his feelings are real?" Kristen asked her now.

"I don't know," she admitted. "But I think I deserve something more than an impulsive and slightly panicked proposal."

"You definitely do," her sister agreed.

"Girls!" Rita called up to her daughters. "Breakfast is ready."

Kayla threw back the covers. "I'm starving."

Her sister laughed. "You're always starving these days."

She walked down the stairs beside Kristen, as she'd done every Christmas morning for as long as she could remember. But this year, Kayla wasn't thinking about presents from the jolly man in the red suit—she was preoccupied with thoughts of a different man...and hoping for a holiday miracle.

Chapter Fourteen

Breakfast was fruit and yogurt, pancakes, and bacon and eggs, and for once her mother didn't give Kayla a disapproving glance when she filled her plate.

She looked around the table as she ate—at her mother and her father, still solid after thirty-five years of marriage; her brother, Jonah, and his wife, Vanessa, still newlyweds; Kristen and her fiancé, blissfully in love and eager to start their life together. She wanted what they each had—the affection and commitment—and she wanted it with Trey.

After everyone had eaten their fill and the kitchen was cleaned up, the family moved into the living room to exchange gifts. Kayla hadn't yet sat down when there was a knock at the door. Her heart quickened.

Though Trey hadn't said anything more about her mother's invitation to join them on Christmas Day, she couldn't imagine who else it might be. Certainly there wasn't anyone else that she wanted to see today as much as she wanted to see him.

"I'll get it," she said, feigning a casualness she didn't feel as she tried not to race to the door.

It *was* Trey—and he looked so incredibly handsome in a black sweater and dark jeans with his leather jacket unzipped. He hadn't shaved, but she didn't mind the light growth of ginger stubble on his jaw. In fact, she thought it made him look even sexier than usual, and just a little bit dangerous.

Dangerous to your heart, she reminded herself, stepping away from the door so he could enter.

"Merry Christmas, Kayla." He took advantage of the fact that they were out of sight of everyone else to steal a quick kiss, touching his lips lightly to hers.

"Merry Christmas," she replied, feeling suddenly and inexplicably shy. After two days of no contact except through text messages, she wasn't sure what to say or how to act around him.

"Is it okay that I'm here?"

"My mother did invite you," she reminded him.

"I meant, is it okay with you?"

"Oh. Of course."

He tipped her chin up. "I've missed you."

"You have?"

"Yes, I have," he confirmed.

"I missed you, too," she admitted.

He smiled at that. "Did Santa bring you everything you wanted for Christmas?"

Everything she wanted was standing right in front of her, but she didn't know how Trey would respond to that kind of declaration. Instead she said, "I don't know yet—we're opening gifts in the front room now."

"Then I'm just in time," he said, holding up the bag of gifts he carried.

Kayla led him into the family room where a fire crackled in the hearth and the lights were lit on an enormous tree beneath which was a small mountain of presents. After greetings and holiday wishes were exchanged all around, Derek began to distribute gifts.

The mountain had been cut down to a moderate hill when her brother passed a heavy square box to her.

Kayla frowned at the tag. "It doesn't say who it's from."

Her family looked from one to the other, all of them shaking their heads. Trey did the same when the attention shifted in his direction.

"It doesn't matter who it's from," Kristen said. "It has your name on it."

So she undid the bow and tore open the paper, but the plain cardboard gave no hint as to its contents. She lifted the lid and found a bottle of something that looked suspiciously like moonshine, beneath which was a note in spidery handwriting.

"What does it say?" Rita asked.

She started to read aloud:

"Dear Ms. Rust Creek Ramblings,

"It didn't take people long to figure out that the wedding punch was doctored but no one knows who did it...or why. Now that you and Trey are together again, I'll fill you in on the story.

"What I saw on the Fourtth of July was more than just a happy couple ready to embark on a life together. I saw a lot of lonely people who needed a little push toward their own happiness. Or maybe more than a little push. Jordyn Leigh Cates, Levi Wyatt, Lani Dalton, Brad Crawford, your sister...and you. All of you sampled Homer Gilmore's Wedding Moonshine—and look at everyone now!

"My work is done. Sincerely, HG"

Kayla was stunned—and already thinking that this confession would make the perfect topic of her next column.

"Homer Gilmore?" Kristen said skeptically. "He doesn't strike me as the romantic type."

"Forget Homer Gilmore," Rita said. "The old coot's clearly off his rocker to think, for even a minute, that Kayla is the Rust Creek Rambler."

"Actually, that's something I need to talk to you all about," Kayla said, her gaze hesitantly shifting around the room from one family member to the next, briefly—and apologetically—encompassing them all.

Everyone was silent for a moment, stunned by the news that sweet, shy Kayla was the source of Rust Creek Falls's juiciest gossip.

Derek recovered his voice first. "Are you saying it's true?" he demanded.

"It's true," she admitted.

"You've been writing gossip for the paper about our friends?" her father asked, his voice heavy with disapproval.

"Not just our friends but our family," Kristen noted. "You wrote about *me*! And Jonah and Vanessa, too!"

"None of it was malicious or untrue," Kayla said defensively.

"Which just goes to prove that people aren't always what they seem," Derek said, looking pointedly from his sister to his high school pal.

"There's something written on the back," Trey noted, trying to deflect attention away from Kayla's revelation and back to Homer's confession.

She turned the page over.

"PS—It was Boyd Sullivan's idea to 'lose' the farm to Brad Crawford. His broken heart just couldn't mend here in Rust Creek Falls. Since he left, he's been living in upstate New York and may have found love again. I'll never regret buying him that train ticket."

"I still can't believe Homer Gilmore could mastermind such a plan," Rita said.

"I still can't believe our daughter is the Rust Creek Rambler," Charles grumbled.

"There's something else in the box," Kayla noted, lifting out a handful of ring boxes and a stack of extra marriage licenses with another note attached. *I didn't get to use them all—maybe one will come in handy for you someday.*

"I guess that answers the question of how Will and Jordyn Leigh were able to get married so easily," Eli noted.

"I guess I should be grateful that I didn't drink any of that punch," Derek muttered.

"If you had, and if you'd actually met someone, you might be a little less cranky," Kristen pointed out.

"There are still presents to be opened," Rita noted, eager to defuse the argument she could sense brewing between her children.

Derek resumed handing out gifts.

"I have one for Kayla," Trey said, then slipped back into the foyer. When he returned, he was carrying an enormous fluffy white teddy bear with a Santa hat on its head.

"It's adorable," Kayla said, hugging the bear to her chest. Then she hugged Trey. "Thank you."

"I think he was expecting a yes or no rather than thank you," Kristen said.

In response to Kayla's blank look, she pointed to the stocking that the bear held between its paws.

On the stocking was embroidered the words "Will you marry me?"

Kayla's breath caught in her throat. She looked from the bear to Trey, who dropped to one knee beside her.

"I promised to give you some time, so that you could be sure—and know that I was sure. And I am. I love you, and what I most want for Christmas is to be your husband and a father to our baby." He reached into the stocking that the bear was holding and pulled out a small box, then flipped open the lid to reveal a gorgeous vintage engagement ring. "So I'm asking now, Kayla Dalton, will you marry me?"

She was glad she was already sitting down, because her knees had turned to jelly. When they were in Kalispell together, it had been easy to disregard his impulsive proposal because she knew he was trying to do the right thing. The fact that he'd chosen to ask her again, putting his heart on the line not just in front of her but her whole family, too, made her realize that his motivation might be a little more complicated than she'd assumed.

What did she need to believe his feelings for her were real? Only this—exactly this.

"Yes, Trey Strickland, I will marry you."

He fumbled a little as he pulled the ring from the box. "I'm not nervous about marrying you," he said, his voice lowered so that only she could hear. "I'm just feeling a little nervous about doing this in front of your whole family."

"So why did you?"

"Because I wanted to prove to you that it wasn't an impulse or an obligation. And because I thought putting a ring on your finger would increase my chances of getting out of here without my backside full of buckshot."

"I can see why you'd be concerned," she told him. "It's a really nice backside."

His brows lifted. "You think so?" He finally slid the ring on her finger and then leaned forward to kiss her softly.

Kayla almost forgot they were in a room filled with her family until everyone applauded. Trey must have, too, because he eased back and smiled sheepishly.

"Now we need to set a date for the wedding," Rita said. "And I think the sooner, the better."

"I agree," Trey said. "In fact, I was thinking today would be perfect."

"Today?" Kayla echoed. "We can't get married today."

"Why not?"

"Because there's paperwork that needs to be filed and—"

"The paperwork's done," he told her. "My grandfather suggested I take care of the administrative details so that we could have a Christmas wedding."

"You're serious," she realized. "You want to get married today."

"I don't want to wait another minute to make you my wife."

"I love the idea," she admitted. "But we need more than a license to make it happen."

"The minister is just waiting for our call."

"But… I don't even have a dress."

"I do," Kristen interjected.

"You just happen to have a wedding dress hanging in your closet?" Kayla asked skeptically, because she knew the gown her sister had ordered for her own wedding wouldn't be ready for several weeks and wouldn't fit Kayla even if she did have it.

"The theater was getting rid of some costumes, including a vintage wedding dress, so I brought it home, certain it could be put to good use one day," Kristen explained.

Kayla laid a hand on her swollen tummy. "I can't imagine anything designed for the stage would fit me in this condition."

"It has an empire waist and a full skirt," Kristen said. Still, she hesitated.

"You should at least try it," her mother suggested.

"What do you think?" she asked Trey.

"I think you're going to be the most beautiful bride ever, no matter what you're wearing."

She glanced down at the simple green tunic-style top that she had on over black leggings. "Well, I'd rather not be wearing this," she admitted.

Kristen took her hand and tugged her to her feet. "Let's go upstairs so you can try it on," she urged.

"While you're doing that, I'm going to call my grandparents to invite them to the wedding."

"Then I guess you'd better call the minister, too," Kayla said.

"I will," he promised.

Trey made the necessary phone calls, then went in search of his high school friend and soon-to-be brother-in-law. He found Derek brooding in the corner, a long-necked bottle in his hand and a dark expression on his face.

"You're pissed," Trey realized.

"Did you expect me to be thrilled to learn that my buddy knocked up my little sister?" Derek challenged.

Trey winced. "It really wasn't like that."

"You weren't drunk on Homer Gilmore's moonshine when you seduced her?"

"The wedding punch might have been a factor," he acknowledged. "But I don't regret what happened, because I love your sister and I'm looking forward to building a life and a family with her."

"You always did have a way with words—and with the ladies," Derek sneered.

"We both did," Trey reminded his friend. "And if you

remember that, you should also remember that when I make a commitment, I honor it. I could tell you that, from this day forward, there will be no one for me but Kayla. The truth is, there hasn't been anyone for me but Kayla since that night we spent together in July."

"The fact you spent that night with her still makes me want to take you out to the barn to go a few rounds," Kayla's brother warned. "The only reason I'm restraining myself is that I know my sister wouldn't forgive me if I was the reason her groom was sporting a black eye on their wedding day."

"I appreciate your restraint," Trey said. "And I'd appreciate it even more if you stood beside me as my best man when I marry her."

Derek considered the offer for a long moment before he finally nodded. "I could do that."

Trey offered his hand. "I'm going to do everything I can to make Kayla happy—to be a good husband to her and a good father to our baby."

"I know you will," his friend agreed grudgingly. "Because if you don't, you'll answer to me."

"I can't believe the theater was going to throw this away," Kayla said, trailing a hand down the lace sleeve of the dress her sister presented to her.

"Lots of costumes and limited storage space," Kristen said matter-of-factly.

"But this is…beautiful."

"It is," her sister agreed. "And it will look even more beautiful on you."

"I'm feeling a little guilty."

"Why?"

"Because you got engaged first but I'm getting married first."

"Actually, I'm happy it turned out this way," Kristen said. "Because after you're married and your baby is born, there will be no distractions from my big day."

Kayla chuckled. "Absolutely not," she promised.

With her sister's help, she stripped down and slipped into the vintage gown.

"Maybe it wasn't just a lack of storage space," Kristen allowed, as she worked on fastening the dozens of tiny buttons that ran down the back of the dress. "It could be that this dress isn't exactly conducive to quick costume changes."

But at last she finished, then turned Kayla around to face her. "Oh, it's perfect." Kristen's eyes misted. "You're perfect. Absolutely perfect."

"You think it's okay that I'm wearing white?"

"I think a bride should wear whatever she wants on her wedding day, but it's actually off-white, so you don't need to worry about anyone wagging a finger in your direction."

"No, it's more likely tongues will be wagging."

"The joys of living in a small town," her sister reminded her. "But at least you've mostly flown under the radar of the Rust Creek Rambler for the past few years."

"Not entirely, though," she pointed out.

"Yeah, there were occasional—and completely forgettable mentions—just enough to ensure that no one ever suspected you were the author of the column."

"I protected you, too," she pointed out.

"Which is probably why people *did* suspect me."

"I guess I didn't think that one through very well," she apologized, as she pinned her hair into a twist at the back of her head.

"It didn't bother me," Kristen assured her. Then, "You need earrings."

"You're right." Kayla lifted the lid of her jewelry box

and selected the sparkly teardrops that had belonged to their grandmother.

"I thought you lost one of those."

"I did," she admitted. "In Trey's bed."

Her sister's brows lifted. "It's a good thing he found it before his grandmother did."

"No kidding," she agreed.

"When did you get it back?"

"Just a few days ago. He said he'd been carrying it with him since that morning, waiting for the right time to return it to me."

Kristen laid a hand on her heart and sighed dramatically. "Just like Prince Charming with the glass slipper."

Kayla felt her cheeks flush. "I don't know if it was just like that, but it was pretty romantic."

There was a tap of knuckles on the door, then Rita peeked her head into her daughter's room. "Everyone is here so anytime— Oh, Kayla." Her mother's eyes filled with tears. "You look so beautiful." She drew in a breath and blinked away the moisture. "But you don't have any flowers."

"I didn't expect to even have a dress," she reminded her mother. "I'm not too worried about the flowers."

"But it's your wedding day. It should be perfect."

"I'm marrying the man I love—it already is perfect."

"You're right," Rita agreed. "And speaking of men, your father would like to give you away."

"I know—he tried to do that the day he found out about my pregnancy."

Her mother flushed.

Kayla touched a hand to her arm. "I'm kidding, Mom. I would very much like to have Dad walk me down the aisle."

"Actually, it's going to be the hall, not an aisle," Kristen pointed out.

"I'll go get him," Rita said, and slipped out of the room, closing the door softly behind her.

"Are you nervous?" Kristen asked.

Kayla shook her head. "Excited. Although I'm still not convinced this isn't all a dream."

"It is a dream," Kristen said. "It's *your* dream come true. Don't question it—just enjoy it."

"I've been in love with Trey since I was twelve years old."

"I know."

"I never thought he'd even notice me, never mind love me back."

"Well, he did and he does," her sister told her. "And right now, he's waiting downstairs to marry you."

Trey shifted from one foot to the other as he waited for Kayla to appear. His grandmother had positioned him in front of the Christmas tree—insisting it would be the best backdrop for pictures—and Derek stood beside him. The minister was there, too, smiling and chatting with guests, assuring them that it wasn't an imposition but a pleasure to be called out to perform a surprise wedding ceremony, even on Christmas Day.

Trey had been in agreement with the plan—the idea of a small family wedding suited him perfectly. But apparently it wasn't going to be as small as he'd anticipated. Not only had his grandparents picked up the minister on their way to the Circle D, they'd also brought Claire, Levi, Bekka, Hadley and Tessa. And while Kayla was doing whatever she was doing upstairs to get ready for the wedding, the mother of the bride had been busy on the phone, because before the bride descended the stairs again, the living room was practically bursting at the seams with people.

There were Kayla's siblings, of course. Jonah and his wife, Vanessa, Kristen's fiancé, Ryan Roarke, and Eli and Derek. Her aunt and uncle, Mary and Ben Dalton were also there, along with their unmarried children—Anderson, Travis and Lindsay. Also in attendance were Caleb and Mallory Dalton with their adopted daughter, Lily; Paige and Sutter Traub with their son, Carter; and Lani Dalton and Russ Campbell.

Then Kayla appeared and everyone else faded away.

He'd meant what he'd said when he'd told her she would look beautiful in whatever she was wearing, but in the white dress with her hair pinned up and a pair of familiar earrings dangling from her lobes, she was absolutely stunning.

He couldn't take his eyes off her while they exchanged their vows, and he didn't want to. A few short weeks earlier, he could not have imagined that he would be married before the end of the year—certainly and not be happy about it. But as Kayla returned his promise to love, honor and cherish "till death do us part," he realized that he was finally where he belonged. It didn't matter if they were in Rust Creek Falls or Thunder Canyon or even Timbuktu—what mattered was that they were together.

Finally, the minister invited the groom to kiss his bride.

Trey lowered his head to hers, pausing before his lips touched hers to whisper, "I love you, Mrs. Strickland."

"And I love you, Mr. Strickland," she whispered back.

He smiled and then—finally—he kissed his wife for the first time.

After that, flutes of champagne and sparkling grape juice were passed around so that guests could toast the newlyweds. Kayla surprised everyone by offering a toast of her own.

"I just want to thank our families and friends who have gathered here today—on very short notice—to celebrate this occasion with us. Christmas has always been my favorite time of the year but now for even more reasons. Because of Trey, I got everything I wanted this year—and more.

"But if I could have one more wish come true, it would be that all of our siblings and cousins and friends will someday be as lucky to share the same love and happiness that I've found with Trey."

Of course, there were many more toasts after that, and everyone wanted to kiss the bride and congratulate the groom. Trey didn't really mind, but he was anxious to be alone with Kayla, and it seemed like forever before they managed to extricate themselves from the crowd to head back to his room at the boarding house.

"Why do I feel like I'm returning to the scene of the crime?" Kayla asked, after Trey had parked his truck and came around to the passenger side to help her out.

"Maybe because you're whispering and tiptoeing," he suggested.

"I feel guilty," she acknowledged.

"Why would you feel guilty?"

"Because we violated your grandparents' rule prohibiting overnight visitors."

"That was five months ago," he reminded her. "Now we're lawfully married and there's no reason to feel guilty."

"I guess it's going to take me a little while to get used to that fact."

"You've got the rest of your life—the rest of our lives," he amended, unlocking the door to his room.

"I'm looking forward to every single day of it."

"Me, too," he said. "And I promise you, now that my ring is on your finger, if you ever try to sneak out in the middle of the night again, I will go after you."

"I guess I didn't handle that very well, did I?"

"You might have saved us some confusion and a lot of lost time if you hadn't disappeared before the sun came up."

"I'm not going anywhere this time," she assured him.

"You won't have a chance—I'm not going to let you out of my arms tonight."

She smiled. "Is that a promise?"

"That is very definitely a promise."

His gaze skimmed over her, slowly, appreciatively, from the top of her head to the toes of the shoes that peeked out beneath the hem of her gown. "Your sister made a good call on this dress," he said. "You look fabulous in it, but I suspect you're going to look even better out of it."

"I'm five-and-a-half months pregnant," she reminded him.

"I know."

"I've gained twelve pounds now."

He framed her face in his hands. "You were beautiful in July, you're beautiful now, and you'll be just as beautiful in April when you can't see your swollen ankles, and even more so when we're celebrating our fiftieth anniversary," he said sincerely.

"What did I ever do to deserve you?"

"You got drunk on Homer's punch." He turned her around and began to unfasten the buttons of her dress.

She laughed softly. "I wasn't drunk. I was in love. I've been in love with you since the day you climbed the big maple tree behind my parents' house to retrieve my favorite doll that Derek had thrown into the top branches."

"I can't say I loved you then," he admitted. "But I love you now. For now and forever."

Her heart sighed with contentment—and then Trey swore under his breath.

She glanced over her shoulder.

"I changed my mind about this dress," he grumbled. "How many damn buttons are on this thing?"

"I don't know," she admitted. "Kristen did it up for me."

He struggled for a few more minutes, then finally had the back opened up enough that he could push the dress off her shoulders and over her hips. He quickly stripped away her undergarments and dispensed with his own attire in record time.

Then he slowed everything down. His lips were patient, his hands gentle, as he aroused her tenderly and very thoroughly. When she was ready for him—almost begging for him—he finally, and again slowly, eased into her. The pressure built inside her the same way—slowly, but steadily, inexorably guiding her toward the culmination of pleasure.

She was close...so close. But she needed something more than what he was giving her, more than soft touches and gentle strokes.

"Trey, please. I need—"

He brushed his lips against hers. "I know."

But he didn't, because he continued at the same leisurely pace, and while it felt good—*really* good—it wasn't enough. She bit back a whimper of frustration as the pleasure continued to build inside her, gentle rolling waves of sensation that teased her with the promise of more.

And then, just when she thought that promise was beyond her reach, her body imploded, shattering into a million little pieces that scattered like stars into the far reaches of the galaxy before they drifted back to earth. Slowly.

It was a long time later before they were both able to breathe normally again, before Trey summoned the energy to tuck her close against him.

"Wow," she said softly.

With her head nestled against his shoulder, she couldn't see his face, but she heard the smile in his voice when he said, "I never thought I'd say this—but I think I'm going to have to thank Homer Gilmore for spiking the wedding punch."

"Maybe we should name our baby after him," Kayla suggested.

"I think we should stick to saying thanks," Trey countered.

She laughed softly. "Okay—we'll do that."

"Did you have any thoughts about names?"

"No, I've tried not to think too far ahead."

"It isn't so far now," he pointed out. "Less than four months."

She shifted so that she was on her side, facing him. "I'm sorry that I didn't tell you sooner, that you missed out on so much."

"I won't miss out next time."

Though she was touched by the confident assurance in his voice, she wanted to enjoy the present with him before scheduling their future. "Could we have this baby before you start planning for the next one?"

"Of course," he agreed. "But I do think we should practice our baby-making technique."

"Again?"

He shrugged. "We missed a lot of months together—and they do say practice makes perfect."

She lifted her arms to his shoulders and drew him down to her. "In that case, we should definitely practice."

Epilogue

When Trey returned to their room at the boarding house, he found his wife exactly where he'd left her: sitting at the desk, staring at the screen of her laptop computer.

"Are you *still* working on that?"

"Just finishing up."

He set down the tray of fruit and cheese he'd snagged from the kitchen along with the two crystal flute glasses he'd borrowed from his grandparents' cabinet, then reached into the mini-fridge for the bottle of nonalcoholic champagne he'd purchased for the occasion. "That's what you said half an hour ago."

"But now it's true," she told him, turning the computer so that he could see the screen.

His brows lifted. "You're giving me a sneak peek?"

"I want an unbiased second opinion before I send it to my editor."

"Then you shouldn't ask me," he pointed out. "How

can I be unbiased about anything written by the woman I love?"

She smiled, as she always did when he told her he loved her. "True, but I want you to read it, anyway."

He stood behind her chair, his hands on her shoulders, as he read her last column for the Rust Creek newspaper.

RUST CREEK RAMBLINGS: OUT WITH THE OLD, IN WITH THE NEW (YEAR) & MISCELLANEOUS OTHER THINGS

2015 was an eventful year for the residents of Rust Creek Falls. In addition to the usual weddings and funerals, engagements and reunions, there was the mystery of the wedding punch served at the Fourth of July nuptials of Braden Traub and Jennifer Mac-Callum. A mystery that was finally solved when Homer Gilmore confessed to spiking the punch with his homemade moonshine in an effort to help the lonely residents of our fair town find their bliss. On many accounts, he succeeded.

As the hours count down and the dawn of a New Year draws ever closer, one cannot help but wonder what events will make headlines in the months ahead. I'll look forward to reading about them rather than writing them myself, as I'm leaving Rust Creek Falls to make my home in Thunder Canyon with my new husband and the family we're going to have together. But don't worry, loyal readers, there is a new Rambler already in your midst, already keeping an ear to the ground and a notepad in hand.

Happy New Year to All!
Your (former) Rust Creek Rambler,
Kayla Dalton Strickland

"You put your name on it," Trey noted with surprise.

His wife nodded. "I thought it was time for the people of Rust Creek Falls to learn the identity of the Rambler."

"You mean that you wanted them to know your sister wasn't responsible for the column," he guessed.

"That, too," she agreed.

"Are you going to miss it?"

She shook her head. "I had a lot of fun with it, but I'm more than ready to move on, to focus on being a wife and—very soon—a mother."

"No regrets about leaving Rust Creek Falls?"

"None," she assured him. "Besides, Thunder Canyon isn't really that far away, and we'll come back to visit whenever we can."

"I'm sure we'll be pressured to come back even more often," Trey said. "Especially after the baby is born."

"And no doubt there will be a convoy from Rust Creek Falls to Thunder Canyon as soon as our families hear that the baby is on his way."

"You're probably right."

She clicked SEND to submit her final edition of "Ramblings" to the newspaper, then shut down the computer.

As Trey handed her a glass of nonalcoholic champagne, she could hear the rest of the family and boarding house guests talking and laughing in the main parlor.

"Are you sure you don't want to go downstairs to ring in the New Year with your cousins and your grandparents?"

"I'm sure," he said. "I want to celebrate our first New Year together with my bride."

"But what if I want to wear a sparkly crown and blow one of those noisy horns?"

He picked up a sparkly crown—pilfered from the box of party stuff his grandmother had amassed for the celebration—and settled it on her head. Then he handed her a noisemaker.

"Once again, you've thought of everything, haven't you?"

"I tried." He touched his lips to hers. "I love you, Kayla."

Her eyes filled with tears.

He pulled back. "What did I do? Why are you crying?"

She managed to laugh at his panicked tone. "Sorry—I'm pregnant and hormonal, and I'm crying because I'm happier than I ever thought possible."

Trey wrapped his arms around her. "That's lucky for us then, because I feel the same way—well, except for the pregnant, hormonal and crying parts."

Kayla laughed again, and as the guests downstairs began their countdown to midnight, she and Trey celebrated the birth of the New Year in their own way.

* * * * *

MILLS & BOON®

Cherish™

EXPERIENCE THE ULTIMATE RUSH OF FALLING IN LOVE

A sneak peek at next month's titles...

In stores from 18th December 2015:

- **Holiday with the Millionaire** – Scarlet Wilson *and*
  Fortune's Secret Heir – Allison Leigh
- **His Princess of Convenience** *and*
  The Texas Ranger's Nanny – Rebecca Winters

In stores from 1st January 2016:

- **Having the Cowboy's Baby** – Judy Duarte *and*
  The Husband She'd Never Met – Barbara Hannay
- **The Widow's Bachelor Bargain** – Teresa Southwick
  and **Unlocking Her Boss's Heart** – Christy McKellen

Available at WHSmith, Tesco, Asda, Eason, Amazon and Apple

Just can't wait?
Buy our books online a month before they hit the shops!
visit www.millsandboon.co.uk

These books are also available in eBook format!

1015_MB514

MILLS & BOON®

Why shop at millsandboon.co.uk?

Each year, thousands of romance readers find their perfect read at millsandboon.co.uk. That's because we're passionate about bringing you the very best romantic fiction. Here are some of the advantages of shopping at www.millsandboon.co.uk:

* **Get new books first**—you'll be able to buy your favourite books one month before they hit the shops

* **Get exclusive discounts**—you'll also be able to buy our specially created monthly collections, with up to 50% off the RRP

* **Find your favourite authors**—latest news, interviews and new releases for all your favourite authors and series on our website, plus ideas for what to try next

* **Join in**—once you've bought your favourite books, don't forget to register with us to rate, review and join in the discussions

Visit **www.millsandboon.co.uk**
for all this and more today!